AUDREY

MARY JOHNSTON

Audrey

Mary Johnston

© 1st World Library, 2007
PO Box 2211
Fairfield, IA 52556
www.1stworldlibrary.com
First Edition

LCCN: 2007927807

Softcover ISBN: 978-1-4218-4558-6
Hardcover ISBN: 978-1-4218-4474-9
eBook ISBN: 978-1-4218-4642-2

Purchase *"Audrey"*
as a traditional bound book at:
www.1stWorldLibrary.com/purchase.asp?ISBN=978-1-4218-4558-6

1st World Library is a literary, educational organization
dedicated to:

- Creating a free internet library of downloadable ebooks

  - Hosting writing competitions and offering book
    publishing scholarships.

Interested in more 1st World Library books?
contact: literacy@1stworldlibrary.com
Check us out at: www.1stworldlibrary.com

1ˢᵗ World Library Literary Society

Giving Back to the World

"If you want to work on the core problem, it's early school literacy."

- James Barksdale, former CEO of Netscape

"No skill is more crucial to the future of a child, or to a democratic and prosperous society, than literacy."

- Los Angeles Times

"Literacy... means far more than learning how to read and write... The aim is to transmit... knowledge and promote social participation."

- UNESCO

"Literacy is not a luxury, it is a right and a responsibility. If our world is to meet the challenges of the twenty-first century we must harness the energy and creativity of all our citizens."

- President Bill Clinton

"Parents should be encouraged to read to their children, and teachers should be equipped with all available techniques for teaching literacy, so the varying needs and capacities of individual kids can be taken into account."

- Hugh Mackay

TO

ELOISE, ANNE, AND ELIZABETH

CONTENTS

CHAPTER I

THE CABIN IN THE VALLEY

The valley lay like a ribbon thrown into the midst of the encompassing hills. The grass which grew there was soft and fine and abundant; the trees which sprang from its dark, rich mould were tall and great of girth. A bright stream flashed through it, and the sunshine fell warm upon the grass and changed the tassels of the maize into golden plumes. Above the valley, east and north and south, rose the hills, clad in living green, mantled with the purpling grape, wreathed morn and eve with trailing mist. To the westward were the mountains, and they dwelt apart in a blue haze. Only in the morning, if the mist were not there, the sunrise struck upon their long summits, and in the evening they stood out, high and black and fearful, against the splendid sky. The child who played beside the cabin door often watched them as the valley filled with shadows, and thought of them as a great wall between her and some land of the fairies which must needs lie beyond that barrier, beneath the splendor and the evening star. The Indians called them the Endless Mountains, and the child never doubted that they ran across the world and touched the floor of heaven.

In the hands of the woman who was spinning the thread

broke and the song died in the white throat of the girl who stood in the doorway. For a moment the two gazed with widening eyes into the green September world without the cabin; then the woman sprang to her feet, tore from the wall a horn, and, running to the door, wound it lustily. The echoes from the hills had not died when a man and a boy, the one bearing a musket, the other an axe, burst from the shadow of the forest, and at a run crossed the greensward and the field of maize between them and the women. The child let fall her pine cones and pebbles, and fled to her mother, to cling to her skirts, and look with brown, frightened eyes for the wonder that should follow the winding of the horn. Only twice could she remember that clear summons for her father: once when it was winter and snow was on the ground, and a great wolf, gaunt and bold, had fallen upon their sheep; and once when a drunken trader from Germanna, with a Pamunkey who had tasted of the trader's rum, had not waited for an invitation before entering the cabin. It was not winter now, and there was no sign of the red-faced trader or of the dreadful, capering Indian. There was only a sound in the air, a strange noise coming to them from the pass between the hills over which rose the sun.

The man with the musket sent his voice before him as he approached the group upon the doorstep: "Alce, woman! What's amiss? I see naught wrong!"

His wife stepped forward to meet him. "There's naught to see, William. It's to hear. There was a noise. Molly and I heard it, and then we lost it. There it is again!"

Fronting the cabin, beyond the maize field and the rich green grass and the placid stream, rose two hills, steep and thickly wooded, and between them ran a narrow, winding, and rocky pass. Down this gorge, to the listening

Mary Johnston

pioneer, now came a confused and trampling sound.

"It is iron striking against the rocks!" he announced. "The hoofs of horses"—

"Iron!" cried his wife. "The horses in Virginia go unshod! And what should a troop of horse do here, beyond the frontier, where even the rangers never come?"

The man shook his head, a frown of perplexity upon his bronzed and bearded face. "It is the sound of the hoofs of horses," he said, "and they are coming through the pass. Hark!"

A trumpet blew, and there came a noise of laughter. The child pressed close to her brother's side. "Oh, Robin, maybe 't is the fairies!"

Out from the gloom of the pass into the sunshine of the valley, splashing through the stream, trampling the long grass, laughing, and calling one rider to the other, burst a company of fifty horsemen. The trumpet blew again, and the entire party, drawing rein, stared at the unexpected maize field, the cabin, and the people about the door.

Between the intruders and the lonely folk, whose nearest neighbors were twenty miles away, was only a strip of sunny grass, dotted over with the stumps of trees that had been felled lest they afford cover for attacking savages. A man, riding at the head of the invading party, beckoned, somewhat imperiously, to the pioneer; and the latter, still with his musket in the hollow of his arm, strode across the greensward, and finding himself in the midst, not of rude traders and rangers, but of easy, smiling, periwigged gentlemen, handsomely dressed and accoutred, dropped the butt of his gun upon the ground, and took off his squirrel-skin cap.

"You are deep in the wilderness, good fellow," said the man who had beckoned, and who was possessed of a stately figure, a martial countenance, and an air of great authority. "How far is it to the mountains?"

The pioneer stared at the long blue range, cloudlike in the distance. "I don't know," he answered. "I hunt to the eastward. Twenty miles, maybe. You're never going to climb them?"

"We are come out expressly to do so," answered the other heartily, "having a mind to drink the King's health with our heads in the clouds! We need another axeman to clear away the fallen trees and break the nets of grapevine. Wilt go along amongst our rangers yonder, and earn a pistole and undying fame?"

The woodsman looked from the knot of gentlemen to the troop of hardy rangers, who, with a dozen ebony servants and four Meherrin Indians, made up the company. Under charge of the slaves were a number of packhorses. Thrown across one was a noble deer; a second bore a brace of wild turkeys and a two-year-old bear, fat and tender; a third had a legion of pots and pans for the cooking of the woodland cheer; while the burden of several others promised heart's content of good liquor. From the entire troop breathed a most enticing air of gay daring and good-fellowship. The gentlemen were young and of cheerful countenances; the rangers in the rear sat their horses and whistled to the woodpeckers in the sugar-trees; the negroes grinned broadly; even the Indians appeared a shade less saturnine than usual. The golden sunshine poured upon them all, and the blue mountains that no Englishman had ever passed seemed for the moment as soft and yielding as the cloud that slept along their summits. And no man knew what might be just beyond the mountains: Frenchmen, certainly, and the great lakes and the South Sea: but, besides these, might there not be gold, glittering stones, new birds and beasts and plants, strange secrets of the hills? It was only westward-ho! for a week or two, with good company and good drink—

The woodsman shifted from one foot to the other, but his wife, who had now crossed the grass to his side, had no doubts.

"You'll not go, William!" she cried. "Remember the smoke that you saw yesterday from the hilltop! If the Northern Indians are on the warpath against the Southern, and are passing between us and the mountains, there may be straying bands. I'll not let you go!"

In her eagerness she clasped his arm with her hands. She was a comely, buxom dame, and the circle on horseback, being for the most part young and gallant, and not having seen a woman for some days, looked kindly upon her.

"And so you saw a smoke, goodwife, and are afraid of roving Indians?" said the gentleman who had spoken before. "That being the case, your husband has our permission to stay behind. On my life, 't is a shame to ride away and leave you in danger of such marauders!"

"Will your Excellency permit me to volunteer for guard duty?" demanded a young man who had pressed his horse to the leader's side. "It's odds, though, that when you return this way you'll find me turned Papist. I'll swear your Excellency never saw in Flanders carved or painted saint so worthy of your prayers as yonder breathing one!"

The girl Molly had followed her parents, and now stood upon a little grassy knoll, surveying with wide brown eyes the gay troop before her. A light wind was blowing, and it wrapped her dress of tender, faded blue around her young limbs, and lifted her loosened hair, gilded by the sunshine into the likeness of an aureole. Her face was serious and wondering, but fair as a woodland flower. She had placed her hand upon the head of the child who was with her, clinging to her dress. The green knoll formed a pedestal; behind was the sky, as blue as that of Italy; the two figures might have been some painted altar-piece.

The sprightly company, which had taken for its motto "Sic juvat transcendere montes," looked and worshiped. There was a moment of silent devotion, broken by one of the gentlemen demanding if 't were not time for dinner; another remarked that they might go much farther and fare much worse, in respect of a cool, sweet spot in which to rest during the heat of the afternoon; and a third boldly proposed that they go no farther at all that day. Their leader settled the question by announcing that, Mr. Mason's suggestion finding favor in his sight, they would forthwith dismount, dine, drink red wine and white, and wear out the heat of the day in this sylvan paradise until four of the clock, when the trumpet should sound for the mount; also, that if the goodwife and her daughter would do them the honor to partake of their rustic fare, their healths should be drunk in nothing less than Burgundy.

As he spoke he swung himself from the saddle, pulled out his ruffles, and raised his hat. "Ladies, permit me,"—a wave of his hand toward his escort, who were now also on foot. "Colonel Robertson, Captain Clonder, Captain Brooke, Mr. Haward, Mr. Beverley, Dr. Robinson, Mr. Fontaine, Mr. Todd, Mr. Mason,—all of the Tramontane Order. For myself, I am Alexander Spotswood, at your service."

The pioneer, standing behind his wife, plucked her by the sleeve. "Ecod, Alce, 't is the Governor himself! Mind your manners!"

Alce, who had been a red-cheeked dairymaid in a great house in England, needed no admonition. Her curtsy was profound; and when the Governor took her by the hand and kissed her still blooming cheek, she curtsied again. Molly, who had no memories of fine gentlemen and the complaisance which was their due, blushed fire-red at the touch of his Excellency's lips, forgot to curtsy, and knew not where to look. When, in her confusion, she turned her head aside, her eyes met those of the young man who had threatened to turn Papist. He bowed, with his hand upon his heart, and she blushed more deeply than before.

By now every man had dismounted, and the valley was ringing with the merriment of the jovial crew. The negroes led the horses down the stream, lightened them of saddle and bridle, and left them tethered to saplings beneath which the grass grew long and green. The rangers gathered fallen wood, and kindled two mighty fires, while the gentlemen of the party threw themselves down beside the stream, upon a little grassy rise shadowed by a huge sugar-tree. A mound of turf, flanked by two spreading roots, was the Governor's chair of state, and Alce and Molly he must needs seat beside him. Not one of his gay company but seemed an adept in the high-flown compliment of the age; out of very idleness and the mirth born of that summer hour they followed his Excellency's lead, and plied the two simple women with all the wordy ammunition that a tolerable acquaintance with the mythology of the ancients and the polite literature of the present could furnish. The mother and daughter did not understand the fine speeches, but liked them passing well. In their lonely lives, a little thing made conversation for many and many a day. As for these golden hours,—the jingle and clank and mellow laughter, the ruffles and gold buttons and fine cloth, these gentlemen, young and handsome, friendly-eyed, silver-tongued, the taste of wine, the taste of flattery, the sunshine that surely was never yet so bright,—ten years from now they would still be talking of these things, still wishing that such a day could come again.

The negroes were now busy around the fires, and soon the cheerful odor of broiling meat rose and blended with the fragrance of the forest. The pioneer, hospitably minded, beckoned to the four Meherrins, and hastening with them to the patch of waving corn, returned with a goodly lading of plump, green ears. A second foraging party, under guidance of the boy, brought into the larder of the gentry half a dozen noble melons, golden within and without. The woman whispered to the child, and the latter ran to the cabin, filled her upgathered skirts with the loaves of her mother's baking, and came back to the group upon the knoll beneath the sugar-tree. The Governor himself took the bread from the little maid, then drew her toward him.

"Thanks, my pretty one," he said, with a smile that for the moment quite dispelled the expression of haughtiness which marred an otherwise comely countenance. "Come, give me a kiss, sweeting, and tell me thy name."

The child looked at him gravely. "My name is Audrey," she answered, "and if you eat all of our bread we'll have none for supper."

The Governor laughed, and kissed the small dark face. "I'll give thee a gold moidore, instead, my maid. Odso!

thou'rt as dark and wild, almost, as was my little Queen of the Saponies that died last year. Hast never been away from the mountains, child?"

Audrey shook her head, and thought the question but a foolish one. The mountains were everywhere. Had she not been to the top of the hills, and seen for herself that they went from one edge of the world to the other? She was glad to slip from the Governor's encircling arm, and from the gay ring beneath the sugar-tree; to take refuge with herself down by the water side, and watch the fairy tale from afar off.

The rangers, with the pioneer and his son for their guests, dined beside the kitchen fire, which they had kindled at a respectful distance from the group upon the knoll. Active, bronzed and daring men, wild riders, bold fighters, lovers of the freedom of the woods, they sprawled upon the dark earth beneath the walnut-trees, laughed and joked, and told old tales of hunting or of Indian warfare. The four Meherrins ate apart and in stately silence, but the grinning negroes must needs endure their hunger until their masters should be served. One black detachment spread before the gentlemen of the expedition a damask cloth; another placed upon the snowy field platters of smoking venison and turkey, flanked by rockahominy and sea-biscuit, corn roasted Indian fashion, golden melons, and a quantity of wild grapes gathered from the vines that rioted over the hillside; while a third set down, with due solemnity, a formidable array of bottles. There being no chaplain in the party, the grace was short. The two captains carved, but every man was his own Ganymede. The wines were good and abundant: there was champagne for the King's health; claret in which to pledge themselves, gay stormers of the mountains; Burgundy for the oreads who were so gracious as to sit beside them, smile upon them, taste of their mortal fare.

Sooth to say, the oreads were somewhat dazed by the company they were keeping, and found the wine a more potent brew than the liquid crystal of their mountain streams. Red roses bloomed in Molly's cheeks; her eyes grew starry, and no longer sought the ground; when one of the gentlemen wove a chaplet of oak leaves, and with it crowned her loosened hair, she laughed, and the sound was so silvery and delightful that the company laughed with her. When the viands were gone, the negroes drew the cloth, but left the wine. When the wine was well-nigh spent, they brought to their masters long pipes and japanned boxes filled with sweet-scented. The fragrant smoke, arising, wrapped the knoll in a bluish haze. A wind had arisen, tempering the blazing sunshine, and making low music up and down the hillsides. The maples blossomed into silver, the restless poplar leaves danced more and more madly, the hemlocks and great white pines waved their broad, dark banners. Above the hilltops the sky was very blue, and the distant heights seemed dream mountains and easy of climbing. A soft and pleasing indolence, born of the afternoon, the sunlight, and the red wine, came to dwell in the valley. One of the company beneath the spreading sugar-tree laid his pipe upon the grass, clasped his hands behind his head, and, with his eyes on the azure heaven showing between branch and leaf, sang the song of Amiens of such another tree in such another forest. The voice was manly, strong, and sweet; the rangers quit their talk of war and hunting to listen, and the negroes, down by the fire which they had built for themselves, laughed for very pleasure.

When the wine was all drunken and the smoke of the tobacco quite blown away, a gentleman who seemed of a somewhat saturnine disposition, and less susceptible than

Mary Johnston

his brother adventurers to the charms of the wood nymphs, rose, and declared that he would go a-fishing in the dark crystal of the stream below. His servant brought him hook and line, while the grasshoppers in the tall grass served for bait. A rock jutting over the flood formed a convenient seat, and a tulip-tree lent a grateful shade. The fish were abundant and obliging; the fisherman was happy. Three shining trophies had been landed, and he was in the act of baiting the hook that should capture the fourth, when his eyes chanced to meet the eyes of the child Audrey, who had left her covert of purple-berried alder, and now stood beside him. Tithonus, green and hale, skipped from between his fingers, and he let fall his line to put out a good-natured hand and draw the child down to a seat upon the rock. "Wouldst like to try thy skill, moppet?" he demanded.

The child shook her head. "Are you a prince?" she asked, "and is the grand gentleman with, the long hair and the purple coat the King?"

The fisherman laughed. "No, little one, I'm only a poor ensign. The gentleman yonder, being the representative in Virginia of my Lord of Orkney and his Majesty King George the First, may somewhat smack of royalty. Indeed, there are good Virginians who think that were the King himself amongst us he could not more thoroughly play my Lord Absolute. But he's only the Governor of Virginia, after all, bright eyes."

"Does he live in a palace, like the King? My father once saw the King's house in a place they call London."

The gentleman laughed again. "Ay, he lives in a palace, a red brick palace, sixty feet long and forty feet deep, with a bauble on top that's all afire on birth-nights. There are green gardens, too, with winding paths, and sometimes pretty ladies walk in them. Wouldst like to see all these fine things?"

The child nodded. "Ay, that I would! Who is the gentleman that sang, and that now sits by Molly? See! with his hand touching her hair. Is he a Governor, too?"

The other glanced in the direction of the sugar-tree, raised his eyebrows, shrugged his shoulders, and returned to his fishing. "That is Mr. Marmaduke Haward," he said, "who, having just come into a great estate, goes abroad next month to be taught the newest, most genteel mode of squandering it. Dost not like his looks, child? Half the ladies of Williamsburgh are enamored of his *beaux yeux*."

Audrey made no answer, for just then the trumpet blew for the mount, and the fisherman must needs draw in and pocket his hook and line. Clear, high, and sweet, the triumphant notes pierced the air, and were answered from the hills by a thousand fairy horns. The martial-minded Governor would play the soldier in the wilderness; his little troop of gentlemen and rangers and ebony servants had come out well drilled for their tilt against the mountains. The echoes were still ringing, when, with laughter, some expenditure of wit, and much cheerful swearing, the camp was struck. The packhorses were again laden, the rangers swung themselves into their saddles, and the gentlemen beneath the sugar-tree rose from the grass, and tendered their farewells to the oreads.

Alce roundly hoped that their Honors would pass that way again upon their return from the high mountains, and the deepening rose of Molly's cheeks and her wistful eyes added weight to her mother's importunity. The Governor swore that in no great time they would dine again in the valley, and his companions confirmed the oath. His Excellency, turning to mount his horse, found the pioneer at the animal's head.

"So, honest fellow," he exclaimed good-naturedly, "you will not with us to grave your name upon the mountain tops? Let me tell you that you are giving Fame the go-by. To march against the mountains and overcome them as though they were so many Frenchmen, and then to gaze into the promised land beyond—Odso, man, we are as great as were Cortez and Pizarro and their crew! We are heroes and paladins! We are the Knights of"—

His horse, impatient to be gone, struck with a ringing sound an iron-shod hoof against a bit of rock. "The Knights of the Horseshoe," said the gentleman nearest the Governor.

Spotswood uttered a delighted exclamation: "'Gad, Mr. Haward, you've hit it! Well-nigh the first horseshoes used in Virginia—the number we were forced to bring along—the sound of the iron against the rocks—the Knights of the Horseshoe! 'Gad, I'll send to London and have little horseshoes—little gold horseshoes—made, and every man of us shall wear one. The Knights of the Golden Horseshoe! It hath an odd, charming sound, eh, gentlemen?"

None of the gentlemen were prepared to deny that it was a quaint and pleasing title. Instead, out of very lightness of heart and fantastic humor, they must needs have the Burgundy again unpacked, that they might pledge at once all valorous discoverers, his Excellency the Governor of Virginia, and their new-named order. And when the wine was drunk, the rangers were drawn up, the muskets were loaded, and a volley was fired that brought the echoes crashing about their heads. The Governor mounted, the trumpet sounded once more, and the joyous company swept down the narrow valley toward the long, blue, distant ranges.

The pioneer, his wife and children, watched them go. One of the gentlemen turned in his saddle and waved his hand. Alce curtsied, but Molly, at whom he had looked, saw him not, because her eyes were full of tears. The company reached and entered a cleft between the hills; a moment, and men and horses were lost to sight; a little longer, and not even a sound could be heard.

It was as though they had taken the sunshine with them; for a cloud had come up from the west, and the sun was hidden. All at once the valley seemed a sombre and lonely place, and the hills with their whispering trees looked menacingly down upon the clearing, the cabin, and the five simple English folk. The glory of the day was gone. After a little more of idle staring, the frontiersman and his son returned to their work in the forest, while Alce and Molly went indoors to their spinning, and Audrey sat down upon the doorstep to listen to the hurry of voices in the trees, and to watch the ever-deepening shadow of the cloud above the valley.

CHAPTER II

THE COURT OF THE ORPHAN

An hour before dusk found the company that had dined in the valley making their way up the dry bed of a stream, through a gorge which cleft a line of precipitous hills. On either hand the bank rose steeply, giving no footing for man or beast. The road was a difficult one; for here a tall, fern-crowned rock left but a narrow passage between itself and the shaggy hillside, and there smooth and slippery ledges, mounting one above the other, spanned the way. In places, too, the drought had left pools of dark, still water, difficult to avoid, and not infrequently the entire party must come to a halt while the axemen cleared from the path a fallen birch or hemlock. Every man was afoot, none caring to risk a fall upon the rocks or into the black, cold water of the pools. The hoofs of the horses and the spurs of the men clanked against the stones; now and then one of the heavily laden packhorses stumbled and was sworn at, and once a warning rattle, issuing from a rank growth of fern on the hillside, caused a momentary commotion. There was no more laughter, or whistling, or calling from the van to the rear guard. The way was arduous, and every man must watch his footsteps; moreover, the last rays of the sun were gilding the hilltops above them, and the level that should form their camping-place must be reached before the falling of the night.

The sunlight had all but faded from the heights, when one of the company, stumbling over a round and mossy rock, measured his length upon the ground, amid his own oaths at his mishap, and the exclamations of the man immediately in his rear, whose progress he had thus unceremoniously blocked. The horse of the fallen man, startled by the dragging at the reins, reared and plunged, and in a moment the entire column was in disorder. When the frightened animals were at last quieted, and the line re-formed, the Governor called out to know who it was that had fallen, and whether any damage had been suffered.

"It was Mr. Haward, sir!" cried two or three; and presently the injured gentleman himself, limping painfully, and with one side of his fine green coat all stained by reason of contact with a bit of muddy ground, appeared before his Excellency.

"I have had a cursed mishap,—saving your presence, sir," he explained. "The right ankle is, I fear, badly sprained. The pain, is exquisite, and I know not how I am to climb mountains."

The Governor uttered an exclamation of concern: "Unfortunate! Dr. Robinson must look to the hurt at once."

"Your Excellency forgets my dispute with Dr. Robinson as to the dose of Jesuit bark for my servant," said the sufferer blandly. "Were I *in extremis* I should not apply to him for relief."

"I'll lay my life that you are not *in extremis* now," retorted the doctor. "If ever I saw a man with a sprained ankle keep his color so marvelously, or heard him speak in so composed a tone! The pain must be of a very unusual degree indeed!"

"It is," answered Mr. Haward calmly. "I cannot possibly go on in this condition, your Excellency, nor can I dream of allowing my unlucky accident to delay this worshipful company in their ascent of the mountains. I will therefore take my servant and ride slowly back to the cabin which we left this afternoon. Doubtless the worthy pioneer will give me shelter until my foot is healed, and I will rejoin your Excellency upon your return through the valley."

As he spoke, for the greater ease of the injured member, he leaned against a towering lock. He was a handsome youth, with a trick of keeping an unmoved countenance under even such a fire of laughter and exclamation as greeted his announcement.

"And for this you would lose the passing of the Appalachian Mountains!" cried Spotswood. "Why, man! from those heights we may almost see Lake Erie; may find out how near we are to the French, how easily the mountains may be traversed, what promise of success should his Majesty determine to plant settlements beyond them or to hold the mountain passes! There is service to be done and honor to be gained, and you would lag behind because of a wrenched ankle! Zoons, sir! at Blenheim I charged a whole regiment of Frenchmen, with a wound in my breast into which you might have thrust your hand!"

The younger man shrugged his shoulders. "Beggars may not be choosers," he said coolly. "The sunlight is fast fading, and if we would be out of this gorge before nightfall we must make no further tarrying. I have your Excellency's permission to depart?"

One of the gentlemen made a low-voiced but audible remark to his neighbor, and another hummed a line from a love song. The horses moved impatiently amongst the loose stones, and the rangers began to mutter that night would be upon them before they reached a safer footing.

"Mr. Haward! Mr. Haward!" said the Governor sternly. "It is in my mind that you meditate inflicting a greater harm than you have received. Let me tell you, sir, if you think to so repay a simple-minded hospitality"—

Mr. Haward's eyes narrowed. "I own Colonel Spotswood for Governor of Virginia," he said, speaking slowly, as was his wont when he was angry. "His office does not, I think, extend farther than that. As for these pleasant-minded gentlemen who are not protected by their rank I beg to inform them that in my fall my sword arm suffered no whit."

Turning, he beckoned to a negro who had worked his way from the servants in the rear, along the line of rangers, to the outskirts of the group of gentlemen gathered around the Governor and the injured man. "Juba," he ordered, "draw your horse and mine to one side. Your Excellency, may I again remind you that it draws toward nightfall, and that this road will be no pleasant one to travel in the dark?"

What he said was true; moreover, upon the setting out of the expedition it had been laughingly agreed that any gentleman who might find his spirits dashed by the dangers and difficulties of the way should be at liberty at

Mary Johnston

any time to turn his back upon the mountains, and his face toward safety and the settlements. The Governor frowned, bit his lips, but finally burst into unwilling laughter.

"You are a very young gentleman, Mr. Marmaduke Haward!" he cried. "Were you a little younger, I know what ointment I should prescribe for your hurt. Go your ways with your broken ankle; but if, when I come again to the cabin in the valley, I find that your own injury has not contented you, look to it that I do not make you build a bridge across the bay itself! Gentlemen, Mr. Haward is bent upon intrusting his cure to other and softer hands than Dr. Robinson's, and the expedition must go forward without him. We sorrow to lose him from our number, but we know better than to reason with—ahem!—a twisted ankle. *En avant*, gentlemen! Mr. Haward, pray have a care of yourself. I would advise that the ankle be well bandaged, and that you stir not from the chimney corner"—

"I thank your Excellency for your advice," said Mr. Haward imperturbably, "and will consider of taking it. I wish your Excellency and these merry gentlemen a most complete victory over the mountains, from which conquest I will no longer detain you."

He bowed as he spoke, and began to move, slowly and haltingly, across the width of the rocky way to where his negro stood with the two horses.

"Mr. Haward!" called the Governor.

The recreant turned his head. "Your Excellency?"

"It was the right foot, was it not?" queried his sometime leader. "Ah, I thought so! Then it were best not to limp with the left."

Homeric laughter shook the air; but while Mr. Haward laughed not, neither did he frown or blush. "I will remember, sir," he said simply, and at once began to limp with the proper foot. When he reached the bank he turned, and, standing with his arm around his horse's neck, watched the company which he had so summarily deserted, as it put itself into motion and went slowly past him up its dusky road. The laughter and bantering farewells moved him not; he could at will draw a line around himself across which few things could step. Not far away the bed of the stream turned, and a hillside, dark with hemlock, closed the view. He watched the train pass him, reach this bend, and disappear. The axemen and the four Meherrins, the Governor and the gentlemen of the Horseshoe, the rangers, the negroes,—all were gone at last. With that passing, and with the ceasing of the laughter and the trampling, came the twilight. A whippoorwill began to call, and the wind sighed in the trees. Juba, the negro, moved closer to his master; then upon an impulse stooped, and lifting above his head a great rock, threw it with might into one of the shallow pools. The crashing sound broke the spell of the loneliness and quiet that had fallen upon the place. The white man drew his breath, shrugged his shoulders, and turned his horse's head down the way up which he had so lately come.

The cabin in the valley was not three miles away. Down this ravine to a level place of pines, through the pines to a strip of sassafras and a poisoned field, past these into a dark, rich wood of mighty trees linked together with the ripening grape, then three low hills, then the valley and the cabin and a pair of starry eyes. It was full moon. Once out from under the stifling walls of the ravine, and the

Mary Johnston

silver would tremble through the leaves, and show the path beneath. The trees, too, that they had blazed,—with white wood pointing to white wood, the backward way should be easy.

The earth, rising sheer in darkness on either hand, shut in the bed of the stream. In the warm, scented dusk the locusts shrilled in the trees, and far up the gorge the whippoorwill called and called. The air was filled with the gold of fireflies, a maze of spangles, now darkening, now brightening, restless and bewildering. The small, round pools caught the light from the yet faintly colored sky, and gleamed among the rocks; a star shone out, and a hot wind, heavy with the smell of the forest, moved the hemlock boughs and rustled in the laurels.

The white man and the negro, each leading his horse, picked their way with caution among the pitfalls of the rocky and uneven road. With the passing of the Governor and his train a sudden cure had been wrought, for now Haward's step was as firm and light as it had been before his fall. The negro looked at him once or twice with a puzzled face, but made no comment and received no enlightenment. Indeed, so difficult was their way that they were left but scant leisure for speech. Moment by moment the darkness deepened, and once Haward's horse came to its knees, crashing down among the rocks and awakening every echo.

The way, if hard, was short. The hills fell farther apart, the banks became low and broad, and fair in front, between two slender pines, shone out the great round moon. Leaving the bed of the stream, the two men entered a pine wood, dim and fragrant and easy to thread. The moon rose higher, and the light fell in wide shafts between trees that stood well apart, with no vines to grapple one to another or undergrowth to press about their knees.

There needed no watchfulness: the ground was smooth, the light was fair; no motion save the pale flicker of the fireflies, no sound save the sigh of the night wind in the boughs that were so high overhead. Master and man, riding slowly and steadily onward through a wood that seemed interminably the same, came at last to think of other things than the road which they were traveling. Their hands lost grasp upon the reins, and their eyes, ceasing to glance now here, now there, gazed steadfastly down the gray and dreamlike vista before them, and saw no longer hole and branch, moonlight and the white scars that the axe had made for guidance. The vision of the slave was of supper at the quarters, of the scraping of the fiddle in the red firelight, of the dancing and the singing. The white man saw, at first, only a girl's face, shy and innocent,—the face of the woodland maid who had fired his fancy, who was drawing him through the wilderness back to the cabin in the valley. But after a while, in the gray stillness, he lost the face, and suddenly thought, instead, of the stone that was to cover his father's grave. The ship that was to bring the great, dark, carven slab should be in by now; the day after his return to Williamsburgh the stone must be put in place, covering in the green sod and that which lay below. *Here, lieth in the hope of a joyful resurrection—*

His mind left the grave in the churchyard at Williamsburgh, and visited the great plantation of which he was now sole master. There was the house, foursquare, high-roofed, many-windowed, built of dark red brick that glowed behind the veil of the walnuts and the oaks. There, too, were the quarters,—the home quarter, that at the creek, that on the ridge. Fifty white servants, three hundred slaves,—and he was the master. The honey-suckles in the garden that had been his father's pride, the shining expanse of the river, the ship—his ship, the Golden Rose—that was to take him home to England,—he forgot the night and the forest, and saw these things quite plainly. Then he fell to thinking of London and the sweets that he meant to taste, the heady wine of youth and life that he meant to drain to the lees. He was young; he could spare the years. One day he would come back to Virginia, to the dim old garden and quiet house. His factor would give account, and he would settle down in the red brick house, with the tobacco to the north and east, the corn to the west, and to the south the mighty river,—the river silvered by the moon, the river that lay just beyond him, gleaming through the trees—

Startled by the sudden tightening of the reins, or by the tearing of some frightened thing through the canes that beset the low, miry bank, the horse sprang aside; then stood trembling with pricked ears. The white man stared at the stream; turned in his saddle and stared at the tree trunks, the patches of moonlight, and the impenetrable shadow that closed each vista. "The blazed trees!" he exclaimed at last. "How long since we saw one?"

The slave shook his head. "Juba forgot to look. He was away by a river that he knew."

"We have passed from out the pines," said Haward. "These are oaks. But what is that water, and how far we are out of our reckoning the Lord only knows!"

As he spoke he pushed his horse through the tall reeds to the bank of the stream. Here in the open, away from the shadow of the trees, the full moon had changed the night-time into a wonderful, silver day. Narrow above and belows the stream widened before him into a fairy basin, rimmed with reeds, unruffled, crystal-clear, stiller than a dream. The trees that grew upon the farther side were faint gray clouds in the moonlight, and the gold of the fireflies was very pale. From over the water, out of the heart of the moonlit wood, came the song of a mockingbird, a tumultuous ecstasy, possessing the air and making elfin the night.

Haward backed his horse from the reeds to the oak beneath which waited the negro. "'Tis plain that we have lost our way, Juba," he said, with a laugh. "If you were an Indian, we should turn and straightway retrace our steps to the blazed trees. Being what you are, you are more valuable in the tobacco fields than in the forest. Perhaps this is the stream which flows by the cabin in the valley. We'll follow it down, and so arrive, at least, at a conclusion."

They dismounted, and, leading their horses, followed the stream for some distance, to arrive at the conclusion that it was not the one beside which they had dined that day. When they were certain of this, they turned and made their way back to the line of reeds which they had broken to mark their starting-point. By now the moon was high, and the mockingbird in the wood across the water was singing madly. Turning from the still, moonlit sheet, the silent reeds, the clear mimicker in the slumbrous wood, the two wayfarers plunged into the darkness beneath the spreading branches of the oak-trees. They could not have ridden far from the pines; in a very little while they might reach and recognize the path which they should tread.

An hour later, the great trees, oak and chestnut, beech and poplar, suddenly gave way to saplings, many, close-set, and overrun with grapevines. So dense was the growth, so unyielding the curtain of vines, that men and horses were brought to a halt as before a fortress wall. Again they turned, and, skirting that stubborn network, came upon a swamp, where leafless trees, white as leprosy, stood up like ghosts from the water that gleamed between the lily-pads. Leaving the swamp they climbed a hill, and at the summit found only the moon and the stars and a long plateau of sighing grass. Behind them were the great mountains; before them, lesser heights, wooded hills, narrow valleys, each like its fellow, each indistinct and shadowy, with no sign of human tenant.

Haward gazed at the climbing moon and at the wide and universal dimness of the world beneath; then turned to the negro, and pointed to a few low trees growing at the eastern end of the plateau.

"Fasten the horses there, Juba," he said. "We will wait upon this hilltop until morning. When the light comes, we may be able to see the clearing or the smoke from the cabin."

When the horses had been tethered, master and man lay down upon the grass. It was so still upon the hilltop, and the heavens pressed so closely, that the slave grew restless and strove to make talk. Failing in this, he began to croon a savage, mournful air, and presently, forgetting himself, to sing outright.

"Be quiet!" ordered his master. "There may be Indians abroad."

The song came to an end as abruptly as it lad begun, and the singer, having nothing better to do, went fast asleep. His companion, more wakeful, lay with his hands behind his head and his eyes upon the splendor of the firmament.

Lying so, he could not see the valleys nor the looming mountains. There were only the dome of the sky, the grass, and himself. He stared at the moon, and made pictures of her shadowy places; then fell to thinking of the morrow, and of the possibility that after all he might never find again the cabin in the valley. While he laughed at this supposition, yet he played with it. He was in a mood to think the loss of the trail of the expedition no great matter. The woods were full of game, the waters of fish; he and Juba had only to keep their faces to the eastward, and a fortnight at most would bring them to the settlements. But the valleys folded among the hills were many; what if the one he sought should still elude him? What if the cabin, the sugar-tree, the crystal stream, had sunk from sight, like the city in one of Monsieur Gralland's fantastic tales? Perhaps they had done so,—the spot had all the air of a bit of fairyland,—and the woodland maid was gone to walk with the elves. Well, perchance for her it would be better so. And yet it would be pleasant if she should climb the hillside now and sit beside him, with her shy dark eyes and floating hair. Her hair was long and fine, and the wind would lift it; her face was fair, and another than the wind should kiss it. The night would not then be so slow in going.

He turned upon his side, and looked along the grassy summit to the woods upon the opposite slope and to the distant mountains. Dull silver, immutable, perpetual, they reared themselves to meet the moonbeams. Between him and those stern and changeless fronts, pallid as with snows, stretched the gray woods. The moon shone very brightly, and there was no wind. So unearthly was the quiet of the night, so solemn the light, so high and still and calm the universe around him, that awe fell upon his soul. It was well to lie upon the hilltop and guess at the riddle of the world; now dimly to see the meaning, now to

lose it quite, to wonder, to think of death. The easy
consciousness that for him death was scores of years
away, that he should not meet the spectre until the wine
was all drunken, the garlands withered, and he, the guest,
ready to depart, made these speculations not at all
unpleasing. He looked at his hand, blanched by the moonlight, lying beside him upon the grass, and thought how
like a dead hand it seemed, and what if he could not move
it, nor his body, nor could ever rise from the grass, but
must lie there upon the lonely hilltop in the untrodden
wilderness, until that which had ridden and hunted and
passed so buoyantly through life should become but a few
dry bones, a handful of dust. He was of his time, and its
laxness of principle and conduct; if he held within himself
the potential scholar, statesman, and philosopher, there
were also the skeptic, the egotist, and the libertine. He
followed the fashion and disbelieved much, but he knew
that if he died to-night his soul would not stay with his
body upon the hilltop. He wondered, somewhat grimly,
what it would do when so much that had clothed it
round—pride of life, love of pleasure, desire, ambition—
should be plucked away. Poor soul! Surely it would feel
itself something shrunken, stripped of warmth,
shiveringly bare to all the winds of heaven. The radiance
of the moon usurped the sky, but behind that veil of light
the invisible and multitudinous stars were shining.
Beyond those stars were other stars, beyond those yet
others; on and on went the stars, wise men said. Beyond
them all, what then? And where was the place of the soul?
What would it do? What heaven or hell would it find or
make for itself? Guesswork all!

The silver pomp of the night began to be oppressive to
him. There was beauty, but it was a beauty cold and
distant, infinitely withdrawn from man and his concerns.
Woods and mountains held aloof, communing with the

stars. They were kindred and of one house; it was man who was alien, a stranger and alone. The hilltop cared not that he lay thereon; the grass would grow as greenly when he was in his grave; all his tragedies since time began he might reenact there below, and the mountains would not bend to look.

He flung his arm across his eyes to shut out the moonlight, and tried to sleep. Finding the attempt a vain one, and that the night pressed more and more heavily upon him, he sat up with the intention of shaking the negro awake, and so providing himself with other company than his own thoughts.

His eyes had been upon the mountains, but now, with the sudden movement, he faced the eastern horizon and a long cleft between the hills. Far down this opening something was on fire, burning fiercely and redly. Some one must have put torch to the forest; and yet it did not burn as trees burn. It was like a bonfire ... it was a bonfire in a clearing! There were not woods about it, but a field— and the glint of water—

The negro, awakened by foot and voice, sprang up, and stood bewildered beside his master. "It is the valley that we have been seeking, Juba," said the latter, speaking rapidly and low. "That burning pile is the cabin, and 't is like that there are Indians between us and it! Leave the horses; we shall go faster without them. Look to the priming of your gun, and make no noise. Now!"

Rapidly descending the hill, they threw themselves into the woods at its base. Here they could not see the fire, but now and then, as they ran, they caught the glow, far down the lines of trees. Though they went swiftly they went warily as well, keeping an eye and ear open and muskets ready. But there was no sound other than their own quick footfalls upon the floor of rotting leaves, or the eager brushing of their bodies through occasional undergrowth; no sight but the serried trees and the checkered light and shade upon the ground.

They came to the shallow stream that flashed through the valley, and crossing it found themselves on cleared ground, with only a long strip of corn between them and what had been a home for English folk. It was that no longer: for lack of fuel the flames were dying down; there was only a charred and smoking pile, out of which leaped here and there a red tongue.

Haward had expected to hear a noise of savage triumph, and to see dark figures moving about their handiwork. There was no noise, and the moonlight showed no living being. The night was changelessly still and bright; the tragedy had been played, and the mountains and the hills and the running water had not looked.

It took but a few minutes to break through the rustling corn and reach the smouldering logs. Once before them, there seemed naught to do but to stand and stare at the ruin, until a tongue of flame caught upon a piece of uncharred wood, and showed them the body of the pioneer lying at a little distance from the stone that had formed his doorstep. At a sign from Haward the negro went and turned it over, then, let it sink again into the seared grass. "Two arrows, Marse Duke," he said, coming back to the other's side. "An' they've taken his scalp."

Three times Haward made the round of the yet burning heap. Was it only ruined and fallen walls, or was it a funeral pyre as well? To know, he must wait for the day and until the fire had burned itself out. If the former were the case, if the dead man alone kept the valley, then now, through the forest and the moonlight, captives were being haled to some Indian village, and to a fate more terrible than that of the man who lay there upon the grass with an arrow through his heart.

If the girl were still alive, yet was she dead to him. He was no Quixote to tilt with windmills. Had a way to rescue her lain fair before him, he would have risked his life without a thought. But the woods were deep and pathless, and only an Indian could find and keep a trail by night. To challenge the wilderness; to strike blindly at the forest, now here, now there; to dare all, and know that it was hopeless daring,—a madman might do this for love. But it was only Haward's fancy that had been touched, and if he lacked not courage, neither did he lack a certain cool good sense which divided for him the possible from that which was impossible, and therefore not to be undertaken.

Turning from the ruin, he walked across the trampled sward to the sugar-tree in whose shade, in the golden afternoon, he had sung to his companions and to a simple girl. Idle and happy and far from harm had the valley seemed.

"Here shall he see
No enemy
But winter and rough weather."

Suddenly he found that he was trembling, and that a sensation of faintness and of dull and sick revolt against all things under the stars was upon him. Sitting down in the shadow of the tree, he rested his face in his hands and shut his eyes, preferring the darkness within to that outer night which hid not and cared not, which was so coldly at

Mary Johnston

peace. He was young, and though stories of such dismal things as that before him were part of the stock in trade of every ancient, garrulous man or woman of his acquaintance, they had been for him but tales; not horrible truths to stare him in the face. He had seen his father die; but he had died, in his bed, and like one who went to sleep.

The negro had followed him, and now stood with his eyes upon the dying flames, muttering to himself some heathenish charm. When it was ended, he looked about him uneasily for a time; then bent and plucked his master by the sleeve. "We cyarn' do nothin' here, Marse Duke," he whispered. "An' the wolves may get the horses."

With a laugh and a groan, the young man rose to his feet. "That is true, Juba," he said. "It's all over here,—we were too late. And it's not a pleasant place to lie awake in, waiting for the morning. We'll go back to the hilltop."

Leaving the tree, they struck across the grass and entered the strip of corn. Something low and dark that had lain upon the ground started up before them, and ran down the narrow way between the stalks. Haward made after it and caught it.

"Child!" he cried. "Where are the others?"

The child had struggled for a moment, desperately if weakly, but at the sound of his voice she lay still in his grasp, with her eyes upon his face. In the moonlight each could see the other quite plainly. Raising her in his arms, Haward bore her to the brink of the stream, laved her face and chafed the small, cold hands.

"Now tell me, Audrey," he said at last. "Audrey is your name, isn't it? Cry, if you like, child, but try to tell me."

Audrey did not cry. She was very, very tired, and she wanted to go to sleep. "The Indians came," she told him in a whisper, with her head upon his breast. "We all waked up, and father fired at them through the hole in the door. Then they broke the door down, and he went outside, and they killed him. Mother put me under the bed, and told me to stay there, and to make no noise. Then the Indians came in at the door, and killed her and Molly and Robin. I don't remember anything after that,—maybe I went to sleep. When I was awake again the Indians were gone, but there was fire and smoke everywhere. I was afraid of the fire, and so I crept from under the bed, and kissed mother and Molly and Robin, and left them lying in the cabin, and came away."

She sighed with weariness, and the hand with which she put back her dark hair that had fallen over her face was almost too heavy to lift. "I sat beside father and watched the fire," she said. "And then I heard you and the black man coming over the stones in the stream. I thought that you were Indians, and I went and hid in the corn."

Her voice failed, and her eyelids drooped. In some anxiety Haward watched her breathing and felt for the pulse in the slight brown wrist; then, satisfied, he lifted the light burden, and, nodding to the negro to go before, recommenced his progress to the hill which he had left an hour agone.

It was not far away. He could see the bare summit above the treetops, and in a little while they were upon its slope. A minute more and they came to the clump of trees, and found the horses in safety, Haward paused to take from the roll strapped behind his saddle a riding cloak; then, leaving the negro with the horses, climbed to the grassy level. Here he spread the cloak upon the ground, and laid the sleeping child upon it, which done, he stood and looked at his new-found charge for a moment; then turning, began to pace up and down upon the hilltop.

It was necessary to decide upon a course of action. They had the horses, the two muskets, powder and shot. The earth was dry and warm, and the skies were cloudless. Was it best to push on to Germanna, or was it best to wait down there in the valley for the return of the Governor and his party? They would come that way, that was certain, and would look to find him there. If they found only the ruined cabin, they might think him dead or taken by the Indians, and an attempt to seek him, as dangerous, perhaps, as fruitless, might be made. He decided that he would wait. To-morrow he would take Juba and the horses and the child and go down into the valley; not back to the sugar-tree and that yet smouldering pyre, but to the woods on this side of the stream.

This plan thought out, he went; and took his seat beside the child. She was moaning in her sleep, and he bent over and soothed her. When she was quiet he still kept her hand in his, as he sat there waiting for the dawn. He gave the child small thought. Together he and Juba must care for her until they could rejoin the expedition: then the Governor, who was so fond of children, might take her in hand, and give her for nurse old Dominick, who was as gentle as a woman. Once at Germanna perhaps some scolding *Hausfrau* would take her, for the sake of the scrubbing and lifting to be gotten out of those small hands and that slender frame. If not, she must on to Williamsburgh and the keeping of the vestry there. The next Orphan Court would bind her to some master or mistress who might (or might not) be kind to her, and so there would be an end to the matter.

The day was breaking. Moon and stars were gone, and the east was dull pink, like faded roses. A ribbon of silver mist, marking the course of the stream below, drew itself like a serpent through the woods that were changing from gray to green. The dank smell of early morning rose from the dew-drenched earth, and in the countless trees of the forest the birds began to sing.

A word or phrase which is as common and familiar as our hand may, in some one minute of time, take on a significance and present a face so keen and strange that it is as if we had never met it before. An Orphan Court! Again he said the words to himself, and then aloud. No doubt the law did its best for the fatherless and motherless, for such waifs and strays as that which lay beside him. When it bound out children, it was most emphatic that they should be fed and clothed and taught; not starved or beaten unduly, or let to grow up ignorant as negroes. Sometimes the law was obeyed, sometimes not.

The roses in the east bloomed again, and the pink of their petals melted into the clear blue of the upper skies. Because their beauty compelled him Haward looked at the heavens. The Court of the Orphan!... *When my father and my mother forsake, me, the Lord taketh me up.* Haward acknowledged with surprise that portions of the Psalter did somehow stick in the memory.

The face of the child was dark and thin, but the eyes were large and there was promise in the mouth. It was a pity—

He looked at her again, and suddenly resolved that he, Marmaduke Haward, would provide for her future. When they met once more, he should tell the Governor and his brother adventurers as much; and if they chose to laugh, why, let them do so! He would take the child to

Williamsburgh with him, and get some woman to tend her until he could find kind and decent folk with whom to bestow her. There were the new minister of Fair View parish and his wife,—they might do. He would give them two thousand pounds of sweet-scented a year for the child's maintenance. Oh, she should be well cared for! He would—if he thought of it—send her gifts from London; and when she was grown, and asked in marriage, he would give her for dowry a hundred acres of land.

As the strengthening rays of the sun, shining alike upon the just and the unjust, warmed his body, so his own benevolence warmed his heart. He knew that he was doing a generous thing, and his soul felt in tune with the beamy light, the caroling of the birds, the freshness and fragrance of the morning. When at last the child awoke, and, the recollection of the night coming full upon her, clung to him, weeping and trembling, he put his arm around her and comforted her with all the pet names his memory could conjure up.

CHAPTER III

DARDEN'S AUDREY

It was May Day in Virginia, in the year 1727. In England there were George the First, by the grace of God of Great Britain, France, and Ireland King and Defender of the Faith; my Lord of Orkney, Governor in chief of Virginia; and William Gooch, newly appointed Lieutenant Governor. In Virginia there were Colonel Robert Carter, President of the Council and Governor *pro tem.*; the Council itself; and Mistress Martha Jaquelin.

By virtue of her good looks and sprightliness, the position of her father in the community, and the fact that this 1st of May was one and the same with her sixteenth birthday, young Mistress Jaquelin was May Queen in Jamestown. And because her father was a worthy gentleman and a gay one, with French blood in his veins and Virginia hospitality in his heart, he had made a feast for divers of his acquaintances, and, moreover, had provided, in a grassy meadow down by the water side, a noble and seasonable entertainment for them, and for the handful of townsfolk, and for all chance comers.

Meadow and woodland and marsh, ploughed earth and blossoming orchards, lay warm in the sunshine. Even the ruined town, fallen from her estate, and become but as a handmaid to her younger sister, put a good face upon her melancholy fortunes. Honeysuckle and ivy embraced and hid crumbling walls, broken foundations, mounds of brick and rubbish, all the untouched memorials of the last burning of the place. Grass grew in the street, and the silent square was strewn with the gold of the buttercups. The houses that yet stood and were lived in might have been counted on the fingers of one hand, with the thumb for the church. But in their gardens the flowers bloomed gayly, and the sycamores and mulberries in the churchyard were haunts of song. The dead below had music, and violets in the blowing grass, and the undertone of the river. Perhaps they liked the peace of the town that was dead as they were dead; that, like them, had seen of the travail of life, and now, with shut eyes and folded hands, knew that it was vanity.

But the Jaquelin house was built to the eastward of the churchyard and the ruins of the town, and, facing the sparkling river, squarely turned its back upon the quiet desolation at the upper end of the island and upon the text from Ecclesiastes.

In the level meadow, around a Maypole gay with garlands and with fluttering ribbons, the grass had been closely mown, for there were to be foot-races and wrestling bouts for the amusement of the guests. Beneath a spreading tree a dozen fiddlers put their instruments in tune, while behind the open windows of a small, ruinous house, dwelt in by the sexton, a rustic choir was trying over "The Beggar's Daughter of Bednall Green." Young men and maidens of the meaner sort, drawn from the surrounding country, from small plantation, store and ordinary, mill and ferry, clad in their holiday best and prone to laughter, strayed here and there, or, walking up and down the river bank, where it commanded a view of both the landing and the road, watched for the coming of the gentlefolk. Children, too, were not lacking, but rolled amidst the buttercups or caught at the ribbons flying from the Maypole, while aged folk sat in the sun, and a procession of wide-lipped negroes, carrying benches and chairs, advanced to the shaven green and put the seats in order about the sylvan stage. It was but nine of the clock, and the shadow of the Maypole was long upon the grass. Along the slightly rising ground behind the meadow stretched an apple orchard in full bloom, and between that line of rose and snow and the lapping of the tide upon the yellow sands lay, for the length of a spring day, the kingdom of all content.

The shadow of the Maypole was not much shrunken when the guests of the house of Jaquelin began to arrive. First to come, and from farthest away, was Mr. Richard Ambler, of Yorktown, who had ridden from that place to Williamsburgh the afternoon before, and had that morning used the planter's pace to Jamestown,—his industry being due to the fact that he was courting the May Queen's elder sister. Following him came five Lees in a chariot, then a delegation of Burwells, then two Digges in a chaise. A Bland and a Bassett and a Randolph came on horseback, while a barge brought up river a bevy of blooming Carters, a white-sailed sloop from Warwick landed a dozen Carys, great and small, and two periaguas, filled with Harrisons, Aliens, and Cockes, shot over from the Surrey shore.

From a stand at one end of the grassy stage, trumpet and drum proclaimed that the company had gathered beneath the sycamores before the house, and was about to enter the meadow. Shrill-voiced mothers warned their children from the Maypole, the fiddlers ceased their twanging, and

Mary Johnston

Pretty Bessee, her name cut in twain, died upon the air. The throng of humble folk—largely made up of contestants for the prizes of the day, and of their friends and kindred—scurried to its appointed place, and with the issuing from the house gates of the May Queen and her court the festivities commenced.

An hour later, in the midst of a bout at quarterstaff between the Jamestown blacksmith and the miller from Princess Creek, a coach and four, accompanied by a horseman, crossed the neck, rolled through the street, and, entering the meadow, drew up a hundred feet from the ring of spectators.

The eyes of the commonalty still hung upon every motion of the blacksmith and the miller, but by the people of quality the cudgelers were for the moment quite forgot. The head of the house of Jaquelin hurried over the grass to the coach door. "Ha, Colonel Byrd! When we heard that you were staying overnight at Green Spring, we hoped that, being so near, you would come to our merrymaking. Mistress Evelyn, I kiss your hands. Though we can't give you the diversions of Spring Garden, yet such as we have are at your feet. Mr. Marmaduke Haward, your servant, sir! Virginia has missed you these ten years and more. We were heartily glad to hear, t'other day, that the Golden Rose had brought you home."

As he spoke the worthy gentleman strove to open the coach door; but the horseman, to whom the latter part of his speech was addressed, and who had now dismounted, was beforehand with him. The door swung open, and a young lady, of a delicate and pensive beauty, placed one hand upon the deferential arm of Mr. Marmaduke Haward and descended from the painted coach to the flower-enameled sward. The women amongst the assembled guests fluttered and whispered; for this was youth, beauty, wealth, London, and the Court, all drawn in the person of Mistress Evelyn Byrd, bred since childhood in the politest society of England, newly returned with her father to his estate of Westover in Virginia, and, from her garlanded gypsy hat to the point of her silken shoe, suggestive of the rainbow world of *mode*.

Her father—alert, vivacious, handsome, with finely cut lips that were quick to smile, and dark eyes that smiled when the lips were still—followed her to the earth, shook out his ruffles, and extended his gold snuffbox to his good friend Mr. Jaquelin. The gentleman who had ridden beside the coach threw the reins of his horse to one of the negroes who had come running from the Jaquelin stables, and, together with their host, the three walked across the strip of grass to the row of expectant gentry. Down went the town-bred lady until the skirt of her blue-green gown lay in folds upon the buttercups; down went the ladies opposite in curtsies as profound, if less exquisitely graceful. Off came the hats of the gentlemen; the bows were of the lowest; snuffboxes were drawn out, hand-kerchiefs of fine holland flourished; the welcoming speeches were hearty and not unpolished.

It was a society less provincial than that of more than one shire that was nearer to London by a thousand leagues. It dwelt upon the banks of the Chesapeake and of great rivers; ships dropped their anchors before its very doors. Now and again the planter followed his tobacco aboard. The sands did not then run so swiftly through the hourglass; if the voyage to England was long, why, so was life! The planters went, sold their tobacco,—Sweet-scented, E. Dees, Oronoko, Cowpen, Non-burning,—talked with their agents, visited their English kindred; saw the town, the opera, and the play,—perhaps, afar off, the

King; and returned to Virginia and their plantations with the last but one novelty in ideas, manner, and dress. Of their sons not a few were educated in English schools, while their wives and daughters, if for the most part they saw the enchanted ground only through the eyes of husband, father, or brother, yet followed its fashions, when learned, with religious zeal. In Williamsburgh, where all men went on occasion, there was polite enough living: there were the college, the Capitol, and the playhouse; the palace was a toy St. James; the Governors that came and went almost as proper gentlemen, fitted to rule over English people, as if they had been born in Hanover and could not speak their subjects' tongue.

So it was that the assembly which had risen to greet Mr. Jaquelin's latest guests, besides being sufficiently well born, was not at all ill bred, nor uninformed, nor untraveled. But it was not of the gay world as were the three whom it welcomed. It had spent only months, not years, in England; it had never kissed the King's hand; it did not know Bath nor the Wells; it was innocent of drums and routs and masquerades; had not even a speaking acquaintance with great lords and ladies; had never supped with Pope, or been grimly smiled upon by the Dean of St. Patrick's, or courted by the Earl of Peterborough. It had not, like the elder of the two men, studied in the Low Countries, visited the Court of France, and contracted friendships with men of illustrious names; nor, like the younger, had it written a play that ran for two weeks, fought a duel in the Field of Forty Footsteps, and lost and won at the Cocoa Tree, between the lighting and snuffing of the candles, three thousand pounds.

Therefore it stood slightly in awe of the wit and manners and fine feathers, curled newest fashion, of its sometime friends and neighbors, and its welcome, if warm at heart, was stiff as cloth of gold with ceremony. The May Queen tripped in her speech as she besought Mistress Evelyn to take the flower-wreathed great chair standing proudly forth from the humbler seats, and colored charmingly at the lady of fashion's smiling shake of the head and few graceful words of homage. The young men slyly noted the length of the Colonel's periwig and the quality of Mr. Hayward's Mechlin, while their elders, suddenly lacking material for discourse, made shift to take a deal of snuff. The Colonel took matters into his own capable hands.

"Mr. Jaquelin, I wish that my tobacco at Westover may look as finely a fortnight hence as does yours to-day! There promise to be more Frenchmen in my fields than Germans at St. James. Mr. Gary, if I come to Denbigh when the peaches are ripe, will you teach me to make persico? Mr. Allen, I hear that you breed cocks as courageous as those of Tanagra. I shall borrow from you for a fight that I mean to give. Ladies, for how much gold will you sell the recipe for that balm of Mecca you must use? There are dames at Court would come barefoot to Virginia for so dazzling a bloom. Why do you patch only upon the Whig side of the face? Are you all of one camp, and does not one of you grow a white rosebush against the 29th of May? May it please your Majesty the May Queen, I shall watch the sports from this seat upon your right hand. Egad, the miller quits himself as though he were the moss-grown fellow of Sherwood Forest!"

The ice had thawed; and by the time the victorious miller had been pushed forward to receive the smart cocked hat which was the Virginia rendition of the crown of wild olive, it had quite melted. Conversation became general, and food was found or made for laughter. When the twelve fiddlers who succeeded the blacksmith and the miller came trooping upon the green, they played, one by one, to perhaps as light-hearted a company as a May Day ever shone upon. All their tunes were gay and lively ones, and the younger men moved their feet to the music, while a Strephon at the lower end of the lists seized upon a blooming Chloe, and the two began to dance "as if," quoth the Colonel, "the musicians were so many tarantula doctors."

A flower-wreathed instrument of his calling went to the player of the sprightliest air; after which awardment, the fiddlers, each to the tune of his own choosing, marched off the green to make room for Pretty Bessee, her father the beggar, and her suitors the innkeeper, the merchant, the gentleman, and the knight.

The high, quick notes of the song suited the sunshiny weather, the sheen of the river, the azure skies. A light wind brought from the orchard a vagrant troop of pink and white petals to camp upon the silken sleeve of Mistress Evelyn Byrd. The gentleman sitting beside her gathered them up and gave them again to the breeze.

"It sounds sweetly enough," he said, "but terribly old-fashioned:—

'I weigh not true love by the weight of the purse,
And beauty is beauty in every degree.'

That's not Court doctrine."

The lady to whom he spoke rested her cheek upon her hand, and looked past the singers to the blossoming slope and the sky above. "So much the worse for the Court," she said. "So much the better for"—

Haward glanced at her. "For Virginia?" he ended, with a

smile. "Do you think that they do not weigh love with gold here in Virginia, Evelyn? It isn't really Arcady."

"So much the better for some place, somewhere," she answered quietly. "I did not say Virginia. Indeed, from what travelers like yourself have told me, I think the country lies not upon this earth. But the story is at an end, and we must applaud with the rest. It sounded sweetly, after all,—though it was only a lying song. What next?"

Her father, from his station beside the May Queen, caught the question, and broke the flow of his smiling compliments to answer it. "A race between young girls, my love,—the lucky fair who proves her descent from Atalanta to find, not a golden apple, but a golden guinea. Here come from the sexton's house the pretty light o' heels!"

The crowd, gentle and simple, arose, and pushed back all benches, stools, and chairs, so as to enlarge the circumference of the ring, and the six girls who were to run stepped out upon the green. The youngest son of the house of Jaquelin checked them off in a shrill treble:—

"The blacksmith's Meg—Mall and Jenny from the crossroads ordinary—the Widow Constance's Barbara—red-headed Bess—Parson Darden's Audrey!"

A tall, thin, grave gentleman, standing behind Haward, gave an impatient jerk of his body and said something beneath his breath. Haward looked over his shoulder. "Ha, Mr. Le Neve! I did not know you were there. I had the pleasure of hearing you read at Williamsburgh last Sunday afternoon,—though this is your parish, I believe? What was that last name that the youngster cried? I failed to catch it."

"Audrey, sir," answered the minister of James City parish; "Gideon Darden's Audrey. You can't but have heard of Darden? A minister of the gospel of the Lord Jesus Christ, sir; and a scandal, a shame, and a stumbling-block to the Church! A foul-mouthed, brawling, learned sot! A stranger to good works, but a frequenter of tippling houses! A brazen, dissembling, atheistical Demas, who will neither let go of the lusts of the flesh nor of his parish,—a sweet-scented parish, sir, with the best glebe in three counties! And he's inducted, sir, inducted, which is more than most of the clergy of Virginia, who neither fight nor drink nor swear, can say for themselves!"

The minister had lost his gravity, and spoke with warmth and bitterness. As he paused for breath, Mistress Evelyn took her eyes from the group of those about to run and opened her fan. "A careless father, at least," she said. "If he hath learning, he should know better than to set his daughter there."

"She's not his own, ma'am. She's an orphan, bound to Darden and his wife, I suppose. There's some story or other about her, but, not being curious in Mr. Darden's affairs, I have never learned it. When I came to Virginia, five years ago, she was a slip of a girl of thirteen or so. Once, when I had occasion to visit Darden, she waylaid me in the road as I was riding away, and asked me how far it was to the mountains, and if there were Indians between them and us."

"Did she so?" asked Haward. "And which is—Audrey?"

"The dark one—brown as a gypsy—with the dogwood in her hair. And mark me, there'll be Darden's own luck and she'll win. She's fleeter than a greyhound. I've seen her running in and out and to and fro in the forest like a wild thing."

Bare of foot and slender ankle, bare of arm and shoulder, with heaving bosom, shut lips, and steady eyes, each of the six runners awaited the trumpet sound that should send her forth like an arrow to the goal, and to the shining guinea that lay thereby. The spectators ceased to talk and laugh, and bent forward, watching. Wagers had been laid, and each man kept his eyes upon his favorite, measuring her chances. The trumpet blew, and the race was on.

When it was over and won, the May Queen rose from her seat and crossed the grass to her fine lady guest. "There are left only the prizes for this and for the boys' race and for the best dancer. Will you not give them, Mistress Evelyn, and so make them of more value?"

More curtsying, more complimenting, and the gold was in Evelyn's white hand. The trumpet blew, the drum beat, the fiddlers swung into a quick, staccato air, and Darden's Audrey, leaving the post which she had touched some seconds in advance of the foremost of those with whom she had raced, came forward to receive the guinea.

The straight, short skirt of dull blue linen could not hide the lines of the young limbs; beneath the thin, white, sleeveless bodice showed the tint of the flesh, the rise and fall of the bosom. The bare feet trod the grass lightly and firmly; the brown eyes looked from under the dogwood chaplet in a gaze that was serious, innocent, and unashamed. To Audrey they were only people out of a fairy tale,—all those gay folk, dressed in silks and with curled hair. They lived in "great houses," and men and women were born to till their fields, to row their boats, to doff hats or curtsy as they passed. They were not real; if you pricked them they would not bleed. In the mountains that she remembered as a dream there were pale masses of bloom far up among the cliffs; very beautiful, but no more to be gained than the moon or than rainbow gold. She looked at the May party before which she had been called much as, when a child, she had looked at the gorgeous, distant bloom,—not without longing, perhaps, but indifferent, too, knowing that it was beyond her reach.

When the gold piece was held out to her, she took it, having earned it; when the little speech with which the lady gave the guinea was ended, she was ready with her curtsy and her "Thank you, ma'am." The red came into her cheeks because she was not used to so many eyes upon her, but she did not blush for her bare feet, nor for her dress that had slipped low over her shoulder, nor for the fact that she had run her swiftest five times around the Maypole, all for the love of a golden guinea, and for mere youth and pure-minded ignorance, and the springtime in the pulses.

The gold piece lay within her brown fingers a thought too lightly, for as she stepped back from the row of gentlefolk it slid from her hand to the ground. A gentleman, sitting beside the lady who had spoken to her, stooped, and picking up the money gave it again into her hand. Though she curtsied to him, she did not look at him, but turned away, glad to be quit of all the eyes, and in a moment had slipped into the crowd from which she had come. It was midday, and old Israel, the fisherman, who had brought her and the Widow Constance's Barbara up the river in his boat, would be going back with the tide. She was not loath to leave: the green meadow, the gaudy Maypole, and the music were good, but the silence on the river, the shadow of the brooding forest, the darting of the fish hawk, were better.

In the meadow the boys' race and the rustic dance were soon over. The dinner at the Jaquelin house to its guests lasted longer, but it too was hurried; for in the afternoon Mr. Harrison's mare Nelly was to run against Major Burwell's Fearnaught, and the stakes were heavy.

Not all of the company went from the banquet back to the meadow, where the humbler folk, having eaten their dinner of bread and meat and ale, were whiling away with sports of their own the hour before the race. Colonel Byrd had business at Williamsburgh, and must reach his lodgings there an hour before sunset. His four black horses brought to the door the great vermilion-and-cream coach; an ebony coachman in scarlet cracked his whip at a couple of negro urchins who had kept pace with the vehicle as it lumbered from the stables, and a light brown footman flung open the door and lowered the steps. The Colonel, much regretting that occasion should call him away, vowed that he had never spent a pleasanter May Day, kissed the May Queen's hand, and was prodigal of well-turned compliments, like the gay and gallant gentleman that he was. His daughter made her graceful adieux in her clear, low, and singularly sweet voice, and together they were swallowed up of the mammoth coach. Mr. Haward took snuff with Mr. Jaquelin; then, mounting his horse,—it was supposed that he too had business in Williamsburgh,—raised his hat and bade farewell to the company with one low and comprehensive bow.

The equipage made a wide turn; the ladies and gentlemen upon the Jaquelin porch fluttered fans and handkerchiefs; the Colonel, leaning from the coach window, waved his hand; and the horseman lifted his hat the second time. The very especial guests were gone; and though the remainder of the afternoon was as merry as heart could wish, yet a bouquet, a flavor, a tang of the Court and the great world, a breath of air that was not colonial, had gone with them. For a moment the women stood in a brown study, revolving in their minds Mistress Evelyn's gypsy hat and the exceeding thinness and fineness of her tucker; while to each of the younger men came, linked to the memory of a charming face, a vision of many-acred Westover.

But the trumpet blew, summoning them to the sport of the afternoon, and work stopped upon castles in Spain. When a horse-race was on, a meadow in Virginia sufficed.

CHAPTER IV

THE ROAD TO WILLIAMSBURGH

April had gone out in rain, and though the sun now shone brightly from a cloudless sky, the streams were swollen and the road was heavy. The ponderous coach and the four black horses made slow progress. The creeping pace, the languid warmth of the afternoon, the scent of flowering trees, the ceaseless singing of redbird, catbird, robin, and thrush, made it drowsy in the forest. In the midst of an agreeable dissertation upon May Day sports of more ancient times the Colonel paused to smother a yawn; and when he had done with the clown, the piper, and the hobby-horse, he yawned again, this time outright.

"What with Ludwell's Burgundy, piquet, and the French peace, we sat late last night. My eyes are as heavy as the road. Have you noticed, my dear, how bland and dreamy is the air? On such an afternoon one is content to be in Virginia, and out of the world. It is a very land of the Lotophagi,—a lazy clime that Ulysses touched at, my love."

The equipage slowly climbed an easy ascent, and as slowly descended to the level again. The road was narrow, and now and then a wild cherry-tree struck the coach with a white arm, or a grapevine swung through the window a fragrant trailer. The woods on either hand were pale green and silver gray, save where they were starred with dogwood, or where rose the pink mist of the Judas-tree. At the foot of the hill the road skirted a mantled pond, choked with broad green leaves and the half-submerged trunks of fallen trees. Upon these logs, basking in the sunlight, lay small tortoises by the score. A snake glided across the road in front of the horses, and from a bit of muddy ground rose a cloud of yellow butterflies.

The Colonel yawned for the third time, looked at his watch, sighed, lifted his finely arched brows with a whimsical smile for his own somnolence; then, with an "I beg your pardon, my love," took out a lace handkerchief, spread it over his face and head, and, crossing his legs, sunk back into the capacious corner of the coach. In three minutes the placid rise and fall of his ruffles bore witness that he slept.

The horseman, who, riding beside the lowered glass, had at intervals conversed with the occupants of the coach, now glanced from the sleeping gentleman to the lady, in whose dark, almond-shaped eyes lurked no sign of drowsiness. The pond had been passed, and before them, between low banks crowned with ferns and overshadowed by beech-trees, lay a long stretch of shady road.

Haward drew rein, dismounted, and motioned to the coachman to check the horses. When the coach had come to a standstill, he opened the door with as little creaking as might be, and held out a petitionary hand. "Will you not walk with me a little way, Evelyn?" he asked, speaking in a low voice that he might not wake the sleeper. "It is much pleasanter out here, with the birds and the flowers."

His eyes and the smile upon his lips added, "and with me." From what he had been upon a hilltop, one moonlight night eleven years before, he had become a somewhat silent, handsome gentleman, composed in manner, experienced, not unkindly, looking abroad from his apportioned mountain crag and solitary fortress upon men, and the busy ways of men, with a tolerant gaze. That to certain of his London acquaintance he was simply the well-bred philosopher and man of letters; that in the minds of others he was associated with the peacock plumage of the world of fashion, with the flare of candles, the hot breath of gamesters, the ring of gold upon the tables; that one clique had tales to tell of a magnanimous spirit and a generous hand, while yet another grew red at mention of his name, and put to his credit much that was not creditable, was perhaps not strange. He, like his neighbors, had many selves, and each in its turn—the scholar, the man of pleasure, the indolent, kindly, reflective self, the self of pride and cool assurance and stubborn will—took its place behind the mask, and went through its allotted part. His self of all selves, the quiet, remote, crowned, and inscrutable *I*, sat apart, alike curious and indifferent, watched the others, and knew how little worth the while was the stir in the ant-hill.

But on a May Day, in the sunshine and the blossoming woods and the company of Mistress Evelyn Byrd, it seemed, for the moment, worth the while. At his invitation she had taken his hand and descended from the coach. The great, painted thing moved slowly forward, bearing the unconscious Colonel, and the two pedestrians walked behind it: he with his horse's reins over his arm and his hat in his hand; she lifting her silken skirts from contact with the ground, and looking, not at her companion, but at the greening boughs, and at the sunlight striking upon smooth, pale beech trunks and the leaf-strewn earth beneath. Out of the woods came a sudden medley of bird notes, clear, sweet, and inexpressibly joyous.

"That is a mockingbird," said Haward. "I once heard one of a moonlight night, beside a still water"—

He broke off, and they listened in silence. The bird flew away, and they came to a brook traversing the road, and flowing in wide meanders through the forest. There were stepping-stones, and Haward, crossing first, turned and held out his hand to the lady. When she was upon his side of the streamlet, and before he released the slender fingers, he bent and kissed them; then, as there was no answering smile or blush, but only a quiet withdrawal of the hand and a remark about the crystal clearness of the brook, looked at her, with interrogation in his smile.

"What is that crested bird upon yonder bough," she asked,—"the one that gave the piercing cry?"

"A kingfisher," he answered, "and cousin to the halcyon of the ancients. If, when next you go to sea, you take its feathers with you, you need have no fear of storms."

A tree, leafless, but purplish pink with bloom, leaned from the bank above them. He broke a branch and gave it to her. "It is the Judas-tree," he told her. "Iscariot hanged himself thereon."

Around the trunk of a beech a lizard ran like a green flame, and they heard the distant barking of a fox. Large white butterflies went past them, and a hummingbird whirred into the heart of a wild honeysuckle that had hasted to bloom. "How different from the English forests!" she said. "I could love these best. What are all those broad-leaved plants with the white, waxen flowers?"

"May-apples. Some call them mandrakes, but they do not rise shrieking, nor kill the wight that plucks them. Will you have me gather them for you?"

"I will not trouble you," she answered, and presently turned aside to pull them for herself.

He looked at the graceful, bending figure and lifted his brows; then, quickening his pace until he was up with the coach, he spoke to the negro upon the box. "Tyre, drive on to that big pine, and wait there for your mistress and me. Sidon,"—to the footman,—"get down and take my horse. If your master wakes, tell him that Mistress Evelyn tired of the coach, and that I am picking her a nosegay."

Tyre and Sidon, Haward's steed, the four black coach horses, the vermilion-and-cream coach, and the slumbering Colonel, all made a progress of an hundred yards to the pine-tree, where the cortege came to a halt. Mistress Evelyn looked up from the flower-gathering to find the road bare before her, and Haward, sitting upon a log, watching her with something between a smile and a frown.

"You think that I, also, weigh true love by the weight of the purse," he said. "I do not care overmuch for your gold, Evelyn."

She did not answer at once, but stood with her head slightly bent, fingering the waxen flowers with a delicate, lingering touch. Now that there was no longer the noise of the wheels and the horses' hoofs, the forest stillness, which is composed of sound, made itself felt. The call of birds, the whir of insects, the murmur of the wind in the treetops, low, grave, incessant, and eternal as the sound of the sea, joined themselves to the slow waves of fragrance, the stretch of road whereon nothing moved, the sunlight lying on the earth, and made a spacious quiet.

"I think that there is nothing for which you care overmuch," she said at last. "Not for gold or the lack of it, not for friends or for enemies, not even for yourself."

"I have known you for many years," he answered. "I have watched you grow from a child into a gracious and beautiful woman. Do you not think that I care for you, Evelyn?"

Near where he sat so many violets were blooming that they made a purple carpet for the ground. Going over to them, she knelt and began to pluck them. "If any danger threatened me," she began, in her clear, low voice, "I believe that you would step between me and it, though at the peril of your life. I believe that you take some pleasure in what you are pleased to style my beauty, some pride in a mind that you have largely formed. If I died early, it would grieve you for a little while. I call you my friend."

"I would be called your lover," he said.

She laid her fan upon the ground, heaped it with violets, and turned again to her reaping. "How might that be," she asked, "when you do not love me? I knew that you would marry me. What do the French call it,—*mariage de convenance*?"

Her voice was even, and her head was bent so that he

could not see her face. In the pause that followed her words treetop whispered to treetop, but the sunshine lay very still and bright upon the road and upon the flowers by the wayside.

"There are worse marriages," Haward said at last. Rising from the log, he moved to the side of the kneeling figure. "Let the violets rest, Evelyn, while we reason together. You are too clear-eyed. Since they offend you, I will drop the idle compliments, the pretty phrases, in which neither of us believes. What if this tinted dream of love does not exist for us? What if we are only friends—dear and old friends"—

He stooped, and, taking her by the busy hands, made her stand up beside him. "Cannot we marry and still be friends?" he demanded, with something like laughter in his eyes. "My dear, I would strive to make you happy; and happiness is as often found in that temperate land where we would dwell as in Love's flaming climate." He smiled and tried to find her eyes, downcast and hidden in the shadow of her hat. "This is no flowery wooing such as women love," he said; "but then you are like no other woman. Always the truth was best with you."

Upon her wrenching her hands from his, and suddenly and proudly raising her head, he was amazed to find her white to the lips.

"The truth!" she said slowly. "Always the truth was best! Well, then, take the truth, and afterwards and forever and ever leave me alone! You have been frank; why should not I, who, you say, am like no other woman, be so, too? I will not marry you, because—because"—The crimson flowed over her face and neck; then ebbed, leaving her whiter than before. She put her hands, that still held the wild flowers, to her breast, and her eyes, dark with pain, met his. "Had you loved me," she said proudly and quietly, "I had been happy."

Haward stepped backwards until there lay between them a strip of sunny earth. The murmur of the wind went on and the birds were singing, and yet the forest seemed more quiet than death. "I could not guess," he said, speaking slowly and with his eyes upon the ground. "I have spoken like a brute. I beg your pardon."

"You might have known! you might have guessed!" she cried, with passion. "But, you walk an even way; you choose nor high nor low; you look deep into your mind, but your heart you keep cool and vacant. Oh, a very temperate land! I think that others less wise than you may also be less blind. Never speak to me of this day! Let it die as these blooms are dying in this hot sunshine! Now let us walk to the coach and waken my father. I have gathered flowers enough."

Side by side, but without speaking, they moved from shadow to sunlight, and from sunlight to shadow, down the road to the great pine-tree. The white and purple flowers lay in her hand and along her bended arm; from the folds of her dress, of some rich and silken stuff, chameleon-like in its changing colors, breathed the subtle fragrance of the perfume then most in fashion; over the thin lawn that half revealed, half concealed neck and bosom was drawn a long and glossy curl, carefully let to escape from the waved and banded hair beneath the gypsy hat. Exquisite from head to foot, the figure had no place in the unpruned, untrained, savage, and primeval beauty of those woods. Smooth sward, with jets of water and carven nymphs embowered in clipped box or yew, should have been its setting, and not this wild and tangled growth, this license of bird and beast and growing things. And yet the incongruous riot, the contrast of profuse, untended beauty, enhanced the value of the picture, gave it piquancy and a completer charm.

When they were within a few feet of the coach and horses and negroes, all drowsing in the sunny road, Haward made as if to speak, but she stopped him with her lifted hand. "Spare me," she begged. "It is bad enough as it is, but words would make it worse. If ever a day might come—I do not think that I am unlovely; I even rate myself so highly as to think that I am worthy of your love. If ever the day shall come when you can say to me, 'Now I see that love is no tinted dream; now I ask you to be my wife indeed,' then, upon that day—But until then ask not of me what you asked back there among the violets. I, too, am proud"—Her voice broke.

"Evelyn!" he cried. "Poor child—poor friend"—

She turned her face upon him. "Don't!" she said, and her lips were smiling, though her eyes were full of tears. "We have forgot that it is May Day, and that we must be light of heart. Look how white is that dogwood-tree! Break me a bough for my chimney-piece at Williamsburgh."

He brought her a branch of the starry blossoms. "Did you notice," she asked, "that the girl who ran—Audrey—wore dogwood in her hair? You could see her heart beat with very love of living. She was of the woods, like a dryad. Had the prizes been of my choosing, she should have had a gift more poetical than a guinea."

Haward opened the coach door, and stood gravely aside while she entered the vehicle and took her seat, depositing her flowers upon the cushions beside her. The Colonel

stirred, uncrossed his legs, yawned, pulled the handkerchief from his face, and opened his eyes.

"Faith!" he exclaimed, straightening himself, and taking
up his radiant humor where, upon falling-asleep, he had
let it drop. "The way must have suddenly become smooth
as a road in Venice, for I've felt no jolting this half hour.
Flowers, Evelyn? and Haward afoot? You've been on a
woodland saunter, then, while I enacted Solomon's
sluggard!" The worthy parent's eyes began to twinkle.
"What flowers did you find? They have strange blooms
here, and yet I warrant that even in these woods one might
come across London pride and none-so-pretty and forget-
me-not"—

His daughter smiled, and asked him some idle question
about the May-apple and the Judas-tree. The master of
Westover was a treasure house of sprightly lore. Within
ten minutes he had visited Palestine, paid his compliments
to the ancient herbalists, and landed again in his own
coach, to find in his late audience a somewhat *distraite*
daughter and a friend in a brown study. The coach was
lumbering on toward Williamsburgh, and Haward, with
level gaze and hand closed tightly upon his horse's reins,
rode by the window, while the lady, sitting in her corner
with downcast eyes, fingered the dogwood blooms that
were not paler than her face.

The Colonel's wits were keen. One glance, a lift of his
arched brows, the merest ghost of a smile, and, dragging
the younger man with him, he plunged into politics.
Invective against a refractory House of Burgesses brought
them a quarter of a mile upon their way; the necessity for
an act to encourage adventurers in iron works carried
them past a milldam; and frauds in the customs enabled
them to reach a crossroads ordinary, where the Colonel

ordered a halt, and called for a tankard of ale. A slipshod, blue-eyed Cherry brought it, and spoke her thanks in broad Scotch for the shilling which the gay Colonel flung tinkling into the measure.

That versatile and considerate gentleman, having had his draught, cried to the coachman to go on, and was beginning upon the question of the militia, when Haward, who had dismounted, appeared at the coach door. "I do not think that I will go on to Williamsburgh with you, sir," he said. "There's some troublesome business with my overseer that ought not to wait. If I take this road and the planter's pace, I shall reach Fair View by sunset. You do not return to Westover this week? Then I shall see you at Williamsburgh within a day or two. Evelyn, good-day."

Her hand lay upon the cushion nearest him. He would have taken it in his own, as for years he had done when he bade her good-by; but though she smiled and gave him "Good-day" in her usual voice, she drew the hand away. The Colonel's eyebrows went up another fraction of an inch, but he was a discreet gentleman who had bought experience. Skillfully unobservant, his parting words were at once cordial and few in number; and after Haward had mounted and had turned into the side road, he put his handsome, periwigged head out of the coach window and called to him some advice about the transplanting of tobacco. This done, and the horseman out of sight, and the coach once more upon its leisurely way to Williamsburgh, the model father pulled out of his pocket a small book, and, after affectionately advising his daughter to close her eyes and sleep out the miles to Williamsburgh, himself retired with Horace to the Sabine farm.

Mary Johnston

CHAPTER V

THE STOREKEEPER

It was now late afternoon, the sun's rays coming slantingly into the forest, and the warmth of the day past and gone. To Haward, riding at a gallop down the road that was scarce more than a bridle path, the rush of the cool air was grateful; the sharp striking of protruding twigs, the violent brushing aside of hanging vines, not unwelcome.

It was of the man that the uppermost feeling in his mind was one of disgust at his late infelicity of speech, and at the blindness which had prompted it. That he had not divined, that he had been so dull as to assume that as he felt, or did not feel, so must she, annoyed him like the jar of rude noises or like sand blowing into face and eyes. It was of him, too, that the annoyance was purely with himself; for her, when at last he came to think of her, he found only the old, placid affection, as far removed from love as from hate. If he knew himself, it would always be as far removed from love as from hate.

All the days of her youth he had come and gone, a welcome guest at her father's house in London. He had grown to be her friend, watching the crescent beauty of face and mind with something of the pride and tenderness which a man might feel for a young and favorite sister; and then, at last, when some turn of affairs sent them all home to Virginia to take lot and part there, he had thought of marriage.

His mind had turned, not unwillingly, from the town and its apples of Sodom to his Virginia plantation that he had not seen for more than ten years. It was his birthplace, and there he had spent his boyhood. Sometimes, in heated rooms, when the candles in the sconces were guttering down, and the dawn looked palely in upon gaming tables and heaped gold, and seamed faces, haggardly triumphant, haggardly despairing, determinedly indifferent, there had come to him visions of cool dawns upon the river, wide, misty expanses of marsh and forest, indistinct and cold and pure. The lonely "great house," too,—the house which his father had built with so much love and pains, that his son and his son's sons should have a worthy home,—appealed to him, and the garden, and the fishing-boats, and the old slaves in the quarters. He told himself that he was glad to go back.

Had men called him ambitious, he would have smiled, and felt truly that they had bungled in the word. Such and such things were simply his appurtenances; in London, the regard due to a gentleman who to a certain distinction in his manner of amusing himself added the achievement of a successful comedy, three lampoons quoted at all London tea-tables, and a piece of Whig invective, so able, stern, and sustained that many cried that the Dean had met his match; in Virginia, the deferential esteem of the colony at large, a place in the Council, and a great estate. An alliance with the master of Westover was in itself a desirable thing, advantageous to purse and to credit; his house must have a mistress, and that mistress must please at every point his fastidious taste.

What better to do than to give it for Mistress Evelyn Byrd? Evelyn, who had had for all her suitors only a slow smile and shake of the head; Evelyn, who was older than her years; Evelyn, who was his friend as he was hers. Love! He had left that land behind, and she had never touched its shores; the geography of the poets to the contrary, it did not lie in the course of all who passed through life. He made his suit, and now he had his answer.

If he did not take trouble to wonder at her confession, or to modestly ask himself how he had deserved her love, neither did he insult her with pity or with any lightness of thought. Nor was he ready to believe that his rejection was final. Apparently indifferent as he was, it was yet his way to move steadily and relentlessly, if very quietly, toward what goal he desired to reach. He thought that Fair View might yet call Evelyn Byrd its mistress.

Since turning into the crossroad that, running south and east, would take him back to the banks of the James and to his own house, he had not slackened speed, but now, as he saw through the trees before him a long zigzag of rail fence, he drew rein. The road turned, and a gate barred his way. When he had opened it and passed through, he was upon his own land.

He had ridden off his irritation, and could now calmly tell himself that the blunder was made and over with, and that it was the duty of the philosopher to remember it only in so far as it must shape his future course. His house of cards had toppled over; but the profound indifferentism of his nature enabled him to view the ruins with composure. After a while he would build the house again. The image of Evelyn, as she had stood, dark-eyed and pale, with the flowers pressed to her bosom, he put from him. He knew her strength of soul; and with the curious hardness of the strong toward the strong, and also not without the delicacy which, upon occasion, he could both feel and exhibit, he shut the door upon that hour in the forest.

He had left the woods, and was now riding through a field of newly planted tobacco. It and the tobacco house in the midst of it were silent, deserted, bathed in the late sunshine. The ground rose slightly, and when he had mounted with it he saw below him the huddle of cabins which formed the ridge quarter, and winding down to it a string of negroes. One turned his head, and saw the solitary horseman upon the summit of the slope behind him; another looked, and another, until each man in line had his head over his shoulder. They knew that the horseman was their master. Some had been upon the plantation when he was a boy; others were more recent acquisitions who knew not his face; but alike they grinned and ducked. The white man walking beside the line took off his hat and pulled a forelock. Haward raised his hand that they might know he saw, and rode on.

Another piece of woods where a great number of felled trees cumbered the ground, more tobacco, and then, in worn fields where the tobacco had been, knee-deep wheat rippling in the evening breeze. The wheat ran down to a marsh, and to a wide, slow creek that, save in the shadow of its reedy banks, was blue as the sky above. Haward, riding slowly beside his green fields and still waters, noted with quiet, half-regretful pleasure this or that remembered feature of the landscape. There had been little change. Here, where he remembered deep woods, tobacco was planted; there, where the tobacco had been, were now fields of wheat or corn, or wild tangles of vine-rid saplings and brushwood: but for this it might have been yesterday that he had last ridden that way.

Presently he saw the river, and then the marshes with brown dots that were his cattle straying over them, and beyond these the home landing and the masts of the Golden Rose. The sun was near its setting; the men had left the fields; over all things were the stillness and peace, the encroaching shadows, the dwindling light, so golden in its quality, of late afternoon. When he crossed the bridge over the creek, the hollow sound that the boards gave forth beneath his horse's hoofs had the depth and resonance of drumbeats, and the cry of a solitary heron in the marsh seemed louder than its wont. He passed the rolling-house and drew near to the river, riding again through tobacco. These plants were Oronoko; the mild sweet-scented took the higher ground. Along the river bank grew a row of tall and stately trees: passing beneath them, he saw the shining water between brown columns or through a veil of slight, unfolding leaves. Soon the trees fell away, and he came to a stretch of bank,—here naked earth, there clad in grass and dewberry vines. Near by was a small landing, with several boats fastened to its piles; and at a little distance beyond it, shadowed by a locust-tree, a strongly built, two-roomed wooden house, with the earth around it trodden hard and bare, and with two or three benches before its open door. Haward recognized the store which his father—after the manner of his kind, merchant and trader as well as planter and maker of laws—had built, and which, through his agent in Virginia, he had maintained.

Before one of the benches a man was kneeling with his back to Haward, who could only see that his garb was that of a servant, and that his hands were busily moving certain small objects this way and that upon the board. At the edge of the space of bare earth were a horse-block and a hitching-post. Haward rode up to them, dismounted, and fastened his horse, then walked over to the man at the bench.

So intent was the latter upon his employment that he heard neither horse nor rider. He had some shells, a few bits of turf, and a double handful of sand, and he was arranging these trifles upon the rough, unpainted boards in a curious and intricate pattern. He was a tall man, with hair that was more red than brown, and he was dressed in a shirt of dowlas, leather breeches, and coarse plantation-made shoes and stockings.

"What are you doing?" asked Haward, after a moment's silent watching of the busy fingers and intent countenance.

There was no start of awakened consciousness upon the other's part. "Why," he said, as if he had asked the question of himself, "with this sand I have traced the shores of Loch-na-Keal. This turf is green Ulva, and this is Gometra, and the shell is Little Colonsay. With this wet sand I have moulded Ben Grieg, and this higher pile is Ben More. If I had but a sprig of heather, now, or a pebble from the shore of Scridain!"

The voice, while harsh, was not disagreeably so, and neither the words nor the manner of using them smacked of the rustic.

"And where are Loch-na-Keal and Ulva and Scridain?" demanded Haward. "Somewhere in North Britain, I presume?"

The second question broke the spell. The man glanced

over his shoulder, saw that he was not alone, and with one sweep of his hand blotting loch and island and mountain out of existence, rose to his feet, and opposed to Haward's gaze a tall, muscular frame, high features slightly pock-marked, and keen dark blue eyes.

"I was dreaming, and did not hear you," he said, civilly enough. "It's not often that any one comes to the store at this time of day. What d' ye lack?"

As he spoke he moved toward the doorway, through which showed shelves and tables piled with the extra-ordinary variety of goods which were deemed essential to the colonial trade. "Are you the storekeeper?" asked Haward, keeping pace with the other's long stride.

"It's the name they call me by," answered the man curtly; then, as he chanced to turn his eyes upon the landing, his tone changed, and a smile irradiated his countenance. "Here comes a customer," he remarked, "that'll make you bide your turn."

A boat, rowed by a young boy and carrying a woman, had slipped out of the creek, and along the river bank to the steps of the landing. When they were reached, the boy sat still, the oars resting across his knees, and his face upturned to a palace beautiful of pearl and saffron cloud; but the woman mounted the steps, and, crossing the boards, came up to the door and the men beside it. Her dress was gray and unadorned, and she was young and of a quiet loveliness.

"Mistress Truelove Taberer," said the storekeeper, "what can you choose, this May Day, that's so fair as yourself?"

A pair of gray eyes were lifted for the sixth part of a

second, and a voice that bad learned of the doves in the forest proceeded to rebuke the flatterer. "Thee is idle in thy speech, Angus MacLean," it declared. "I am not fair; nor, if I were, should thee tell me of it. Also, friend, it is idle and tendeth toward idolatry to speak of the first day of the fifth month as May Day. My mother sent me for a paper of White-chapel needles, and two of manikin pins. Has thee them in thy store of goods?"

"Come you in and look for yourself," said the storekeeper. "There's woman's gear enough, but it were easier for me to recount the names of all the children of Gillean-ni-Tuaidhe than to remember how you call the things you wear."

So saying he entered the store. The Quakeress followed, and Haward, tired of his own thoughts, and in the mood to be amused by trifles, trod in their footsteps.

Door and window faced the west, and the glow from the sinking sun illumined the thousand and one features of the place. Here was the glint of tools and weapons; there pewter shone like silver, and brass dazzled the eyes. Bales of red cotton, blue linen, flowered Kidderminster, scarlet serge, gold and silver drugget, all sorts of woven stuffs from lockram to brocade, made bright the shelves. Pendent skins of buck and doe showed like brown satin, while looking-glasses upon the wall reflected green trees and painted clouds. In one dark corner lurked kegs of powder and of shot; another was the haunt of aqua vitae and right Jamaica. Playing-cards, snuffboxes, and fringed gloves elbowed a shelf of books, and a full-bottomed wig ogled a lady's headdress of ribbon and malines. Knives and hatchets and duffel blankets for the Indian trade were not wanting.

Haward, leaning against a table laden with so singular a miscellany that a fine saddle with crimson velvet holsters took the head of the board, while the foot was set with blue and white china, watched the sometime moulder of peak and islet draw out a case filled with such small and womanish articles as pins and needles, tape and thread, and place it before his customer. She made her choice, and the storekeeper brought a great book, and entered against the head of the house of Taberer so many pounds of tobacco; then, as the maiden turned to depart, heaved a sigh so piteous and profound that no tender saint in gray could do less than pause, half turn her head, and lift two compassionate eyes.

"Mistress Truelove, I have read the good book that you gave me, and I cannot deny that I am much beholden to you," and her debtor sighed like a furnace.

The girl's quiet face flushed to the pink of a seashell, and her eyes grew eager.

"Then does thee not see the error of thy ways, Angus MacLean? If it should be given me to pluck thee as a brand from the burning! Thee will not again brag of war and revenge, nor sing vain and ruthless songs, nor use dice or cards, nor will thee swear any more?"

The voice was persuasion's own. "May I be set overtide on the Lady's Rock, or spare a false Campbell when I meet him, or throw up my cap for the damned Hogan Mogan that sits in Jamie's place, if I am not entirely convert!" cried the neophyte. "Oh, the devil! what have I said? Mistress Truelove—Truelove"—

But Truelove was gone,—not in anger or in haste, for that would have been unseemly, but quietly and steadily, with no looking back. The storekeeper, leaping over a keg of nails that stood in the way, made for the door, and together with Haward, who was already there, watched her go. The path to the landing and the boat was short; she had taken her seat, and the boy had bent to the oars, while the unlucky Scot was yet alternately calling out protestations of amendment and muttering maledictions upon his unguarded tongue. The canoe slipped from the rosy, unshadowed water into the darkness beneath the overhanging trees, reached the mouth of the creek, and in a moment disappeared from sight.

CHAPTER VI

MASTER AND MAN

The two men, left alone, turned each toward the interior of the store, and their eyes met. Alike in gray eyes and in dark blue there was laughter. "Kittle folk, the Quakers," said the storekeeper, with a shrug, and went to put away his case of pins and needles. Haward, going to the end of the store, found a row of dusty bottles, and breaking the neck of one with a report like that of a pistol set the Madeira to his lips, and therewith quenched his thirst. The wine cellar abutted upon the library. Taking off his riding glove he ran his finger along the bindings, and plucking forth The History of a Coy Lady looked at the first page, read the last paragraph, and finally thrust the thin brown and gilt volume into his pocket. Turning, he found himself face to face with the storekeeper.

"I have not the honor of knowing your name, sir," remarked the latter dryly. "Do you buy at this store, and upon whose account?"

Haward shook his head, and applied himself again to the Madeira.

"Then you carry with you coin of the realm with which to

settle?" continued the other. "The wine is two shillings; the book you may have for twelve-pence."

"Here I need not pay, good fellow," said Haward negligently, his eyes upon a row of dangling objects. "Fetch me down yonder cane; 't is as delicately tapered and clouded as any at the Exchange."

"Pay me first for the wine and the book," answered the man composedly. "It's a dirty business enough, God knows, for a gentleman to put finger to; but since needs must when the devil drives, and he has driven me here, why, I, Angus MacLean, who have no concerns of my own, must e'en be faithful to the concerns of another. Wherefore put down the silver you owe the Sassenach whose wine you have drunken and whose book you have taken."

"And if I do not choose to pay?" asked Haward, with a smile.

"Then you must e'en choose to fight," was the cool reply. "And as I observe that you wear neither sword nor pistols, and as jack boots and a fine tight-buttoned riding coat are not the easiest clothes to wrestle in, it appears just possible that I might win the cause."

"And when you've thrown me, what then?"

"Oh, I would just draw a rope around you and yonder cask of Jamaica, and leave you to read your stolen book in peace until Saunderson (that's the overseer, and he's none so bad if he was born in Fife) shall come. You can have it out with him; or maybe he'll hale you before the man that owns the store. I hear they expect him home."

Haward laughed, and abstracting another bottle from the shelf broke its neck. "Hand me yonder cup," he said easily, "and we'll drink to his home-coming. Good fellow, I am Mr. Marmaduke Haward, and I am glad to find so honest a man in a place of no small trust. Long absence and somewhat too complaisant a reference of all my Virginian affairs to my agent have kept me much in ignorance of the economy of my plantation. How long have you been my storekeeper?"

Neither cup for the wine nor answer to the question being forthcoming, Haward looked up from his broken bottle. The man was standing with his body bent forward and his hand pressed against the wood of a great cask behind him until the finger-nails showed white. His head was high, his face dark red and angry, his brows drawn down until the gleaming eyes beneath were like pin points.

So sudden and so sinister was the change that Haward was startled. The hour was late, the place deserted; as the man had discovered, he had no weapons, nor, strong, active, and practiced as he was, did he flatter himself that he could withstand the length of brawn and sinew before him. Involuntarily, he stepped backward until there was a space between them, casting at the same moment a glance toward the wall where hung axe and knife and hatchet.

The man intercepted the look, and broke into a laugh. The sound was harsh and gibing, but not menacing. "You need not be afraid," he said. "I do not want the feel of a rope around my neck,—though God knows why I should care! Here is no clansman of mine, and no cursed Campbell either, to see my end!"

"I am not afraid," Haward answered calmly. Walking to the shelf that held an array of drinking vessels, he took two cups, filled them with wine, and going back to his former station, set one upon the cask beside the storekeeper. "The wine is good," he said. "Will you drink?"

The other loosened the clasp of his hand upon the wood and drew himself upright. "I eat the bread and drink the water which you give your servants," he answered, speaking with the thickness of hardly restrained passion. "The wine cup goes from equal to equal."

As he spoke he took up the peace offering, eyed it for a moment with a bitter smile, then flung it with force over his shoulder. The earthen floor drank the wine; the china shivered into a thousand fragments. "I have neither silver nor tobacco with which to pay for my pleasure," continued the still smiling storekeeper. "When I am come to the end of my term, then, an it please you, I will serve out the damage."

Haward sat down upon a keg of powder, crossed his knees, and, with his chin upon his hand, looked from between the curled lengths of his periwig at the figure opposite. "I am glad to find that in Virginia, at least, there is honesty," he said dryly. "I will try to remember the cost of the cup and the wine against the expiry of your indenture. In the mean time, I am curious to know why you are angry with me whom you have never seen before to-day."

With the dashing of the wine to earth the other's passion had apparently spent itself. The red slowly left his face, and he leaned at ease against the cask, drumming upon its head with his fingers. The sunlight, shrinking from floor and wall, had left but a single line of gold. In the half light strange and sombre shapes possessed the room; through the stillness, beneath the sound of the tattoo upon the cask head, the river made itself heard.

"For ten years and more you have been my—master," said the storekeeper. "It is a word for which I have an invincible distaste. It is not well—having neither love nor friendship to put in its place—to let hatred die. When I came first to this slavery, I hated all Campbells, all Whigs, Forster that betrayed us at Preston, and Ewin Mor Mackinnon. But the years have come and the years have gone, and I am older than I was at twenty-five. The Campbells I can never reach: they walk secure, overseas, through Lorn and Argyle, couching in the tall heather above Etive, tracking the red deer in the Forest of Dalness. Forster is dead. Ewin Mackinnon is dead, I know; for five years ago come Martinmas night I saw his perjured soul on its way to hell. All the world is turning Whig. A man may hate the world, it is true, but he needs a single foe."

"And in that capacity you have adopted me?" demanded Haward.

MacLean let his gaze travel over the man opposite him, from the looped hat and the face between the waves of hair to the gilt spurs upon the great boots; then turned his eyes upon his own hand and coarsely clad arm stretched across the cask. "I, too, am a gentleman, the brother of a chieftain," he declared. "I am not without schooling. I have seen something of life, and of countries more polite than the land where I was born, though not so dear. I have been free, and have loved my freedom. Do you find it so strange that I should hate you?"

There was a silence; then, "Upon my soul, I do not know that I do," said Haward slowly. "And yet, until this day I did not know of your existence."

"But I knew of yours," answered the storekeeper. "Your agent hath an annoying trick of speech, and the overseers have caught it from him. 'Your master' this, and 'your master' that; in short, for ten years it hath been, 'Work, you dog, that your master may play!' Well, I have worked; it was that, or killing myself, or going mad. I have worked for you in the fields, in the smithy, in this close room. But when you bought my body, you could not buy my soul. Day after day, and night after night, I sent it away; I would not let it bide in these dull levels, in this cursed land of heat and stagnant waters. At first it went home to its own country,—to its friends and its foes, to the torrent and the mountain and the music of the pipes; but at last the pain outweighed the pleasure, and I sent it there no more. And then it began to follow you."

"To follow me!" involuntarily exclaimed Haward.

"I have been in London," went on the other, without heeding the interruption. "I know the life of men of quality, and where they most resort. I early learned from your other servants, and from the chance words of those who had your affairs in charge, that you were young, well-looking, a man of pleasure. At first when I thought of you the blood came into my cheek, but at last I thought of you constantly, and I felt for you a constant hatred. It began when I knew that Ewin Mackinnon was dead. I had no need of love; I had need of hate. Day after day, my body slaving here, my mind has dogged your footsteps. Up and down, to and fro, in business and in pleasure, in whatever place I have imagined you to be, there have I been also. Did you never, when there seemed none by, look over your shoulder, feeling another presence than your own?"

He ceased to speak, and the hand upon the cask was still.

The sunshine was clean gone from the room, and without the door the wind in the locust-tree answered the voice of the river. Haward rose from his seat, but made no further motion toward departing. "You have been frank," he said quietly. "Had you it in mind, all this while, so to speak to me when we should meet?"

"No," answered the other. "I thought not of words, but of"—

"But of deeds," Haward finished for him. "Rather, I imagine, of one deed."

Composed as ever in voice and manner, he drew out his watch, and held it aslant that the light might strike upon the dial. "'T is after six," he remarked as he put it away, "and I am yet a mile from the house." The wine that he had poured for himself had been standing, untouched, upon the keg beside him. He took it up and drank it off; then wiped his lips with his handkerchief, and passing the storekeeper with a slight inclination of his head walked toward the door. A yard beyond the man who had so coolly shown his side of the shield was a rude table, on which were displayed hatchets and hunting knives. Haward passed the gleaming steel; then, a foot beyond it, stood still, his face to the open door, and his back to the storekeeper and the table with its sinister lading.

"You do wrong to allow so much dust and disorder," he said sharply. "I could write my name in that mirror, and there is a piece of brocade fallen to the floor. Look to it that you keep the place more neat."

There was dead silence for a moment; then MacLean spoke in an even voice: "Now a fool might call you as brave as Hector. For myself, I only give you credit for some knowledge of men. You are right. It is not my way to strike in the back an unarmed man. When you are gone, I will wipe off the mirror and pick up the brocade."

He followed Haward outside. "It's a brave evening for riding," he remarked, "and you have a bonny bit of horse-flesh there. You'll get to the house before candlelight."

Beside one of the benches Haward made another pause. "You are a Highlander and a Jacobite," he said. "From your reference to Forster, I gather that you were among the prisoners taken at Preston and transported to Virginia."

"In the Elizabeth and Anne of Liverpool, *alias* a bit of hell afloat; the master, Captain Edward Trafford, *alias* Satan's first mate," quoth the other grimly.

He stooped to the bench where lay the debris of the coast and mountains he had been lately building, and picked up a small, deep shell. "My story is short," he began. "It could be packed into this. I was born in the island of Mull, of my father a chieftain, and my mother a lady. Some schooling I got in Aberdeen, some pleasure in Edinburgh and London, and some service abroad. In my twenty-third year—being at home at that time—I was asked to a hunting match at Braemar, and went. No great while afterwards I was bidden to supper at an Edinburgh tavern, and again I accepted the invitation. There was a small entertainment to follow the supper,—just the taking of Edinburgh Castle. But the wine was good, and we waited to powder our hair, and the entertainment could hardly be called a success. Hard upon that convivial evening, I, with many others, was asked across the Border to join a number of gentlemen who drank to the King after our fashion, and had a like fancy for oak boughs and white roses. The weather was pleasant, the company of the best, the roads very noble after our Highland sheep tracks. Together with our English friends, and enlivened by much good claret and by music of bagpipe and drum, we strolled on through a fine, populous country until we came to a town called Preston, where we thought we would tarry for a day or two. However, circumstances arose which detained us somewhat longer. (I dare say you have heard the story?) When finally we took our leave, some of us went to heaven, some to hell, and some to Barbadoes and Virginia. I was among those dispatched to Virginia, and to all intents and purposes I died the day I landed. There, the shell is full!"

He tossed it from him, and going to the hitching-post loosed Haward's horse. Haward took the reins from his hand. "It hath been ten years and more since Virginia got her share of the rebels taken at Preston. If I remember aright, their indentures were to be made for seven years. Why, then, are you yet in my service?"

MacLean laughed. "I ran away," he replied pleasantly, "and when I was caught I made off a second time. I wonder that you planters do not have a Society for the Encouragement of Runaways. Seeing that they are nearly always retaken, and that their escapades so lengthen their term of service, it would surely be to your advantage! There are yet several years in which I am to call you master."

He laughed again, but the sound was mirthless, and the eyes beneath the half-closed lids were harder than steel. Haward mounted his horse and gathered up the reins. "I am not responsible for the laws of the realm," he said calmly, "nor for rebellions and insurrections, nor for the practice of transporting overseas those to whom have been given the ugly names of 'rebel' and 'traitor.' Destiny that set you there put me here. We are alike pawns; what the player means we have no way of telling. Curse Fate and the gods, if you choose,—and find that your cursing does small good,—but regard me with indifference, as one neither more nor less the slave of circumstances than yourself. It has been long since I went this way. Is there yet the path by the river?"

"Ay," answered the other. "It is your shortest road."

"Then I will be going," said Haward. "It grows late, and I am not looked for before to-morrow. Good-night."

As he spoke he raised his hat and bowed to the gentleman from whom he was parting. That rebel to King George gave a great start; then turned very red, and shot a piercing glance at the man on horseback. The latter's mien was composed as ever, and, with his hat held beneath his arm and his body slightly inclined, he was evidently awaiting a like ceremony of leave-taking on the store-keeper's part. MacLean drew a long breath, stepped back a pace or two, and bowed to his equal. A second "Good-night," and one gentleman rode off in the direction of the great house, while the other went thoughtfully back to the store, got a cloth and wiped the dust from the mirror.

It was pleasant riding by the river in the cool evening wind, with the colors of the sunset yet gay in sky and water. Haward went slowly, glancing now at the great, bright stream, now at the wide, calm fields and the rim of woodland, dark and distant, bounding his possessions. The smell of salt marshes, of ploughed ground, of leagues of flowering forests, was in his nostrils. Behind him was the crescent moon; before him a terrace crowned with lofty trees. Within the ring of foliage was the house; even as he looked a light sprang up in a high window, and shone like a star through the gathering dusk. Below the hill the home landing ran its gaunt black length far out into the carmine of the river; upon the Golden Rose lights burned like lower stars; from a thicket to the left of the bridle path sounded the call of a whippoorwill. A gust of wind blowing from the bay made to waver the lanterns of the Golden Rose, broke and darkened the coral peace of the river, and pushed rudely against the master of those parts. Haward laid his hand upon his horse that he loved. "This is better than the Ring, isn't it, Mirza?" he asked genially, and the horse whinnied under his touch.

The land was quite gray, the river pearl-colored, and the fireflies beginning to sparkle, when he rode through the home gates. In the dusk of the world, out of the deeper shadow of the surrounding trees, his house looked grimly upon him. The light had been at the side; all the front was stark and black with shuttered windows. He rode to the back of the house and hallooed to the slaves in the home quarter, where were lights and noisy laughter, and one deep voice singing in an unknown tongue.

It was but a stone's throw to the nearest cabin, and Haward's call made itself heard above the babel. The noise suddenly lessened, and two or three negroes, starting up from the doorstep, hurried across the grass to horse and rider. Quickly as they came, some one within the house was beforehand with them. The door swung open; there was the flare of a lighted candle, and a voice cried out to know what was wanted.

"Wanted!" exclaimed Haward. "Ingress into my own house is wanted! Where is Juba?"

One of the negroes pressed forward. "Heah I is, Marse

Duke! House all ready for you, but you done sont word"—

"I know,—I know," answered Haward impatiently. "I changed my mind. Is that you, Saunderson, with the light? Or is it Hide?"

The candle moved to one side, and there was disclosed a large white face atop of a shambling figure dressed in some coarse, dark stuff. "Neither, sir," said an expressionless voice. "Will it please your Honor to dismount?"

Haward swung himself out of the saddle, tossed the reins to a negro, and, with Juba at his heels, climbed the five low stone steps and entered the wide hall running through the house and broken only by the broad, winding stairway. Save for the glimmer of the solitary candle all was in darkness; the bare floor, the paneled walls, echoed to his tread. On either hand squares of blackness proclaimed the open doors of large, empty rooms, and down the stair came a wind that bent the weak flame. The negro took the light from the hand of the man who had opened the door, and, pressing past his master, lit three candles in a sconce upon the wall.

"Yo' room's all ready, Marse Duke," he declared. "Dere's candles enough, an' de fire am laid an' yo' bed aired. Ef you wan' some supper, I kin get you bread an' meat, an' de wine was put in yesterday."

Haward nodded, and taking the candle began to mount the stairs. Half way up he found that the man in the sad-colored raiment was following him. He raised his brows, but being in a taciturn humor, and having, moreover, to shield the flame from the wind that drove down the stair, he said nothing, going on in silence to the landing, and to the great eastward-facing room that had been his father's, and which now he meant to make his own. There were candles on the table, the dresser, and the mantelshelf. He lit them all, and the room changed from a place of shadows and monstrous shapes to a gentleman's bed-chamber,—somewhat sparsely furnished, but of a comfortable and cheerful aspect. A cloth lay upon the floor, the windows were curtained, and the bed had fresh hangings of green and white Kidderminster. Over the mantel hung a painting of Haward and his mother, done when he was six years old. Beneath the laughing child and the smiling lady, young and flower-crowned, were crossed two ancient swords. In the middle of the room stood a heavy table, and pushed back, as though some one had lately risen from it, was an armchair of Russian leather. Books lay upon the table; one of them open, with a horn snuffbox keeping down the leaf.

Haward seated himself in the great chair, and looked around him with a thoughtful and melancholy smile. He could not clearly remember his mother. The rings upon her fingers and her silvery laughter were all that dwelt in his mind, and now only the sound of that merriment floated back to him and lingered in the room. But his father had died upon that bed, and beside the dead man, between the candles at the head and the candles at the foot, he had sat the night through. The curtains were half drawn, and in their shadow his imagination laid again that cold, inanimate form. Twelve years ago! How young he had been that night, and how old he had thought himself as he watched beside the dead, chilled by the cold of the crossed hands, awed by the silence, half frighted by the shadows on the wall; now filled with natural grief, now with surreptitious and shamefaced thoughts of his changed estate,—yesterday son and dependent, to-day heir and master! Twelve years! The sigh and the smile were not for the dead father, but for his own dead youth, for the unjaded freshness of the morning, for the world that had been, once upon a time.

Turning in his seat, his eyes fell upon the man who had followed him, and who was now standing between the table and the door. "Well, friend?" he demanded.

The man came a step or two nearer. His hat was in his hand, and his body was obsequiously bent, but there was no discomposure in his lifeless voice and manner. "I stayed to explain my presence in the house, sir," he said. "I am a lover of reading, and, knowing my weakness, your overseer, who keeps the keys of the house, has been so good as to let me, from time to time, come here to this room to mingle in more delectable company than I can choose without these walls. Your Honor doubtless remembers yonder goodly assemblage?" He motioned with his hand toward a half-opened door, showing a closet lined with well-filled bookshelves.

"I remember," replied Haward dryly. "So you come to my room alone at night, and occupy yourself in reading? And when you are wearied you refresh yourself with my wine?" As he spoke he clinked together the bottle and glass that stood beside the books.

"I plead guilty to the wine," answered the intruder, as lifelessly as ever, "but it is my only theft. I found the bottle below, and did not think it would be missed. I trust that your Honor does not grudge it to a poor devil who tastes Burgundy somewhat seldomer than does your Worship. And my being in the house is pure innocence. Your overseer knew that I would neither make nor meddle with aught but the books, or he would not have given me the key to the little door, which I now restore to

your Honor's keeping." He advanced, and deposited upon the table a large key.

"What is your name?" demanded Haward, leaning back in his chair.

"Bartholomew Paris, sir. I keep the school down by the swamp, where I impart to fifteen or twenty of the youth of these parts the rudiments of the ancient and modern tongues, mathematics, geography, fortifications, navigation, philosophy"—

Haward yawned, and the schoolmaster broke the thread of his discourse. "I weary you, sir," he said. "I will, with your permission, take my departure. May I make so bold as to beg your Honor that you will not mention to the gentlemen hereabouts the small matter of this bottle of wine? I would wish not to be prejudiced in the eyes of my patrons and scholars."

"I will think of it," Haward replied. "Come and take your snuffbox—if it be yours—from the book where you have left it."

"It is mine," said the man. "A present from the godly minister of this parish."

As he spoke he put out his hand to take the snuffbox. Haward leaned forward, seized the hand, and, bending back the fingers, exposed the palm to the light of the candles upon the table.

"The other, if you please," he commanded.

For a second—no longer—a wicked soul looked blackly out of the face to which he had raised his eyes. Then the window shut, and the wall was blank again. Without any change in his listless demeanor, the schoolmaster laid his left hand, palm out, beside his right.

"Humph!" exclaimed Haward. "So you have stolen before to-night? The marks are old. When were you branded, and where?"

"In Bristol, fifteen years ago," answered the man unblushingly. "It was all a mistake. I was as innocent as a newborn babe"—

"But unfortunately could not prove it," interrupted Haward. "That is of course. Go on."

"I was transported to South Carolina, and there served out my term. The climate did not suit me, and I liked not the society, nor—being of a peaceful disposition—the constant alarms of pirates and buccaneers. So when I was once more my own man I traveled north to Virginia with a party of traders. In my youth I had been an Oxford servitor, and schoolmasters are in demand in Virginia. Weighed in the scales with a knowledge of the humanities and some skill in imparting them, what matters a little mishap with hot irons? My patrons are willing to let bygones be bygones. My school flourishes like a green bay-tree, and the minister of this parish will speak for the probity and sobriety of my conduct. Now I will go, sir."

He made an awkward but deep and obsequious reverence, turned and went out of the door, passing Juba, who was entering with a salver laden with bread and meat and a couple of bottles. "Put down the food, Juba," said Haward, "and see this gentleman out of the house."

An hour later the master dismissed the slave, and sat

down beside the table to finish the wine and compose himself for the night. The overseer had come hurrying to the great house, to be sent home again by a message from the owner thereof that to-morrow would do for business; the negro women who had been called to make the bed were gone; the noises from the quarter had long ceased, and the house was very still. In his rich, figured Indian nightgown and his silken nightcap, Haward sat and drank his wine, slowly, with long pauses between the emptying and the filling of the slender, tall-stemmed glass. A window was open, and the wind blowing in made the candles to flicker. With the wind came a murmur of leaves and the wash of the river,—stealthy and mournful sounds that sorted not with the lighted room, the cheerful homeliness of the flowered hangings, the gleeful lady and child above the mantelshelf. Haward felt the incongruity: a slow sea voyage, and a week in that Virginia which, settled one hundred and twenty years before, was yet largely forest and stream, had weaned him, he thought, from sounds of the street, and yet to-night he missed them, and would have had the town again. When an owl hooted in the walnut-tree outside his window, and in the distance, as far away as the creek quarter, a dog howled, and the silence closed in again, he rose, and began to walk to and fro, slowly, thinking of the past and the future. The past had its ghosts,—not many; what spectres the future might raise only itself could tell. So far as mortal vision went, it was a rose-colored future; but on such a night of silence that was not silence, of loneliness that was filled with still, small voices, of heavy darkness without, of lights burning in an empty house, it was rather of ashes of roses that one thought.

Haward went to the open window, and with one knee upon the window seat looked out into the windy, starlit night. This was the eastern face of the house, and, beyond the waving trees, there were visible both the river and the second and narrower creek which on this side bounded the plantation. The voice with which the waters swept to the sea came strongly to him. A large white moth sailed out of the darkness to the lit window, but his presence scared it away.

Looking through the walnut branches, he could see a light that burned steadily, like a candle set in a window. For a moment he wondered whence it shone; then he remembered that the glebe lands lay in that direction. The parish was building a house for its new minister, when he left Virginia, those many years ago. Suddenly he recalled that the minister—who had seemed to him a bluff, downright, honest fellow—had told him of a little room looking out upon an orchard, and had said that it should be the child's.

It was possible that the star which pierced the darkness might mark that room. He knit his brows in an effort to remember when, before this day, he had last thought of a child whom he had held in his arms and comforted, one splendid dawn, upon a hilltop, in a mountainous region. He came to the conclusion that he must have forgotten her quite six years ago. Well, she would seem to have thriven under his neglect,—and he saw again the girl who had run for the golden guinea. It was true that when he had put her there where that light was shining, it was with some shadowy idea of giving her gentle breeding, of making a lady of her. But man's purposes are fleeting, and often gone with the morrow. He had forgotten his purpose; and perhaps it was best this way,—perhaps it was best this way.

For a little longer he looked at the light and listened to the voice of the river; then he rose from the window seat, drew the curtains, and began thoughtfully to prepare for bed.

CHAPTER VII

THE RETURN OF MONSIEUR JEAN HUGON

To the north the glebe was bounded by a thick wood, a rank and dense "second growth" springing from earth where had once stood, decorously apart, the monster trees of the primeval forest; a wild maze of young trees, saplings and underbrush, overrun from the tops of the slender, bending pines to the bushes of dogwood and sassafras, and the rotting, ancient stumps and fallen logs, by the uncontrollable, all-spreading vine. It was such a fantastic thicket as one might look to find in fairyland, thorny and impenetrable: here as tall as a ten years' pine, there sunken away to the height of the wild honeysuckles; everywhere backed by blue sky, heavy with odors, filled, with the flash of wings and the songs of birds. To the east the thicket fell away to low and marshy grounds, where tall cypresses grew, and myriads of myrtle bushes. Later in the year women and children would venture in upon the unstable earth for the sake of the myrtle berries and their yield of fragrant wax, and once and again an outlying slave had been tracked by men and dogs to the dark recesses of the place; but for the most part it was given over to its immemorial silence. To the south and the west the tobacco fields of Fair View closed in upon the glebe, taking the fertile river bank, and pressing down to the

Mary Johnston

crooked, slow-moving, deeply shadowed creek, upon whose farther bank stood the house of the Rev. Gideon Darden.

A more retired spot, a completer sequestration from the world of mart and highway, it would have been hard to find. In the quiet of the early morning, when the shadows of the trees lay across the dewy grass, it was an angle of the earth as cloistral and withdrawn as heart of scholar or of anchorite could wish. On one side of the house lay a tiny orchard, and the windows of the living room looked out upon a mist of pink and white apple blooms. The fragrance of the blossoms had been in the room, but could not prevail against the odor of tobacco and rum lately introduced by the master of the house and minister of the parish. Audrey, sitting beside a table which had been drawn in front of the window, turned her face aside, and was away, sense and soul, out of the meanly furnished room into the midst of the great bouquets of bloom, with the blue between and above. Darden, walking up and down, with his pipe in his mouth, and the tobacco smoke curling like an aureole around his bullet head, glanced toward the window.

"When you have written that which I have told you to write, say so, Audrey," he commanded. "Don't sit there staring at nothing!"

Audrey came back to the present with a start, took up a pen, and drew the standish nearer. "'Answer of Gideon Darden, Minister of Fair View Parish, in Virginia, to the several Queries contained in my Lord Bishop of London's Circular Letter to the Clergy in Virginia,'" she read, and poised her pen in air.

"Read out the questions," ordered Darden, "and write my

answer to each in the space beneath. No blots, mind you, and spell not after the promptings of your woman's nature."

Going to a side table, be mixed for himself, in an old battered silver cap, a generous draught of bombo; then, with the drink in his hand, walked heavily across the uncarpeted floor to his armchair, which creaked under his weight as he sank into its leathern lap. He put down the rum and water with so unsteady a hand that the liquor spilled, and when he refilled his pipe half the contents of his tobacco box showered down upon his frayed and ancient and unclean coat and breeches. From the pocket of the latter he now drew forth a silver coin, which he balanced for a moment upon his fat forefinger, and finally sent spinning across the table to Audrey.

"'Tis the dregs of thy guinea, child, that Paris and Hugon and I drank at the crossroads last night. 'Burn me,' says I to them, 'if that long-legged lass of mine shan't have a drop in the cup!' And say Hugon"—

What Hugon said did not appear, or was confided to the depths of the tankard which the minister raised to his lips. Audrey looked at the splendid shilling gleaming upon the table beside her, but made no motion toward taking it into closer possession. A little red had come into the clear brown of her cheeks. She was a young girl, with her dreams and fancies, and the golden guinea would have made a dream or two come true.

"'Query the first,'" she read slowly, "'How long since you went to the plantations as missionary?'"

Darden, leaning back in his chair, with his eyes uplifted through the smoke clouds to the ceiling, took his pipe from his mouth, for the better answering of his diocesan. "'My Lord, thirteen years come St. Swithin's day,'" he dictated. "'Signed, Gideon Darden.' Audrey, do not forget thy capitals. Thirteen years! Lord, Lord, the years, how they fly! Hast it down, Audrey?"

Audrey, writing in a slow, fair, clerkly hand, made her period, and turned to the Bishop's second question: "'Had you any other church before you came to that which you now possess?'"

"'No, my Lord,'" said the minister to the Bishop; then to the ceiling: "I came raw from the devil to this parish. Audrey, hast ever heard children say that Satan comes and walks behind me when I go through the forest?"

"Yes," said Audrey, "but their eyes are not good. You go hand in hand."

Darden paused in the lifting of his tankard. "Thy wits are brightening, Audrey; but keep such observations to thyself. It is only the schoolmaster with whom I walk. Go on to the next question."

The Bishop desired to know how long the minister addressed had been inducted into his living. The minister addressed, leaning forward, laid it off to his Lordship how that the vestries in Virginia did not incline to have ministers inducted, and, being very powerful, kept the poor servants of the Church upon uneasy seats; but that he, Gideon Darden, had the love of his flock, rich and poor, gentle and simple, and that in the first year of his ministry the gentlemen of his vestry had been pleased to present his name to the Governor for induction. Which explanation made, the minister drank more rum, and looked out of the window at the orchard and at his neighbor's tobacco.

"You are only a woman, and can hold no office, Audrey," he said, "but I will impart to you words of wisdom whose price is above rubies. Always agree with your vestry. Go, hat in hand, to each of its members in turn, craving advice as to the management of your own affairs. Thunder from the pulpit against Popery, which does not exist in this colony, and the Pretender, who is at present in Italy. Wrap a dozen black sheep of inferior breed in white sheets and set them arow at the church door, but make it stuff of the conscience to see no blemish in the wealthier and more honorable portion of your flock. So you will thrive, and come to be inducted into your living, whether in Virginia or some other quarter of the globe. What's the worthy Bishop's next demand? Hasten, for Hugon is coming this morning, and there's settlement to be made of a small bet, and a hand at cards."

By the circular letter and the lips of Audrey the Bishop proceeded to propound a series of questions, which the minister answered with portentous glibness. In the midst of an estimate of the value of a living in a sweet-scented parish a face looked in at the window, and a dark and sinewy hand laid before Audrey a bunch of scarlet columbine.

"The rock was high," said a voice, "and the pool beneath was deep and dark. Here are the flowers that waved from the rock and threw colored shadows upon the pool."

The girl shrank as from a sudden and mortal danger. Her lips trembled, her eyes half closed, and with a hurried and passionate gesture she rose from her chair, thrust from her the scarlet blooms, and with one lithe movement of her body put between her and the window the heavy writing table. The minister laid by his sum in arithmetic.

"Ha, Hugon, dog of a trader!" he cried. "Come in, man. Hast brought the skins? There's fire-water upon the table, and Audrey will be kind. Stay to dinner, and tell us what lading you brought down river, and of your kindred in the forest and your kindred in Monacan-Town."

The man at the window shrugged his shoulders, lifted his brows, and spread his hands. So a captain of Mousquetaires might have done; but the face was dark-skinned, the cheek-bones were high, the black eyes large, fierce, and restless. A great bushy peruke, of an ancient fashion, and a coarse, much-laced cravat gave setting and lent a touch of grotesqueness and of terror to a countenance wherein the blood of the red man warred with that of the white.

"I will not come in now," said the voice again. "I am going in my boat to the big creek to take twelve doeskins to an old man named Taberer. I will come back to dinner. May I not, ma'm'selle?"

The corners of the lips went up, and the thicket of false hair swept the window sill, so low did the white man bow; but the Indian eyes were watchful. Audrey made no answer; she stood with her face turned away and her eyes upon the door, measuring her chances. If Darden would let her pass, she might reach the stairway and her own room before the trader could enter the house. There were bolts to its heavy door, and Hugon might do as he had done before, and talk his heart out upon the wrong side of the wood. Thanks be! lying upon her bed and pressing the pillow over her ears, she did not have to hear.

At the trader's announcement that his present path led past

the house, she ceased her stealthy progress toward her own demesne, and waited, with her back to the window, and her eyes upon one long ray of sunshine that struck high against the wall.

"I will come again," said the voice without, and the apparition was gone from the window. Once more blue sky and rosy bloom spanned the opening, and the sunshine lay in a square upon the floor. The girl drew a long breath, and turning to the table began to arrange the papers upon it with trembling hands.

"'Sixteen thousand pounds of sweet-scented, at ten shillings the hundredweight; for marriage by banns, five shillings; for the preaching of a funeral sermon, forty shillings; for christening'"—began Darden for the Bishop's information. Audrey took her pen and wrote; but before the list of the minister's perquisites had come to an end the door flew open, and a woman with the face of a vixen came hurriedly into the room. With her entered the breeze from the river, driving before it the smoke wreaths, and blowing the papers from the table to the floor.

Darden stamped his foot. "Woman, I have business, I tell ye,—business with the Bishop of London! I've kept his Lordship at the door this se'nnight, and if I give him not audience Blair will presently be down uon me with tooth and nail and his ancient threat of a visitation. Begone and keep the house! Audrey, where are you, child?"

"Audrey, leave the room!" commanded the woman. "I have something to say that's not for your ears. Let her go, Darden. There's news, I tell you."

The minister glanced at his wife; then knocked the ashes from his pipe and nodded dismissal to Audrey. His late secretary slipped from her seat and left the room, not without alacrity.

"Well?" demanded Darden, when the sound of the quick young feet had died away. "Open your budget, Deborah. There's naught in it, I'll swear, but some fal-lal about your flowered gown or an old woman's black cat and corner broomstick."

Mistress Deborah Darden pressed her thin lips together, and eyed her lord and master with scant measure of conjugal fondness. "It's about some one nearer home than your bishops and commissaries," she said. "Hide passed by this morning, going to the river field. I was in the garden, and he stopped to speak to me. Mr. Haward is home from England. He came to the great house last night, and he ordered his horse for ten o'clock this morning, and asked the nearest way through the fields to the parsonage."

Darden whistled, and put down his drink untasted.

"Enter the most powerful gentleman of my vestry!" he exclaimed. "He'll be that in a month's time. A member of the Council, too, no doubt, and with the Governor's ear. He's a scholar and fine gentleman. Deborah, clear away this trash. Lay out my books, fetch a bottle of Canary, and give me my Sunday coat. Put flowers on the table, and a dish of bonchretiens, and get on your tabby gown. Make your curtsy at the door; then leave him to me."

"And Audrey?" said his wife.

Darden, about to rise, sank back again and sat still, a hand upon either arm of his chair. "Eh!" he said; then, in a meditative tone, "That is so,—there is Audrey."

"If he has eyes, he'll see that for himself," retorted Mistress Deborah tartly. "'More to the purpose,' he'll say, 'where is the money that I gave you for her?'"

"Why, it's gone," answered Darden "Gone in maintenance,—gone in meat and drink and raiment. He didn't want it buried. Pshaw, Deborah, he has quite forgot his fine-lady plan! He forgot it years ago, I'll swear."

"I'll send her now on an errand to the Widow Constance's," said the mistress of the house. "Then before he comes again I'll get her a gown"—

The minister brought his hand down upon the table. "You'll do no such thing!" he thundered. "The girl's got to be here when he comes. As for her dress, can't she borrow from you? The Lord knows that though only the wife of a poor parson, you might throw for gewgaws with a bona roba! Go trick her out, and bring her here. I'll attend to the wine and the books."

When the door opened again, and Audrey, alarmed and wondering, slipped with the wind into the room, and stood in the sunshine before the minister, that worthy first frowned, then laughed, and finally swore.

"'Swounds, Deborah, your hand is out! If I hadn't taken you from service, I'd swear that you were never inside a fine lady's chamber. What's the matter with the girl's skirt?"

"She's too tall!" cried the sometime waiting woman angrily. "As for that great stain upon the silk, the wine made it when you threw your tankard at me, last Sunday but one."

"That manteau pins her arms to her sides," interrupted the minister calmly, "and the lace is dirty. You've hidden all her hair under that mazarine, and too many patches become not a brown skin. Turn around, child!"

While Audrey slowly revolved, the guardian of her fortunes, leaning back in his chair, bent his bushy brows and gazed, not at the circling figure in its tawdry apparel, but into the distance. When she stood still and looked at him with a half-angry, half-frightened face, he brought his bleared eyes to bear upon her, studied her for a minute, then motioned to his wife.

"She must take off this paltry finery, Deborah," he announced. "I'll have none of it. Go, child, and don your Cinderella gown."

"What does it all mean?" cried Audrey, with heaving bosom. "Why did she put these things upon me, and why will she tell me nothing? If Hugon has hand in it"—

The minister made a gesture of contempt. "Hugon! Hugon, half Monacan and half Frenchman, is bartering skins with a Quaker. Begone, child, and when you are transformed return to us."

When the door had closed he turned upon his wife. "The girl has been cared for," he said. "She has been fed,—if not with cates and dainties, then with bread and meat; she has been clothed,—if not in silk and lace, then in good blue linen and penistone. She is young and of the springtime, hath more learning than had many a princess of old times, is innocent and good to look at. Thou and the rest of thy sex are fools, Deborah, but wise men died not with Solomon. It matters not about her dress."

Rising, he went to a shelf of battered, dog-eared books, and taking down an armful proceeded to strew the volumes upon the table. The red blooms of the columbine being in the way, he took up the bunch and tossed it out of the window. With the light thud of the mass upon the ground eyes of husband and wife met.

"Hugon would marry the girl," said the latter, twisting the hem of her apron with restless fingers.

Without change of countenance, Darden leaned forward, seized her by the shoulder and shook her violently. "You are too given to idle and meaningless words, Deborah," he declared, releasing her. "By the Lord, one of these days I'll break you of the habit for good and all! Hugon, and scarlet flowers, and who will marry Audrey, that is yet but a child and useful about the house,—what has all this to do with the matter in hand, which is simply to make ourselves and our house presentable in the eyes of my chief parishioner? A man would think that thirteen years in Virginia would teach any fool the necessity of standing well with a powerful gentleman such as this. I'm no coward. Damn sanctimonious parsons and my Lord Bishop's Scotch hireling! If they yelp much longer at my heels, I'll scandalize them in good earnest! It's thin ice, though,—it's thin ice; but I like this house and glebe, and I'm going to live and die in them,—and die drunk, if I choose, Mr. Commissary to the contrary! It's of import, Deborah, that my parishioners, being easy folk, willing to live and let live, should like me still, and that a majority of my vestry should not be able to get on without me. With this in mind, get out the wine, dust the best chair, and be ready with thy curtsy. It will be time enough to cry Audrey's banns when she is asked in marriage."

Audrey, in her brown dress, with the color yet in her

cheeks, entering at the moment, Mistress Deborah attempted no response to her husband's adjuration. Darden turned to the girl. "I've done with the writing for the nonce, child," he said, "and need you no longer. I'll smoke a pipe and think of my sermon. You're tired; out with you into the sunshine! Go to the wood or down by the creek, but not beyond call, d'ye mind."

Audrey looked from one to the other, but said nothing. There were many things in the world of other people which she did not understand; one thing more or less made no great difference. But she did understand the sunlit roof, the twilight halls, the patterned floor of the forest. Blossoms drifting down, fleeing shadows, voices of wind and water, and all murmurous elfin life spoke to her. They spoke the language of her land; when she stepped out of the door into the air and faced the portals of her world, they called to her to come. Lithe and slight and light of foot, she answered to their piping. The orchard through which she ran was fair with its rosy trees, like gayly dressed curtsying dames; the slow, clear creek that held the double of the sky enticed, but she passed it by. Straight as an arrow she pierced to the heart of the wood that lay to the north. Thorn and bramble, branch of bloom and entangling vine, stayed her not; long since she had found or had made for herself a path to the centre of the labyrinth. Here was a beech-tree, older by many a year than the young wood,—a solitary tree spared by the axe what time its mates had fallen. Tall and silver-gray the column of the trunk rose to meet wide branches and the green lace-work of tender leaves. The earth beneath was clean swept, and carpeted with the leaves of last year; a wide, dry, pale brown enchanted ring, against whose borders pressed the riot of the forest. Vine and bush, flower and fern, could not enter; but Audrey came and laid herself down upon a cool and shady bed.

By human measurement the house that she had left was hard by; even from under the beech-tree Mistress Deborah's thin call could draw her back to the walls which sheltered her, which she had been taught to call her home. But it was not her soul's home, and now the veil of the kindly woods withdrew it league on league, shut it out, made it as if it had never been. From the charmed ring beneath the beech-tree she took possession of her world; for her the wind murmured, the birds sang, insects hummed or shrilled, the green saplings nodded their heads. Flowers, and the bedded moss, and the little stream that leaped from a precipice of three feet into the calm of a hand-deep pool spoke to her. She was happy. Gone was the house and its inmates; gone Paris the schoolmaster, who had taught her to write, and whose hand touching hers in guidance made her sick and cold; gone Hugon the trader, whom she feared and hated. Here were no toil, no annoy, no frightened flutterings of the heart; she had passed the frontier, and was safe in her own land.

She pressed her cheek against the dead leaves, and, with the smell of the earth in her nostrils, looked sideways with half-closed eyes and made a radiant mist of the forest round about. A drowsy warmth was in the air; the birds sang far away; through a rift in the foliage a sunbeam came and rested beside her like A gilded snake.

For a time, wrapped in the warmth and the green and gold mist, she lay as quiet as the sunbeam; of the earth earthy, in pact with the mould beneath the leaves, with the slowly crescent trunks, brown or silver-gray, with moss and lichened rock, and with all life that basked or crept or flew. At last, however, the mind aroused, and she opened her eyes, saw, and thought of what she saw. It was pleasant in the forest. She watched the flash of a bird, as blue as the sky, from limb to limb; she listened to the elfin waterfall; she drew herself with hand and arm across the leaves to the edge of the pale brown ring, plucked a honeysuckle bough and brought it back to the silver column of the beech; and lastly, glancing up from the rosy sprig within her hand, she saw a man coming toward her, down the path that she had thought hidden, holding his arm before him for shield against brier and branch, and looking curiously about him as for a thing which he had come out to seek.

CHAPTER VIII

UNDER THE GREENWOOD TREE

In the moment in which she sprang to her feet she saw that it was not Hugon, and her heart grew calm again. In her torn gown, with her brown hair loosed from its fastenings, and falling over her shoulders in heavy waves whose crests caught the sunlight, she stood against the tree beneath which she had lain, gazed with wide-open eyes at the intruder, and guessed from his fine coat and the sparkling toy looping his hat that he was a gentleman. She knew gentlemen when she saw them: on a time one had cursed her for scurrying like a partridge across the road before his horse, making the beast come nigh to unseating him; another, coming upon her and the Widow Constance's Barbara gathering fagots in the November woods, had tossed to each a sixpence; a third, on vestry business with the minister, had touched her beneath the chin, and sworn that an she were not so brown she were fair; a fourth, lying hidden upon the bank of the creek, had caught her boat head as she pushed it into the reeds, and had tried to kiss her. They had certain ways, had gentlemen, but she knew no great harm of them. There was one, now—but he would be like a prince. When at eventide the sky was piled with pale towering clouds, and she looked, as she often looked, down the river, toward the bay and the sea beyond, she always saw this prince that she had woven—warp of memory, woof of dreams—stand erect in the pearly light. There was a gentleman indeed!

As to the possessor of the title now slowly and steadily making his way toward her she was in a mere state of wonder. It was not possible that he had lost his way; but if so, she was sorry that, in losing it, he had found the slender zigzag of her path. A trustful child,—save where Hugon was concerned,—she was not in the least afraid, and being of a friendly mind looked at the approaching figure with shy kindliness, and thought that he must have come from a distant part of the country. She thought that had she ever seen him before she would have remembered it.

Upon the outskirts of the ring, clear of the close embrace of flowering bush and spreading vine, Haward paused, and looked with smiling eyes at this girl of the woods, this forest creature that, springing from the earth, had set its back against the tree.

"Tarry awhile," he said. "Slip not yet within the bark. Had I known, I should have brought oblation of milk and honey."

"This is the thicket between Fair View and the glebe lands," said Audrey, who knew not what bark of tree and milk and honey had to do with the case. "Over yonder, sir, is the road to the great house. This path ends here; you must go back to the edge of the wood, then turn to the south"—

"I have not lost my way," answered Haward, still smiling. "It is pleasant here in the shade, after the warmth of the open. May I not sit down upon the leaves and talk to you for a while? I came out to find you, you know."

As he spoke, and without waiting for the permission which he asked, he crossed the rustling leaves, and threw himself down upon the earth between two branching roots. Her skirt brushed his knee; with a movement quick and shy she put more distance between them, then stood and looked at him with wide, grave eyes. "Why do you say that you came here to find me?" she asked. "I do not know you."

Haward laughed, nursing his knee and looking about him. "Let that pass for a moment. You have the prettiest woodland parlor, child! Tell me, do they treat you well over there?" with a jerk of his thumb toward the glebe house. "Madam the shrew and his reverence the bully, are they kind to you? Though they let you go like a beggar maid,"—he glanced kindly enough at her bare feet and torn gown,—"yet they starve you not, nor beat you, nor deny you aught in reason?"

Audrey drew herself up. She had a proper pride, and she chose to forget for this occasion a bruise upon her arm and the thrusting upon her of Hugon's company. "I do not know who you are, sir, that ask me such questions," she said sedately. "I have food and shelter and—and— kindness. And I go barefoot only of week days"—

It was a brave beginning, but of a sudden she found it hard to go on. She felt his eyes upon her and knew that he was unconvinced, and into her own eyes came the large tears. They did not fall, but through them she saw the forest swim in green and gold. "I have no father or mother," she said, "and no brother or sister. In all the world there is no one that is kin to me."

Her voice, that was low and full and apt to fall into minor cadences, died away, and she stood with her face raised and slightly turned from the gentleman who lay at her feet, stretched out upon the sere beech leaves. He did not seem inclined to speech, and for a time the little brook and the birds and the wind in the trees sang undisturbed.

"These woods are very beautiful," said Haward at last, with his gaze upon her, "but if the land were less level it were more to my taste. Now, if this plain were a little valley couched among the hills, if to the westward rose dark blue mountains like a rampart, if the runlet yonder were broad and clear, if this beech were a sugar-tree"—

He broke off, content to see her eyes dilate, her bosom rise and fall, her hand go trembling for support to the column of the beech.

"Oh, the mountains!" she cried. "When the mist lifted, when the cloud rested, when the sky was red behind them! Oh, the clear stream, and the sugar-tree, and the cabin! Who are you? How did you know about these things? Were you—were you there?"

She turned upon him, with her soul in her eyes. As for him, lying at length upon the ground, he locked his hands beneath his head and began to sing, though scarce above his breath. He sang the song of Amiens:—

"Under the greenwood tree,
Who loves to lie with me."

When he had come to the end of the stanza he half rose, and turned toward the mute and breathless figure leaning against the beech-tree. For her the years had rolled back: one moment she stood upon the doorstep of the cabin, and the air was filled with the trampling of horses, with quick laughter, whistling, singing, and the call of a trumpet; the next she ran, in night-time and in terror, between rows of rustling corn, felt again the clasp of her pursuer, heard at her ear the comfort of his voice. A film came between her eyes and the man at whom she stared, and her heart grew cold.

"Audrey," said Haward, "come here, child."

The blood returned to her heart, her vision cleared, and her arm fell from its clasp upon the tree. The bark opened not; the hamadryad had lost the spell. When at his repeated command she crossed to him, she went as the trusting, dumbly loving, dumbly grateful child whose life he had saved, and whose comforter, protector, and guardian he had been. When he took her hands in his she was glad to feel them there again, and she had no blushes ready when he kissed her upon the forehead. It was sweet to her who hungered for affection, who long ago had set his image up, loving him purely as a sovereign spirit or as a dear and great elder brother, to hear him call her again "little maid;" tell her that she had not changed save in height; ask her if she remembered this or that adventure, what time they had strayed in the woods together. Remember! When at last, beneath his admirable management, the wonder and the shyness melted away, and she found her tongue, memories came in a torrent. The hilltop, the deep woods and the giant trees, the house he had built for her out of stones and moss, the grapes they had gathered, the fish they had caught, the thunderstorm when he had snatched her out of the path of a stricken and falling pine, an alarm of Indians, an alarm of wolves, finally the first faint sounds of the returning expedition, the distant trumpet note, the nearer approach, the bursting again into the valley of the Governor and his party, the journey from that loved spot to Williamsburgh,—all sights and sounds, thoughts and emotions, of that time, fast held through lonely years, came at her call, and passed again in procession before them. Haward, first amazed, then touched, reached at length the conclusion that the years of her residence beneath the minister's roof could not have been happy; that she must always have put from her with shuddering and horror the memory of the night which orphaned her; but that she had passionately nursed, cherished, and loved all that she had of sweet and dear, and that this all was the memory of her childhood in the valley, and of that brief season when he had been her savior, protector, friend, and playmate. He learned also— for she was too simple and too glad either to withhold the information or to know that she had given it—that in her girlish and innocent imaginings she had made of him a fairy knight, clothing him in a panoply of power, mercy, and tenderness, and setting him on high, so high that his very heel was above the heads of the mortals within her ken.

Keen enough in his perceptions, he was able to recognize that here was a pure and imaginative spirit, strongly yearning after ideal strength, beauty, and goodness. Given such a spirit, it was not unnatural that, turning from sordid or unhappy surroundings as a flower turns from shadow to the full face of the sun, she should have taken a memory of valiant deeds, kind words, and a protecting arm, and have created out of these a man after her own heart, endowing him with all heroic attributes; at one and the same time sending him out into the world, a knight-errant without fear and without reproach, and keeping him by her side—the side of a child—in her own private wonderland. He saw that she had done this, and he was ashamed. He did not tell her that that eleven-years-distant fortnight was to him but a half-remembered incident of a crowded life, and that to all intents and purposes she herself had been forgotten. For one thing, it would have hurt her; for another, he saw no reason why he should tell her. Upon occasion he could be as ruthless as a stone; if he were so now he knew it not, but in deceiving her deceived himself. Man of a world that was corrupt enough, he was of course quietly assured that he could bend this woodland creature—half child, half dryad—to the form of his bidding. To do so was in his power, but not his pleasure. He meant to leave her as she was; to accept the adoration of the child, but to attempt no awakening of the woman. The girl was of the mountains, and their higher, colder, purer air; though he had brought her body thence, he would not have her spirit leave the climbing earth, the dreamlike summits, for the hot and dusty plain. The plain, God knew, had dwellers enough.

She was a thing of wild and sylvan grace, and there was fulfillment in a dark beauty all her own of the promise she had given as a child. About her was a pathos, too,—the pathos of the flower taken from its proper soil, and drooping in earth which nourished it not. Haward, looking at her, watching the sensitive, mobile lips, reading in the dark eyes, beneath the felicity of the present, a hint and prophecy of woe, felt for her a pity so real and great that for the moment his heart ached as for some sorrow of his own. She was only a young girl, poor and helpless, born of poor and helpless parents dead long ago. There was in her veins no gentle blood; she had none of the world's goods; her gown was torn, her feet went bare. She had youth, but not its heritage of gladness: beauty, but none to see it; a nature that reached toward light and height, and for its home the house which he had lately left. He was a man older by many years than the girl beside him, knowing good and evil; by instinct preferring the former, but at times stooping, open-eyed, to that degree of the latter which a lax and gay world held to be not incompatible with a convention somewhat misnamed "the honor of a gentleman." Now, beneath the beech-tree in the forest which touched upon one side the glebe, upon the other his own lands, he chose at this time the good; said to himself, and believed the thing he said, that in word and in deed he would prove himself her friend.

Putting out his hand he drew her down upon the leaves; and she sat beside him, still and happy, ready to answer him when he asked her this or that, readier yet to sit in blissful, dreamy silence. She was as pure as the flower which she held in her hand, and most innocent in her imaginings. This was a very perfect knight, a great gentleman, good and pitiful, that had saved her from the Indians when she was a little girl, and had been kind to her,—ah, so kind! In that dreadful night when she had lost father and mother and brother and sister, when in the darkness her childish heart was a stone for terror, he had come, like God, from the mountains, and straightway she was safe. Now into her woods, from over the sea, he had come again, and at once the load upon her heart, the dull longing and misery, the fear of Hugon, were lifted. The chaplet which she laid at his feet was not loosely woven of gay-colored flowers, but was compact of austerer blooms of gratitude, reverence, and that love which is only a longing to serve. The glamour was at hand, the enchanted light which breaks not from the east or the west or the north or the south was upon its way; but she knew it not, and she was happy in her ignorance.

"I am tired of the city," he said. "Now I shall stay in Virginia. A longing for the river and the marshes and the house where I was born came upon me"—

"I know," she answered. "When I shut my eyes I see the

cabin in the valley, and when I dream it is of things which happen in a mountainous country."

"I am alone in the great house," he continued, "and the floors echo somewhat loudly. The garden, too; beside myself there is no one to smell the roses or to walk in the moonlight. I had forgotten the isolation of these great plantations. Each is a province and a despotism. If the despot has neither kith nor kin, has not yet made friends, and cares not to draw company from the quarters, he is lonely. They say that there are ladies in Virginia whose charms well-nigh outweigh their dowries of sweet-scented and Oronoko. I will wed such an one, and have laughter in my garden, and other footsteps than my own in my house."

"There are beautiful ladies in these parts," said Audrey. "There is the one that gave me the guinea for my running yesterday. She was so very fair. I wished with all my heart that I were like her."

"She is my friend," said Haward slowly, "and her mind is as fair as her face. I will tell her your story."

The gilded streak upon the earth beneath the beech had crept away, but over the ferns and weeds and flowering bushes between the slight trees without the ring the sunshine gloated. The blue of the sky was wonderful, and in the silence Haward and Audrey heard the wind whisper in the treetops. A dove moaned, and a hare ran past.

"It was I who brought you from the mountains and placed you here," said Haward at last. "I thought it for the best, and that when I sailed away I left you to a safe and happy life. It seems that I was mistaken. But now that I am at home again, child, I wish you to look upon me, who am so much your elder, as your guardian and protector still. If there is anything which you lack, if you are misused, are in need of help, why, think that your troubles are the Indians again, little maid, and turn to me once more for help!"

Having spoken honestly and well and very unwisely, he looked at his watch and said that it was late. When he rose to his feet Audrey did not move, and when he looked down upon her he saw that her eyes, that had been wet, were overflowing. He put out his hand, and she took it and touched it with her lips; then, because he said that he had not meant to set her crying, she smiled, and with her own hand dashed away the tears.

"When I ride this way I shall always stop at the minister's house," said Haward, "when, if there is aught which you need or wish, you must tell me of it. Think of me as your friend, child."

He laid his hand lightly and caressingly upon her head. The ruffles at his wrist, soft, fine, and perfumed, brushed her forehead and her eyes. "The path through your labyrinth to its beechen heart was hard to find," he continued, "but I can easily retrace it. No, trouble not yourself, child. Stay for a time where you are. I wish to speak to the minister alone."

His hand was lifted. Audrey felt rather than saw him go. Only a few feet, and the dogwood stars, the purple mist of the Judas-tree, the white fragrance of a wild cherry, came like a painted arras between them. For a time she could hear the movement of the branches as he put them aside; but presently this too ceased, and the place was left to her and to all the life that called it home.

It was the same wood, surely, into which she had run two hours before, and yet—and yet—When her tears were spent, and she stood up, leaning, with her loosened hair and her gown that was the color of oak bark, against the beech-tree, she looked about her and wondered. The wonder did not last, for she found an explanation.

"It has been blessed," said Audrey, with all reverence and simplicity, "and that is why the light is so different."

CHAPTER IX

MACLEAN TO THE RESCUE

Saunderson, the overseer, having laboriously written and signed a pass, laid down the quill, wiped his inky fore-finger upon his sleeve, and gave the paper to the storekeeper, who sat idly by.

"Ye'll remember that the store chiefly lacks in broadcloth of Witney, frieze and camlet, and in women's shoes, both silk and callimanco. And dinna forget to trade with Alick Ker for three small swords, a chafing dish, and a dozen mourning and hand-and-heart rings. See that you have the skins' worth. Alick's an awfu' man to get the upper hand of."

"I'm thinking a MacLean should have small difficulty with a Ker," said the storekeeper dryly. "What I'm wanting to know is why I am saddled with the company of Monsieur Jean Hugon." He jerked his thumb toward the figure of the trader standing within the doorway. "I do not like the gentleman, and I'd rather trudge it to Williamsburgh alone."

"Ye ken not the value of the skins, nor how to show them off," answered the other. "Wherefore, for the consideration of a measure of rum, he's engaged to help you in the trading. As for his being half Indian, Gude guide us! It's been told me that no so many centuries ago the Highlandmen painted their bodies and went into battle without taking advantage even of feathers and silk grass. One half of him is of the French nobeelity; he told me as much himself. And the best of ye—sic as the Campbells—are no better than that."

He looked at MacLean with a caustic smile. The latter shrugged his shoulders. "So long as you tie him neck and heels with a Campbell I am content," he answered. "Are you going? I'll just bar the windows and lock the door, and then I'll be off with yonder copper cadet of a French house. Good-day to you. I'll be back to-night."

"Ye'd better," said the overseer, with another widening of his thin lips. "For myself, I bear ye no ill-will; for my grandmither—rest her soul!—came frae the north, and I aye thought a Stewart better became the throne than a foreign-speaking body frae Hanover. But if the store is not open the morn I'll raise hue and cry, and that without wasting time. I've been told ye're great huntsmen in the Highlands; if ye choose to turn red deer yourself, I'll give ye a chase, *and trade ye down, man, and track ye down.*"

MacLean half turned from the window. "I have hunted the red deer," he said, "in the land where I was born, and which I shall see no more, and I have been myself hunted in the land where I shall die. I have run until I have fallen, and I have felt the teeth of the dogs. Were God to send a miracle—which he will not do—and I were to go back to the glen and the crag and the deep birch woods, I suppose that I would hunt again, would drive the stag to bay, holloing to my hounds, and thinking the sound of the horns sweet music in my ears. It is the way of the earth.

Hunter and hunted, we make the world and the pity of it."

Setting to work again, he pushed to the heavy shutters. "You'll find them open in the morning," he said, "and find me selling,—selling clothing that I may not wear, wine that I may not drink, powder and shot that I may not spend, swords that I may not use; and giving,—giving pride, manhood, honor, heart's blood"—

He broke off, shot to the bar across the shutters, and betook himself in silence to the other window, where presently he burst into a fit of laughter. The sound was harsh even to savagery. "Go your ways, Saunderson," he said. "I've tried the bars of the cage; they're too strong. Stop on your morning round, and I'll give account of my trading."

The overseer gone, the windows barred, and the heavy door shut and locked behind him, MacLean paused upon the doorstep to look down upon his appointed companion. The trader, half sitting, half reclining upon a log, was striking at something with the point of his hunting-knife, lightly, delicately, and often. The something was a lizard, about which, as it lay in the sunshine upon the log, he had wrought a pen of leafy twigs. The creature, darting for liberty this way and that, was met at every turn by the steel, and at every turn suffered a new wound. MacLean looked; then bent over and with a heavy stick struck the thing out of its pain.

"There's a time to work and a time to play, Hugon," he said coolly. "Playtime's over now. The sun is high, and Isaac and the oxen must have the skins well-nigh to Williamsburgh. Up with you!"

Hugon rose to his feet, slid his knife into its sheath, and

announced in good enough English that he was ready. He had youth, the slender, hardy, perfectly moulded figure of the Indian, a coloring and a countenance that were not of the white and not of the brown. When he went a-trading up the river, past the thickly settled country, past the falls, past the French town which his Huguenot father had helped to build, into the deep woods and to the Indian village whence had strayed his mother, he wore the clothing that became the woods,—beaded moccasins, fringed leggings, hunting-shirt of deerskin, cap of fur,—looked his part and played it well. When he came back to an English country, to wharves and stores, to halls and porches of great houses and parlors of lesser ones, to the streets and ordinaries of Williamsburgh, he pulled on jack boots, shrugged himself into a coat with silver buttons, stuck lace of a so-so quality at neck and wrists, wore a cocked hat and a Blenheim wig, and became a figure alike grotesque and terrible. Two thirds of the time his business caused him to be in the forests that were far away; but when he returned to civilization, to stare it in the face and brag within himself, "I am lot and part of what I see!" he dwelt at the crossroads ordinary, drank and gamed with Paris the schoolmaster and Darden the minister, and dreamed (at times) of Darden's Audrey.

The miles to Williamsburgh were long and sunny, with the dust thick beneath the feet. Warm and heavy, the scented spring possessed the land. It was a day for drowsing in the shade: for them who must needs walk in the sunshine, languor of thought overtook them, and sparsity of speech. They walked rapidly, step with step, their two lean and sinewy bodies casting the same length of shadow; but they kept their eyes upon the long glare of white dust, and told not their dreams. At a point in the road where the storekeeper saw only confused marks and a powdering of dust upon the roadside bushes, the half-breed announced that there had been that morning a scuffle in a gang of negroes; that a small man had been thrown heavily to the earth, and a large man had made off across a low ditch into the woods; that the overseer had parted the combatants, and that some one's back had bled. No sooner was this piece of clairvoyance aired than he was vexed that he had shown a hall-mark of the savage, and hastily explained that life in the woods, such as a trader must live, would teach any man—an Englishman, now, as well as a Frenchman—how to read what was written on the earth. Farther on, when they came to a miniature glen between the semblance of two hills, down which, in mockery of a torrent, brabbled a slim brown stream, MacLean stood still, gazed for a minute, then, whistling, caught up with his companion, and spoke at length upon the subject of the skins awaiting them at Williamsburgh.

The road had other travelers than themselves. At intervals a cloud of dust would meet or overtake them, and out of the windows of coach or chariot or lighter chaise faces would glance at them. In the thick dust wheels and horses' hoofs made no noise, the black coachmen sat still upon the boxes, the faces were languid with the springtime. A moment and all were gone. Oftener there passed a horseman. If he were riding the planter's pace, he went by like a whirlwind, troubling only to curse them out of his path; if he had more leisure, he threw them a good-morning, or perhaps drew rein to ask this or that of Hugon. The trader was well known, and was an authority upon all matters pertaining to hunting or trapping. The foot passengers were few, for in Virginia no man walked that could ride, and on a morn of early May they that walked were like to be busy in the fields. An ancient seaman, lame and vagabond, lurched beside them for a while, then lagged behind; a witch, old and bowed and bleared of eye, crossed their path; and a Sapony hunter, with three wolves' heads slung across his shoulder, slipped by them on his way to claim the reward decreed by the Assembly. At a turn of the road they came upon a small ordinary, with horses fastened before it, and with laughter, oaths, and the rattling of dice issuing from the open windows. The trader had money; the storekeeper had none. The latter, though he was thirsty, would have passed on; but Hugon twitched him by the sleeve, and producing from the depths of his great flapped pocket a handful of crusadoes, ecues, and pieces of eight, indicated with a flourish that he was prepared to share with his less fortunate companion.

They drank standing, kissed the girl who served them, and took to the road again. There were no more thick woods, the road running in a blaze of sunshine past clumps of cedars and wayside tangles of blackberry, sumac, and elder. Presently, beyond a group of elms, came into sight the goodly college of William and Mary, and, dazzling white against the blue, the spire of Bruton church.

Within a wide pasture pertaining to the college, close to the roadside and under the boughs of a vast poplar, half a score of students were at play. Their lithe young bodies were dark of hue and were not overburdened with clothing; their countenances remained unmoved, without laughter or grimacing; and no excitement breathed in the voices with which they called one to another. In deep gravity they tossed a ball, or pitched a quoit, or engaged in wrestling. A white man, with a singularly pure and gentle face, sat upon the grass at the foot of the tree, and watched the studious efforts of his pupils with an approving smile.

"Wildcats to purr upon the hearth, and Indians to go to

school!" quoth MacLean. "Were you taught here, Hugon, and did you play so sadly?"

The trader, his head held very high, drew out a large and bedizened snuffbox, and took snuff with ostentation. "My father was of a great tribe—I would say a great house—in the country called France," he explained, with dignity. "Oh, he was of a very great name indeed! His blood was—what do you call it?—*blue*. I am the son of my father: I am a Frenchman. *Bien*! My father dies, having always kept me with him at Monacan-Town; and when they have laid him full length in the ground, Monsieur le Marquis calls me to him. 'Jean,' says he, and his voice is like the ice in the stream, 'Jean, you have ten years, and your father—may *le bon Dieu* pardon his sins!—has left his wishes regarding you and money for your mainte- nance. To-morrow Messieurs de Sailly and de Breuil go down the river to talk of affairs with the English Governor. You will go with them, and they will leave you at the Indian school which the English have built near to the great college in their town of Williamsburgh. There you will stay, learning all that Englishmen can teach you, until you have eighteen years. Come back to me then, and with the money left by your father you shall be fitted out as a trader. Go!' ... Yes, I went to school here; but I learned fast, and did not forget the things I learned, and I played with the English boys—there being no scholars from France—on the other side of the pasture."

He waved his hand toward an irruption of laughing, shouting figures from the north wing of the college. The white man under the tree had been quietly observant of the two wayfarers, and he now rose to his feet, and came over to the rail fence against which they leaned.

"Ha, Jean Hugon!" he said pleasantly, touching with his

thin white hand the brown one of the trader. "I thought it had been my old scholar! Canst say the belief and the Commandments yet, Jean? Yonder great fellow with the ball is Meshawa,—Meshawa that was a little, little fellow when you went away. All your other playmates are gone,—though you did not play much, Jean, but gloomed and gloomed because you must stay this side of the meadow with your own color. Will you not cross the fence and sit awhile with your old master?"

As he spoke he regarded with a humorous smile the dusty glories of his sometime pupil, and when he had come to an end he turned and made as if to beckon to the Indian with the ball. But Hugon drew his hand away, straightened himself, and set his face like a flint toward the town. "I am sorry, I have no time to-day," he said stiffly. "My friend and I have business in town with men of my own color. My color is white. I do not want to see Meshawa or the others. I have forgotten them."

He turned away, but a thought striking him his face brightened, and plunging his hand into his pocket he again brought forth his glittering store. "Nowadays I have money," he said grandly. "It used to be that Indian braves brought Meshawa and the others presents, because they were the sons of their great men. I was the son of a great man, too; but he was not Indian and he was lying in his grave, and no one brought me gifts. Now I wish to give presents. Here are ten coins, master. Give one to each Indian boy, the largest to Meshawa."

The Indian teacher, Charles Griffin by name, looked with a whimsical face at the silver pieces laid arow upon the top rail. "Very well, Jean," he said. "It is good to give of thy substance. Meshawa and the others will have a feast. Yes, I will remember to tell them to whom they owe it.

Good-day to you both."

The meadow, the solemnly playing Indians, and their gentle teacher were left behind, and the two men, passing the long college all astare with windows, the Indian school, and an expanse of grass starred with buttercups, came into Duke of Gloucester Street. Broad, unpaved, deep in dust, shaded upon its ragged edges by mulberries and poplars, it ran without shadow of turning from the gates of William and Mary to the wide sweep before the Capitol. Houses bordered it, flush with the street or set back in fragrant gardens; other and narrower ways opened from it; half way down its length wide greens, where the buttercups were thick in the grass, stretched north and south. Beyond these greens were more houses, more mulberries and poplars, and finally, closing the vista, the brick facade of the Capitol.

The two from Fair View plantation kept their forest gait; for the trader was in a hurry to fulfill his part of the bargain, which was merely to exhibit and value the skins. There was an ordinary in Nicholson Street that was to his liking. Sailors gamed there, and other traders, and half a dozen younger sons of broken gentlemen. It was as cleanly dining in its chief room as in the woods, and the aqua vitae, if bad, was cheap. In good humor with himself, and by nature lavish with his earnings, he offered to make the storekeeper his guest for the day. The latter curtly declined the invitation. He had bread and meat in his wallet, and wanted no drink but water. He would dine beneath the trees on the market green, would finish his business in town, and be half way back to the plantation while the trader—being his own man, with no fear of hue and cry if he were missed—was still at hazard.

This question settled, the two kept each other company

for several hours longer, at the end of which time they issued from the store at which the greater part of their business had been transacted, and went their several ways,—Hugon to the ordinary in Nicholson Street, and MacLean to his dinner beneath the sycamores on the green. When the frugal meal had been eaten, the latter recrossed the sward to the street, and took up again the round of his commissions.

It was after three by the great clock in the cupola of the Capitol when he stood before the door of Alexander Ker, the silversmith, and found entrance made difficult by the serried shoulders of half a dozen young men standing within the store, laughing, and making bantering speeches to some one hidden from the Highlander's vision. Presently an appealing voice, followed by a low cry, proclaimed that the some one was a woman.

MacLean had a lean and wiry strength which had stood him in good stead upon more than one occasion in his checkered career. He now drove an arm like a bar of iron between two broadcloth coats, sent the wearers thereof to right and left, and found himself one of an inner ring and facing Mistress Truelove Taberer, who stood at bay against the silversmith's long table. One arm was around the boy who had rowed her to the Fair View store a week agone; with the other she was defending her face from the attack of a beribboned gallant desirous of a kiss. The boy, a slender, delicate lad of fourteen, struggled to free himself from his sister's restraining arm, his face white with passion and his breath coming in gasps. "Let me go, Truelove!" he commanded. "If I am a Friend, I am a man as well! Thou fellow with the shoulder knots, thee shall pay dearly for thy insolence!"

Truelove tightened her hold. "Ephraim, Ephraim! If a man

compel thee to go with him a mile, thee is to go with him twain; if he take thy cloak, thee is to give him thy coat also; if he—Ah!" She buried her profaned cheek in her arm and began to cry, but very softly.

Her tormentors, flushed with wine and sworn to obtain each one a kiss, laughed more loudly, and one young rake, with wig and ruffles awry, lurched forward to take the place of the coxcomb who had scored. Ephraim wrenched himself free, and making for this gentleman might have given or received bodily injury, had not a heavy hand falling upon his shoulder stopped him in mid-career.

"Stand aside, boy," said MacLean, "This quarrel's mine by virtue of my making it so. Mistress Truelove, you shall have no further annoyance. Now, you Lowland cowards that cannot see a flower bloom but you wish to trample it in the mire, come taste the ground yourself, and be taught that the flower is out of reach!"

As he spoke he stepped before the Quakeress, weapon-less, but with his eyes like steel. The half dozen spendthrifts and ne'er-do-weels whom he faced paused but long enough to see that this newly arrived champion had only his bare hands, and was, by token of his dress, undoubtedly their inferior, before setting upon him with drunken laughter and the loudly avowed purpose of administering a drubbing. The one that came first he sent rolling to the floor. "Another for Hector!" he said coolly.

The silversmith, ensconced in safety behind the table, wrung his hands. "Sirs, sirs! Take your quarrel into the street! I'll no have fighting in my store. What did ye rin in here for, ye Quaker baggage? Losh! did ye ever see the like of that! Here, boy, ye can get through the window.

Rin for the constable! Rin, I tell ye, or there'll be murder done!"

A gentleman who had entered the store unobserved drew his rapier, and with it struck up a heavy cane which was in the act of descending for the second time upon the head of the unlucky Scot. "What is all this?" he asked quietly. "Five men against one,—that is hardly fair play. Ah, I see there were six; I had overlooked the gentleman on the floor, who, I hope, is only stunned. Five to one,—the odds are heavy. Perhaps I can make them less so." With a smile upon his lips, he stepped backward a foot or two until he stood with the weaker side.

Now, had it been the constable who so suddenly appeared upon the scene, the probabilities are that the fight, both sides having warmed to it, would, despite the terrors of the law, have been carried to a finish. But it was not the constable; it was a gentleman recently returned from England, and become in the eyes of the youth of Williamsburgh the glass of fashion and the mould of form. The youngster with the shoulder knots had copied color and width of ribbon from a suit which this gentleman had worn at the Palace; the rake with the wig awry, who passed for a wit, had done him the honor to learn by heart portions of his play, and to repeat (without quotation marks) a number of his epigrams; while the pretty fellow whose cane he had struck up practiced night and morning before a mirror his bow and manner of presenting his snuffbox. A fourth ruffler desired office, and cared not to offend a prospective Councilor. There was rumor, too, of a grand entertainment to be given at Fair View; it was good to stand well with the law, but it was imperative to do so with Mr. Marmaduke Haward. Their hands fell; they drew back a pace, and the wit made himself spokesman. Roses were rare so early in the year;

for him and his companions, they had but wished to compliment those that bloomed in the cheeks of the pretty Quakeress. This servant fellow, breathing fire like a dragon, had taken it upon himself to defend the roses,—which likely enough were grown for him,—and so had been about to bring upon himself merited chastisement. However, since it was Mr. Marmaduke Haward who pleaded for him—A full stop, a low bow, and a flourish. "Will Mr. Haward honor me? 'Tis right Macouba, and the box—if the author of 'The Puppet Show' would deign to accept it"—

"Rather to change with you, sir," said the other urbanely, and drew out his own chased and medallioned box.

The gentleman upon the floor had now gotten unsteadily to his feet. Mr. Haward took snuff with each of the six; asked after the father of one, the brother of another; delicately intimated his pleasure in finding the noble order of Mohocks, that had lately died in London, resurrected in Virginia; and fairly bowed the flattered youths out of the store. He stood for a moment upon the threshold watching them go triumphantly, if unsteadily, up the street; then turned to the interior of the store to find MacLean seated upon a stool, with his head against the table, submitting with a smile of pure content to the ministrations of the dove-like mover of the late turmoil, who with trembling fingers was striving to bind her kerchief about a great cut in his forehead.

CHAPTER X

HAWARD AND EVELYN

MacLean put aside with much gentleness the hands of his surgeon, and, rising to his feet, answered the question in Haward's eyes by producing a slip of paper and gravely proffering it to the man whom he served. Haward took it, read it, and handed it back; then turned to the Quaker maiden. "Mistress Truelove Taberer," he said courteously. "Are you staying in town? If you will tell me where you lodge, I will myself conduct you thither."

Truelove shook her head, and slipped her hand into that of her brother Ephraim. "I thank thee, friend," she said, with gentle dignity, "and thee, too, Angus MacLean, though I grieve that thee sees not that it is not given us to meet evil with evil, nor to withstand force with force. Ephraim and I can now go in peace. I thank thee again, friend, and thee." She gave her hand first to Haward, then to MacLean. The former, knowing the fashion of the Quakers, held the small fingers a moment, then let them drop; the latter, knowing it, too, raised them to his lips and imprinted upon them an impassioned kiss. Truelove blushed, then frowned, last of all drew her hand away.

With the final glimpse of her gray skirt the Highlander

came back to the present. "Singly I could have answered for them all, one after the other," he said stiffly. "Together they had the advantage. I pay my debt and give you thanks, sir."

"That is an ugly cut across your forehead," replied Haward. "Mr. Ker had best bring you a basin of water. Or stay! I am going to my lodging. Come with me, and Juba shall dress the wound properly."

MacLean turned his keen blue eyes upon him. "Am I to understand that you give me a command, or that you extend to me an invitation? In the latter case, I should prefer"—

"Then take it as a command," said Haward imperturbably. "I wish your company. Mr. Ker, good-day; I will buy the piece of plate which you showed me yesterday."

The two moved down the room together, but at the door MacLean, with his face set like a flint, stood aside, and Haward passed out first, then waited for the other to come up with him.

"When I drink a cup I drain it to the dregs," said the Scot. "I walk behind the man who commands me. The way, you see, is not broad enough for you and me and hatred."

"Then let hatred lag behind," answered Haward coolly. "I have negroes to walk at my heels when I go abroad. I take you for a gentleman, accept your enmity an it please you, but protest against standing here in the hot sunshine."

With a shrug MacLean joined him. "As you please," he said. "I have in spirit moved with you through London streets. I never thought to walk with you in the flesh."

It was yet warm and bright in the street, the dust thick, the air heavy with the odors of the May. Haward and MacLean walked in silence, each as to the other, one as to the world at large. Now and again the Virginian must stop to bow profoundly to curtsying ladies, or to take snuff with some portly Councilor or less stately Burgess who, coming from the Capitol, chanced to overtake them. When he paused his storekeeper paused also, but, having no notice taken of him beyond a glance to discern his quality, needed neither a supple back nor a ready smile.

Haward lodged upon Palace Street, in a square brick house, lived in by an ancient couple who could remember Puritan rule in Virginia, who had served Sir William Berkeley, and had witnessed the burning of Jamestown by Bacon. There was a grassy yard to the house, and the path to the door lay through an alley of lilacs, purple and white. The door was open, and Haward and MacLean, entering, crossed the hall, and going into a large, low room, into which the late sunshine was streaming, found the negro Juba setting cakes and wine upon the table.

"This gentleman hath a broken head, Juba," said the master. "Bring water and linen, and bind it up for him."

As he spoke he laid aside hat and rapier, and motioned MacLean to a seat by the window. The latter obeyed the gesture in silence, and in silence submitted to the ministrations of the negro. Haward, sitting at the table, waited until the wound had been dressed; then with a wave of the hand dismissed the black.

"You would take nothing at my hands the other day," he said to the grim figure at the window. "Change your mind, my friend,—or my foe,—and come sit and drink with me."

Mary Johnston

MacLean reared himself from his seat, and went stiffly over to the table. "I have eaten and drunken with an enemy before to-day," he said. "Once I met Ewin Mor Mackinnon upon a mountain side. He had oatcake in his sporran, and I a flask of usquebaugh. We couched in the heather, and ate and drank together, and then we rose and fought. I should have slain him but that a dozen Mackinnons came up the glen, and he turned and fled to them for cover. Here I am in an alien land; a thousand fiery crosses would not bring one clansman to my side; I cannot fight my foe. Wherefore, then, should I take favors at his hands?"

"Why should you be my foe?" demanded Haward. "Look you, now! There was a time, I suppose, when I was an insolent youngster like any one of those who lately set upon you; but now I call myself a philosopher and man of a world for whose opinions I care not overmuch. My coat is of fine cloth, and my shirt of holland; your shirt is lockram, and you wear no coat at all: *ergo*, saith a world of pretty fellows, we are beings of separate planets. 'As the cloth is, the man is,'—to which doctrine I am at times heretic. I have some store of yellow metal, and spend my days in ridding myself of it,—a feat which you have accomplished. A goodly number of acres is also counted unto me, but in the end my holding and your holding will measure the same. I walk a level road; you have met with your precipice, and, bruised by the fall, you move along stony ways; but through the same gateway we go at last. Fate, not I, put you here. Why should you hate me who am of your order?"

MacLean left the table, and twice walked the length of the room, slowly and with knitted brows. "If you mean the world-wide order,—the order of gentlemen,"—he said, coming to a pause with the breadth of the table between him and Haward, "we may have that ground in common. The rest is debatable land. I do not take you for a sentimentalist or a redresser of wrongs. I am your storekeeper, purchased with that same yellow metal of which you so busily rid yourself; and your storekeeper I shall remain until the natural death of my term, two years hence. We are not countrymen; we own different kings; I may once have walked your level road, but you have never moved in the stony ways; my eyes are blue, while yours are gray; you love your melting Southern music, and I take no joy save in the pipes; I dare swear you like the smell of lilies which I cannot abide, and prefer fair hair in women where I would choose the dark. There is no likeness between us. Why, then"—

Haward smiled, and drawing two glasses toward him slowly filled them with wine. "It is true," he said, "that it is not my intention to become a petitioner for the pardon of a rebel to his serene and German Majesty the King; true also that I like the fragrance of the lily. I have my fancies. Say that I am a man of whim, and that, living in a lonely house set in a Sahara of tobacco fields, it is my whim to desire the acquaintance of the only gentleman within some miles of me. Say that my fancy hath been caught by a picture drawn for me a week agone; that, being a philosopher, I play with the idea that your spirit, knife in hand, walked at my elbow for ten years, and I knew it not. Say that the idea has for me a curious fascination. Say, finally, that I plume myself that, given the chance, I might break down this airy hatred."

He set down the bottle, and pushed one of the brimming glasses across the table. "I should like to make trial of my strength," he said, with, a laugh. "Come! I did you a service to-day; in your turn do me a pleasure."

MacLean dragged a chair to the table, and sat down. "I will drink with you," he said, "and forget for an hour. A man grows tired—It is Burgundy, is it not? Old Borlum and I emptied a bottle between us, the day he went as hostage to Wills; since then I have not tasted wine. 'Tis a pretty color."

Haward lifted his glass. "I drink to your future. Freedom, better days, a stake in a virgin land, friendship with a sometime foe." He bowed to his guest and drank.

"In my country," answered MacLean, "where we would do most honor, we drink not to life, but to death. *Crioch onarach!* Like a gentleman may you die." He drank, and sighed with pleasure.

"The King!" said Haward. There was a china bowl, filled with red anemones, upon the table. MacLean drew it toward him, and, pressing aside the mass of bloom, passed his glass over the water in the bowl. "The King! with all my heart," he said imperturbably.

Haward poured more wine. "I have toasted at the Kit-Kat many a piece of brocade and lace less fair than yon bit of Quaker gray that cost you a broken head. Shall we drink to Mistress Truelove Taberer?"

By now the Burgundy had warmed the heart and loosened the tongue of the man who had not tasted wine since the surrender of Preston. "It is but a mile from the store to her father's house," he said. "Sometimes on Sundays I go up the creek upon the Fair View side, and when I am over against the house I holloa. Ephraim comes, in his boat and rows me across, and I stay for an hour. They are strange folk, the Quakers. In her sight and in that of her people I am as good a man as you. 'Friend Angus MacLean,'

'Friend Marmaduke Haward,'—world's wealth and world's rank quite beside the question."

He drank, and commended the wine. Haward struck a silver bell, and bade Juba bring another bottle.

"When do you come again to the house at Fair View?" asked the storekeeper.

"Very shortly. It is a lonely place, where ghosts bear me company. I hope that now and then, when I ask it, and when the duties of your day are ended, you will come help me exorcise them. You shall find welcome and good wine." He spoke very courteously, and if he saw the humor of the situation his smile betrayed him not.

MacLean took a flower from the bowl, and plucked at its petals with nervous fingers. "Do you mean that?" he asked at last.

Haward leaned across the table, and their eyes met. "On my word I do," said the Virginian.

The knocker on the house door sounded loudly, and a moment later a woman's clear voice, followed by a man's deeper tones, was heard in the hall.

"More guests," said Haward lightly. "You are a Jacobite; I drink my chocolate at St. James' Coffee House; the gentleman approaching—despite his friendship for Orrery and for the Bishop of Rochester—is but a Hanover Tory; but the lady,—the lady wears only white roses, and every 10th of June makes a birthday feast."

The storekeeper rose hastily to take his leave, but was prevented both by Haward's restraining gesture and by the entrance of the two visitors who were now ushered in by the grinning Juba. Haward stepped forward. "You are very welcome, Colonel. Evelyn, this is kind. Your woman told me this morning that you were not well, else"—

"A migraine," she answered, in her clear, low voice. "I am better now, and my father desired me to take the air with him."

"We return to Westover to-morrow," said that sprightly gentleman. "Evelyn is like David of old, and pines for water from the spring at home. It also appears that the many houses and thronged streets of this town weary her, who, poor child, is used to an Arcady called London! When will you come to us at Westover, Marmaduke?"

"I cannot tell," Haward answered. "I must first put my own house in order, so that I may in my turn entertain my friends."

As he spoke he moved aside, so as to include in the company MacLean, who stood beside the table. "Evelyn," he said, "let me make known to you—and to you, Colonel—a Scots gentleman who hath broken his spear in his tilt with fortune, as hath been the luck of many a gallant man before him. Mistress Evelyn Byrd, Colonel Byrd—Mr. MacLean, who was an officer in the Highland force taken at Preston, and who has been for some years a prisoner of war in Virginia."

The lady's curtsy was low; the Colonel bowed as to his friend's friend. If his eyebrows went up, and if a smile twitched the corners of his lips, the falling curls of his periwig hid from view these tokens of amused wonder. MacLean bowed somewhat stiffly, as one grown rusty in such matters. "I am in addition Mr. Marmaduke Haward's storekeeper," he said succinctly, then turned to the master of Fair View. "It grows late," he announced, "and I must be back at the store to-night. Have you any message for Saunderson?"

"None," answered Haward. "I go myself to Fair View to-morrow, and then I shall ask you to drink with me again."

As he spoke he held out his hand. MacLean looked at it, sighed, then touched it with his own. A gleam as of wintry laughter came into his blue eyes. "I doubt that I shall have to get me a new foe," he said, with regret in his voice.

When he had bowed to the lady and to her father, and had gone out of the room and down the lilac-bordered path and through the gate, and when the three at the window had watched him turn into Duke of Gloucester Street, the master of Westover looked at the master of Fair View and burst out laughing. "Ludwell hath for an overseer the scapegrace younger son of a baronet; and there are three brothers of an excellent name under indentures to Robert Carter. I have at Westover a gardener who annually makes the motto of his house to spring in pease and asparagus. I have not had him to drink with me yet, and t'other day I heard Ludwell give to the baronet's son a hound's rating."

"I do not drink with the name," said Haward coolly. "I drink with the man. The churl or coward may pass me by, but the gentleman, though his hands be empty, I stop."

The other laughed again; then dismissed the question with a wave of his hand, and pulled out a great gold watch with cornelian seals. "Carter swears that Dr. Contesse hath a specific that is as sovereign for the gout as is St. Andrew's cross for a rattlesnake bite. I've had twinges lately, and the doctor lives hard by. Evelyn, will you rest here while I go petition AEsculapius? Haward, when I have the recipe I will return, and impart it to you against the time when you need it. No, no, child, stay where you are! I will be back anon."

Having waved aside his daughter's faint protest, the Colonel departed,—a gallant figure of a man, with a pretty wit and a heart that was benevolently gay. As he went down the path he paused to gather a sprig of lilac. "Westover—Fair View," he said to himself, and smiled, and smelled the lilac; then—though his ills were some-what apocryphal—walked off at a gouty pace across the buttercup-sprinkled green toward the house of Dr. Contesse.

Haward and Evelyn, left alone, kept silence for a time in the quiet room that was filled with late sunshine and the fragrance of flowers. He stood by the window, and she sat in a great chair, with her hands folded in her lap, and her eyes upon them. When silence had become more loud than speech, she turned in her seat and addressed herself to him.

"I have known you do many good deeds," she said slowly. "That gentleman that was here is your servant, is he not, and an exile, and unhappy? And you sent him away comforted. It was a generous thing."

Haward moved restlessly. "A generous thing," he answered. "Ay, it was generous. I can do such things at times, and why I do them who can tell? Not I! Do you think that I care for that grim Highlander, who drinks my death in place of my health, who is of a nation that I dislike, and a party that is not mine?"

She shook her head. "I do not know. And yet you helped him."

Haward left the window, and came and sat beside her. "Yes, I helped him. I am not sure, but I think I did it because, when first we met, he told me that he hated me, and meant the thing he said. It is my humor to fix my own position in men's minds; to lose the thing I have that I may gain the thing I have not; to overcome, and never prize the victory; to hunt down a quarry, and feel no ardor in the chase; to strain after a goal, and yet care not if I never reach it."

He took her fan in his hand, and fell to counting the slender ivory sticks. "I tread the stage as a fine gentle-man," he said. "It is the part for which I was cast, and I play it well with proper mien and gait. I was not asked if I would like the part, but I think that I do like it, as much as I like anything. Seeing that I must play it, and that there is that within me which cries out against slovenliness, I play it as an artist should. Magnanimity goes with it, does it not, and generosity, courtesy, care for the thing which is, and not for that which seems? Why, then, with these and other qualities I strive to endow the character."

He closed the fan, and, leaning back in his chair, shaded his eyes with his hand. "When the lights are out," he said; "when forever and a night the actor bids the stage farewell; when, stripped of mask and tinsel, he goes home to that Auditor who set him his part, then perhaps he will be told what manner of man he is. The glass that now he dresses before tells him not; but he thinks a truer glass would show a shrunken figure."

He sat in silence for a moment; then laughed, and gave her back her fan. "Am I to come to Westover, Evelyn?" he asked. "Your father presses, and I have not known what answer to make him."

"You will give us pleasure by your coming," she said gently and at once. "My father wishes your advice as to the ordering of his library; and you know that my pretty stepmother likes you well."

"Will it please you to have me come?" he asked, with his eyes upon her face.

She met his gaze very quietly. "Why not?" she answered simply. "You will help me in my flower garden, and sing with me in the evening, as of old."

"Evelyn," he said, "if what I am about to say to you distresses you, lift your hand, and I will cease to speak. Since a day and an hour in the woods yonder, I have been thinking much. I wish to wipe that hour from your memory as I wipe it from mine, and to begin afresh. You are the fairest woman that I know, and the best. I beg you to accept my reverence, homage, love; not the boy's love, perhaps; perhaps not the love that some men have to squander, but *my* love. A quiet love, a lasting trust, deep pride and pleasure"—

At her gesture he broke off, sat in silence for a moment, then rising went to the window, and with slightly contracted brows stood looking out at the sunshine that was slipping away. Presently he was aware that she stood beside him.

She was holding out her hand. "It is that of a friend," she said. "No, do not kiss it, for that is the act of a lover. And you are not my lover,—oh, not yet, not yet!" A soft, exquisite blush stole over her face and neck, but she did not lower her lovely candid eyes. "Perhaps some day, some summer day at Westover, it will all be different," she breathed, and turned away.

Haward caught her hand, and bending pressed his lips upon it. "It is different now!" he cried. "Next week I shall come to Westover!"

He led her back to the great chair, and presently she asked some question as to the house at Fair View. He plunged into an account of the cases of goods which had followed him from England by the Falcon, and which now lay in the rooms that were yet to be swept and garnished; then spoke lightly and whimsically of the solitary state in which he must live, and of the entertainments which, to be in the Virginia fashion, he must give. While he talked she sat and watched him, with the faint smile upon her lips. The sunshine left the floor and the wall, and a dankness from the long grass and the closing flowers and the heavy trees in the adjacent churchyard stole into the room. With the coming of the dusk conversation languished, and the two sat in silence until the return of the Colonel.

If that gentleman did not light the darkness like a star, at least his entrance into a room invariably produced the effect of a sudden accession of was lights, very fine and clear and bright. He broke a jest or two, bade laughing farewell to the master of Fair View, and carried off his daughter upon his arm. Haward walked with them to the gate, and came back alone, stepping thoughtfully between the lilac bushes.

It was not until Juba had brought candles, and he had taken his seat at table before the half-emptied bottle of wine, that it came to Haward that he had wished to tell

Evelyn of the brown girl who had run for the guinea, but had forgotten to do so.

CHAPTER XI

AUDREY OF THE GARDEN

The creek that ran between Fairview and the glebe lands was narrow and deep; upon it, moored to a stake driven into a bit of marshy ground below the orchard, lay a crazy boat belonging to the minister. To this boat, of an early, sunny morning, came Audrey, and, standing erect, pole in hand, pushed out from the reedy bank into the slow-moving stream. It moved so slowly and was so clear that its depth seemed the blue depth of the sky, with now and then a tranquil cloud to be glided over. The banks were low and of the greenest grass, save where they sank still lower and reeds abounded, or where some colored bush, heavy with bloom, bent to meet its reflected image. It was so fair that Audrey began to sing as she went down the stream; and without knowing why she chose it, she sang a love song learned out of one of Darden's ungodly books, a plaintive and passionate lay addressed by some cavalier to his mistress of an hour. She sang not loudly, but very sweetly; carelessly, too, and as if to herself; now and then repeating a line twice or maybe thrice; pleased with the sweet melancholy of the notes, but not thinking overmuch of the meaning of the words. They died upon her lips when Hugon rose from a lair of reeds and called to her to stop. "Come to the shore, ma'm'selle!" he cried. "See, I have brought you a ribbon from the town. Behold!" and he fluttered a crimson streamer.

Audrey caught her breath; then gazed, reassured, at the five yards of water between her and the bank. Had Hugon stood there in his hunting dress, she would have felt them no security; but he was wearing his coat and breeches of fine cloth, his ruffled shirt, and his great black periwig. A wetting would not be to his mind.

As she answered not, but went on her way, silent now, and with her slender figure bending with the motion of the pole, he frowned and shrugged; then took up his pilgrimage, and with his light and swinging stride kept alongside of the boat. The ribbon lay across his arm, and he turned it in the sunshine. "If you come not and get it," he wheedled, "I will throw it in the water."

The angry tears sprang to Audrey's eyes. "Do so, and save me the trouble," she answered, and then was sorry that she had spoken.

The red came into the swarthy cheeks of the man upon the bank. "You love me not," he said. "Good! You have told me so before. But here I am!"

"Then here is a coward!" said Audrey. "I do not wish you to walk there. I do not wish you to speak to me. Go back!"

Hugon's teeth began to show. "I go not," he answered, with something between a snarl and a smirk. "I love you, and I follow on your path,—like a lover."

"Like an Indian!" cried the girl.

The arrow pierced the heel. The face which he turned

upon her was the face of a savage, made grotesque and horrible, as war-paint and feathers could not have made it, by the bushy black wig and the lace cravat.

"Audrey!" he called. "Morning Light! Sunshine in the Dark! Dancing Water! Audrey that will not be called 'mademoiselle' nor have the wooing of the son of a French chief! Then shall she have the wooing of the son of a Monacan woman. I am a hunter. I will woo as they woo in the woods."

Audrey bent to her pole, and made faster progress down the creek. Her heart was hot and angry, and yet she was afraid. All dreadful things, all things that oppressed with horror, all things that turned one white and cold, so cold and still that one could not run away, were summed up for her in the word "Indian." To her the eyes of Hugon were basilisk eyes,—they drew her and held her; and when she looked into them, she saw flames rising and bodies of murdered kindred; then the mountains loomed above her again, and it was night-time, and she was alone save for the dead, and mad with fear and with the quiet.

The green banks went by, and the creek began to widen. "Where are you going?" called the trader. "Wheresoever you go, at the end of your path stand my village and my wigwam. You cannot stay all day in that boat. If you come not back at the bidden hour, Darden's squaw will beat you. Come over, Morning Light, come over, and take me in your boat, and tie your hair with my gift. I will not hurt you. I will tell you the French love songs that my father sang to my mother. I will speak of land that I have bought (oh, I have prospered, ma'm'selle!), and of a house that I mean to build, and of a woman that I wish to put in the house,—a Sunshine in the Dark to greet me when I come from my hunting in the great forests beyond the falls, from my trading with the nation of the Tuscaroras, with the villages of the Monacans. Come over to me, Morning Light!"

The creek widened and widened, then doubled a grassy cape all in the shadow of a towering sycamore. Beyond the point, crowning the low green slope of the bank, and topped with a shaggy fell of honeysuckle and ivy, began a red brick wall. Half way down its length it broke, and six shallow steps led up to an iron gate, through whose bars one looked into a garden. Gazing on down the creek past the farther stretch of the wall, the eye came upon the shining reaches of the river.

Audrey turned the boat's head toward the steps and the gate in the wall. The man on the opposite shore let fall an oath.

"So you go to Fair View house!" he called across the stream. "There are only negroes there, unless"—he came to a pause, and his face changed again, and out of his eyes looked the spirit of some hot, ancestral French lover, cynical, suspicious, and jealously watchful—"unless their master is at home," he ended, and laughed.

Audrey touched the wall, and over a great iron hook projecting therefrom threw a looped rope, and fastened her boat.

"I stay here until you come forth!" swore Hugon from across the creek. "And then I follow you back to where you must moor the boat. And then I shall walk with you to the minister's house. Until we meet again, ma'm'selle!"

Audrey answered not, but sped up the steps to the gate. A sick fear lest it should be locked possessed her; but it opened at her touch, disclosing a long, sunny path, paved with brick, and shut between lines of tall, thick, and smoothly clipped box. The gate clanged to behind her; ten steps, and the boat, the creek, and the farther shore were hidden from her sight. With this comparative bliss came a faintness and a trembling that presently made her slip down upon the warm and sunny floor, and lie there, with her face within her arm and the tears upon her cheeks. The odor of the box wrapped her like a mantle; a lizard glided past her; somewhere in open spaces birds were singing; finally a greyhound came down the path, and put its nose into the hollow of her hand.

She rose to her knees, and curled her arm around the dog's neck; then, with a long sigh, stood up, and asked of herself if this were the way to the house. She had never seen the house at close range, had never been in this walled garden. It was from Williamsburgh that the minister had taken her to his home, eleven years before. Sometimes from the river, in those years, she had seen, rising above the trees, the steep roof and the upper windows; sometimes upon the creek she had gone past the garden wall, and had smelled the flowers upon the other side.

In her lonely life, with the beauty of the earth about her to teach her that there might be greater beauty that she yet might see with a daily round of toil and sharp words to push her to that escape which lay in a world of dreams, she had entered that world, and thrived therein. It was a world that was as pure as a pearl, and more fantastic than an Arabian tale. She knew that when she died she could take nothing out of life with her to heaven. But with this other world it was different, and all that she had or dreamed of that was fair she carried through its portals. This house was there. Long closed, walled in, guarded by tall trees, seen at far intervals and from a distance, as through a glass darkly, it had become to her an enchanted spot, about which played her quick fancy, but where her feet might never stray.

But now the spell which had held the place in slumber was snapped, and her feet was set in its pleasant paths. She moved down the alley between the lines of box, and the greyhound went with her. The branches of a walnut-tree drooped heavily across the way; when she had passed them she saw the house, square, dull red, bathed in sunshine. A moment, and the walk led her between squat pillars of living green into the garden out of the fairy tale.

Dim, fragrant, and old time; walled in; here sunshiny spaces, there cool shadows of fruit-trees; broken by circles and squares of box; green with the grass and the leaves, red and purple and gold and white with the flowers; with birds singing, with the great silver river murmuring by without the wall at the foot of the terrace, with the voice of a man who sat beneath a cherry-tree reading aloud to himself,—such was the garden that she came upon, a young girl, and heavy at heart.

She was so near that she could hear the words of the reader, and she knew the piece that he was reading; for you must remember that she was not untaught, and that Darden had books.

> "'When from the censer clouds of fragrance roll,
> And swelling organs lift the rising soul,
> One thought of thee puts all the pomp to flight,
> Priests, tapers, temples, swim before my sight'"—

The greyhound ran from Audrey to the man who was reading these verses with taste and expression, and also with a smile half sad and half cynical. He glanced from his page, saw the girl where she stood against the dark pillar of the box, tossed aside the book, and went to her down the grassy path between rows of nodding tulips. "Why, child!" he said. "Did you come up like a flower? I am glad to see you in my garden, little maid. Are there Indians without?"

At least, to Audrey, there were none within. She had been angered, sick at heart and sore afraid, but she was no longer so. In this world that she had entered it was good to be alive; she knew that she was safe, and of a sudden she felt that the sunshine was very golden, the music very sweet. To Haward, looking at her with a smile, she gave a folded paper which she drew from the bosom of her gown. "The minister sent me with it," she explained, and curtsied shyly.

Haward took the paper, opened it, and fell to poring over the crabbed characters with which it was adorned. "Ay? Gratulateth himself that this fortunate parish hath at last for vestryman Mr. Marmaduke Haward; knoweth that, seeing I am what I am, my influence will be paramount with said vestry; commendeth himself to my favor; beggeth that I listen not to charges made by a factious member anent a vastly magnified occurrence at the French ordinary; prayeth that he may shortly present himself at Fair View, and explain away certain calumnies with which his enemies have poisoned the ears of the Commissary; hopeth that I am in good health; and is my very obedient servant to command. Humph!"

He let the paper flutter to the ground, and turned to Audrey with a kindly smile. "I am much afraid that this man of the church, whom I gave thee for guardian, child, is but a rascal, after all, and a wolf in sheep's clothing. But let him go hang while I show you my garden."

Going closer, he glanced at her keenly; then went nearer still, and touched her cheek with his forefinger. "You have been crying," he said. "There *were* Indians, then. How many and how strong, Audrey?"

The dark eyes that met his were the eyes of the child who, in the darkness, through the corn, had run from him, her helper. "There was one," she whispered, and looked over her shoulder.

Haward drew her to the seat beneath the cherry-tree, and there, while he sat beside her, elbow on knee and chin on hand, watching her, she told him of Hugon. It was so natural to tell him. When she had made an end of her halting, broken sentences, and he spoke to her gravely and kindly, she hung upon his words, and thought him wise and wonderful as a king. He told her that he would speak to Darden, and did not despair of persuading that worthy to forbid the trader his house. Also he told her that in this settled, pleasant, every-day Virginia, and in the eighteenth century, a maid, however poor and humble, might not be married against her will. If this half-breed had threats to utter, there was always the law of the land. A few hours in the pillory or a taste of the sheriff's whip might not be amiss. Finally, if the trader made his suit again, Audrey must let him know, and Monsieur Jean Hugon should be taught that he had another than a helpless, friendless girl to deal with.

Audrey listened and was comforted, but the shadow did not quite leave her eyes. "He is waiting for me now," she said fearfully to Haward, who had not missed the shadow. "He followed me down the creek, and is waiting over against the gate in the wall. When I go back he will follow me again, and at last I will have to cross to his side. And then he will go home with me, and make me listen to him. His eyes burn me, and when his hand touches me I see—I see"—

Her frame shook, and she raised to his gaze a countenance suddenly changed into Tragedy's own. "I don't know why," she said, in a stricken voice, "but of them all that I kissed good-by that night I now see only Molly. I suppose she was about as old as I am when they killed her. We were always together. I can't remember her face very clearly; only her eyes, and how red her lips were. And her hair: it came to her knees, and mine is just as long. For a long, long time after you went away, when I could not sleep because it was dark, or when I was frightened or Mistress Deborah beat me, I saw them all; but now I see only Molly,—Molly lying there *dead*."

There was a silence in the garden, broken presently by Haward. "Ay, Molly," he said absently.

With his hand covering his lips and his eyes upon the ground, he fell into a brown study. Audrey sat very still for fear that she might disturb him, who was so kind to her. A passionate gratitude filled her young heart; she would have traveled round the world upon her knees to serve him. As for him, he was not thinking of the mountain girl, the oread who, in the days when he was younger and his heart beat high, had caught his light fancy, tempting him from his comrades back to the cabin in the valley, to look again into her eyes and touch the brown waves of her hair. She was ashes, and the memory of her stirred him not.

At last he looked up. "I myself will take you home, child. This fellow shall not come near you. And cease to think of these gruesome things that happened long ago. You are young and fair; you should be happy. I will see to it that"—

He broke off, and again looked thoughtfully at the ground. The book which he had tossed aside was lying upon the grass, open at the poem which he had been reading. He stooped and raised the volume, and, closing it, laid it upon the bench beside her. Presently he laughed. "Come, child!" he said. "You have youth. I begin to think my own not past recall. Come and let me show you my dial that I have just had put up."

There was no load at Audrey's heart: the vision of Molly had passed; the fear of Hugon was a dwindling cloud. She was safe in this old sunny garden, with harm shut without. And as a flower opens to the sunshine, so because she was happy she grew more fair. Audrey every day, Audrey of the infrequent speech and the wide dark eyes, the startled air, the shy, fugitive smiles,—that was not Audrey of the garden. Audrey of the garden had shining eyes, a wild elusive grace, laughter as silvery as that which had rung from her sister's lips, years agone, beneath the sugar-tree in the far-off blue mountains, quick gestures, quaint fancies which she feared not to speak out, the charm of mingled humility and spirit; enough, in short, to make Audrey of the garden a name to conjure with.

They came to the sun-dial, and leaned thereon. Around its rim were graved two lines from Herrick, and Audrey traced the letters with her finger. "The philosophy is sound," remarked Haward, "and the advice worth the taking. Let us go see if there are any rosebuds to gather from the bushes yonder. Damask buds should look well against your hair, child."

When they came to the rosebushes he broke for her a few scarce-opened buds, and himself fastened them in the coils of her hair. Innocent and glad as she was,—glad even that he thought her fair,—she trembled beneath his touch, and knew not why she trembled. When the rosebuds were in place they went to see the clove pinks, and when they had seen the clove pinks they walked slowly up another alley of box, and across a grass plot to a side door of the house; for he had said that he must show her in what great, lonely rooms he lived.

Audrey measured the height and breadth of the house with her eyes. "It is a large place for one to live in alone," she said, and laughed. "There's a book at the Widow Constance's; Barbara once showed it to me. It is all about a pilgrim; and there's a picture of a great square house, quite like this, that was a giant's castle,—Giant Despair. Good giant, eat me not!"

Child, woman, spirit of the woodland, she passed before him into a dim, cool room, all littered with books. "My library," said Haward, with a wave of his hand. "But the curtains and pictures are not hung, nor the books in place. Hast any schooling, little maid? Canst read?"

Audrey flushed with pride that she could tell him that she was not ignorant; not like Barbara, who could not read the giant's name in the pilgrim book.

"The crossroads schoolmaster taught me," she explained. "He has a scar in each hand, and is a very wicked man, but he knows more than the Commissary himself. The minister, too, has a cupboard filled with books, and he buys the new ones as the ships bring them in. When I have time, and Mistress Deborah will not let me go to the woods, I read. And I remember what I read. I could"—

A smile trembled upon her lips, and her eyes grew brighter. Fired by the desire that he should praise her learning, and in her very innocence bold as a Wortley or a Howe, she began to repeat the lines which he had been reading beneath the cherry-tree:—

"'When from the censer clouds of fragrance roll'"—

The rhythm of the words, the passion of the thought, the pleased surprise that she thought she read in his face, the gesture of his hand, all spurred her on from line to line, sentence to sentence. And now she was not herself, but that other woman, and she was giving voice to all her passion, all her woe. The room became a convent cell; her ragged dress the penitent's trailing black. That Audrey, lithe of mind as of body; who in the woods seemed the spirit of the woods, in the garden the spirit of the garden, on the water the spirit of the water,—that this Audrey, in using the speech of the poet, should embody and become the spirit of that speech was perhaps, considering all things, not so strange. At any rate, and however her power came about, at that moment, in Fair View house, a great actress was speaking.

"'Fresh blooming Hope, gay daughter of the skies,
And Faith'"—

The speaker lost a word, hesitated, became confused. Finally silence; then the Audrey of a while before, standing with heaving bosom, shy as a fawn, fearful that she had not pleased him, after all. For if she had done so, surely he would have told her as much. As it was, he had said but one word, and that beneath his breath, "*Eloisa!*"

It would seem that her fear was unfounded; for when he did speak, there were, God wot, sugar-plums enough. And

Audrey, who in her workaday world was always blamed, could not know that the praise that was so sweet was less wholesome than the blame.

Leaving the library they went into the hall, and from the hall looked into great, echoing, half-furnished rooms. All about lay packing-cases, many of them open, with rich stuffs streaming from them. Ornaments were huddled on tables, mirrors and pictures leaned their faces to the walls; everywhere was disorder.

"The negroes are careless, and to-day I held their hands," said Haward. "I must get some proper person to see to this gear."

Up stairs and down they went through the house, that seemed very large and very still, and finally they came out of the great front door, and down the stone steps on to the terrace. Below them, sparkling in the sunshine, lay the river, the opposite shore all in a haze of light. "I must go home," Audrey shyly reminded him, whereat he smiled assent, and they went, not through the box alley to the gate in the wall, but down the terrace, and out upon the hot brown boards of the landing. Haward, stepping into a boat, handed her to a seat in the stern, and himself took the oars. Leaving the landing, they came to the creek and entered it. Presently they were gliding beneath the red brick wall with the honeysuckle atop. On the opposite grassy shore, seated in a blaze of noon sunshine, was Hugon.

They in the boat took no notice. Haward, rowing, spoke evenly on, his theme himself and the gay and lonely life he had led these eleven years; and Audrey, though at first sight of the waiting figure she had paled and trembled, was too safe, too happy, to give to trouble any part of this magic morning. She kept her eyes on Haward's face, and almost forgot the man who had risen from the grass and in silence was following them.

Now, had the trader, in his hunting shirt and leggings, his moccasins and fur cap, been walking in the great woods, this silence, even with others in company, would have been natural enough to his Indian blood; but Monsieur Jean Hugon, in peruke and laced coat, walking in a civilized country, with words a-plenty and as hot as fire-water in his heart, and none upon his tongue, was a figure strange and sinister. He watched the two in the boat with an impassive face, and he walked like an Indian on an enemy's trail, so silently that he scarce seemed to breathe, so lightly that his heavy boots failed to crush the flowers or the tender grass.

Haward rowed on, telling Audrey stories of the town, of great men whose names she knew, and beautiful ladies of whom she had never heard; and she sat before him with her slim brown hands folded in her lap and the rosebuds withering in her hair, while through the reeds and the grass and the bushes of the bank over against them strode Hugon in his Blenheim wig and his wine-colored coat. Well-nigh together the three reached the stake driven in among the reeds, a hundred yards below the minister's house. Haward fastened the boat, and, motioning to Audrey to stay for the moment where she was, stepped out upon the bank to confront the trader, who, walking steadily and silently as ever, was almost upon them.

But it was broad daylight, and Hugon, with his forest instincts, preferred, when he wished to speak to the point, to speak in the dark. He made no pause; only looked with his fierce black eyes at the quiet, insouciant, fine gentleman standing with folded arms between him and the boat;

then passed on, going steadily up the creek toward the bend where the water left the open smiling fields and took to the forest. He never looked back, but went like a hunter with his prey before him. Presently the shadows of the forest touched him, and Audrey and Haward were left alone.

The latter laughed. "If his courage is of the quality of his lace—What, cowering, child, and the tears in your eyes! You were braver when you were not so tall, in those mountain days. Nay, no need to wet your shoe."

He lifted her in his arms, and set her feet upon firm grass. "How long since I carried you across a stream and up a dark hillside!" he said. "And yet to-day it seems but yesternight! Now, little maid, the Indian has run away, and the path to the house is clear."

*   *   *   *

In his smoke-filled, untidy best room Darden sat at table, his drink beside him, his pipe between his fingers, and open before him a book of jests, propped by a tome of divinity. His wife coming in from the kitchen, he burrowed in the litter upon the table until he found an open letter, which he flung toward her. "The Commissary threatens again, damn him!" he said between smoke puffs. "It seems that t'other night, when I was in my cups at the tavern, Le Neve and the fellow who has Ware Creek parish—I forget his name—must needs come riding by. I was dicing with Paris. Hugon held the stakes. I dare say we kept not mum. And out of pure brotherly love and charity, my good, kind gentlemen ride on to Williamsburgh on a tale-bearing errand! Is that child never coming back, Deborah?"

"She's coming now," answered his wife, with her eyes upon the letter. "I was watching from the upper window. He rowed her up the creek himself."

The door opened, and Audrey entered the room. Darden turned heavily in his chair, and took the long pipe from between his teeth. "Well?" he said. "You gave him my letter?"

Audrey nodded. Her eyes were dreamy; the red of the buds in her hair had somehow stolen to her cheeks; she could scarce keep her lips from smiling. "He bade me tell you to come to supper with him on Monday," she said. "And the Falcon that we saw come in last week brought furnishing for the great house. Oh, Mistress Deborah, the most beautiful things! The rooms are all to be made fine; and the negro women do not the work aright, and he wants some one to oversee them. He says that he has learned that in England Mistress Deborah was own woman to my Lady Squander, and so should know about hangings and china and the placing of furniture. And he asks that she come to Fair View morning after morning until the house is in order. He wishes me to come, too. Mistress Deborah will much oblige him, he says, and he will not forget her kindness."

Somewhat out of breath, but very happy, she looked with eager eyes from one guardian to the other. Darden emptied and refilled his pipe, scattering the ashes upon the book of jests. "Very good," he said briefly.

Into the thin visage of the ex-waiting-woman, who had been happier at my Lady Squander's than in a Virginia parsonage, there crept a tightened smile. In her way, when she was not in a passion, she was fond of Audrey; but, in temper or out of temper, she was fonder of the fine things which for a few days she might handle at Fair View house. And the gratitude of the master thereof might appear in coins, or in an order on his store for silk and lace. When, in her younger days, at Bath or in town, she had served fine mistresses, she had been given many a guinea for carrying a note or contriving an interview, and in changing her estate she had not changed her code of morals. "We must oblige Mr. Haward, of course," she said complacently. "I warrant you that I can give things an air! There's not a parlor in this parish that does not set my teeth on edge! Now at my Lady Squander's"—She embarked upon reminiscences of past splendor, checked only by her husband's impatient demand for dinner.

Audrey, preparing to follow her into the kitchen, was stopped, as she would have passed the table, by the minister's heavy hand. "The roses at Fair View bloom early," he said, turning her about that he might better see the red cluster in her hair. "Look you, Audrey! I wish you no great harm, child. You mind me at times of one that I knew many years ago, before ever I was chaplain to my Lord Squander or husband to my Lady Squander's waiting-woman. A hunter may use a decoy, and he may also, on the whole, prefer to keep that decoy as good as when 'twas made. Buy not thy roses too dearly, Audrey."

To Audrey he spoke in riddles. She took from her hair the loosened buds, and looked at them lying in her hand. "I did not buy them," she said. "They grew in the sun on the south side of the great house, and Mr. Haward gave them to me."

CHAPTER XII

THE PORTRAIT OF A GENTLEMAN

June came to tide-water Virginia with long, warm days and with the odor of many roses. Day by day the cloudless sunshine visited the land: night by night the large pale stars looked into its waters. It was a slumberous land, of many creeks and rivers that were wide, slow, and deep, of tobacco fields and lofty, solemn forests, of vague marshes, of white mists, of a haze of heat far and near. The moon of blossoms was past, and the red men—few in number now—had returned from their hunting, and lay in the shade of the trees in the villages that the English had left them, while the women brought them fish from the weirs, and strawberries from the vines that carpeted every poisoned field or neglected clearing. The black men toiled amidst the tobacco and the maize; at noontide it was as hot in the fields as in the middle passage, and the voices of those who sang over their work fell to a dull crooning. The white men who were bound served listlessly; they that were well were as lazy as the weather; they that were newly come over and ill with the "seasoning" fever tossed upon their pallets, longing for the cooling waters of home. The white men who were free swore that the world, though fair, was warm, and none walked if he could ride. The sunny, dusty roads were left for shadowed bridle paths; in a land where most places could be reached by boat, the water would have been the highway but that the languid air would not fill the sails. It was agreed that the heat was unnatural, and that, likely enough, there would be a deal of fever during the summer.

But there was thick shade in the Fair View garden, and when there was air at all it visited the terrace above the river. The rooms of the house were large and high-pitched; draw to the shutters, and they became as cool as caverns. Around the place the heat lay in wait: heat of wide, shadowless fields, where Haward's slaves toiled from morn to eve; heat of the great river, unstirred by any wind, hot and sleeping beneath the blazing sun; heat of sluggish creeks and of the marshes, shadeless as the fields. Once reach the mighty trees drawn like a cordon around house and garden, and there was escape.

To and fro and up and down in the house went the erst waiting-woman to my Lady Squander, carrying matters with a high hand. The negresses who worked under her eye found her a hard taskmistress. Was a room clean to-day, to-morrow it was found that there was dust upon the polished floor, finger marks on the paneled walls. The same furniture must be placed now in this room, now in that; china slowly washed and bestowed in one closet transferred to another; an eternity spent upon the household linen, another on the sewing and resewing, the hanging and rehanging, of damask curtains. The slaves, silent when the greenish eyes and tight, vixenish face were by, chattered, laughed, and sung when they were left alone. If they fell idle, and little was done of a morning, they went unrebuked; thoroughness, and not haste, appearing to be Mistress Deborah's motto.

The master of Fair View found it too noisy in his house to

sit therein, and too warm to ride abroad. There were left the seat built round the cherry-tree in the garden, the long, cool box walk, and the terrace with a summer-house at either end. It was pleasant to read out of doors, pacing the box walk, or sitting beneath the cherry-tree, with the ripening fruit overhead. If the book was long in reading, if morning by morning Haward's finger slipped easily in between the selfsame leaves, perhaps it was the fault of poet or philosopher. If Audrey's was the fault, she knew it not.

How could she know it, who knew herself, that she was a poor, humble maid, whom out of pure charity and knightly tenderness for weak and sorrowful things he long ago had saved, since then had maintained, now was kind to; and knew him, that he was learned and great and good, the very perfect gentle knight who, as he rode to win the princess, yet could stoop from his saddle to raise and help the herd girl? She had found of late that she was often wakeful of nights; when this happened, she lay and looked out of her window at the stars and wondered about the princess. She was sure that the princess and the lady who had given her the guinea were one.

In the great house she would have worked her fingers to the bone. Her strong young arms lifted heavy weights; her quick feet ran up and down stairs for this or that; she would have taken the waxed cloths from the negroes, and upon her knees and with willing hands have made to shine like mirrors the floors that were to be trodden by knight and princess. But almost every morning, before she had worked an hour, Haward would call to her from the box walk or the seat beneath the cherry-tree; and "Go, child," would say Mistress Deborah, looking up from her task of the moment.

The garden continued to be the enchanted garden. To gather its flowers, red and white, to pace with him cool paved walks between walls of scented box, to sit beside him beneath the cherry-tree or upon the grassy terrace, looking out upon the wide, idle river,—it was dreamy bliss, a happiness too rare to last. There was no harm; not that she ever dreamed there could be. The house overlooked garden and terrace; the slaves passed and repassed the open windows; Juba came and went; now and then Mistress Deborah herself would sally forth to receive instructions concerning this or that from the master of the house. And every day, at noon, the slaves drew to all the shutters save those of the master's room, and the minister's wife and ward made their curtsies and went home. The latter, like a child, counted the hours upon the clock until the next morning; but then she was not used to happiness, and the wine of it made her slightly drunken.

The master of Fair View told himself that there was infection in this lotus air of Virginia. A fever ran in his veins that made him languid of will, somewhat sluggish of thought, willing to spend one day like another, and all in a long dream. Sometimes, in the afternoons, when he was alone in the garden or upon the terrace, with the house blank and silent behind him, the slaves gone to the quarters, he tossed aside his book, and, with his chin upon his hand and his eyes upon the sweep of the river, first asked himself whither he was going, and then, finding no satisfactory answer, fell to brooding. Once, going into the house, he chanced to come upon his full-length reflection in a mirror newly hung, and stopped short to gaze upon himself. The parlor of his lodgings at Williamsburgh and the last time that he had seen Evelyn came to him, conjured up by the memory of certain words of his own.

"A truer glass might show a shrunken figure," he repeated, and with a quick and impatient sigh he looked at the image in the mirror.

To the eye, at least, the figure was not shrunken. It was that of a man still young, and of a handsome face and much distinction of bearing. The dress was perfect in its quiet elegance; the air of the man composed,—a trifle sad, a trifle mocking. Haward snapped his fingers at the reflection. "The portrait of a gentleman," he said, and passed on.

That night, in his own room, he took from an escritoire a picture of Evelyn Byrd, done in miniature after a painting by a pupil of Kneller, and, carrying it over to the light of the myrtle candles upon the table, sat down and fell to studying it. After a while he let it drop from his hand, and leaned back in his chair, thinking.

The night air, rising slightly, bent back the flame of the candles, around which moths were fluttering, and caused strange shadows upon the walls. They were thick about the curtained bed whereon had died the elder Haward,—a proud man, choleric, and hard to turn from his purposes. Into the mind of his son, sitting staring at these shadows, came the fantastic notion that amongst them, angry and struggling vainly for speech, might be his father's shade. The night was feverish, of a heat and lassitude to foster grotesque and idle fancies. Haward smiled, and spoke aloud to his imaginary ghost.

"You need not strive for speech," he said. "I know what you would say. *Was it for this I built this house, bought land and slaves?... Fair View and Westover, Westover and Fair View. A lady that will not wed thee because she loves thee! Zoons, Marmaduke! thou puttest me beside my patience!... As for this other, set no nameless, barefoot wench where sat thy mother! King Cophetua and the beggar maid, indeed! I warrant you Cophetua was something under three-and-thirty!"*

Haward ceased to speak for his father, and sighed for himself. "Moral: Three-and-thirty must be wiser in his day and generation." He rose from his chair, and began to walk the room. "If not Cophetua, what then,—what then?" Passing the table, he took up the miniature again. "The villain of the piece, I suppose, Evelyn?" he asked.

The pure and pensive face seemed to answer him. He put the picture hastily down, and recommenced his pacing to and fro. From the garden below came the heavy odor of lilies, and the whisper of the river tried the nerves. Haward went to the window, and, leaning out, looked, as now each night he looked, up and across the creek toward the minister's house. To-night there was no light to mark it; it was late, and all the world without his room was in darkness. He sat down in the window seat, looked out upon the stars and listened to the river. An hour had passed before he turned back to the room, where the candles had burned low. "I will go to Westover to-morrow," he said. "God knows, I should be a villain"—

He locked the picture of Evelyn within his desk, drank his wine and water, and went to bed, strongly resolved upon retreat. In the morning he said, "I will go to Westover this afternoon;" and in the afternoon he said, "I will go to-morrow." When the morrow came, he found that the house lacked but one day of being finished, and that there was therefore no need for him to go at all.

Mistress Deborah was loath, enough to take leave of damask and mirrors and ornaments of china,—the latter fine enough and curious enough to remind her of Lady Squander's own drawing-room; but the leaf of paper which Haward wrote upon, tore from his pocket-book, and gave her provided consolation. Her thanks were very glib, her curtsy was very deep. She was his most obliged, humble servant, and if she could serve him again he would make her proud. Would he not, now, some day, row up creek to their poor house, and taste of her perry and Shrewsbury cakes? Audrey, standing by, raised her eyes, and made of the request a royal invitation.

For a week or more Haward abode upon his plantation, alone save for his servants and slaves. Each day he sent for the overseer, and listened gravely while that worthy expounded to him all the details of the condition and conduct of the estate; in the early morning and the late afternoon he rode abroad through his fields and forests. Mill and ferry and rolling house were visited, and the quarters made his acquaintance. At the creek quarter and the distant ridge quarter were bestowed the newly bought, the sullen and the refractory of his chattels. When, after sunset, and the fields were silent, he rode past the cabins, coal-black figures, new from the slave deck, still seamed at wrist and ankle, mowed and jabbered at him from over their bowls of steaming food; others, who had forgotten the jungle and the slaver, answered, when he spoke to them, in strange English; others, born in Virginia, and remembering when he used to ride that way with his father, laughed, called him "Marse Duke," and agreed with him that the crop was looking mighty well. With the dark he reached the great house, and negroes from the home quarter took—his horse, while Juba lighted him through the echoing hall into the lonely rooms.

From the white quarter he procured a facile lad who could read and write, and who, through too much quickness of wit, had failed to prosper in England. Him he installed as secretary, and forthwith began a correspondence with friends in England, as well as a long poem which was to serve the double purpose of giving Mr. Pope a rival and of occupying the mind of Mr. Marmaduke Haward. The letters were witty and graceful, the poem was the same; but on the third day the secretary, pausing for the next word that should fall from his master's lips, waited so long that he dropped asleep. When he awoke, Mr. Haward was slowly tearing into bits the work that had been done on the poem. "It will have to wait upon my mood," he said. "Seal up the letter to Lord Hervey, boy, and then begone to the fields. If I want you again, I will send for you."

The next day he proposed to himself to ride to Williamsburgh and see his acquaintances there. But even as he crossed the room to strike the bell for Juba a distaste for the town and its people came upon him. It occurred to him that instead he might take the barge and be rowed up the river to the Jaquelins' or to Green Spring; but in a moment this plan also became repugnant. Finally he went out upon the terrace, and sat there the morning through, staring at the river. That afternoon he sent a negro to the store with a message for the storekeeper.

The Highlander, obeying the demand for his company,— the third or fourth since his day at Williamsburgh,—came shortly before twilight to the great house, and found the master thereof still upon the terrace, sitting beneath an oak, with a small table and a bottle of wine beside him.

"Ha, Mr. MacLean!" he cried, as the other approached. "Some days have passed since last we laid the ghosts! I had meant to sooner improve our acquaintance. But my house has been in disorder, and I myself,"—he passed his hand across his face as if to wipe away the expression into which it had been set,—"I myself have been poor company. There is a witchery in the air of this place. I am become but a dreamer of dreams."

As he spoke he motioned his guest to an empty chair, and began to pour wine for them both. His hand was not quite steady, and there was about him a restlessness of aspect most unnatural to the man. The storekeeper thought him looking worn, and as though he had passed sleepless nights.

MacLean sat down, and drew his wineglass toward Mm. "It is the heat," he said. "Last night, in the store, I felt that I was stifling; and I left it, and lay on the bare ground without. A star shot down the sky, and I wished that a wind as swift and strong would rise and sweep the land out to sea. When the day comes that I die, I wish to die a fierce death. It is best to die in battle, for then the mind is raised, and you taste all life in the moment before you go. If a man achieves not that, then struggle with earth or air or the waves of the sea is desirable. Driving sleet, armies of the snow, night and trackless mountains, the leap of the torrent, swollen lakes where kelpies lie in wait, wind on the sea with the black reef and the charging breakers,—it is well to dash one's force against the force of these, and to die after fighting. But in this cursed land of warmth and ease a man dies like a dog that is old and hath lain winter and summer upon the hearthstone." He drank his wine, and glanced again at Haward. "I did not know that you were here," he said. "Saunderson told me that you were going to Westover."

"I was,—I am," answered Haward briefly. Presently he roused himself from the brown study into which he had fallen.

"'Tis the heat, as you say. It enervates. For my part, I am willing that your wind should arise. But it will not blow to-night. There is not a breath; the river is like glass." He raised the wine to his lips, and drank deeply. "Come," he said, laughing. "What did you at the store to-day? And does Mistress Truelove despair of your conversion to *thee* and *thou*, and peace with all mankind? Hast procured an enemy to fill the place I have vacated? I trust he's no scurvy foe."

"I will take your questions in order," answered the other sententiously. "This morning I sold a deal of fine china to a parcel of fine ladies who came by water from Jamestown, and were mightily concerned to know whether your worship was gone to Westover, or had instead (as 't was reported) shut yourself up in Fair View house. And this afternoon came over in a periagua, from the other side, a very young gentleman with money in hand to buy a silver-fringed glove. 'They are sold in pairs,' said I. 'Fellow, I require but one,' said he. 'If Dick Allen, who hath slandered me to Mistress Betty Cocke, dareth to appear at the merrymaking at Colonel Harrison's to-night, his cheek and this glove shall come together!' 'Nathless, you must pay for both,' I told him; and the upshot is that he leaves with me a gold button as earnest that he will bring the remainder of the price before the duel to-morrow. That Quaker maiden of whom you ask hath a soul like the soul of Colna-dona, of whom Murdoch, the harper of Coll, used to sing. She is fair as a flower after winter, and as tender as the rose flush in which swims yonder star. When I am with her, almost she persuades me to think ill of honest hatred, and to pine no longer that it was not I that had the killing of Ewin Mackinnon." He gave a short laugh, and stooping picked up an oak twig from the ground, and with deliberation broke it into many small pieces. "Almost, but not quite," he said. "There was in that feud nothing illusory or fantastic; nothing of the quality that marked, mayhap, another feud of my own making. If I have found that in this latter case I took a wraith and dubbed it my enemy; that, thinking I followed a foe, I followed a friend instead"—He threw away the bits of bark, and straightened himself. "A friend!" he said, drawing his breath. "Save for this Quaker family, I have had no friend for many a year! And I cannot talk to them of honor and warfare and the wide world." His speech was sombre, but in his eyes there was an eagerness not without pathos.

The mood of the Gael chimed with the present mood of the Saxon. As unlike in their natures as their histories, men would have called them; and yet, far away, in dim recesses of the soul, at long distances from the flesh, each recognised the other. And it was an evening, too, in which to take care of other things than the ways and speech of every day. The heat, the hush, and the stillness appeared well-nigh preternatural. A sadness breathed over the earth; all things seemed new and yet old; across the spectral river the dim plains beneath the afterglow took the seeming of battlefields.

"A friend!" said Haward. "There are many men who call themselves my friends. I am melancholy to-day, restless, and divided against myself. I do not know one of my acquaintance whom I would have called to be melancholy with me as I have called you." He leaned across the table and touched MacLean's hand that was somewhat hurriedly fingering the wineglass. "Come!" he said. "Loneliness may haunt the level fields as well as the ways that are rugged and steep. How many times have we held converse since that day I found you in charge of my store? Often enough, I think, for each to know the other's quality. Our lives have been very different, and yet I believe that we are akin. For myself, I should be glad to hold as my friend so gallant though so unfortunate a gentleman." He smiled and made a gesture of courtesy. "Of course Mr. MacLean may very justly not hold me in a like esteem, nor desire a closer relation."

MacLean rose to his feet, and stood gazing across the river at the twilight shore and the clear skies. Presently he turned, and his eyes were wet. He drew his hand across them; then looked curiously at the dew upon it. "I have not done this," he said simply, "since a night at Preston when I wept with rage. In my country we love as we hate, with all the strength that God has given us. The brother of my spirit is to me even as the brother of my flesh.... I used to dream that my hand was at your throat or my sword through your heart, and wake in anger that it was not so ... and now I could love you well."

Haward stood up, and the two men clasped hands. "It is a pact, then," said the Englishman. "By my faith, the world looks not so melancholy gray as it did awhile ago. And here is Juba to say that supper waits. Lay the table for two, Juba. Mr. MacLean will bear me company."

The storekeeper stayed late, the master of Fair View being an accomplished gentleman, a very good talker, and an adept at turning his house for the nonce into the house of his guest. Supper over they went into the library, where their wine was set, and where the Highlander, who was no great reader, gazed respectfully at the wit and wisdom arow before him. "Colonel Byrd hath more volumes at Westover," quoth Haward, "but mine are of the choicer quality." Juba brought a card table, and lit more candles, while his master, unlocking a desk, took from it a number of gold pieces. These he divided into two equal portions: kept one beside him upon the polished table, and, with a fine smile, half humorous, half deprecating, pushed the other across to his guest. With an, imperturbable face MacLean stacked the gold before him, and they fell to piquet, playing briskly, and with occasional application to the Madeira upon the larger table, until ten of the clock. The Highlander, then declaring that he must be no longer away from his post, swept his heap of coins across to swell his opponent's store, and said good-night. Haward went with him to the great door, and watched him stride off through the darkness whistling "The Battle of Harlaw."

That night Haward slept, and the next morning four negroes rowed him up the river to Jamestown. Mr. Jaquelin was gone to Norfolk upon business, but his beautiful wife and sprightly daughters found Mr. Marmaduke Haward altogether charming. "'Twas as good as going to court," they said to one another, when the gentleman, after a two hours' visit, bowed himself out of their drawing-room. The object of their encomiums, going down river in his barge, felt his spirits lighter than they had been for some days. He spoke cheerfully to his negroes, and when the barge passed a couple of fishing-boats he called to the slim brown lads that caught for the plantation to know their luck. At the landing he found the overseer, who walked to the great house with him. The night before Tyburn Will had stolen from the white quarters, and had met a couple of seamen from the Temperance at the crossroads ordinary, which ordinary was going to get into trouble for breaking the law which forbade the harboring of sailors ashore. The three had taken in full lading of kill-devil rum, and Tyburn Will, too drunk to run any farther, had been caught by Hide near Princess Creek, three hours agone. What were the master's orders? Should the rogue go to the court-house whipping post, or should Hide save the trouble of taking him there?

In either case, thirty-nine lashes well laid on—

The master pursed his lips, dug into the ground with the ferrule of his cane, and finally proposed to the astonished overseer that the rascal be let off with a warning. "'Tis too fair a day to poison with ugly sights and sounds," he said, whimsically apologetic for his own weakness. "'Twill do no great harm to be lenient, for once, Saunderson, and I am in the mood to-day to be friends with all men, including myself."

The overseer went away grumbling, and Haward entered the house. The room where dwelt his books looked cool and inviting. He walked the length of the shelves, took out a volume here and there for his evening reading, and upon the binding of others laid an affectionate, lingering touch. "I have had a fever, my friends," he announced to the books, "but I am about to find myself happily restored to reason and serenity; in short, to health."

Some hours later he raised his eyes from the floor which he had been studying for a great while, covered them for a moment with his hand, then rose, and, with the air of a sleepwalker, went out of the lit room into a calm and fragrant night. There was no moon, but the stars were many, and it did not seem dark. When he came to the verge of the landing, and the river, sighing in its sleep, lay clear below him, mirroring the stars, it was as though he stood between two firmaments. He descended the steps, and drew toward him a small rowboat that was softly rubbing against the wet and glistening piles. The tide was out, and the night was very quiet.

Haward troubled not the midstream, but rowing in the shadow of the bank to the mouth of the creek that slept beside his garden, turned and went up this narrow water.

Until he was free of the wall the odor of honeysuckle and box clung to the air, freighting it heavily; when it was left behind the reeds began to murmur and sigh, though not loudly, for there was no wind. When he came to a point opposite the minister's house, rising fifty yards away from amidst low orchard trees, he rested upon his oars. There was a light in an upper room, and as he looked Audrey passed between the candle and the open window. A moment later and the light was out, but he knew that she was sitting at the window. Though it was dark, he found that he could call back with precision the slender throat, the lifted face, and the enshadowing hair. For a while he stayed, motionless in his boat, hidden by the reeds that whispered and sighed; but at last he rowed away softly through the darkness, back to the dim, slow-moving river and the Fair View landing.

This was of a Friday. All the next day he spent in the garden, but on Sunday morning he sent word to the stables to have Mirza saddled. He was going to church, he told Juba over his chocolate, and he would wear the gray and silver.

CHAPTER XIII

A SABBATH DAY'S JOURNEY

Although the house of worship which boasted as its ornament the Reverend Gideon Darden was not so large and handsome as Bruton church, nor could rival the painted glories of Poplar Spring, it was yet a building good enough,—of brick, with a fair white spire and a decorous mantle of ivy. The churchyard, too, was pleasant, though somewhat crowded with the dead. There were oaks for shade, and wild roses for fragrance, and the grass between the long gravestones, prone upon mortal dust, grew very thick and green. Outside the gates,—a gift from the first master of Fair View,—between the churchyard and the dusty highroad ran a long strip of trampled turf, shaded by locust-trees and by one gigantic gum that became in the autumn a pillar of fire.

Haward, arriving somewhat after time, found drawn up upon this piece of sward a coach, two berlins, a calash, and three chaises, while tied to hitching-posts, trees, and the fence were a number of saddle-horses. In the shade of the gum-tree sprawled half a dozen negro servants, but on the box of the coach, from which the restless horses had been taken, there yet sat the coachman, a mulatto of powerful build and a sullen countenance. The vehicle

Mary Johnston

stood in the blazing sunshine, and it was both cooler and merrier beneath the tree,—a fact apparent enough to the coachman, but the knowledge of which, seeing that he was chained to the box, did him small good. Haward glanced at the figure indifferently; but Juba, following his master upon Whitefoot Kate, grinned from ear to ear. "Larnin' not to run away, Sam? Road's clear: why don' you carry off de coach?"

Haward dismounted, and leaving Juba first to fasten the horses, and then join his fellows beneath the gum-tree, walked into the churchyard. The congregation had assembled, and besides himself there were none without the church save the negroes and the dead. The service had commenced. Through the open door came to him Darden's voice: "*Dearly beloved brethren*"—

Haward waited, leaning against a tomb deep graven with a coat of arms and much stately Latin, until the singing clave the air, when he entered the building, and passed down the aisle to his own pew, the chiefest in the place. He was aware of the flutter and whisper on either hand,—perhaps he did not find it unpleasing. Diogenes may have carried his lantern not merely to find a man, but to show one as well, and a philosopher in a pale gray riding dress, cut after the latest mode, with silver lace and a fall of Mechlin, may be trusted to know the value as well as the vanity of sublunary things.

Of the gathering, which was not large, two thirds, perhaps, were people of condition; and in the country, where occasions for display did not present themselves uncalled, it was highly becoming to worship the Lord in fine clothes. So there were broken rainbows in the tall pews, with a soft waving of fans to and fro in the essenced air, and a low rustle of silk. The men went as fine as the women, and the June sunshine, pouring in upon all this lustre and color, made a flower-bed of the assemblage. Being of the country, it was vastly better behaved than would have been a fashionable London congregation; but it certainly saw no reason why Mr. Marmaduke Haward should not, during the anthem, turn his back upon altar, minister, and clerk, and employ himself in recognizing with a smile and an inclination of his head his friends and acquaintances. They smiled back,—the gentlemen bowing slightly, the ladies making a sketch of a curtsy. All were glad that Fair View house was open once more, and were kindly disposed toward the master thereof.

The eyes of that gentleman were no longer for the gay parterre. Between it and the door, in uncushioned pews or on rude benches, were to be found the plainer sort of Darden's parishioners, and in this territory, that was like a border of sober foliage to the flower-bed in front, he discovered whom he sought.

Her gaze had been upon him since he passed the minister's pew, where she stood between my Lady Squander's ex-waiting-woman and the branded school-master, but now their eyes came full together. She was dressed in some coarse dark stuff, above which rose the brown pillar of her throat and the elusive, singular beauty of her face. There was a flower in her hair, placed as he had placed the rosebuds. A splendor leaped into her eyes, but her cheek did not redden; it was to his face that the color rushed. They had but a moment in which to gaze at each other, for the singing, which to her, at least, had seemed suddenly to swell into a great ascending tide of sound, with somewhere, far away, the silver calling of a trumpet, now came to an end, and with another silken rustle and murmur the congregation sat down.

Haward did not turn again, and the service went drowsily on. Darden was bleared of eye and somewhat thick of voice; the clerk's whine was as sleepy a sound as the buzzing of the bees in and out of window, or the soft, incessant stir of painted fans. A churchwarden in the next pew nodded and nodded, until he nodded his peruke awry, and a child went fast asleep, with its head in its mother's lap. One and all worshiped somewhat languidly, with frequent glances at the hourglass upon the pulpit. They prayed for King George the First, not knowing that he was dead, and for the Prince, not knowing that he was King. The minister preached against Quakers and witch-craft, and shook the rafters with his fulminations. Finally came the benediction and a sigh of relief.

In that country and time there was no unsociable and undignified scurrying homeward after church. Decorous silence prevailed until the house was exchanged for the green and shady churchyard: but then tongues were loosened, and the flower-bed broken into clusters. One must greet one's neighbors; present or be presented to what company might be staying at the various great houses within the parish; talk, laugh, coquet, and ogle; make appointments for business or for pleasure; speak of the last horse-race, the condition of wheat and tobacco, and the news brought in by the Valour, man-of-war, that the King was gone to Hanover. In short, for the nonce, the churchyard became a drawing-room, with the sun for candles, with no painted images of the past and gone upon the walls, but with the dead themselves beneath the floor.

The minister, having questions to settle with clerk and sexton, tarried in the vestry room; but his wife, with Audrey and the schoolmaster, waited for him outside, in the shade of an oak-tree that was just without the pale of the drawing-room. Mistress Deborah, in her tarnished amber satin and ribbons that had outworn their youth, bit her lip and tapped her foot upon the ground. Audrey watched her apprehensively. She knew the signs, and that when they reached home a storm might break that would leave its mark upon her shoulders. The minister's wife was not approved of by the ladies of Fair View parish, but had they seen how wistful was the face of the brown girl with her, they might have turned aside, spoken, and let the storm go by. The girl herself was scarcely noticed. Few had ever heard her story, or, hearing it, had remembered; the careless many thought her an orphan, bound to Darden and his wife,—in effect their servant. If she had beauty, the ladies and gentlemen who saw her, Sunday after Sunday, in the minister's pew, had scarce discovered it. She was too dark, too slim, too shy and strange of look, with her great brown eyes and that startled turn of her head. Their taste was for lilies and roses, and it was not an age that counted shyness a grace.

Mr. Marmaduke Haward was not likely to be accused of diffidence. He had come out of church with the sleepy-headed churchwarden, who was now wide awake and mightily concerned to know what horse Mr. Haward meant to enter for the great race at Mulberry Island, while at the foot of the steps he was seized upon by another portly vestryman, and borne off to be presented to three blooming young ladies, quick to second their papa's invitation home to dinner. Mr. Haward was ready to curse his luck that he was engaged elsewhere; but were not these Graces the children to whom he had used to send sugar-plums from Williamsburgh, years and years ago? He vowed that the payment, which he had never received, he would take now with usury, and proceeded to salute the cheek of each protesting fair. The ladies found him vastly agreeable; old and new friends crowded around him; he put forth his powers and charmed all hearts,—and all the while inwardly cursed the length of way to the gates, and the tardy progress thereto of his friends and neighbors.

But however slow in ebbing, the tide was really set toward home and dinner. Darden, coming out of the vestry room, found the churchyard almost cleared, and the road in a cloud of dust. The greater number of those who came a-horseback were gone, and there had also departed both berlins, the calash, and two chaises. Mr. Haward was handing the three Graces into the coach with the chained coachman, Juba standing by, holding his master's horse. Darden grew something purpler in the face, and, rumbling oaths, went over to the three beneath the oak. "How many spoke to you to-day?" he asked roughly of his wife. "Did *he* come and speak?"

"No, he didn't!" cried Mistress Deborah tartly. "And all the gentry went by; only Mr. Bray stopped to say that everybody knew of your fight with Mr. Bailey at the French ordinary, and that the Commissary had sent for Bailey, and was going to suspend him. I wish to Heaven I knew why I married you, to be looked down upon by every Jill, when I might have had his Lordship's own man! Of all the fools"—

"You were not the only one," answered her husband grimly. "Well, let's home; there's dinner yet. What is it, Audrey?" This in answer to an inarticulate sound from the girl.

The schoolmaster answered for her: "Mr. Marmaduke Haward has not gone with the coach. Perhaps he only waited until the other gentlefolk should be gone. Here he comes."

The sward without the gates was bare of all whose presence mattered, and Haward had indeed reentered the churchyard, and was walking toward them. Darden went to meet him. "These be fine tales I hear of you, Mr. Darden," said his parishioner calmly. "I should judge you were near the end of your rope. There's a vestry meeting Thursday. Shall I put in a good word for your reverence? Egad, you need it!"

"I shall be your honor's most humble, most obliged servant," quoth the minister. "The affair at the French ordinary was nothing. I mean to preach next Sunday upon calumny,—calumny that spareth none, not even such as I. You are for home, I see, and our road for a time is the same. Will you ride with us?"

"Ay," said Haward briefly. "But you must send yonder fellow with the scarred hands packing. I travel not with thieves."

He had not troubled to lower his voice, and as he and Darden were now themselves within the shadow of the oak, the schoolmaster overheard him and answered for himself. "Your honor need not fear my company," he said, in his slow and lifeless tones. "I am walking, and I take the short cut through the woods. Good-day, worthy Gideon. Madam Deborah and Audrey, good-day."

He put his uncouth, shambling figure into motion, and, indifferent and lifeless in manner as in voice, was gone, gliding like a long black shadow through the churchyard and into the woods across the road. "I knew him long ago in England," the minister explained to their new companion. "He's a learned man, and, like myself, a calumniated one. The gentlemen of these parts value him highly as an instructor of youth. No need to send their sons to college if they've been with him for a year or two! My good Deborah, Mr. Haward will ride with us toward Fair View."

Mistress Deborah curtsied; then chided Audrey for not minding her manners, but standing like a stock or stone, with her thoughts a thousand miles away. "Let her be," said Haward. "We gave each other good-day in church."

Together the four left the churchyard. Darden brought up two sorry horses; lifted his wife and Audrey upon one, and mounted the other. Haward swung himself into his saddle, and the company started, Juba upon Whitefoot Kate bringing up the rear. The master of Fair View rode beside the minister, and only now and then spoke to the women. The road was here sunny, there shady; the excessive heat broken, the air pleasant enough. Everywhere, too, was the singing of birds, while the fields that they passed of tobacco and golden, waving wheat were charming to the sight. The minister was, when sober, a man of parts, with some education and a deal of mother wit; in addition, a close and shrewd observer of the times and people. He and Haward talked of matters of public moment, and the two women listened, submissive and admiring. It seemed that they came very quickly to the bridge across the creek and the parting of their ways. Would Mr. Haward ride on to the glebe house?

It appeared that Mr. Haward would. Moreover, when the house was reached, and Darden's one slave came running from a broken-down stable to take the horses, he made no motion toward returning to the bridge which led across the creek to his own plantation, but instead dismounted, flung his reins to Juba, and asked if he might stay to dinner.

Now, by the greatest good luck, considered Mistress Deborah, there chanced to be in her larder a haunch of venison roasted most noble; the ducklings and asparagus, too, cooked before church, needed but to be popped into the oven; and there was also an apple tart with cream. With elation, then, and eke with a mind at rest, she added her shrill protests of delight to Darden's more moderate assurances, and, leaving Audrey to set chairs in the shade of a great apple-tree, hurried into the house to unearth her damask tablecloth and silver spoons, and to plan for the morrow a visit to the Widow Constance, and a casual remark that Mr. Marmaduke Haward had dined with the minister the day before. Audrey, her task done, went after her, to be met with graciousness most unusual. "I'll see to the dinner, child. Mr. Haward will expect one of us to sit without, and you had as well go as I. If he's talking to Darden, you might get some larkspur and gilliflowers for the table. La! the flowers that used to wither beneath the candles at my Lady Squander's!"

Audrey, finding the two men in conversation beneath the apple-tree, passed on to the ragged garden, where clumps of hardy, bright-colored flowers played hide-and-seek with currant and gooseberry bushes. Haward saw her go, and broke the thread of his discourse. Darden looked up, and the eyes of the two men met; those of the younger were cold and steady. A moment, and his glance had fallen to his watch which he had pulled out. "'Tis early yet," he said coolly, "and I dare say not quite your dinner time,—which I beg that Mistress Deborah will not advance on my account. Is it not your reverence's habit to rest within doors after your sermon? Pray do not let me detain you. I will go talk awhile with Audrey."

He put up his watch and rose to his feet. Darden cleared his throat. "I have, indeed, a letter to write to Mr.

Commissary, and it may be half an hour before Deborah has dinner ready. I will send your servant to fetch you in."

Haward broke the larkspur and gilliflowers, and Audrey gathered up her apron and filled it with the vivid blooms. The child that had thus brought loaves of bread to a governor's table spread beneath a sugar-tree, with mountains round about, had been no purer of heart, no more innocent of rustic coquetry. When her apron was filled she would have returned to the house, but Haward would not have it so. "They will call when dinner is ready," he said. "I wish to talk to you, little maid. Let us go sit in the shade of the willow yonder."

It was almost a twilight behind the cool green rain of the willow boughs. Through that verdant mist Haward and Audrey saw the outer world but dimly. "I had a fearful dream last night," said Audrey. "I think that that must have been why I was to glad to see you come into church to-day. I dreamed that you had never come home again, overseas, in the Golden Rose. Hugon was beside me, in the dream, telling me that you were dead in England: and suddenly I knew that I had never really seen you; that there was no garden, no terrace, no roses, no *you*. It was all so cold and sad, and the sun kept growing smaller and smaller. The woods, too, were black, and the wind cried in them so that I was afraid. And then I was in Hugon's house, holding the door,—there was a wolf without,—and through the window I saw the mountains; only they were so high that my heart ached to look upon them, and the wind cried down the cleft in the hills. The wolf went away, and then, somehow, I was upon the hilltop.... There was a dead man lying in the grass, but it was too dark to see. Hugon came up behind me, stooped, and lifted the hand.... Upon the finger was that ring you wear, burning in the moonlight.... Oh me!"

The remembered horror of her dream contending with present bliss shook her spirit to its centre. She shuddered violently, then burst into a passion of tears.

Haward's touch upon her hair, Haward's voice in her ear, all the old terms of endearment for a frightened child,— "little maid," "little coward," "Why, sweetheart, these things are shadows, they cannot hurt thee!" She controlled her tears, and was the happier for her weeping. It was sweet to sit there in the lush grass, veiled and shadowed from the world by the willow's drooping green, and in that soft and happy light to listen to his voice, half laughing, half chiding, wholly tender and caressing. Dreams were naught, he said. Had Hugon troubled her waking hours?

He had come once to the house, it appeared; but she had run away and hidden in the wood, and the minister had told him she was gone to the Widow Constance's. That was a long time ago; it must have been the day after she and Mistress Deborah had last come from Fair View.

"A long time," said Haward. "It was a week ago. Has it seemed a long time, Audrey?"

"Yes,—oh yes!"

"I have been busy. I must learn to be a planter, you know. But I have thought of you, little maid."

Audrey was glad of that, but there was yet a weight upon her heart. "After that dream I lay awake all night, and it came to me how wrongly I had done. Hugon is a wicked man,—an Indian. Oh, I should never have told you, that first day in the garden, that he was waiting for me outside! For now, because you took care of me and would not let him come near, he hates you. He is so wicked that he might do you a harm." Her eyes widened, and the hand that touched his was cold and trembling. "If ever hurt came to you through me, I would drown myself in the river yonder. And then I thought—lying awake last night—that perhaps I had been troublesome to you, those days at Fair View, and that was why you had not come to see the minister, as you had said you would." The dark eyes were pitifully eager; the hand that went to her heart trembled more and more. "It is not as it was in the mountains," she said. "I am older now, and safe, and— and happy. And you have many things to do and to think of, and many friends—gentlemen and beautiful ladies—to go to see. I thought—last night—that when I saw you I would ask your pardon for not remembering that the mountains were years ago; for troubling you with my matters, sir; for making too free, forgetting my place"— Her voice sank; the shamed red was in her cheeks, and her eyes, that she had bravely kept upon his face, fell to the purple and gold blooms in her lap.

Haward rose from the grass, and, with his back to the gray hole of the willow, looked first at the veil of leaf and stem through which dimly showed house, orchard, and blue sky, then down upon the girl at his feet. Her head was bent and she sat very still, one listless, upturned hand upon the grass beside her, the other lying as quietly among her flowers.

"Audrey," he said at last, "you shame me in your thoughts of me. I am not that knight without fear and without reproach for which you take me. Being what I am, you must believe that you have not wearied me; that I think of you and wish to see you. And Hugon, having possibly some care for his own neck, will do me no harm; that is a very foolish notion, which you must put from you. Now listen." He knelt beside her and took her hand in his. "After a while, perhaps, when the weather is cooler, and I must open my house and entertain after the fashion of the country; when the new Governor comes in, and all this gay little world of Virginia flocks to Williamsburgh; when I am a Councilor, and must go with the rest, and must think of gold and place and people,—why, then, maybe, our paths will again diverge, and only now and then will I catch the gleam of your skirt, mountain maid, brown Audrey! But now in these midsummer days it is a sleepy world, that cares not to go bustling up and down. I am alone in my house; I visit not nor am visited, and the days hang heavy. Let us make believe for a time that the mountains are all around us, that it was but yesterday we traveled together. It is only a little way from Fair View to the glebe house, from the glebe house to Fair View. I will see you often, little maid, and you must dream no more as you dreamed last night." He paused; his voice changed, and he went on as to himself: "It is a lonely land, with few to see and none to care. I will drift with the summer, making of it an idyl, beautiful,—yes, and innocent! When autumn comes I will go to Westover."

Of this speech Audrey caught only the last word. A wonderful smile, so bright was it, and withal so sad, came into her face. "Westover!" she said to herself. "That is where the princess lives."

"We will let thought alone," continued Haward. "It suits not with this charmed light, this glamour of the summer." He made a laughing gesture. "Hey, presto! little maid, there go the years rolling back! I swear I see the mountains through the willow leaves."

"There was one like a wall shutting out the sun when he went down," answered Audrey. "It was black and grim, and the light flared like a fire behind it. And there was the one above which the moon rose. It was sharp, pointing like a finger to heaven, and I liked it best. Do you remember how large was the moon pushing up behind the pine-trees? We sat on the dark hillside watching it, and you told me beautiful stories, while the moon rose higher and higher and the mockingbirds began to sing."

Haward remembered not, but he said that he did so. "The moon is full again," he continued, "and last night I heard a mockingbird in the garden. I will come in the barge to-morrow evening, and the negroes shall row us up and down the river—you and me and Mistress Deborah—between the sunset and the moonrise. Then it is lonely and sweet upon the water. The roses can be smelled from the banks, and if you will speak to the mockingbirds we shall have music, dryad Audrey, brown maid of the woods!"

Audrey's laugh, was silver-clear and sweet, like that of a forest nymph indeed. She was quite happy again, with all her half-formed doubts and fears allayed. They had never been of him,—only of herself. The two sat within the green and swaying fountain of the willow, and time went by on eagle wings. Too soon came the slave to call them to the house; the time within, though spent in the company of Darden and his wife, passed too soon; too soon came the long shadows of the afternoon and Haward's call for his horse.

Audrey watched him ride away, and the love light was in her eyes. She did not know that it was so. That night, in her bare little room, when the candle was out, she kneeled by the window and looked at the stars. There was one very fair and golden, an empress of the night. "That is the princess," said Audrey, and smiled upon the peerless star.

Far from that light, scarce free from the murk of the horizon, shone a little star, companionless in the night. "And that is I," said Audrey, and smiled upon herself.

CHAPTER XIV

THE BEND IN THE ROAD

"'Brave Derwentwater he is dead;
From his fair body they took the head:
But Mackintosh and his friends are fled,
And they'll set the hat upon another head'"—

chanted the Fair View storekeeper, and looked aside at
Mistress Truelove Taberer, spinning in the doorway of
her father's house.

Truelove answered naught, but her hands went to and fro,
and her eyes were for her work, not for MacLean, sitting
on the doorstep at her feet.

"'And whether they're gone beyond the sea'"—

The exile broke off and sighed heavily. Before the two a
little yard, all gay with hollyhocks and roses, sloped down
to the wider of the two creeks between which stretched
the Fair View plantation. It was late of a holiday
afternoon. A storm was brewing, darkening all the water,
and erecting above the sweep of woods monstrous towers
of gray cloud. There must have been an echo, for
MacLean's sigh came back to him faintly, as became

an echo.

"Is there not peace here, 'beyond the sea'?" said Truelove softly. "Thine must be a dreadful country, Angus MacLean!"

The Highlander looked at her with kindling eyes. "Now had I the harp of old Murdoch!" he said.

"'Dear is that land to the east,
Alba of the lakes!
Oh, that I might dwell there forever'"—

He turned upon the doorstep, and taking between his fingers the hem of Truelove's apron fell to plaiting it. "A woman named Deirdre, who lived before the days of Gillean-na-Tuaidhe, made that song. She was not born in that land, but it was dear to her because she dwelt there with the man whom she loved. They went away, and the man was slain; and where he was buried, there Deirdre cast herself down and died." His voice changed, and all the melancholy of his race, deep, wild, and tender, looked from his eyes. "If to-day you found yourself in that loved land, if this parched grass were brown heather, if it stretched down to a tarn yonder, if that gray cloud that hath all the seeming of a crag were crag indeed, and eagles plied between the tarn and it,"—he touched her hand that lay idle now upon her knee,—"if you came like Deirdre lightly through the heather, and found me lying here, and found more red than should be in the tartan of the MacLeans, what would you do, Truelove? What would you cry out, Truelove? How heavy would be thy heart, Truelove?"

Truelove sat in silence, with her eyes upon the sky above the dream crags. "How heavy would grow thy heart,

Truelove, Truelove?" whispered the Highlander.

Up the winding water, to the sedges and reeds below the little yard, glided the boy Ephraim in his boat. The Quakeress started, and the color flamed into her gentle face. She took up the distaff that she had dropped, and fell to work again. "Thee must not speak to me so, Angus MacLean," she said. "I trust that my heart is not hard. Thy death would grieve me, and my father and my mother and Ephraim"—

"I care not for thy father and mother and Ephraim!" MacLean began impetuously. "But you do right to chide me. Once I knew a green glen where maidens were fain when paused at their doors Angus, son of Hector, son of Lachlan, son of Murdoch, son of Angus that was named for Angus Mor, who was great-grandson of Hector of the Battles, who was son of Lachlan Lubanach! But here I am a landless man, with none to do me honor,—a wretch bereft of liberty"—

"To me, to all Friends," said Truelove sweetly, halting a little in her work, "thee has now what thee thyself calls freedom. For God meant not that one of his creatures should say to another: 'Lo, here am I! Behold thy God!' To me, and my father and mother and Ephraim, thee is no bond servant of Marmaduke Haward. But thee is bond servant to thy own vain songs; thy violent words; thy idle pride, that, vaunting the cruel deeds of thy forefathers, calls meekness and submission the last worst evil; thy shameless reverence for those thy fellow creatures, James Stewart and him whom thee calls the chief of thy house,—forgetting that there is but one house, and that God is its head; thy love of clamor and warfare; thy hatred of the ways of peace"—

MacLean laughed. "I hate not all its ways. There is no hatred in my heart for this house which is its altar, nor for the priestess of the altar. Ah! now you frown, Truelove"—

Across the clouds ran so fierce a line of gold that Truelove, startled, put her hand before her eyes. Another dart of lightning, a low roll of thunder, a bending apart of the alder bushes on the far side of the creek; then a woman's voice calling to the boy in the boat to come ferry her over.

"Who may that be?" asked Truelove wonderingly.

It was only a little way to the bending alders. Ephraim rowed across the glassy water, dark beneath the approach of the storm; the woman stepped into the boat, and the tiny craft came lightly back to its haven beneath the bank.

"It is Darden's Audrey," said the storekeeper.

Truelove shrank a little, and her eyes darkened. "Why should she come here? I never knew her. It is true that we may not think evil, but—but"—

MacLean moved restlessly. "I have seen the girl but twice," he said. "Once she was alone, once—It is my friend of whom I think. I know what they say, but, by St. Kattan! I hold him a gentleman too high of mind, too noble—There was a tale I used to hear when I was a boy. A long, long time ago a girl lived in the shadow of the tower of Duart, and the chief looked down from his walls and saw her. Afterwards they walked together by the shore and through the glens, and he cried her health when he drank in his hall, sitting amongst his tacksmen. Then what the men whispered the women spoke aloud; and so,

Mary Johnston

more quickly than the tarie is borne, word went to a man of the MacDonalds who loved the Duart maiden. Not like a lover to his tryst did he come. In the handle of his dirk the rich stones sparkled as they rose and fell with the rise and fall of the maiden's white bosom. She prayed to die in his arms; for it was not Duart that she loved, but him. She died, and they snooded her hair and buried her. Duart went overseas; the man of the MacDonalds killed himself. It was all wrought with threads of gossamer,—idle fancy, shrugs, smiles, whispers, slurring speech,—and it was long ago. But there is yet gossamer to be had for the gathering; it gleams on every hand these summer mornings."

By now Darden's Audrey had left the boat and was close upon them. MacLean arose, and Truelove hastily pushed aside her wheel. "Is thee seeking shelter from the storm?" she asked tremulously, and with her cheeks as pink as a seashell. "Will thee sit here with us? The storm will not break yet awhile."

Audrey heeded her not, her eyes being for MacLean. She had been running,—running more swiftly than for a thousand May Day guineas. Even now, though her breath came short, every line of her slender figure was tense, and she was ready to be off like an arrow. "You are Mr. Haward's friend?" she cried. "I have heard him say that you were so—call you a brave gentleman"—

MacLean's dark face flushed. "Yes, we are friends,—I thank God for it. What have you to do with that, my lass?"

"I also am his friend," said Audrey, coming nearer. Her hands were clasped, her bosom heaving. "Listen! To-day I was sent on an errand to a house far up this creek.

Coming back, I took the short way home through the woods because of the storm. It led me past the school-house down by the big swamp. I thought that no one was there, and I went and sat down upon the steps to rest a moment. The door behind me was partly open. Then I heard two voices: the schoolmaster and Jean Hugon were inside—close to me—talking. I would have run away, but I heard Mr. Haward's name." Her hand went to her heart, and she drew a sobbing breath.

"Well!" cried MacLean sharply.

"Mr. Haward went yesterday to Williamsburgh—alone—without Juba. He rides back—alone—to Fair View late this afternoon—he is riding now. You know the sharp bend in the road, with the steep bank above and the pond below?"

"Ay, where the road nears the river. Well?"

"I heard all that Hugon and the schoolmaster said. I hid behind a fallen tree and watched them leave the schoolhouse; then I followed them, making no noise, back to the creek, where Hugon had a boat. They crossed the creek, and fastened the boat on this side. I could follow them no farther; the woods hid them; but they have gone downstream to that bend in the road. Hugon had his hunting-knife and pistols; the schoolmaster carried a coil of rope." She flung back her head, and her hands went to her throat as though she were stifling. "The turn in the road is very sharp. Just past the bend they will stretch the rope from side to side, fastening it to two trees. He will be hurrying home before the bursting of the storm—he will be riding the planter's pace"—

"Man and horse will come crashing down!" cried the

storekeeper, with a great oath "And then"—

"Hugon's knife, so there will be no noise.... They think he has gold upon him: that is for the schoolmaster.... Hugon is an Indian, and he will hide their trail. Men will think that some outlying slave was in the woods, and set upon and killed him."

Her voice broke; then went on, gathering strength: "It was so late, and I knew that he would ride fast because of the storm. I remembered this house, and thought that, if I called, some one might come and ferry me over the creek. Now I will run through the woods to the road, for I must reach it before he passes on his way to where they wait." She turned her face toward the pine wood beyond the house.

"Ay, that is best!" agreed the storekeeper. "Warned, he can take the long way home, and Hugon and this other may be dealt with at his leisure. Come, my girl; there's no time to lose."

They left behind them the creek, the blooming dooryard, the small white house, and the gentle Quakeress. The woods received them, and they came into a world of livid greens and grays dashed here and there with ebony,—a world that, expectant of the storm, had caught and was holding its breath. Save for the noise of their feet upon dry leaves that rustled like paper, the wood was soundless. The light that lay within it, fallen from skies of iron, was wild and sinister; there was no air, and the heat wrapped them like a mantle. So motionless were all things, so fixed in quietude each branch and bough, each leaf or twig or slender needle of the pine, that they seemed to be fleeing through a wood of stone, jade and malachite, emerald and agate.

They hurried on, not wasting breath in speech. Now and again MacLean glanced aside at the girl, who kept beside him, moving as lightly as presently would move the leaves when the wind arose. He remembered certain scurrilous words spoken in the store a week agone by a knot of purchasers, but when he looked at her face he thought of the Highland maiden whose story he had told. As for Audrey, she saw not the woods that she loved, heard not the leaves beneath her feet, knew not if the light were gold or gray. She saw only a horse and rider riding from Williamsburgh, heard only the rapid hoofbeats. All there was of her was one dumb prayer for the rider's safety. Her memory told her that it was no great distance to the road, but her heart cried out that it was so far away,—so far away! When the wood thinned, and they saw before them the dusty strip, pallid and lonely beneath the storm clouds, her heart leaped within her; then grew sick for fear that he had gone by. When they stood, ankle-deep in the dust, she looked first toward the north, and then to the south. Nothing moved; all was barren, hushed, and lonely.

"How can we know? How can we know?" she cried, and wrung her hands.

MacLean's keen eyes were busily searching for any sign that a horseman had lately passed that way. At a little distance above them a shallow stream of some width flowed across the way, and to this the Highlander hastened, looked with attention at the road-bed where it emerged from the water, then came back to Audrey with a satisfied air. "There are no hoof-prints," he said. "No marks upon the dust. None can have passed for some hours."

A rotted log, streaked with velvet moss and blotched with

fan-shaped, orange-colored fungi, lay by the wayside, and the two sat down upon it to wait for the coming horseman. Overhead the thunder was rolling, but there was as yet no breath of wind, no splash of raindrops. Opposite them rose a gigantic pine, towering above the forest, red-brown trunk and ultimate cone of deep green foliage alike outlined against the dead gloom of the sky. Audrey shook back her heavy hair and raised her face to the roof of the world; her hands were clasped upon her knee; her bare feet, slim and brown, rested on a carpet of moss; she was as still as the forest, of which, to the Highlander, she suddenly seemed a part. When they had kept silence for what seemed a long time, he spoke to her with some hesitation: "You have known Mr. Haward but a short while; the months are very few since he came from England."

The name brought Audrey down to earth again. "Did you not know?" she asked wonderingly. "You also are his friend,—you see him often. I thought that at times he would have spoken of me." For a moment her face was troubled, though only for a moment. "But I know why he did not so," she said softly to herself. "He is not one to speak of his good deeds." She turned toward MacLean, who was attentively watching her, "But I may speak of them," she said, with pride. "I have known Mr. Haward for years and years. He saved my life; he brought me here from the Indian country; he was, he is, so kind to me!"

Since the afternoon beneath the willow-tree, Haward, while encouraging her to speak of her long past, her sylvan childhood, her dream memories, had somewhat sternly checked every expression of gratitude for the part which he himself had played or was playing, in the drama of her life. Walking in the minister's orchard, sitting in the garden or upon the terrace of Fair View house, drifting on the sunset river, he waved that aside, and went on to teach her another lesson. The teaching was exquisite; but when the lesson for the day was over, and he was alone, he sat with one whom he despised. The learning was exquisite; it was the sweetest song, but she knew not its name, and the words were in a strange tongue. She was Audrey, that she knew; and he,—he was the plumed knight, who, for the lack of a better listener, told her gracious tales of love, showed her how warm and beautiful was this world that she sometimes thought so sad, sang to her sweet lines that poets had made. Over and through all she thought she read the name of the princess. She had heard him say that with the breaking of the heat he should go to Westover, and one day, early in summer, he had shown her the miniature of Evelyn Byrd. Because she loved him blindly, and because he was wise in his generation, her trust in him was steadfast as her native hills, large as her faith in God. Now it was sweet beneath her tongue to be able to tell one that was his friend how worthy of all friendship— nay, all reverence—he was. She spoke simply, but with that strange power of expression which nature had given her. Gestures with her hands, quick changes in the tone of her voice, a countenance that gave ample utterance to the moment's thought,—as one morning in the Fair View library she had brought into being that long dead Eloisa whose lines she spoke, so now her auditor of to-day thought that he saw the things of which she told.

She had risen, and was standing in the wild light, against the background of the forest that was breathless, as if it too listened, "And so he brought me safely to this land," she said. "And so he left me here for ten years, safe and happy, he thought. He has told me that all that while he thought of me as safe and happy. That I was not so,— why, that was not his fault! When he came back I was both. I have never seen the sunshine so bright or the woods so fair as they have been this summer. The people with whom I live are always kind to me now,—that is his doing. And ah! it is because he would not let Hugon scare or harm me that that wicked Indian waits for him now beyond the bend in the road." At the thought of Hugon she shuddered, and her eyes began to widen. "Have we not been here a long time?" she cried. "Are you sure? Oh, God! perhaps he has passed!"

"No, no," answered MacLean, with his hand upon her arm. "There is no sign that he has done so. It is not late; it is that heavy cloud above our heads that has so darkened the air. Perhaps he has not left Williamsburgh at all: perhaps, the storm threatening, he waits until to-morrow."

From the cloud above came a blinding light and a great crash of thunder,—the one so intense, the other so tremendous, that for a minute the two stood as if stunned. Then, "The tree!" cried Audrey. The great pine, blasted and afire, uprooted itself and fell from them like a reed that the wind has snapped. The thunder crash, and the din with which the tree met its fellows of the forest, bore them down, and finally struck the earth from which it came, seemed an alarum to waken all nature from its sleep. The thunder became incessant, and the wind suddenly arising the forest stretched itself and began to speak with no uncertain voice. MacLean took his seat again upon the log, but Audrey slipped into the road, and stood in the whirling dust, her arm raised above her eyes, looking for the horseman whose approach she could not hope to hear through the clamor of the storm. The wind lifted her long hair, and the rising dust half obscured her form, bent against the blast. On the lonesome road, in the partial light, she had the seeming of an apparition, a creature tossed like a ball from the surging forest. She had made herself a world, and she had become its product. In all her ways, to the day of her death, there was about her a touch of mirage, illusion, fantasy. The Highlander, imaginative like all his race, and a believer in things not of heaven nor of earth, thought of spirits of the glen and the shore.

There was no rain as yet; only the hurly-burly of the forest, the white dust cloud, and the wild commotion overhead. Audrey turned to MacLean, watching her in silence. "He is coming!" she cried. "There is some one with him. Now, now he is safe!"

CHAPTER XV

HUGON SPEAKS HIS MIND

MacLean sprang up from the log, and, joining her, saw indeed two horsemen galloping toward them, their heads bent and riding cloaks raised to shield them from the whirlwind of dust, dead leaves, and broken twigs. He knew Haward's powerful steed Mirza, but the other horse was strange.

The two rode fast. A moment, and they were splashing through the stream; another, and the horses, startled by Audrey's cry and waving arms and by the sudden and violent check on the part of their riders, were rearing and curveting across the road. "What the devil!" cried one of the horsemen. "Imp or sprite, or whatever you are, look out! Haward, your horse will trample her!"

But Audrey, with her hand on Mirza's bridle, had no fears. Haward stared at her in amazement. "Child, what are you doing here? Angus, you too!" as the storekeeper advanced. "What rendezvous is this? Mirza, be quiet!"

Audrey left her warning to be spoken by MacLean. She was at peace, her head against Mirza's neck, her eyes upon Haward's face, clear in the flashing lightning. That gentleman heard the story with his usual calmness; his companion first swore, and then laughed.

"Here's a Canterbury tale!" he cried. "Egad, Haward, are we to take this skipping rope, vault it as though we were courtiers of Lilliput? Neither of us is armed. I conceive that the longest way around will prove our shortest way home."

"My dear Colonel, I want to speak with these two gentlemen."

"But at your leisure, my friend, at your leisure, and not in dying tones! I like not what I hear of Monsieur Jean Hugon's pistols. Flank an ambush; don't ride into it open-eyed."

"Colonel Byrd is right," said the storekeeper earnestly. "Ride back, the two of you, and take the bridle path that will carry you to Fair View by way of the upper bridge. In the mean time, I will run through the woods to Mr. Taberer's house, cross there, hurry to the quarters, rouse the overseer, and with a man or two we will recross the creek by the lower bridge, and coming upon these rogues unawares, give them a taste of their own medicine! We'll hale them to the great house; you shall have speech of them in your own hall."

Neither of the riders being able to suggest a better plan, the storekeeper, with a wave of his hand, plunged into the forest, and was soon lost to view amidst its serried trunks and waving branches. Haward stooped from his saddle; Audrey set her bare foot upon his booted one, and he swung her up behind him. "Put thine arm around me, child," he told her. "We will ride swiftly through the storm. Now, Colonel, to turn our backs upon the enemy!"

The lightning was about them, and they raced to the booming of the thunder. Heavy raindrops began to fall, and the wind was a power to drive the riders on. Its voice shrilled above the diapason of the thunder; the forest swung to its long cry. When the horses turned from the wide into the narrow road, they could no longer go abreast. Mirza took the lead, and the bay fell a length behind. The branches now hid the sky; between the flashes there was Stygian gloom, but when the lightning came it showed far aisles of the forest. There was the smell of rain upon dusty earth, there was the wine of coolness after heat, there was the sense of being borne upon the wind, there was the leaping of life within the veins to meet the awakened life without. Audrey closed her eyes, and wished to ride thus forever. Haward, too, traveling fast through mist and rain a road whose end was hidden, facing the wet wind, hearing the voices of earth and sky, felt his spirit mount with the mounting voices. So to ride with Love to doom! On, and on, and on! Left behind the sophist, the apologist, the lover of the world with his tinsel that was not gold, his pebbles that were not gems! Only the man thundering on,—the man and his mate that was meant for him since time began! He raised his face to the strife above, he drew his breath, his hand closed over the hand of the woman riding with him. At the touch a thrill ran through them both; had the lightning with a sword of flame cut the world from beneath their feet, they had passed on, immortal in their happiness. But the bolts struck aimlessly, and the moment fled. Haward was Haward again; he recognized his old acquaintance with a half-humorous, half-disdainful smile. The road was no longer a road that gleamed athwart all time and space; the wind had lost its trumpet tone; Love spoke not in the thunder, nor seemed so high a thing as the lit heaven. Audrey's hand was yet within his clasp; but it was flesh and blood that he touched, not spirit, and he was glad that it was so. For her, her cheek burned, and she hid her eyes. She had looked unawares, as by the lightning glare, into a world of which she had not dreamed. Its portals had shut; she rode on in the twilight again, and she could not clearly remember what she had seen. But she was sure that the air of that country was sweet, she was faint with its beauty, her heart beat with violence to its far echoes. Moreover, she was dimly aware that in the moment when she had looked there had been a baptism. She had thought of herself as a child, as a girl; now and for evermore she was a woman.

They left the forest behind, and came to open fields where the tobacco had been beaten to earth. The trees now stood singly or in shivering copses. Above, the heavens were bare to their gaze, and the lightning gave glimpses of pale castles overhanging steel-gray, fathomless abysses. The road widened, and the bay was pushed by its rider to Mirza's side. Fields of corn where the long blades wildly clashed, a wood of dripping cedars, a patch of Oronoko, tobacco house in midst, rising ground and a vision of the river, then a swift descent to the lower creek, and the bridge across which lay the road that ran to the minister's house. Audrey spoke earnestly to the master of Fair View, and after a moment's hesitation he drew rein. "We will not cross, Colonel," he declared. "My preserver will have it that she has troubled us long enough; and indeed it is no great distance to the glebe house, and the rain has stopped. Have down with thee, then, obstinate one!"

Audrey slipped to the earth, and pushed back her hair from her eyes. Colonel Byrd observed her curiously. "Faith," he exclaimed, "'tis the Atalanta of last May Day! Well, child, I believe thou hast saved our lives. Come, here are three gold baubles that may pass for Hippomenes' apples!"

Audrey put her hands behind her. "I want no money, sir. What I did was a gift; it has no price." She was only Darden's Audrey, but she spoke as proudly as a princess might have spoken. Haward smiled to hear her; and seeing the smile, she was comforted. "For he understands," she said to herself. "He would never hurt me so." It did not wound her that he said no word, but only lifted his hat, when she curtsied to them both. There was to-morrow, and he would praise her then for her quickness of wit and her courage in following Hugon, whom she feared so much.

The riders watched her cross the bridge and turn into the road that led to the glebe house, then kept their own road in silence until it brought them to the doors of Fair View.

It was an hour later, and drawing toward dusk, when the Colonel, having changed his wet riding clothes for a suit of his friend's, came down the stairs and entered the Fair View drawing-room. Haward, in green, with rich lace at throat and wrist, was there before him, walking up and down in the cheerful light of a fire kindled against the dampness. "No sign of our men," he said, as the other entered. "Come to the fire. Faith, Colonel, my russet and gold becomes you mightily! Juba took you the aqua vitae?"

"Ay, in one of your great silver goblets, with a forest of mint atop. Ha, this is comfort!" He sank into an armchair, stretched his legs before the blaze, and began to look about him. "I have ever said, Haward, that of all the gentlemen of my acquaintance you have the most exact taste. I told Bubb Dodington as much, last year, at Eastbury. Damask, mirrors, paintings, china, cabinets,— all chaste and quiet, extremely elegant, but without ostentation! It hath an air, too. I would swear a woman had the placing of yonder painted jars!"

"You are right," said Haward, smiling. "The wife of the minister of this parish was good enough to come to my assistance."

"Ah!" said the Colonel dryly. "Did Atalanta come as well? She is his reverence's servant, is she not?"

"No," answered Haward shortly to the last question, and, leaning across, stirred the fire.

The light caused to sparkle a jeweled pin worn in the lace of his ruffles, and the toy caught the Colonel's eye. "One of Spotswood's golden horseshoes!" he exclaimed. "I had them wrought for him in London. Had they been so many stars and garters, he could have made no greater pother! 'Tis ten years since I saw one."

Haward detached the horseshoe-shaped bauble from the lace, and laid it on the other's palm. The master of Westover regarded it curiously, and read aloud the motto engraved upon its back: "'Sic Juvat Transcendere Montes.' A barren exploit! But some day I too shall please myself and cross these sun-kissing hills. And so the maid with the eyes is not his reverence's servant? What is she?"

Haward took the golden horseshoe in his own hand, and fell to studying it in the firelight. "I wore this to-night," he said at length, with deliberation, "in order that it might bring to your mind that sprightly ultramontane expedition in which, my dear Colonel, had you not been in England, you had undoubtedly borne a part. You have asked me a question; I will answer it with a story, and so the time may pass more rapidly until the arrival of Mr. MacLean with our friends who set traps." He turned the mimic horseshoe this way and that, watching the small gems, that simulated nails, flash in the red light. "Some days to the west of Germanna," he said, "when about us were the lesser mountains, and before us those that propped the sky, we came one sunny noon upon a valley, a little valley, very peaceful below the heights. A stream shone through it, and there were noble trees, and beside the stream the cabin of a frontiersman."

On went the story. The fire crackled, reflecting itself in mirrors and polished wood and many small window panes. Outside, the rain had ceased, but the wind and the river murmured loudly, and the shadows of the night were gathering. When the narrative was ended, he who had spoken and he who had listened sat staring at the fire. "A pretty story!" said the Colonel at last. "Dick Steele should have had it; 'twould have looked vastly well over against his Inkle and Yarico. There the maid the savior, here the man; there perfidy, here plain honesty; there for the woman a fate most tragical, here"—

"Here?" said Haward, as the other paused.

The master of Westover took out his snuffbox. "And here the continued kindness of a young and handsome preserver," he said suavely, and extended the box to his host.

"You are mistaken," said Haward. He rose, and stood leaning against the mantel, his eyes upon the older man's somewhat coldly smiling countenance. "She is as inno-cent, as high of soul, and as pure of heart as—as Evelyn."

The Colonel clicked to the lid of his box. "You will be so good as to leave my daughter's name out of the conversation."

"As you please," Haward answered, with hauteur.

Another silence, broken by the guest. "Why did you hang that kit-kat of yourself behind the door, Haward?" he asked amiably. "'Tis too fine a piece to be lost in shadow. I would advise a change with yonder shepherdess."

"I do not know why," said Haward restlessly. "A whim. Perhaps by nature I court shadows and dark corners."

"That is not so," Byrd replied quietly. He had turned in his chair, the better to observe the distant portrait that was now lightened, now darkened, as the flames rose and fell. "A speaking likeness," he went on, glancing from it to the original and back again. "I ever thought it one of Kneller's best. The portrait of a gentleman. Only—you have noticed, I dare say, how in the firelight familiar objects change aspect many times?—only just now it seemed to me that it lost that distinction"—

"Well?" said Haward, as he paused.

The Colonel went on slowly: "Lost that distinction, and became the portrait of"—

"Well? Of whom?" asked Haward, and, with his eyes shaded by his hand, gazed not at the portrait, but at the connoisseur in gold and russet.

"Of a dirty tradesman," said the master of Westover lightly. "In a word, of an own brother to Mr. Thomas Inkle."

A dead silence; then Haward spoke calmly: "I will not take offense, Colonel Byrd. Perhaps I should not take it even were it not as my guest and in my drawing-room that you have so spoken. We will, if you please, consign my portrait to the obscurity from which it has been dragged. In good time here comes Juba to light the candles and set the shadows fleeing."

Leaving the fire he moved to a window, and stood looking out upon the windy twilight. From the back of the house came a sound of voices and of footsteps. The Colonel put up his snuffbox and brushed a grain from his ruffles. "Enter two murderers!" he said briskly. "Will you have them here, Haward, or shall we go into the hall?"

"Light all the candles, Juba," ordered the master. "Here, I think, Colonel, where the stage will set them off. Juba, go ask Mr. MacLean and Saunderson to bring their prisoners here."

As he spoke, he turned from the contemplation of the night without to the brightly lit room. "This is a murderous fellow, this Hugon," he said, as he took his seat in a great chair drawn before a table. "I have heard Colonel Byrd argue in favor of imitating John Rolfe's early experiment, and marrying the white man to the heathen. We are about to behold the result of such an union."

"I would not have the practice universal," said the Colonel coolly, "but 'twould go far toward remedying loss of scalps in this world, and of infidel souls hereafter. Your sprightly lover is a most prevailing missionary. But here is our Huguenot-Monacan."

MacLean, very wet and muddy, with one hand wrapped in a blood-stained rag, came in first. "We found them hidden in the bushes at the turn of the road," he said hastily. "The schoolmaster was more peaceably inclined than any

Quaker, but Hugon fought like the wolf that he is. Can't you hang him out of hand, Haward? Give me a land where the chief does justice while the king looks the other way!" He turned and beckoned. "Bring them in, Saunderson."

There was no discomposure in the schoolmaster's dress, and as little in his face or manner. He bowed to the two gentlemen, then shambled across to the fire, and as best he could held out his bound hands to the grateful blaze. "May I ask, sir," he said, in his lifeless voice, "why it is that this youth and I, resting in all peace and quietness beside a public road, should be set upon by your servants, overpowered, bound, and haled to your house as to a judgment bar?"

Haward, to whom this speech was addressed, gave it no attention. His gaze was upon Hugon, who in his turn glared at him alone. Haward had a subtle power of forcing and fixing the attention of a company; in crowded rooms, without undue utterance or moving from his place, he was apt to achieve the centre of the stage, the head of the table. Now, the half-breed, by very virtue of the passion which, false to his Indian blood, shook him like a leaf, of a rage which overmastered and transformed, reached at a bound the Englishman's plane of distinction. His great wig, of a fashion years gone by, was pulled grotesquely aside, showing the high forehead and shaven crown beneath; his laced coat and tawdry waistcoat and ruffled shirt were torn and foul with mud and mould, but the man himself made to be forgotten the absurdity of his trappings. Gone, for him, were his captors, his accomplice, the spectator in gold and russet; to Haward, also, sitting very cold, very quiet, with narrowed eyes, they were gone. He was angered, and in the mood to give rein after his own fashion to that anger. MacLean and the master of Westover, the overseer and the schoolmaster, were forgotten, and he and Hugon met alone as they might have met in the forest. Between them, and without a spoken word, the two made this fact to be recognized by the other occupants of the drawing-room. Colonel Byrd, who had been standing with his hand upon the table, moved backward until he joined MacLean beside the closed door: Saunderson drew near to the schoolmaster: and the centre of the room was left to the would-be murderer and the victim that had escaped him.

"Monsieur le Monacan," said Haward.

Hugon snarled like an angry wolf, and strained at the rope which bound his arms.

Haward went on evenly: "Your tribe has smoked the peace pipe with the white man. I was not told it by singing birds, but by the great white father at Williamsburgh. They buried the hatchet very deep; the dead leaves of many moons of Cohonks lie thick upon the place where they buried it. Why have you made a warpath, treading it alone of your color?"

"Diable!" cried Hugon. "Pig of an Englishman! I will kill you for"—

"For an handful of blue beads," said Haward, with a cold smile. "And I, dog of an Indian! I will send a Nottoway to teach the Monacans how to lay a snare and hide a trail."

The trader, gasping with passion, leaned across the table until his eyes were within a foot of Haward's unmoved face. "Who showed you the trail and told you of the snare?" he whispered. "Tell me that, you Englishman,— tell me that!"

"A storm bird," said Haward calmly. "Okee is perhaps angry with his Monacans, and sent it."

"Was it Audrey?"

Haward laughed. "No, it was not Audrey. And so, Monacan, you have yourself fallen into the pit which you digged."

From the fireplace came the schoolmaster's slow voice: "Dear sir, can you show the pit? Why should this youth desire to harm you? Where is the storm bird? Can you whistle it before a justice of the peace or into a court room?"

If Haward heard, it did not appear. He was leaning back in his chair, his eyes fixed upon the trader's twitching face in a cold and smiling regard. "Well, Monacan?" he demanded.

The half-breed straightened himself, and with a mighty effort strove in vain for a composure that should match the other's cold self-command,—a command which taunted and stung now at this point, now at that. "I am a Frenchman!" he cried, in a voice that broke with passion. "I am of the noblesse of the land of France, which is a country that is much grander than Virginia! Old Pierre at Monacan-Town told me these things. My father changed his name when he came across the sea, so I bear not the *de* which is a sign of a great man. Listen, you Englishman! I trade, I prosper, I buy me land, I begin to build me a house. There is a girl that I see every hour, every minute, while I am building it. She says she loves me not, but nevertheless I shall wed her. Now I see her in this room, now in that; she comes down the stair, she smiles at the window, she stands on the doorstep to welcome me when I come home from my hunting and trading in the woods so far away. I bring her fine skins of the otter, the beaver, and the fawn; beadwork also from the villages and bracelets of copper and pearl. The flowers bloom around her, and my heart sings to see her upon my doorstep.... The flowers are dead, and you have stolen the girl away.... There was a stream, and the sun shone upon it, and you and she were in a boat. I walked alone upon the bank, and in my heart I left building my house and fell to other work. You laughed; one day you will laugh no more. That was many suns ago. I have watched"—

Foam was upon his lips, and he strained without ceasing at his bonds. Already pulled far awry, his great peruke, a cataract of hair streaming over his shoulders, shading and softening the swarthy features between its curled waves, now slipped from his head and fell to the floor. The change which its absence wrought was startling. Of the man the moiety that was white disappeared. The shaven head, its poise, its features, were Indian; the soul was Indian, and looked from Indian eyes. Suddenly, for the last transforming touch, came a torrent of words in a strange tongue, the tongue of his mother. Of what he was speaking, what he was threatening, no one of them could tell; he was a savage giving voice to madness and hate.

Haward pushed back his chair from the table, and, rising, walked across the room to the window. Hugon followed him, straining at the rope about his arms and speaking thickly. His eyes were glaring, his teeth bared. When he was so close that the Virginian could feel his hot breath, the latter turned, and uttering an oath of disgust struck the back of his hand across his lips. With the cry of an animal, Hugon, bound as he was, threw himself bodily upon his foe, who in his turn flung the trader from him with a violence that sent him reeling against the wall.

Here Saunderson, a man of powerful build, seized him by the shoulders, holding him fast; MacLean, too, hurriedly crossed from the door. There was no need, for the half-breed's frenzy was spent. He stood with glittering eyes following Haward's every motion, but quite silent, his frame rigid in the overseer's grasp.

Colonel Byrd went up to Haward and spoke in a low voice: "Best send them at once to Williamsburgh."

Haward shook his head. "I cannot," he said, with a gesture of impatience. "There is no proof."

"No proof!" exclaimed his guest sharply. "You mean"—

The other met his stare of surprise with an imperturbable countenance. "What I say," he answered quietly. "My servants find two men lurking beside a road that I am traveling. Being somewhat over-zealous, they take them up upon suspicion of meaning mischief and bring them before me. It is all guesswork why they were at the turn of the road, and what they wanted there. There is no proof, no witness"—

"I see that there is no witness that you care to call," said the Colonel coldly.

Haward waved his hand. "There is no witness," he said, without change of tone. "And therefore, Colonel, I am about to dismiss the case."

With a slight bow to his guest he left the window, and advanced to the group in the centre of the room. "Saunderson," he said abruptly, "take these two men to the quarter and cut their bonds. Give them a start of fifty yards, then loose the dogs and hunt them from the plantation. You have men outside to help you? Very well; go! Mr. MacLean, will you see this chase fairly started?"

The Highlander, who had become very thoughtful of aspect since entering the room, and who had not shared Saunderson's start of surprise at the master's latest orders, nodded assent. Haward stood for a moment gazing steadily at Hugon, but with no notice to bestow upon the bowing schoolmaster; then walked over to the harpsichord, and, sitting down, began to play an old tune, soft and slow, with pauses between the notes. When he came to the final chord he looked over his shoulder at the Colonel, standing before the mantel, with his eyes upon the fire. "So they have gone," he said. "Good riddance! A pretty brace of villains!"

"I should be loath to have Monsieur Jean Hugon for my enemy," said the Colonel gravely.

Haward laughed. "I was told at Williamsburgh that a party of traders go to the Southern Indians to-morrow, and he with them. Perhaps a month or two of the woods will work a cure."

He fell to playing again, a quiet, plaintive air. When it was ended, he rose and went over to the fire to keep his guest company; but finding him in a mood for silence, presently fell silent himself, and took to viewing structures of his own building in the red hollows between the logs. This mutual taciturnity lasted until the announcement of supper, and was relapsed into at intervals during the meal; but when they had returned to the drawing-room the two talked until it was late, and the fire had sunken to ash and embers. Before they parted for the night it was agreed that the master of Westover should remain with the master of Fair View for a day or so, at the end of which time the latter gentleman would accompany the former to Westover for a visit of indefinite length.

CHAPTER XVI

AUDREY AND EVELYN

Hugon went a-trading to the Southern Indians, but had lately returned to his lair at the crossroads ordinary, when, upon a sunny September morning, Audrey and Mistress Deborah, mounted upon the sorriest of Darden's sorry steeds, turned from Duke of Gloucester into Palace Street. They had parted with the minister before his favorite ordinary, and were on their way to the house where they themselves were to lodge during the three days of town life which Darden had vouchsafed to offer them.

For a month or more Virginia had been wearing black ribbons for the King, who died in June, but in the last day or so there had been a reversion to bright colors. This cheerful change had been wrought by the arrival in the York of the Fortune of Bristol, with the new governor on board. His Excellency had landed at Yorktown, and, after suitable entertainment at the hands of its citizens, had proceeded under escort to Williamsburgh. The entry into the town was triumphal, and when, at the doorway of his Palace, the Governor turned, and addressed a pleasing oration to the people whom he was to rule in the name of the King and my Lord of Orkney, enthusiasm reached its height. At night the town was illuminated, and well-nigh all its ladies and gentlemen visited the Palace, in order to pay their duty to its latest occupant. It was a pleasure-loving people, and the arrival of a governor an occasion of which the most must be made. Gentlemen of consideration had come in from every county, bringing with them wives and daughters. In the mild, sunshiny weather the crowded town overflowed into square and street and garden. Everywhere were bustle and gayety,—gayety none the less for the presence of thirty or more ministers of the Established Church. For Mr. Commissary Blair had convoked a meeting of the clergy for the consideration of evils affecting that body,—not, alas! from without alone. The Governor, arriving so opportunely, must, too, be addressed upon the usual subjects of presentation, induction, and all-powerful vestries. It was fitting, also, that the college of William and Mary should have its say upon the occasion, and the brightest scholar thereof was even now closeted with the Latin master. That the copy of verses giving the welcome of so many future planters, Burgesses, and members of Council would be choice in thought and elegant in expression, there could be no reasonable doubt. The Council was to give an entertainment at the Capitol; one day had been set aside for a muster of militia in the meadow beyond the college, another for a great horse-race; many small parties were arranged; and last, but not least, on the night of the day following Darden's appearance in town, his Excellency was to give a ball at the Palace. Add to all this that two notorious pirates were standing their trial before a court-martial, with every prospect of being hanged within the se'ennight; that a deputation of Nottoways and Meherrins, having business with the white fathers in Williamsburgh, were to be persuaded to dance their wildest, whoop their loudest, around a bonfire built in the market square; that at the playhouse Cato was to be given with extraordinary magnificence, and one may readily see that there might have been found, in this sunny September week, places less entertaining than Williamsburgh.

Darden's old white horse, with its double load, plodded along the street that led to the toy Palace of this toy capital. The Palace, of course, was not its riders' destination; instead, when they had crossed Nicholson Street, they drew up before a particularly small white house, so hidden away behind lilac bushes and trellised grapevines that it gave but here and there a pale hint of its existence. It was planted in the shadow of a larger building, and a path led around it to what seemed a pleasant, shady, and extensive garden.

Mistress Deborah gave a sigh of satisfaction. "Seven years come Martinmas since I last stayed overnight with Mary Stagg! And we were born in the same village, and at Bath what mighty friends we were! She was playing Dorinda,—that's in 'The Beaux' Stratagem,' Audrey,—and her dress was just an old striped Persian, vastly unbecoming. Her Ladyship's pink alamode, that Major D—spilt a dish of chocolate over, she gave to me for carrying a note; and I gave it to Mary (she was Mary Baker then),—for I looked hideous in pink,—and she was that grateful, as well she might be! Mary, Mary!"

A slender woman, with red-brown hair and faded cheeks, came running from the house to the gate. "At last, my dear Deborah! I vow I had given you up! Says I to Mirabell an hour ago,—you know that is my name for Charles, for 'twas when he played Mirabell to my Millamant that we fell in love,—'Well,' says I, 'I'll lay a gold-furbelowed scarf to a yard of oznaburg that Mr. Darden, riding home through the night, and in liquor, perhaps, has fallen and broken his neck, and Deborah can't come.' And says Mirabell—But la, my dear, there you stand in your safeguard, and I'm keeping the gate shut on you! Come in. Come in, Audrey. Why, you've grown to be a woman! You were just a brown slip of a thing, that Lady Day, two years ago, that I spent with Deborah. Come in the both of you. There are cakes and a bottle of Madeira."

Audrey fastened the horse against the time that Darden should remember to send for it, and then followed the ex-waiting-woman and the former queen of a company of strollers up a grassy path and through a little green door into a pleasant room, where grape leaves wreathed the windows and cast their shadows upon a sanded floor. At one end of the room stood a great, rudely built cabinet, and before it a long table, strewn with an orderly litter of such slender articles of apparel as silk and tissue scarfs, gauze hoods, breast knots, silk stockings, and embroidered gloves. Mistress Deborah must needs run and examine these at once, and Mistress Mary Stagg, wife of the lessee, manager, and principal actor of the Williamsburgh theatre, looked complacently over her shoulder. The minister's wife sighed again, this time with envy.

"What with the theatre, and the bowling green, and tea in your summer-house, and dancing lessons, and the sale of these fine things, you and Charles must turn a pretty penny! The luck that some folk have! *You* were always fortunate, Mary."

Mistress Stagg did not deny the imputation. But she was a kindly soul, who had not forgotten the gift of my Lady Squander's pink alamode. The chocolate stain had not been so very large.

"I've laid by a pretty piece of sarcenet of which to make

you a capuchin," she said promptly. "Now, here's the wine. Shan't we go into the garden, and sip it there? Peggy," to the black girl holding a salver, "put the cake and wine on the table in the arbor; then sit here by the window, and call me if any come. My dear Deborah, I doubt if I have so much as a ribbon left by the end of the week. The town is that gay! I says to Mirabell this morning, says I, 'Lord, my dear, it a'most puts me in mind of Bath!' And Mirabell says—But here's the garden door. Now, isn't it cool and pleasant out here? Audrey may gather us some grapes. Yes, they're very fine, full bunches; it has been a bounteous year."

The grape arbor hugged the house, but beyond it was a pretty, shady, fancifully laid out garden, with shell-bordered walks, a grotto, a summer-house, and a gate opening into Nicholson Street. Beyond the garden a glimpse was to be caught through the trees of a trim bowling green. It had rained the night before, and a delightful, almost vernal freshness breathed in the air. The bees made a great buzzing amongst the grapes, and the birds in the mulberry-trees sang as though it were nesting time. Mistress Stagg and her old acquaintance sat at a table placed in the shadow of the vines, and sipped their wine, while Audrey obediently gathered clusters of the purple fruit, and thought the garden very fine, but oh, not like—There could be no garden in the world so beautiful and so dear as that! And she had not seen it for so long, so long a time. She wondered if she would ever see it again.

When she brought the fruit to the table, Mistress Stagg made room for her kindly enough; and she sat and drank her wine and went to her world of dreams, while her companions bartered town and country gossip. It has been said that the small white house adjoined a larger building. A window in this structure, which had much the appearance of a barn, was now opened, with the result that a confused sound, as of several people speaking at once, made itself heard. Suddenly the noise gave place to a single high-pitched voice:—

"'Welcome, my son! Here lay him down, my friends,
Full in my sight, that I may view at leisure
The bloody corse, and count those glorious wounds.'"

A smile irradiated Mistress Stagg's faded countenance, and she blew a kiss toward the open window. "He does Cato so extremely well; and it's a grave, dull, odd character, too. But Mirabell—that's Charles, you know—manages to put a little life in it, a *Je ne sais quoi*, a touch of Sir Harry Wildair. Now—now he's pulling out his laced handkerchief to weep over Rome! You should see him after he has fallen on his sword, and is brought on in a chair, all over blood. This is the third rehearsal; the play's ordered for Monday night. Who is it, Peggy? Madam Travis! It's about the lace for her damask petticoat, and there's no telling how long she may keep me! My dear Deborah, when you have finished your wine, Peggy shall show you your room. You must make yourself quite at home. For says I to Mirabell this morning, 'Far be it from me to forget past kindnesses, and in those old Bath days Deborah was a good friend to me,—which was no wonder, to be sure, seeing that when we were little girls we went to the same dame school, and always learned our book and worked our samplers together.' And says Mirabell—Yes, yes, ma'am, I'm coming!"

She disappeared, and the black girl showed the two guests through the hall and up a tiny stairway into a little dormer-windowed, whitewashed room. Mistress Deborah, who still wore remnants of my Lady Squander's ancient gifts of spoiled finery, had likewise failed to discard the second-hand fine-lady airs acquired during her service. She now declared herself excessively tired by her morning ride, and martyr, besides, to a migraine. Moreover, it was enough to give one the spleen to hear Mary Stagg's magpie chatter and to see how some folk throve, willy-nilly, while others just as good—Here tears of vexation ensued, and she must lie down upon the bed and call in a feeble voice for her smelling salts. Audrey hurriedly searched in the ragged portmanteau brought to town the day before in the ox-cart of an obliging parishioner, found the flask, and took it to the bedside, to receive in exchange a sound box of the ear for her tardiness. The blow reddened her cheek, but brought no tears to her eyes. It was too small a thing to weep for; tears were for blows upon the heart.

It was a cool and quiet little room, and Mistress Deborah, who had drunk two full glasses of the Madeira, presently fell asleep. Audrey sat very still, her hands folded in her lap and her eyes upon them, until their hostess's voice announced from the foot of the stairs that Madam Travis had taken her departure. She then slipped from the room, and was affably received below, and taken into the apartment which they had first entered. Here Mistress became at once extremely busy. A fan was to be mounted; yards of silk gathered into furbelows; breast knots, shoulder knots, sword knots, to be made up. Her customers were all people of quality, and unless she did her part not one of them could go to the ball. Audrey shyly proffered her aid, and was set to changing the ribbons upon a mask.

Mistress Stagg's tongue went as fast as her needle: "And Deborah is asleep! Poor soul! she's sadly changed from what she was in old England thirteen years ago. As neat a shape as you would see in a day's journey, with the prettiest color, and eyes as bright as those marcasite buttons! And she saw the best of company at my Lady Squander's,—no lack there of kisses and guineas and fine gentlemen, you may be sure! There's a deal of change in this mortal world, and it's generally for the worse. Here, child, you may whip this lace on Mr. Lightfoot's ruffles. I think myself lucky, I can tell you, that there are so few women in Cato. If 'tweren't so, I should have to go on myself; for since poor, dear, pretty Jane Day died of the smallpox, and Oriana Jordan ran away with the rascally Bridewell fellow that we bought to play husbands' parts, and was never heard of more, but is supposed to have gotten clean off to Barbadoes by favor of the master of the Lady Susan, we have been short of actresses. But in this play there are only Marcia and Lucia. 'It is extremely fortunate, my dear,' said I to Mirabell this very morning, 'that in this play, which is the proper compliment to a great gentleman just taking office, Mr. Addison should have put no more than two women.' And Mirabell says— Don't put the lace so full, child; 'twon't go round."

"A chair is stopping at the gate," said Audrey, who sat by the window. "There's a lady in it."

The chair was a very fine painted one, borne by two gayly dressed negroes, and escorted by a trio of beribboned young gentlemen, prodigal of gallant speeches, amorous sighs, and languishing glances. Mistress Stagg looked, started up, and, without waiting to raise from the floor the armful of delicate silk which she had dropped, was presently curtsying upon the doorstep.

The bearers set down their load. One of the gentlemen opened the chair door with a flourish, and the divinity, compressing her hoop, descended. A second cavalier flung back Mistress Stagg's gate, and the third, with a low bow, proffered his hand to conduct the fair from the gate to the doorstep. The lady shook her head; a smiling word or two, a slight curtsy, the wave of a painted fan, and her attendants found themselves dismissed. She came up the path alone, slowly, with her head a little bent. Audrey, watching her from the window, knew who she was, and her heart beat fast. If this lady were in town, then so was he; he would not have stayed behind at Westover. She would have left the room, but there was not time. The mistress of the house, smiling and obsequious, fluttered in, and Evelyn Byrd followed.

There had been ordered for her a hood of golden tissue, with wide and long streamers to be tied beneath the chin, and she was come to try it on. Mistress Stagg had it all but ready,—there was only the least bit of stitchery; would Mistress Evelyn condescend to wait a very few minutes? She placed a chair, and the lady sank into it, finding the quiet of the shadowed room pleasant enough after the sunlight and talkativeness of the world without. Mistress Stagg, in her role of milliner, took the gauzy trifle, called by courtesy a hood, to the farthest window, and fell busily to work.

It seemed to grow more and more quiet in the room: the shadow of the leaves lay still upon the floor; the drowsy humming of the bees outside the windows, the sound of locusts in the trees, the distant noises of the town,—all grew more remote, then suddenly appeared to cease.

Audrey raised her eyes, and met the eyes of Evelyn. She knew that they had been upon her for a long time, in the quiet of the room. She had sat breathless, her head bowed over her work that lay idly in her lap, but at last she must look. The two gazed at each other with a sorrowful steadfastness; in the largeness of their several natures there was no room for self-consciousness; it was the soul of each that gazed. But in the mists of earthly ignorance they could not read what was written, and they erred in their guessing. Audrey went not far wide. This was the princess, and, out of the fullness of a heart that ached with loss, she could have knelt and kissed the hem of her robe, and wished her long and happy life. There was no bitterness in her heart; she never dreamed that she had wronged the princess. But Evelyn thought: "This is the girl they talk about. God knows, if he had loved worthily, I might not so much have minded!"

From the garden came a burst of laughter and high voices. Mistress Stagg started up. "'Tis our people, Mistress Evelyn, coming from the playhouse. We lodge them in the house by the bowling green, but after rehearsals they're apt to stop here. I'll send them packing. The hood is finished. Audrey will set it upon your head, ma'am, while I am gone. Here, child! Mind you don't crush it." She gave the hood into Audrey's hands, and hurried from the room.

Evelyn sat motionless, her silken draperies flowing around her, one white arm bent, the soft curve of her cheek resting upon ringed fingers. Her eyes yet dwelt upon Audrey, standing as motionless, the mist of gauze and lace in her hands. "Do not trouble yourself," she said, in her low, clear voice. "I will wait until Mistress Stagg returns."

The tone was very cold, but Audrey scarce noticed that it was so. "If I may, I should like to serve you, ma'am," she said pleadingly. "I will be very careful."

Leaving the window, she came and knelt beside Evelyn;

but when she would have put the golden hood upon her head, the other drew back with a gesture of aversion, a quick recoil of her entire frame. The hood slipped to the floor. After a moment Audrey rose and stepped back a pace or two. Neither spoke, but it was the one who thought no evil whose eyes first sought the floor. Her dark cheek paled, and her lips trembled; she turned, and going back to her seat by the window took up her fallen work. Evelyn, with a sharp catch of her breath, withdrew her attention from the other occupant of the room, and fixed it upon a moted sunbeam lying like a bar between the two.

Mistress Stagg returned. The hood was fitted, and its purchaser prepared to leave. Audrey rose and made her curtsy, timidly, but with a quick, appealing motion of her hand. Was not this the lady whom he loved, that people said he was to wed? And had he not told her, long ago, that he would speak of her to Mistress Evelyn Byrd, and that she too would be her friend? Last May Day, when the guinea was put into her hand, the lady's smile was bright, her voice sweet and friendly. Now, how changed! In her craving for a word, a look, from one so near him, one that perhaps had seen him not an hour before; in her sad homage for the object of his love, she forgot her late repulse, and grew bold. When Evelyn would have passed her, she put forth a trembling hand and began to speak, to say she scarce knew what; but the words died in her throat. For a moment Evelyn stood, her head averted, an angry red staining neck and bosom and beautiful, down-bent face. Her eyes half closed, the long lashes quivering against her cheek, and she smiled faintly, in scorn of the girl and scorn of herself. Then, freeing her skirt from Audrey's clasp, she passed in silence from the room.

Audrey stood at the window, and with wide, pained eyes watched her go down the path. Mistress Stagg was with her, talking volubly, and Evelyn seemed to listen with smiling patience. One of the bedizened negroes opened the chair door; the lady entered, and was borne away. Before Mistress Stagg could reenter her house Audrey had gone quietly up the winding stair to the little white-washed room, where she found the minister's wife astir and restored to good humor. Her sleep had helped her; she would go down at once and see what Mary was at. Darden, too, was coming as soon as the meeting at the church had adjourned. After dinner they would walk out and see the town, until which time Audrey might do as she pleased. When she was gone, Audrey softly shut herself in the little room, and lay down upon the bed, very still, with her face hidden in her arm.

With twelve of the clock came Darden, quite sober, distrait in manner and uneasy of eye, and presently interrupted Mistress Stagg's flow of conversation by a demand to speak with his wife alone. At that time of day the garden was a solitude, and thither the two repaired, taking their seats upon a bench built round a mulberry-tree.

"Well?" queried Mistress Deborah bitterly. "I suppose Mr. Commissary showed himself vastly civil? I dare say you're to preach before the Governor next Sunday? Or maybe they've chosen Bailey? He boasts that he can drink you under the table! One of these fine days you'll drink and curse and game yourself out of a parish!"

Darden drew figures on the ground with his heavy stick. "On such a fine day as this," he said, in a suppressed voice, and looked askance at the wife whom he beat upon occasion, but whose counsel he held in respect.

She turned upon him. "What do you mean? They talk and

talk, and cry shame,—and a shame it is, the Lord knows! But it never comes to anything"—

"It has come to this," interrupted Darden, with an oath: "that this Governor means to sweep in the corners; that the Commissary—damned Scot!—to-day appointed a committee to inquire into the charges made against me and Bailey and John Worden; that seven of my vestrymen are dead against me; and that 'deprivation' has suddenly become a very common word!"

"Seven of the vestry?" said his wife, after a pause. "Who are they?"

Darden told her.

"If Mr. Haward"—she began slowly, her green eyes steady upon the situation. "There's not one of that seven would care to disoblige him. I warrant you he could make them face about. They say he knew the Governor in England, too; and there's his late gift to the college,—the Commissary wouldn't forget that. If Mr. Haward would"—She broke off, and with knit brows studied the problem more intently.

"If he would, he could," Darden finished for her. "With his interest this cloud would go by, as others have done before. I know that, Deborah. And that's the card I'm going to play."

"If you had gone to him, hat in hand, a month ago, he'd have done you any favor," said his helpmate sourly. "But it is different now. He's over his fancy; and besides, he's at Westover."

"He's in Williamsburgh, at Marot's ordinary," said the

other. "As for his being over his fancy,—I'll try that. Fancy or no fancy, if a woman asked him for a fairing, he would give it her, or I don't know my gentleman. We'll call his interest a ribbon or some such toy, and Audrey shall ask him for it."

"Audrey is a fool!" cried Mistress Deborah. "And you had best be careful, or you'll prove yourself another! There's been talk enough already. Audrey, village innocent that she is, is the only one that doesn't know it. The town's not the country; if he sets tongues a-clacking here"—

"He won't," said Darden roughly. "He's no hare-brained one-and-twenty! And Audrey's a good girl. Go send her here, Deborah. Bid her fetch me Stagg's inkhorn and a pen and a sheet of paper. If he does anything for me, it will have to be done quickly. They're in haste to pull me out of saddle, the damned canting pack! But I'll try conclusions with them!"

His wife departed, muttering to herself, and the reverend Gideon pulled out of his capacious pocket a flask of usquebaugh. In five minutes from the time of his setting it to his lips the light in which he viewed the situation turned from gray to rose color. By the time he espied Audrey coming toward him through the garden he felt a moral certainty that when he came to die (if ever he died) it would be in his bed in the Fair View glebe house.

CHAPTER XVII

WITHIN THE PLAYHOUSE

Haward, sitting at the table in Marot's best room, wrote an answer to Audrey's letter, and tore it up; wrote another, and gave it to Juba, to be given to the messenger waiting below; recalled the negro before he could reach the door, destroyed the second note, and wrote a third. The first had been wise and kind, telling her that he was much engaged, lightly and skillfully waving aside her request—the only one she made—that she might see him that day. The second had been less wise. The last told her that he would come at five o'clock to the summer-house in Mistress Stagg's garden.

When he was alone in the room, he sat for some time very still, with his eyes closed and his head thrown back against the tall woodwork of his chair. His face was stern in repose: a handsome, even a fine face, with a look of power and reflection, but to-day somewhat worn and haggard of aspect. When presently he roused himself and took up the letter that lay before him, the paper shook in his hand. "Wine, Juba," he said to the slave, who now reentered the room. "And close the window; it is growing cold."

There were but three lines between the "Mr. Haward" and "Audrey;" the writing was stiff and clerkly, the words very simple,—a child's asking of a favor. He guessed rightly that it was the first letter of her own that she had ever written. Suddenly a wave of passionate tenderness took him; he bowed his head and kissed the paper; for the moment many-threaded life and his own complex nature alike straightened to a beautiful simplicity. He was the lover, merely; life was but the light and shadow through which moved the woman whom he loved. He came back to himself, and tried to think it out, but could not. Finally, with a weary impatience, he declined to think at all. He was to dine at the Governor's. Evelyn would be there.

Only momentarily, in those days of early summer, had he wavered in his determination to make this lady his wife. Pride was at the root of his being,—pride and a deep self-will; though because they were so sunken, and because poisonous roots can flower most deceivingly, he neither called himself nor was called of others a proud and willful man. He wished Evelyn for his wife; nay, more, though on May Day he had shown her that he loved her not, though in June he had offered her a love that was only admiring affection, yet in the past month at Westover he had come almost to believe that he loved her truly. That she was worthy of true love he knew very well. With all his strength of will, he had elected to forget the summer that lay behind him at Fair View, and to live in the summer that was with him at Westover. His success had been gratifying; in the flush of it, he persuaded himself that a chamber of the heart had been locked forever, and the key thrown away. And lo now! a touch, the sudden sight of a name, and the door had flown wide; nay, the very walls were rived away! It was not a glance over the shoulder; it was full presence in the room so lately sealed.

He knew that Evelyn loved him. It was understood of all their acquaintance that he was her suitor; months ago he had formally craved her father's permission to pay his addresses. There were times in those weeks at Westover when she had come nigh to yielding, to believing that he loved her; he was certain that with time he would have his way.... But the room, the closed room, in which now he sat!

He buried his face in his hands, and was suddenly back in spirit in his garden at Fair View. The cherries were ripe; the birds were singing: great butterflies went by. The sunshine beat on the dial, on the walks, and the smell of the roses was strong as wine. His senses swam with the warmth and fragrance; the garden enlarged itself, and blazed in beauty. Never was sunshine so golden as that; never were roses so large, never odors so potent-sweet. A spirit walked in the garden paths: its name was Audrey.... No, it was speaking, speaking words of passion and of woe.... Its name was Eloisa!

When he rose from his chair, he staggered slightly, and put his hand to his head. Recovering himself in a moment, he called for his hat and cane, and, leaving the ordinary, turned his face toward the Palace. A garrulous fellow Councilor, also bidden to his Excellency's dinner party, overtook him, and, falling into step, began to speak first of the pirates' trial, and then of the weather. A hot and feverish summer. 'Twas said that a good third of the servants arriving in the country since spring had died of their seasoning. The slaver lying in the York had thrown thirty blacks overboard in the ran from Barbadoes,—some strange sickness or other. Adsbud! He would not buy from the lot the master landed; had they been white, they had showed like spectres! September was the worst month of the year. He did not find Mr. Haward in looks now.

Best consult Dr. Contesse, though indeed he himself had a preventive of fever which never failed. First he bled; then to so much of Peruvian bark—

Mr. Haward declared that he was very well, and turned the conversation piratewards again.

The dinner at the Palace was somewhat hurried, the gentlemen rising with the ladies, despite the enticements of Burgundy and champagne. It was the afternoon set apart for the Indian dance. The bonfire in the field behind the magazine had been kindled; the Nottoways and Meherrins were waiting, still as statues, for the gathering of their audience. Before the dance the great white father was to speak to them; the peace pipe, also, was to be smoked. The town, gay of mood and snatching at enjoyment, emptied its people into the sunny field. Only they who could not go stayed at home. Those light-hearted folk, ministers to a play-loving age, who dwelt in the house by the bowling green or in the shadow of the theatre itself, must go, at all rates. Marcia and Lucia, Syphax, Sempronius, and the African prince made off together, while the sons of Cato, who chanced to be twin brothers, followed with a slower step. Their indentures would expire next month, and they had thoughts, the one of becoming an overseer, the other of moving up country and joining a company of rangers: hence their somewhat haughty bearing toward their fellow players, who—except old Syphax, who acted for the love of it—had not even a bowing acquaintance with freedom.

Mr. and Mrs. Stagg saw their minions depart, and then themselves left the little white house in Palace Street. Mistress Deborah was with them, but not Audrey. "She can't abide the sight of an Indian," said the minister's wife indifferently. "Besides, Darden will be here from the church presently, and he may want her to write for him. She and Peggy can mind the house."

The Capitol clock was telling five when Haward entered the garden by the Nicholson Street gate. There had arisen a zephyr of the evening, to loosen the yellow locust leaves and send them down upon the path, to lay cool fingers upon his forehead that burned, and to whisper low at his ear. House and garden and silent street seemed asleep in the late sunshine, safe folded from the storm of sound that raged in the field on the border of the town. Distance muffled the Indian drums, and changed the scream of the pipes into a far-off wailing. Savage cries, bursts of applause and laughter,—all came softly, blent like the hum of the bees, mellow like the sunlight. There was no one in the summer-house. Haward walked on to the grape arbor, and found there a black girl, who pointed to an open door, pertaining not to the small white house, but to that portion of the theatre which abutted upon the garden. Haward, passing a window of Mr. Stagg's domicile, was aware of Darden sitting within, much engaged with a great book and a tankard of sack. He made no pause for the vision, and another moment found him within the playhouse.

The sunlight entered in at the door and at one high window, but yet the place was dim. The gallery and the rude boxes were all in shadow; the sunbeams from the door struck into the pit, while those from the high window let fall a shaft of misty light upon the stage itself, set for a hall in Utica, with five cane chairs, an ancient settle, and a Spanish table. On the settle, in the pale gold of the falling light, sat Audrey, her hands clasped over her knees, her head thrown back, and her eyes fixed upon the shadowy, chill, and soundless space before her. Upon Haward's speaking her name she sighed, and, loosing her hands, turned toward him. He came and leaned upon the back of the settle. "You sent for me, Audrey," he said, and laid his hand lightly upon her hair.

She shrank from his touch. "The minister made me write the letter," she said, in a low voice. "I did not wish to trouble you, sir."

Upon her wrist were dark marks. "Did Darden do that?" demanded Haward, as he took his seat beside her.

Audrey looked at the bruise indifferently; then with her other hand covered it from sight. "I have a favor to ask of Mr. Haward," she said. "I hope that after his many kindnesses he will not refuse to do me this greatest one. If he should grant my request, the gratitude which I must needs already feel toward him will be increased tenfold." The words came precisely, in an even voice.

Haward smiled. "Child, you have conned your lesson well. Leave the words of the book, and tell me in your own language what his reverence wants."

Audrey told him, but it seemed to her that he was not listening. When she had come to an end of the minister's grievances, she sat, with downcast eyes, waiting for him to speak, wishing that he would not look at her so steadily. She meant never to show him her heart,—never, never; but beneath his gaze it was hard to keep her cheek from burning, her lip from quivering.

At last he spoke: "Would it please you, Audrey, if I should save this man from his just deserts?"

Audrey raised her eyes. "He and Mistress Deborah are all my friends," she said. "The glebe house is my home."

Deep sadness spoke in voice and eye. The shaft of light, moving, had left her in the outer shadow: she sat there with a listless grace; with a dignity, too, that was not without pathos. There had been a forlorn child; there had been an unfriended girl; there was now a woman, for Life to fondle or to wreak its rage upon. The change was subtle; one more a lover or less a lover than Haward might not have noted it. "I will petition the Commissary to-night," he said, "the Governor to-morrow. Is your having in friends so slight as you say, little maid?"

Oh, he could reach to the quick! She was sure that he had not meant to accuse her of ingratitude, and pitifully sure that she must have seemed guilty of it. "No, no!" she cried. "I have had a friend"—Her voice broke, and she started to her feet, her face to the door, all her being quiveringly eager to be gone. She had asked that which she was bidden to ask, had gained that which she was bidden to gain; for the rest, it was far better that she should go. Better far for him to think her dull and thankless as a stone than see—than see—

When Haward caught her by the hand, she trembled and drew a sobbing breath. "'I have had a friend,' Audrey?" he asked. "Why not 'I have a friend'?"

"Why not?" thought Audrey. "Of course he would think, why not? Well, then"—

"I have a friend," she said aloud. "Have you not been to me the kindest friend, the most generous"—She faltered, but presently went on, a strange courage coming to her. She had turned slightly toward him, though she looked not at him, but upward to where the light streamed through the high window. It fell now upon her face. "It is a great thing to save life," she said. "To save a soul alive, how much greater! To have kept one soul in the knowledge that there is goodness, mercy, tenderness, God; to have given it bread to eat where it sat among the stones, water to drink where all the streams were dry,—oh, a king might be proud of that! And that is what you have done for me.... When you sailed away, so many years ago, and left me with the minister and his wife, they were not always kind. But I knew that you thought them so, and I always said to myself, 'If he knew, he would be sorry for me.' At last I said, 'He is sorry for me; there is the sea, and he cannot come, but he knows, and is sorry.' It was make-believe,—for you thought that I was happy, did you not?—but it helped me very much. I was only a child, you know, and I was so very lonely. I could not think of mother and Molly, for when I did I saw them as—as I had seen them last. The dark scared me, until I found that I could pretend that you were holding my hand, as you used to do when night came in the valley. After a while I had only to put out my hand, and yours was there waiting for it. I hope that you can understand—I want you to know how large is my debt.... As I grew, so did the debt. When I was a girl it was larger than when I was a child. Do you know with whom I have lived all these years? There is the minister, who comes reeling home from the crossroads ordinary, who swears over the dice, who teaches cunning that he calls wisdom, laughs at man and scarce believes in God. His hand is heavy; this is his mark." She held up her bruised wrist to the light, then let the hand drop. When she spoke of the minister, she made a gesture toward the shadows growing ever thicker and darker in the body of the house. It was as though she saw him there, and was pointing him out. "There is the minister's wife," she said, and the motion of her hand again accused the shadows. "Oh, their roof has sheltered me; I have eaten of their bread. But truth is truth. There is the schoolmaster with the branded hands. He taught me, you know. There is"—she was looking with wide eyes into the deepest of the shadows—"there is Hugon!" Her voice died away. Haward did not move or speak, and for a minute there was silence in the dusky playhouse. Audrey broke it with a laugh, soft, light, and clear, that came oddly upon the mood of the hour. Presently she was speaking again: "Do you think it strange that I should laugh? I laughed to think I have escaped them all. Do you know that they call me a dreamer? Once, deep in the woods, I met the witch who lives at the head of the creek. She told me that I was a dream child, and that all my life was a dream, and I must pray never to awake; but I do not think she knew, for all that she is a witch. They none of them know,—none, none! If I had not dreamed, as they call it,—if I had watched, and listened, and laid to heart, and become like them,—oh, then I should have died of your look when at last you came! But I 'dreamed;' and in that long dream you, though you were overseas, you showed me, little by little, that the spirit is not bond, but free,—that it can walk the waves, and climb to the sunset and the stars. And I found that the woods were fair, that the earth was fair and kind as when I was a little child. And I grew to love and long for goodness. And, day by day, I have had a life and a world where flowers bloomed, and the streams ran fresh, and there was bread indeed to eat. And it was you that showed me the road, that opened for me the gates!"

She ceased to speak, and, turning fully toward him, took his hand and put it to her lips. "May you be very happy!" she said. "I thank you, sir, that when you came at last you did not break my dream. The dream fell short!"

The smile upon her face was very sweet, very pure and noble. She would have gone without another word, but Haward caught her by the sleeve. "Stay awhile!" he cried.

"I too am a dreamer, though not like you, you maid of Dian, dark saint, cold vestal, with your eyes forever on the still, white flame! Audrey, Audrey, Audrey! Do you know what a pretty name you have, child, or how dark are your eyes, or how fine this hair that a queen might envy? Westover has been dull, child."

Audrey shook her head and smiled, and thought that he was laughing at her. A vision of Evelyn, as Evelyn had looked that morning, passed before her. She did not believe that he had found Westover dull.

"I am coming to Fair View, dark Audrey," he went on. "In its garden there are roses yet blooming for thy hair; there are sweet verses calling to be read; there are cool, sequestered walks to be trodden, with thy hand in mine,— thy hand in mine, little maid. Life is but once; we shall never pass this way again. Drink the cup, wear the roses, live the verses! Of what sing all the sweetest verses, dark-eyed witch, forest Audrey?"

"Of love," said Audrey simply. She had freed her hand from his clasp, and her face was troubled. She did not understand; never had she seen him like this, with shining eyes and hot, unsteady touch.

"There is the ball at the Palace to-morrow night," he went on. "I must be there, for a fair lady and I are to dance together." He smiled. "Poor Audrey, who hath never been to a ball; who only dances with the elves, beneath the moon, around a beechen tree! The next day I will go to Fair View, and you will be at the glebe house, and we will take up the summer where we left it, that weary month ago."

"No, no," said Audrey hurriedly, and shook her head. A

vague and formless trouble had laid its cold touch upon her heart; it was as though she saw a cloud coming up, but it was no larger than a man's hand, and she knew not what it should portend, nor that it would grow into a storm. He was strange to-day,—that she felt; but then all her day since the coming of Evelyn had been sad and strange.

The shaft of sunshine was gone from the stage, and all the house was in shadow. Audrey descended the two or three steps leading into the pit, and Haward followed her. Side by side they left the playhouse, and found themselves in the garden, and also in the presence of five or six ladies and gentlemen, seated upon the grass beneath a mulberry-tree, or engaged in rifling the grape arbor of its purple fruit.

The garden was a public one, and this gay little party, having tired of the Indian spectacle, had repaired hither to treat of its own affairs. Moreover, it had been there, scattered upon the grass in view of the playhouse door, for the better part of an hour. Concerned with its own wit and laughter, it had caught no sound of low voices issuing from the theatre; and for the two who talked within, all outward noise had ranked as coming from the distant, crowded fields.

A young girl, her silken apron raised to catch the clusters which a gentleman, mounted upon a chair, threw down, gave a little scream and let fall her purple hoard. "'Gad!" cried the gentleman. One and another exclaimed, and a withered beauty seated beneath the mulberry-tree laughed shrilly.

A moment, an effort, a sharp recall of wandering thoughts, and Haward had the situation in hand. An easy greeting to the gentlemen, debonair compliments for the ladies, a question or two as to the entertainment they had left, then a negligent bringing forward of Audrey. "A little brown ward and ancient playmate of mine,—shot up in the night to be as tall as a woman. Make thy curtsy, child, and go tell the minister what I have said on the subject he wots of."

Audrey curtsied and went away, having never raised her eyes to note the stare of curiosity, the suppressed smile, the glance from eye to eye, which had trod upon her introduction to the company. Haward, remaining with his friends and acquaintances, gathered grapes for the blooming girl and the withered beauty, and for a little, smiling woman who was known for as arrant a scandal-monger as could be found in Virginia.

CHAPTER XVIII

A QUESTION OF COLORS

Evelyn, seated at her toilette table, and in the hands of Mr. Timothy Green, hairdresser in ordinary to Williamsburgh, looked with unseeing eyes at her own fair reflection in the glass before her. Chloe, the black handmaiden who stood at the door, latch in hand, had time to grow tired of waiting before her mistress spoke. "You may tell Mr. Haward that I am at home, Chloe. Bring him here."

The hairdresser drew a comb through the rippling brown tresses and commenced his most elaborate arrangement, working with pursed lips, and head bent now to this side, now to that. He had been a hard-pressed man since sunrise, and the lighting of the Palace candles that night might find him yet employed by some belated dame. Evelyn was very pale, and shadows were beneath her eyes. Moved by a sudden impulse, she took from the table a rouge pot, and hastily and with trembling fingers rubbed bloom into her cheeks; then the patch box,—one, two, three Tory partisans. "Now I am less like a ghost," she said, "Mr. Green, do I not look well and merry, and as though my sleep had been sound and dreamless?"

In his high, cracked voice, the hairdresser was sure that,

pale or glowing, grave or gay, Mistress Evelyn Byrd would be the toast at the ball that night. The lady laughed, for she heard Haward's step upon the landing. He entered to the gay, tinkling sound, tent over the hand she extended, then, laying aside hat and cane, took his seat beside the table.

"'Fair tresses man's imperial race insnare,
And beauty draws us with a single hair,'"

he quoted, with a smile. Then: "Will you take our hearts in blue to-night, Evelyn? You know that I love you best in blue."

She lifted her fan from the table, and waved it lightly to and fro. "I go in rose color," she said. "'Tis the gown I wore at Lady Rich's rout. I dare say you do not remember it? But my Lord of Peterborough said"—She broke off, and smiled to her fan.

Her voice was sweet and slightly drawling. The languid turn of the wrist, the easy grace of attitude, the beauty of bared neck and tinted face, of lowered lids and slow, faint smile,—oh, she was genuine fine lady, if she was not quite Evelyn! A breeze blowing through the open windows stirred their gay hangings of flowered cotton; the black girl sat in a corner and sewed; the supple fingers of the hairdresser went in and out of the heavy hair; roses in a deep blue bowl made the room smell like a garden. Haward sighed, so pleasant was it to sit quietly in this cool chamber, after the glare and wavering of the world without. "My Lord of Peterborough is magnificent at compliments," he said kindly, "but 'twould be a jeweled speech indeed that outdid your deserving, Evelyn. Come, now, wear the blue! I will find you white roses; you shall wear them for a breast knot, and in the minuet return me one again."

Evelyn waved her fan. "I dance the minuet with Mr. Lee." Her tone was still sweetly languid, her manner most indifferent. The thick and glossy tress that, drawn forward, was to ripple over white neck and bosom was too loosely curled. She regarded it in the mirror with an anxious frown, then spoke of it to the hairdresser.

Haward, smiling, watched her with heavy-lidded eyes. "Mr. Lee is a fortunate gentleman," he said. "I may gain the rose, perhaps, in the country dance?"

"That is better," remarked the lady, surveying with satisfaction the new-curled lock. "The country dance? For that Mr. Lightfoot hath my promise."

"It seems that I am a laggard," said Haward.

The knocker sounded below. "I am at home, Chloe," announced the mistress; and the slave, laying aside her work, slipped from the room.

Haward played with the trifles upon the dressing table. "Wherein have I offended, Evelyn?" he asked, at last.

The lady arched her brows, and the action made her for the moment very like her handsome father. "Why, there is no offense!" she cried. "An old acquaintance, a family friend! I step a minuet with Mr. Lee; I stand up for a country dance with Mr. Lightfoot; I wear pink instead of blue, and have lost my liking for white roses,—what is there in all this that needs such a question? Ah, you have broken my silver chain!"

"I am clumsy to-day!" he exclaimed. "A thousand

pardons!" He let the broken toy slip from his fingers to the polished surface of the table, and forgot that it was there. "Since Colonel Byrd (I am sorry to learn) keeps his room with a fit of the gout, may I—an old acquaintance, a family friend—conduct you to the Palace to-night?"

The fan waved on. "Thank you, but I go in our coach, and need no escort." The lady yawned, very delicately, behind her slender fingers; then dropped the fan, and spoke with animation: "Ah, here is Mr. Lee! In a good hour, sir! I saw the bracelet that you mended for Mistress Winston. Canst do as much for my poor chain here? See! it and this silver heart have parted company."

Mr. Lee kissed her hand, and took snuff with Mr. Haward; then, after an ardent speech crammed with references to Vulcan and Venus, chains that were not slight, hearts that were of softer substance, sat down beside this kind and dazzling vision, and applied his clever fingers to the problem in hand. He was a personable young gentleman, who had studied at Oxford, and who, proudly conscious that his tragedy of Artaxerxes, then reposing in the escritoire at home, much outmerited Haward's talked-of comedy, felt no diffidence in the company of the elder fine gentleman. He rattled on of this and that, and Evelyn listened kindly, with only the curve of her cheek visible to the family friend. The silver heart was restored to its chain; the lady smiled her thanks; the enamored youth hitched his chair some inches nearer the fair whom he had obliged, and, with his hand upon his heart, entered the realm of high-flown speech. The gay curtains waved; the roses were sweet; black Chloe sewed and sewed; the hairdresser's hands wove in and out, as though he were a wizard making passes.

Haward rose to take his leave. Evelyn yielded him her

hand; it was cold against his lips. She was nonchalant and smiling; he was easy, unoffended, admirably the fine gentleman. For one moment their eyes met. "I had been wiser," thought the man, "I had been wiser to have myself told her of that brown witch, that innocent sorceress! Why something held my tongue I know not. Now she hath read my idyl, but all darkened, all awry." The woman thought: "Cruel and base! You knew that my heart was yours to break, cast aside, and forget!"

Out of the house the sunlight beat and blinded. Houses of red brick, houses of white wood; the long, wide, dusty Duke of Gloucester Street; gnarled mulberry-trees broadleafed against a September sky, deeply, passionately blue; glimpses of wood and field,—all seemed remote without distance, still without stillness, the semblance of a dream, and yet keen and near to oppression. It was a town of stores, of ordinaries and public places; from open door and window all along Duke of Gloucester Street came laughter, round oaths, now and then a scrap of drinking song. To Haward, giddy, ill at ease, sickening of a fever, the sounds were now as a cry in his ear, now as the noise of a distant sea. The minister of James City parish and the minister of Ware Creek were walking before him, arm in arm, set full sail for dinner after a stormy morning. "For lo! the wicked prospereth!" said one, and "Fair View parish bound over to the devil again!" plained the other. "He's firm in the saddle; he'll ride easy to the day he drinks himself to death, thanks to this sudden complaisance of Governor and Commissary!"

"Thanks to"—cried the other sourly, and gave the thanks where they were due.

Haward heard the words, but even in the act of quickening his pace to lay a heavy hand upon the speaker's shoulder a listlessness came upon him, and he forbore. The memory of the slurring speech went from him; his thoughts were thistledown blown hither and yon by every vagrant air. Coming to Marot's ordinary he called for wine; then went up the stair to his room, and sitting down at the table presently fell asleep, with his head upon his arms.

After a while the sounds from the public room below, where men were carousing, disturbed his slumber. He stirred, and awoke refreshed. It was afternoon, but he felt no hunger, only thirst, which he quenched with the wine at hand. His windows gave upon the Capitol and a green wood beyond; the waving trees enticed, while the room was dull and the noises of the house distasteful. He said to himself that he would walk abroad, would go out under the beckoning trees and be rid of the town. He remembered that the Council was to meet that afternoon. Well, it might sit without him! He was for the woods, where dwelt the cool winds and the shadows deep and silent.

A few yards, and he was quit of Duke of Gloucester Street; behind him, porticoed Capitol, gaol, and tiny vineclad debtor's prison. In the gaol yard the pirates sat upon a bench in the sunshine, and one smoked a long pipe, and one brooded upon his irons. Gold rings were in their ears, and their black hair fell from beneath colored handkerchiefs twisted turbanwise around their brows. The gaoler watched them, standing in his doorway, and his children, at play beneath a tree, built with sticks a mimic scaffold, and hanged thereon a broken puppet. There was a shady road leading through a wood to Queen's Creek and the Capitol Landing, and down this road went Haward. His step was light; the dullness, the throbbing pulses, the oppression of the morning, had given way to a restlessness and a strange exaltation of spirit. Fancy was quickened, imagination heightened; to himself he seemed to see the heart of all things. Across his mind flitted fragments of verse,—now a broken line just hinting beauty, now the pure passion of a lovely stanza. His thoughts went to and fro, mobile as the waves of the sea; but firm as the reefs beneath them stood his knowledge that presently he was going back to Fair View. To-morrow, when the Governor's ball was over, when he could decently get away, he would leave the town; he would go to his house in the country. Late flowers bloomed in his garden; the terrace was fair above the river; beneath the red brick wall, on the narrow little creek shining like a silver highway, lay a winged boat; and the highway ran past a glebe house; and in the glebe house dwelt a dryad whose tree had closed against her. Audrey!—a fair name. Audrey, Audrey!—the birds were singing it; out of the deep, Arcadian shadows any moment it might come, clearly cried by satyr, Pan, or shepherd. Hark! there was song—

It was but a negro on the road behind, singing to himself as he went about his master's business. The voice was the voice of the race, mellow, deep, and plaintive; perhaps the song was of love in a burning land. He passed the white man, and the arching trees hid him, but the wake of music was long in fading. The road leading through a cool and shady dell, Haward left it, and took possession of the mossy earth beneath a holly-tree. Here, lying on the ground, he could see the road through the intervening foliage; else the place had seemed the heart of an ancient wood.

It was merry lying where were glimpses of blue sky, where the leaves quivered and a squirrel chattered and a robin sang a madrigal. Youth the divine, half way down the stair of misty yesterdays, turned upon his heel and came back to him. He pillowed his head upon his arm, and was content. It was well to be so filled with fancies, so iron of will, so headstrong and gay; to be friends once more with a younger Haward, with the Haward of a mountain pass, of mocking comrades and an irate Excellency.

From the road came a rumble of oaths. Sailors, sweating and straining, were rolling a very great cask of tobacco from a neighboring warehouse down to the landing and some expectant sloop. Haward, lying at ease, smiled at their weary task, their grunting and swearing; when they were gone, smiled at the blankness of the road. All things pleased. There was food for mirth in the call of a partridge, in the inquisitive gaze of a squirrel, in the web of a spider gaoler to a gilded fly. There was food for greater mirth in the appearance on the road of a solitary figure in a wine-colored coat and bushy black peruke.

Haward sat up. "Ha, Monacan!" he cried, with a laugh, and threw a stick to attract the man's attention.

Hugon turned, stood astare, then left the road and came down into the dell.

"What fortune, trader?" smiled Haward. "Did your traps hold in the great forest? Were your people easy to fool, giving twelve deerskins for an old match-coat? There is charm in a woodsman life. Come, tell me of your journeys, dangers, and escapes."

The half-breed looked down upon him with a twitching face. "What hinders me from killing you now?" he demanded, with a backward look at the road. "None may pass for many minutes."

Haward lay back upon the moss, with his hands locked beneath his head. "What indeed?" he answered calmly. "Come, here is a velvet log, fit seat for an emperor—or a sachem; sit and tell me of your life in the woods. For peace pipe let me offer my snuffbox." In his mad humor he sat up again, drew from his pocket, and presented with the most approved flourish, his box of chased gold. "Monsieur, c'est le tabac pour le nez d'un inonarque," he said lazily.

Hugon sat down upon the log, helped himself to the mixture with a grand air, and shook the yellow dust from his ruffles. The action, meant to be airy, only achieved fierceness. From some hidden sheath he drew a knife, and began to strip from the log a piece of bark. "Tell me, you," he said. "Have you been to France? What manner of land is it?"

"A gay country," answered Haward; "a land where the men are all white, and where at present, periwigs are worn much shorter than the one monsieur affects."

"He is a great brave, a French gentleman? Always he kills the man he hates?"

"Not always," said the other. "Sometimes the man he hates kills him."

By now one end of the piece of bark in the trader's hands was shredded to tinder. He drew from his pocket his flint and steel, and struck a spark into the frayed mass. It flared up, and he held first the tips of his fingers, then the palm of his hand, then his bared forearm, in the flame that licked and scorched the flesh. His face was perfectly unmoved, his eyes unchanged in their expression of hatred. "Can he do this?" he asked.

"Perhaps not," said Haward lightly. "It is a very foolish thing to do."

The flame died out, and the trader tossed aside the charred bit of bark. "There was old Pierre at Monacan-Town who taught me to pray to *le bon Dieu*. He told me how grand and fine is a French gentleman, and that I was the son of many such. He called the English great pigs, with brains as dull and muddy as the river after many rains. My mother was the daughter of a chief. She had strings of pearl for her neck, and copper for her arms, and a robe of white doeskin, very soft and fine. When she was dead and my father was dead, I came from Monacan-Town to your English school over yonder. I can read and write. I am a white man and a Frenchman, not an Indian. When I go to the villages in the woods, I am given a lodge apart, and the men and women gather to hear a white man speak.... You have done me wrong with that girl, that Ma'm'selle Audrey that I wish for wife. We are enemies: that is as it should be. You shall not have her,—never, never! But you despise me; how is that? That day upon the creek, that night in your cursed house, you laughed"—

The Haward of the mountain pass, regarding the twitching face opposite him and the hand clenched upon the handle of a knife, laughed again. At the sound the trader's face ceased to twitch. Haward felt rather than saw the stealthy tightening of the frame, the gathering of forces, the closer grasp upon the knife, and flung out his arm. A hare scurried past, making for the deeper woods. From the road came the tramp of a horse and a man's voice, singing,—

"'To all you ladies now on land'"—

while an inquisitive dog turned aside from the road, and

plunged into the dell.

The rider, having checked his horse and quit his song in order to call to his dog, looked through the thin veil of foliage and saw the two men beneath the holly-tree. "Ha, Jean Hugon!" he cried. "Is that you? Where is that packet of skins you were to deliver at my store? Come over here, man!"

The trader moistened his dry lips with his tongue, and slipped the knife back into its sheath. "Had we been a mile in the woods," he said, "you would have laughed no more."

Haward watched him go. The argument with the rider was a lengthy one. He upon horseback would not stand still in the road to finish it, but put his beast into motion. The trader, explaining and gesticulating, walked beside his stirrup; the voices grew fainter and fainter,—were gone. Haward laughed to himself; then, with his eyes raised to the depth on depth of blue, serene beyond the grating of thorn-pointed leaves, sent his spirit to his red brick house and silent, sunny garden, with the gate in the ivied wall, and the six steps down to the boat and the lapping water.

The shadows lengthened, and a wind of the evening entered the wood. Haward shook off the lethargy that had kept him lying there for the better part of an afternoon, rose to his feet, and left the green dell for the road, all shadow now, winding back to the toy metropolis, to Marot's ordinary, to the ball at the Palace that night.

The ball at the Palace!—he had forgotten it. Flare of lights, wail of violins, a painted, silken crowd, laughter, whispers, magpie chattering, wine, and the weariness of the dance, when his soul would long to be with the night outside, with the rising wind and the shining stars. He half determined not to go. What mattered the offense that would be taken? Did he go he would repent, wearied and ennuye, watching Evelyn, all rose-colored, moving with another through the minuet; tied himself perhaps to some pert miss, or cornered in a card-room by boisterous gamesters, or, drinking with his peers, called on to toast the lady of his dreams. Better the dull room at Marot's ordinary, or better still to order Mirza, and ride off at the planter's pace, through the starshine, to Fair View. On the river bank before the store MacLean might be lying, dreaming of a mighty wind and a fierce death. He would dismount, and sit beside that Highland gentleman, Jacobite and strong man, and their moods would chime as they had chimed before. Then on to the house and to the eastern window! Not to-night, but to-morrow night, perhaps, would the darkness be pierced by the calm pale star that marked another window. It was all a mistake, that month at Westover,—days lost and wasted, the running of golden sands ill to spare from Love's brief glass....

His mood had changed when, with the gathering dusk, he entered his room at Marot's ordinary. He would go to the Palace that night; it would be the act of a boy to fling away through the darkness, shirking a duty his position demanded. He would go and be merry, watching Evelyn in the gown that Peterborough had praised.

When Juba had lighted the candles, he sat and drank and drank again of the red wine upon the table. It put maggots in his brain, fired and flushed him to the spirit's core. An idea came, at which he laughed. He bade it go, but it would not. It stayed, and his fevered fancy played around it as a moth around a candle. At first he knew it for a notion, bizarre and absurd, which presently he would dismiss. All day strange thoughts had come and gone, appearing, disappearing, like will-o'-the-wisps for which a man upon a firm road has no care. Never fear that he will follow them! He sees the marsh, that it has no footing. So with this Jack-o'-lantern conception,—it would vanish as it came.

It did not so. Instead, when he had drunken more wine, and had sat for some time methodically measuring, over and over again, with thumb and forefinger, the distance from candle to bottle, and from bottle to glass, the idea began to lose its wildfire aspect. In no great time it appeared an inspiration as reasonable as happy. When this point had been reached, he stamped upon the floor to summon his servant from the room below. "Lay out the white and gold, Juba," he ordered, when the negro appeared, "and come make me very fine. I am for the Palace,—I and a brown lady that hath bewitched me! The white sword knot, sirrah; and cock my hat with the diamond brooch"—

It was a night that was thronged with stars, and visited by a whispering wind. Haward, walking rapidly along the almost deserted Nicholson Street, lifted his burning forehead to the cool air and the star-strewn fields of heaven. Coming to the gate by which he had entered the afternoon before, he raised the latch and passed into the garden. By now his fever was full upon him, and it was a man scarce to be held responsible for his actions that presently knocked at the door of the long room where, at the window opening upon Palace Street, Audrey sat with Mistress Stagg and watched the people going to the ball.

CHAPTER XIX

THE GOVERNOR'S BALL

For an hour it had been very quiet, very peaceful, in the small white house on Palace Street. Darden was not there; for the Commissary had sent for him, having certain inquiries to make and a stern warning to deliver. Mistress Deborah had been asked to spend the night with an acquaintance in the town, so she also was out and gone. Mistress Stagg and Audrey kept the lower rooms, while overhead Mr. Charles Stagg, a man that loved his art, walked up and down, and, with many wavings of a laced handkerchief and much resort to a gilt snuffbox, reasoned with Plato of death and the soul. The murmur of his voice came down to the two women, and made the only sound in the house. Audrey, sitting by the window, her chin upon her hand and her dark hair shadowing her face, looked out upon the dooryard and the Palace Street beyond. The street was lit by torches, and people were going to the ball in coaches and chariots, on foot and in painted chairs. They went gayly, light of heart, fine of person, a free and generous folk. Laughter floated over to the silent watcher, and the torchlight gave her glimpses of another land than her own.

Many had been Mistress Stagg's customers since morning,

and something had she heard besides admiration of her wares and exclamation at her prices. Now, as she sat with some gay sewing beneath her nimble fingers, she glanced once and again at the shadowed face opposite her. If the look was not one of curiosity alone, but had in it an admixture of new-found respect; if to Mistress Stagg the Audrey of yesterday, unnoted, unwhispered of, was a being somewhat lowlier than the Audrey of to-day, it may be remembered for her that she was an actress of the early eighteenth century, and that fate and an old mother to support had put her in that station.

The candles beneath their glass shades burned steadily; the house grew very quiet; the noises of the street lessened and lessened, for now nearly all of the people were gone to the ball. Audrey watched the round of light cast by the nearest torch. For a long time she had watched it, thinking that he might perhaps cross the circle, and she might see him in his splendor. She was still watching when he knocked at the garden door.

Mistress Stagg, sitting in a dream of her own, started violently. "La, now, who may that be?" she exclaimed. "Go to the door, child. If 'tis a stranger, we shelter none such, to be taken up for the harboring of runaways!"

Audrey went to the door and opened it. A moment's pause, a low cry, and she moved backward to the wall, where she stood with her slender form sharply drawn against the white plaster, and with the fugitive, elusive charm of her face quickened into absolute beauty, imperious for attention. Haward, thus ushered into the room, gave the face its due. His eyes, bright and fixed, were for it alone. Mistress Stagg's curtsy went unacknowledged save by a slight, mechanical motion of his hand, and her inquiry as to what he lacked that she could supply received no answer. He was a very handsome man, of a bearing both easy and commanding, and to-night he was splendidly dressed in white satin with embroidery of gold. To one of the women he seemed the king, who could do no wrong; to the other, more learned in the book of the world, he was merely a fine gentleman, whose way might as well be given him at once, since, spite of denial, he would presently take it.

Haward sat down, resting his clasped hands upon the table, gazing steadfastly at the face, dark and beautiful, set like a flower against the wall. "Come, little maid!" he said. "We are going to the ball together, you and I. Hasten, or we shall not be in time for the minuet."

Audrey smiled and shook her head, thinking that it was his pleasure to laugh at her a little. Mistress Stagg likewise showed her appreciation of the pleasantry. When he repeated his command, speaking in an authoritative tone and with a glance at his watch, there was a moment of dead silence; then, "Go your ways, sir, and dance with Mistress Evelyn Byrd!" cried the scandalized ex-actress. "The Governor's ball is not for the likes of Audrey!"

"I will be judge of that," he answered. "Come, let us be off, child! Or stay! hast no other dress than that?" He looked toward the mistress of the house. "I warrant that Mistress Stagg can trick you out! I would have you go fine, Audrey of the hair! Audrey of the eyes! Audrey of the full brown throat! Dull gold,—have you that, now, mistress, in damask or brocade? Soft laces for her bosom, and a yellow bloom in her hair. It should be dogwood, Audrey, like the coronal you wore on May Day. Do you remember, child? The white stars in your hair, and the Maypole all aflutter, and your feet upon the green grass"—

"Oh, I was happy then!" cried Audrey and wrung her hands. Within a moment, however, she was calm again, and could look at him with a smile. "I am only Audrey," she said. "You know that the ball is not for me. Why then do you tell me that I must go? It is your kindness; I know that it is your kindness that speaks. But yet—but yet"— She gazed at him imploringly: then from his steady smile caught a sudden encouragement. "Oh!" she exclaimed with a gesture of quick relief, and with tremulous laughter in her face and voice,—"oh, you are mocking me! You only came to show how a gentleman looks who goes to a Governor's ball!"

For the moment, in her relief at having read his riddle, there slipped from her the fear of she knew not what,— the strangeness and heaviness of heart that had been her portion since she came to Williamsburgh. Leaving the white wall against which she had leaned, she came a little forward, and with gayety and grace dropped him a curtsy. "Oh, the white satin like the lilies in your garden!" she laughed. "And the red heels to your shoes, and the gold-fringed sword knot, and the velvet scabbard! Ah, let me see your sword, how bright and keen it is!"

She was Audrey of the garden, and Haward, smiling, drew his rapier and laid it in her hands. She looked at the golden hilt, and passed her brown fingers along the gleaming blade. "Stainless," she said, and gave it back to him.

Taking it, he took also the hand that had proffered it. "I was not laughing, child," he said. "Go to the ball thou shalt, and with me. What! Thou art young and fair. Shalt have no pleasure"—

"What pleasure in that?" cried Audrey. "I may not go, sir;

nay, I will not go!"

She freed her hand, and stood with heaving bosom and eyes that very slowly filled with tears. Haward saw no reason for her tears. It was true that she was young and fair; true, also, that she had few pleasures. Well, he would change all that. The dance,—was it not woven by those nymphs of old, those sprites of open spaces in the deep woods, from whose immemorial company she must have strayed into this present time? Now at the Palace the candles were burning for her, for her the music was playing. Her welcome there amidst the tinsel people? Trust him for that: he was what he was, and could compass greater things than that would be. Go she should, because it pleased him to please her, and because it was certainly necessary for him to oppose pride with pride, and before the eyes of Evelyn demonstrate his indifference to that lady's choice of Mr. Lee for the minuet and Mr. Lightfoot for the country dance. This last thought had far to travel from some unused, deep-down quagmire of the heart, but it came. For the rest, the image of Audrey decked in silk and lace, turned by her apparel into a dark Court lady, a damsel in waiting to Queen Titania, caught his fancy in both hands. He wished to see her thus,—wished it so strongly that he knew it would come to pass. He was a gentleman who had acquired the habit of having his own way. There had been times when the price of his way had seemed too dear; when he had shrugged his shoulders and ceased to desire what he would not buy. To-night he was not able to count the cost. But he knew—he knew cruelly well—how to cut short this fruitless protest of a young girl who thought him all that was wise and great and good.

"So you cannot say 'yes' to my asking, little maid?" he began, quiet and smiling. "Cannot trust me that I have reasons for the asking? Well, I will not ask again, Audrey, since it is so great a thing'"—"Oh," cried Audrey, "you know that I would die for you!" The tears welled over, but she brushed them away with a trembling hand; then stood with raised face, her eyes soft and dewy, a strange smile upon her lips. She spoke at last as simply as a child: "Why you want me, that am only Audrey, to go with you to the Palace yonder, I cannot tell. But I will go, though I am only Audrey, and I have no other dress than this"—

Haward got unsteadily to his feet, and lightly touched the dark head that she bowed upon her hands. "Why, now you are Audrey again," he said approvingly. "Why, child, I would do you a pleasure!" He turned to the player's wife. "She must not go in this guise. Have you no finery stowed away?"

Now, Mistress Stagg, though much scandalized, and very certain that all this would never do, was in her way an artist, and could see as in a mirror what bare throat and shoulders, rich hair drawn loosely up, a touch of rouge, a patch or two, a silken gown, might achieve for Audrey. And after all, had not Deborah told her that the girl was Mr. Haward's ward, not Darden's, and that though Mr. Haward came and went as he pleased, and was very kind to Audrey, so that Darden was sure of getting whatever the girl asked for, yet she was a good girl, and there was no harm? For the talk that day,—people were very idle, and given to thinking the forest afire when there was only the least curl of smoke. And in short and finally it was none of her business; but with the aid of a certain chest upstairs, she knew what she could do! To the ball might go a beauty would make Mistress Evelyn Byrd look to her laurels!

"There's the birthday dress that Madam Carter sent us

only last week," she began hesitatingly. "It's very beautiful, and a'most as good as new, and 'twould suit you to a miracle—But I vow you must not go, Audrey!... To be sure, the damask is just the tint for you, and there are roses would answer for your hair. But la, sir, you know 'twill never do, never in this world."

Half an hour later, Haward rose from his chair and bowed low as to some highborn and puissant dame. The fever that was now running high in his veins flushed his cheek and made his eyes exceedingly bright. When he went up to Audrey, and in graceful mockery of her sudden coming into her kingdom, took her hand and, bending, kissed it, the picture that they made cried out for some painter to preserve it. Her hand dropped from his clasp, and buried itself in rich folds of flowered damask; the quick rise and fall of her bosom stirred soft, yellowing laces, and made to flash like diamonds some ornaments of marcasite; her face was haunting in its pain and bewilderment and great beauty, and in the lie which her eyes gave to the false roses beneath those homes of sadness and longing. She had no word to say, she was "only Audrey," and she could not understand. But she wished to do his bidding, and so, when he cried out upon her melancholy, and asked her if 'twere indeed a Sunday in New England instead of a Saturday in Virginia, she smiled, and strove to put on the mind as well as the garb of a gay lady who might justly go to the Governor's ball.

Half frightened at her own success, Mistress Stagg hovered around her, giving this or that final touch to her costume; but it was Haward himself who put the roses in her hair. "A little longer, and we will walk once more in my garden at Fair View," he said. "June shall come again for us, and we will tread the quiet paths, my sweet, and all the roses shall bloom again for us. There, you are crowned! Hail, Queen!"

Audrey felt the touch of his lips upon her forehead, and shivered. All her world was going round; she could not steady it, could not see aright, knew not what was happening. The strangeness made her dizzy. She hardly heard Mistress Stagg's last protest that it would never do,—never in the world; hardly knew when she left the house. She was out beneath the stars, moving toward a lit Palace whence came the sound of violins. Haward's arm was beneath her hand; his voice was in her ear, but it was as the wind's voice, whose speech she did not understand. Suddenly they were within the Palace garden, with its winding, torchlit walks, and the terraces at the side; suddenly again, they had mounted the Palace steps, and the doors were open, and she was confronted with lights and music and shifting, dazzling figures. She stood still, clasped her hands, and gave Haward a piteous look. Her face, for all its beauty and its painted roses, was strangely the child's face that had lain upon his breast, where he knelt amid the corn, in the valley between the hills, so long ago. He gave her mute appeal no heed. The Governor's guests, passing from room to room, crossed and recrossed the wide hall, and down the stairway, to meet a row of gallants impatient at its foot, came fair women, one after the other, the flower of the colony, clothed upon like the lilies of old. Haward, entering with Audrey, saw Mr. Lee at the stairfoot, and, raising his eyes, was aware of Evelyn descending alone and some-what slowly, all in rose color, and with a smile upon her lips.

She was esteemed the most beautiful woman in Virginia, the most graceful and accomplished. Wit and charm and fortune were hers, and the little gay world of Virginia had mated her with Mr. Marmaduke Haward of Fair View.

Therefore that portion of it that chanced to be in the hall of the Governor's house withdrew for the moment its attention from its own affairs, and bestowed it upon those of the lady descending the stairs, and of the gold-and-white gentleman who, with a strange beauty at his side, stood directly in her path. It was a very wise little world, and since yesterday afternoon had been fairly bursting with its own knowledge. It knew all about that gypsy who had come to town from Fair View parish,—"La, my dear, just the servant of a minister!"—and knew to a syllable what had passed in the violent quarrel to which Mr. Lee owed his good fortune.

That triumphant gentleman now started forward, and, with a low bow, extended his hand to lead to the ballroom this rose-colored paragon and cynosure of all eyes. Evelyn smiled upon him, and gave him her scarf to hold, but would not be hurried; must first speak to her old friend Mr. Haward, and tell him that her father's foot could now bear the shoe, and that he might appear before the ball was over. This done, she withdrew her gaze, from Haward's strangely animated, vividly handsome countenance, and turned it upon the figure at his side. "Pray present me!" she said quickly. "I do not think I have the honor of knowing"—

Audrey raised her head, that had been bent, and looked again, as she had looked yesterday, with all her innocent soul and heavy heart, into the eyes of the princess. The smile died from Evelyn's lips, and a great wave of indignant red surged over face and neck and bosom. The color fled, but not the bitter anger. So he could bring his fancy there! Could clothe her that was a servant wench in a splendid gown, and flaunt her before the world—before the world that must know—oh, God! must know how she herself loved him! He could do this after that month at

Westover! She drew her breath, and met the insult fairly. "I withdraw my petition," she said clearly. "Now that I bethink me, my acquaintance is already somewhat too great. Mr. Lee, shall we not join the company? I have yet to make my curtsy to his Excellency."

With head erect, and with no attention to spare from the happy Mr. Lee, she passed the sometime suitor for her hand and the apple of discord which it had pleased him to throw into the assembly. A whisper ran around the hall. Audrey heard suppressed laughter, and heard a speech which she did not understand, but which was uttered in an angry voice, much like Mistress Deborah's when she chided. A sudden terror of herself and of Haward's world possessed her. She turned where she stood in her borrowed plumage, and clung to his hand and arm. "Let me go," she begged. "It is all a mistake,—all wrong. Let me go,—let me go."

He laughed at her, shaking his head and looking into her beseeching face with shining, far-off eyes. "Thou dear fool!" he said. "The ball is made for thee, and all these folk are here to do thee honor!" Holding her by the hand, he moved with her toward a wide doorway, through which could be seen a greater throng of beautifully dressed ladies and gentlemen. Music came from this room, and she saw that there were dancers, and that beyond them, upon a sort of dais, and before a great carved chair, stood a fine gentleman who, she knew, must be his Excellency the Governor of Virginia.

CHAPTER XX

THE UNINVITED GUEST

"Mistress Audrey?" said the Governor graciously, as the lady in damask rose from her curtsy. "Mistress Audrey whom? Mr. Haward, you gave me not the name of the stock that hath flowered in so beauteous a bloom."

"Why, sir, the bloom is all in all,'" answered Haward. "What root it springs from matters not. I trust that your Excellency is in good health,—that you feel no touch of our seasoning fever?"

"I asked the lady's name, sir," said the Governor pointedly. He was standing in the midst of a knot of gentlemen, members of the Council and officers of the colony. All around the long room, seated in chairs arow against the walls, or gathered in laughing groups, or moving about with a rustle and gleam of silk, were the Virginians his guests. From the gallery, where were bestowed the musicians out of three parishes, floated the pensive strains of a minuet, and in the centre of the polished floor, under the eyes of the company, several couples moved and postured through that stately dance.

"The lady is my ward," said Haward lightly. "I call her

Audrey. Child, tell his Excellency your other name."

If he thought at all, he thought that she could do it. But such an estray, such a piece of flotsam, was Audrey, that she could not help him out. "They call me Darden's Audrey," she explained to the Governor. "If I ever heard my father's name, I have forgotten it."

Her voice, though low, reached all those who had ceased from their own concerns to stare at this strange guest, this dark-eyed, shrinking beauty, so radiantly attired. The whisper had preceded her from the hall: there had been fluttering and comment enough as, under the fire of all those eyes, she had passed with Haward to where stood the Governor receiving his guests. But the whisper had not reached his Excellency's ears. In London he had been slightly acquainted with Mr. Marmaduke Haward, and now knew him for a member of his Council, and a gentleman of much consequence in that Virginia which he had come to rule. Moreover, he had that very morning granted a favor to Mr. Haward, and by reason thereof was inclined to think amiably of the gentleman. Of the piece of dark loveliness whom the Virginian had brought forward to present, who could think otherwise? But his Excellency was a formal man, punctilious, and cautious of his state. The bow with which he received the strange lady's curtsy had been profound; in speaking to her he had made his tones honey-sweet, while his compliment quite capped the one just paid to Mistress Evelyn Byrd. And now it would appear that the lady had no name! Nay, from the looks that were being exchanged, and from the tittering that had risen amongst the younger of his guests, there must be more amiss than that! His Excellency frowned, drew himself up, and turned what was meant to be a searching and terrible eye upon the recreant in white satin. Audrey caught the look, for which Haward cared no whit. Oh, she knew that she had no business there,—she that only the other day had gone barefoot on Darden's errands, had been kept waiting in hall or kitchen of these people's houses! She knew that, for all her silken gown, she had no place among them; but she thought that they were not kind to stare and whisper and laugh, shaming her before one another and before him. Her heart swelled; to the dreamy misery of the day and evening was added a passionate sense of hurt and wrong and injustice. Her pride awoke, and in a moment taught her many things, though among them was no distrust of him. Brought to bay, she put out her hand and found a gate; pushed it open, and entered upon her heritage of art.

The change was so sudden that those who had stared at her sourly or scornfully, or with malicious amusement or some stirrings of pity, drew their breath and gave ground a little. Where was the shrinking, frightened, unbidden guest of a moment before, with downcast eyes and burning cheeks? Here was a proud and easy and radiant lady, with witching eyes and a wonderful smile. "I am only Audrey, your Excellency," she said, and curtsied as she spoke. "My other name lies buried in a valley amongst far-off mountains." She slightly turned, and addressed herself to a portly, velvet-clad gentleman, of a very authoritative air, who, arriving late, had just shouldered himself into the group about his Excellency. "By token," she smiled, "of a gold moidore that was paid for a loaf of bread."

The new Governor appealed to his predecessor. "What is this, Colonel Spotswood, what is this?" he demanded, somewhat testily, of the open-mouthed gentleman in velvet.

"Odso!" cried the latter. "'Tis the little maid of the

sugar-tree!—Marmaduke Haward's brown elf grown into the queen of all the fairies!" Crossing to Audrey he took her by the hand. "My dear child," he said, with a benevolence that sat well upon him, "I always meant to keep an eye upon thee, to see that Mr. Haward did by thee all that he swore he would do. But at first there were cares of state, and now for five years I have lived at Germanna, half way to thy mountains, where echoes from the world seldom reach me. Permit me, my dear." With a somewhat cumbrous gallantry, the innocent gentleman, who had just come to town and knew not the gossip thereof, bent and kissed her upon the cheek.

Audrey curtsied with a bright face to her old acquaintance of the valley and the long road thence to the settled country. "I have been cared for, sir," she said. "You see that I am happy."

She turned to Haward, and he drew her hand within his arm. "Ay, child," he said. "We are keeping others of the company from their duty to his Excellency. Besides, the minuet invites. I do not think I have heard music so sweet before to-night. Your Excellency's most obedient servant! Gentlemen, allow us to pass." The crowd opened before them, and they found themselves in the centre of the room. Two couples were walking a minuet; when they were joined by this dazzling third, the ladies bridled, bit their lips, and shot Parthian glances.

It was very fortunate, thought Audrey, that the Widow Constance had once, long ago, taught her to dance, and that, when they were sent to gather nuts or myrtle berries or fagots in the woods, she and Barbara were used to taking hands beneath the trees and moving with the glancing sunbeams and the nodding saplings and the swaying grapevine trailers. She that had danced to the wind in the pine tops could move with ease to the music of this night. And since it was so that with a sore and frightened and breaking heart one could yet, in some strange way, become quite another person,—any person that one chose to be,—these cruel folk should not laugh at her again! They had not laughed since, before the Governor yonder, she had suddenly made believe that she was a carefree, great lady. Well, she would make believe to them still.

Her eyes were as brilliant as Haward's that shone with fever; a smile stayed upon her lips; she moved with dignity through the stately dance, scarce erring once, graceful and fine in all that she did. Haward, enamored, his wits afire, went mechanically through the oft-trod measure, and swore to himself that he held in his hand the pearl of price, the nonpareil of earth. In this dance and under cover of the music they could speak to each other unheard of those about them.

"'Queen of all the fairies,' did he call you?" he asked. "That was well said. When we are at Fair View again, thou must show me where thou wonnest with thy court, in what moonlit haunt, by what cool stream"—

"I would I were this night at Fair View glebe house," said Audrey. "I would I were at home in the mountains."

Her voice, sunken with pain and longing, was for him alone. To the other dancers, to the crowded room at large, she seemed a brazen girl, with beauty to make a goddess, wit to mask as a great lady, effrontery to match that of the gentleman who had brought her here. The age was free, and in that London which was dear to the hearts of the Virginians ladies of damaged reputation were not so unusual a feature of fashionable entertainments as to receive any especial notice. But Williamsburgh was not London, and the dancer yonder, who held her rose-crowned head so high, was no lady of fashion. They knew her now for that dweller at Fair View gates of whom, during the summer just past, there had been whispering enough. Evidently, it was not for naught that Mr. Marmaduke Haward had refused invitations, given no entertainments, shut himself up at Fair View, slighting old friends and evincing no desire to make new ones. Why, the girl was a servant,—nothing more nor less; she belonged to Gideon Darden, the drunken minister; she was to have married Jean Hugon, the half-breed trader. Look how the Governor, enlightened at last, glowered at her; and how red was Colonel Spotswood's face; and how Mistress Evelyn Byrd, sitting in the midst of a little court of her own, made witty talk, smiled upon her circle of adorers, and never glanced toward the centre of the room, and the dancers there!

"You are so sweet and gay to-night," said Haward to Audrey. "Take your pleasure, child, for it is a sad world, and the blight will fall. I love to see you happy."

"Happy!" she answered. "I am not happy!"

"You are above them all in beauty," he went on. "There is not one here that's fit to tie your shoe."

"Oh me!" cried Audrey. "There is the lady that you love, and that loves you. Why did she look at me so, in the hall yonder? And yesterday, when she came to Mistress Stagg's, I might not touch her or speak to her! You told me that she was kind and good and pitiful. I dreamed that she might let me serve her when she came to Fair View."

"She will never come to Fair View," he said, "nor shall I

go again to Westover. I am for my own house now, you brown enchantress, and my own garden, and the boat upon the river. Do you remember how sweet were our days in June? We will live them over again, and there shall come for us, besides, a fuller summer"—

"It is winter now," said Audrey, with a sobbing breath, "and cold and dark! I do not know myself, and you are strange. I beg you to let me go away. I wish to wash off this paint, to put on my own gown. I am no lady; you do wrong to keep me here. See, all the company are frowning at me! The minister will hear what I have done and be angry, and Mistress Deborah will beat me. I care not for that, but you—Oh, you have gone far away,—as far as Fair View, as far as the mountains! I am speaking to a stranger"—

In the dance their raised hands met again. "You see me, you speak to me at last," he said ardently. "That other, that cold brother of the snows, that paladin and dream knight that you yourself made and dubbed him me,—he has gone, Audrey; nay, he never was! But I myself, I am not abhorrent to you?"

"Oh," she answered, "it is all dark! I cannot see—I cannot understand"—

The time allotted to minuets having elapsed, the musicians after a short pause began to play an ancient, lively air, and a number of ladies and gentlemen, young, gayly dressed, and light of heart as of heels, engaged in a country dance. When they were joined by Mr. Marmaduke Haward and his shameless companion, there arose a great rustling and whispering. A young girl in green taffeta was dancing alone, wreathing in and out between the silken, gleaming couples, coquetting with the men by means of fan and eyes, but taking hands and moving a step or two with each sister of the dance. When she approached Audrey, the latter smiled and extended her hand, because that was the way the lady nearest her had done. But the girl in green stared coldly, put her hand behind her, and, with the very faintest salute to Mr. Marmaduke Haward, danced on her way. For one moment the smile died on Audrey's lips; then it came resolutely back, and she held her head high.

The men, forming in two rows, drew their rapiers with a flourish, and, crossing them overhead, made an arch of steel under which the women must pass. Haward's blade touched that of an old acquaintance. "I have been leaning upon the back of a lady's chair," said the latter gruffly, under cover of the music and the clashing steel,—"a lady dressed in rose color, who's as generous (to all save one poor devil) as she is fair. I promised her I would take her message; the Lord knows I would go to the bottom of the sea to give her pleasure! She says that you are not yourself; begs that you will—go quietly away"—

An exclamation from the man next him, and a loud murmur mixed with some laughter from those in the crowded room who were watching the dancers, caused the gentleman to break off in the middle of his message. He glanced over his shoulder; then, with a shrug, turned to his vis-a-vis in white satin. "Now you see that 'twill not answer,—not in Virginia. The women—bless them!—have a way of cutting Gordian knots."

A score of ladies, one treading in the footsteps of another, should have passed beneath the flashing swords. But there had thrust itself into their company a plague spot, and the girl in green taffeta and a matron in silver brocade, between whom stood the hateful presence, indignantly stepped out of line and declined to dance. The fear of infection spreading like wildfire, the ranks refused to close, and the company was thrown into confusion. Suddenly the girl in green, by nature a leader of her kind, walked away, with a toss of her head, from the huddle of those who were uncertain what to do, and joined her friends among the spectators, who received her with acclaim. The sound and her example were warranty enough for the cohort she had quitted. A moment, and it was in virtuous retreat, and the dance was broken up.

The gentlemen, who saw themselves summarily deserted, abruptly lowered their swords. One laughed; another, flown with wine, gave utterance to some coarse pleasantry; a third called to the musicians to stop the music. Darden's Audrey stood alone, brave in her beautiful borrowed dress and the color that could not leave her cheeks. But her lips had whitened, the smile was gone, and her eyes were like those of a hunted deer. She looked mutely about her: how could she understand, who trusted so completely, who lived in a labyrinth without a clue, who had built her dream world so securely that she had left no way of egress for herself? These were cruel people! She was mad to get away, to tear off this strange dress, to fling herself down in the darkness, in the woods, hiding her face against the earth! But though she was only Audrey and so poor a thing, she had for her portion a dignity and fineness of nature that was a stay to her steps. Barbara, though not so poor and humble a maid, might have burst into tears, and run crying from the room and the house; but to do that Audrey would have been ashamed.

"It was you, Mr. Corbin, that laughed, I think?" said Haward. "To-morrow I shall send to know the reason of your mirth. Mr. Everard, you will answer to me for that pretty oath. Mr. Travis, there rests the lie that you uttered just now: stoop and take it again." He flung his glove at Mr. Travis's feet.

A great hubbub and exclamation arose. Mr. Travis lifted the glove with the point of his rapier, and in a loud voice repeated the assertion which had given umbrage to Mr. Haward of Fair View. That gentleman sprang unsteadily forward, and the blades of the two crossed in dead earnest. A moment, and the men were forced apart; but by this time the whole room was in commotion. The musicians craned their necks over the gallery rail, a woman screamed, and half a dozen gentlemen of years and authority started from the crowd of witnesses to the affair and made toward the centre of the room, with an eye to preventing further trouble. Where much wine had been drunken and twenty rapiers were out, matters might go from bad to worse.

Another was before them. A lady in rose color had risen from her chair and glided across the polished floor to the spot where trouble was brewing. "Gentlemen, for shame!" she cried. Her voice was bell-like in its clear sweetness, final in its grave rebuke and its recall to sense and decency. She was Mistress Evelyn Byrd, who held sovereignty in Virginia, and at the sound of her voice, the command of her raised hand, the clamor suddenly ceased, and the angry group, parting, fell back as from the presence of its veritable queen.

Evelyn went up to Audrey and took her by the hand. "I am not tired of dancing, as were those ladies who have left us," she said, with a smile, and in a sweet and friendly voice. "See, the gentlemen are waiting I Let us finish out this measure, you and me."

At her gesture of command the lines that had so summarily broken re-formed. Back into the old air swung the musicians; up went the swords, crossing overhead with a ringing sound, and beneath the long arch of protecting steel moved to the music the two women, the dark beauty and the fair, the princess and the herdgirl. Evelyn led, and Audrey, following, knew that now indeed she was walking in a dream.

A very few moments, and the measure was finished. A smile, a curtsy, a wave of Evelyn's hand, and the dancers, disbanding, left the floor. Mr. Corbin, Mr. Everard, and Mr. Travis, each had a word to say to Mr. Haward of Fair View, as they passed that gentleman.

Haward heard, and answered to the point; but when presently Evelyn said, "Let us go into the garden," and he found himself moving with her and with Audrey through the buzzing, staring crowd toward the door of the Governor's house, he thought that it was into Fair View garden they were about to descend. And when they came out upon the broad, torchlit walk, and he saw gay parties of ladies and gentlemen straying here and there beneath the trees, he thought it strange that he had forgotten that he had guests this night. As for the sound of the river below his terrace, he had never heard so loud a murmur. It grew and filled the night, making thin and far away the voices of his guests.

There was a coach at the gates, and Mr. Grymes, who awhile ago had told him that he had a message to deliver, was at the coach door. Evelyn had her hand upon his arm, and her voice was speaking to him from as far away as across the river. "I am leaving the ball," it said, "and I will take the girl in my coach to the place where she is staying. Promise me that you will not go back to the house yonder;

promise me that you will go away with Mr. Grymes, who is also weary of the ball"—

"Oh," said Mr. Grymes lightly, "Mr. Haward agrees with me that Marot's best room, cool and quiet, a bottle of Burgundy, and a hand at piquet are more alluring than the heat and babel we have left. We are going at once, Mistress Evelyn. Haward, I propose that on our way to Marot's we knock up Dr. Contesse, and make him free of our company."

As he spoke, he handed into the coach the lady in flowered damask, who had held up her head, but said no word, and the lady in rose-colored brocade, who, through the length of the ballroom and the hall and the broad walk where people passed and repassed, had kept her hand in Audrey's, and had talked, easily and with smiles, to the two attending gentlemen. He shut to the coach door, and drew back, with a low bow, when Haward's deeply flushed, handsome face appeared for a moment at the lowered glass.

"Art away to Westover, Evelyn?" he asked. "Then 't is 'Good-by, sweetheart!' for I shall not go to Westover again. But you have a fair road to travel,—there are violets by the wayside; for it is May Day, you know, and the woods are white with dogwood and purple with the Judas-tree. The violets are for you; but the great white blossoms, and the boughs of rosy mist, and all the trees that wave in the wind are for Audrey." His eyes passed the woman whom he would have wed, and rested upon her companion in the coach. "Thou fair dryad!" he said. "Two days hence we will keep tryst beneath the beech-tree in the woods beyond the glebe house."

The man beside him put a hand upon his shoulder and

plucked him back, nor would look at Evelyn's drawn and whitened face, but called to the coachman to go on. The black horses put themselves into motion, the equipage made a wide turn, and the lights of the Palace were left behind.

Evelyn lodged in a house upon the outskirts of the town, but from the Palace to Mistress Stagg's was hardly more than a stone's throw. Not until the coach was drawing near the small white house did either of the women speak. Then Audrey broke into an inarticulate murmur, and stooping would have pressed her cheek against the hand that had clasped hers only a little while before. But Evelyn snatched her hand away, and with a gesture of passionate repulsion shrank into her corner of the coach. "Oh, how dare you touch me!" she cried. "How dare you look at me, you serpent that have stung me so!" Able to endure no longer, she suddenly gave way to angry laughter. "Do you think I did it for you,—put such humiliation upon myself for you? Why, you wanton, I care not if you stand in white at every church door in Virginia! It was for him, for Mr. Marmaduke Haward of Fair View, for whose name and fame, if he cares not for them himself, his friends have yet some care!" The coach stopped, and the footman opened the door. "Descend, if you please," went on Evelyn clearly and coldly. "You have had your triumph. I say not there is no excuse for him,—you are very beautiful. Good-night."

Audrey stood between the lilac bushes and watched the coach turn from Palace into Duke of Gloucester Street; then went and knocked at the green door. It was opened by Mistress Stagg in person, who drew her into the parlor, where the good-natured woman had been sitting all alone, and in increasing alarm as to what might be the outcome of this whim of Mr. Marmaduke Haward's. Now she was full of inquiries, ready to admire and to nod approval, or to shake her head and cry, "I told you so!" according to the turn of the girl's recital.

But Audrey had little to say, little to tell. Yes, oh yes, it had been a very grand sight.... Yes, Mr. Haward was kind; he had always been kind to her.... She had come home with Mistress Evelyn Byrd in her coach.... Might she go now to her room? She would fold the dress very carefully.

Mistress Stagg let her go, for indeed there was no purpose to be served in keeping her, seeing that the girl was clearly dazed, spoke without knowing what she said, and stood astare like one of Mrs. Salmon's beautiful was ladies. She would hear all about it in the morning, when the child had slept off her excitement. They at the Palace couldn't have taken her presence much amiss, or she would never in the world have come home in the Westover coach.

CHAPTER XXI

AUDREY AWAKES

There had lately come to Virginia, and to the convention of its clergy at Williamsburgh, one Mr. Eliot, a minister after the heart of a large number of sober and godly men whose reputation as a body suffered at the hands of Mr. Darden, of Fair View parish, Mr. Bailey, of Newport, Mr. Worden, of Lawn's Creek, and a few kindred spirits. Certainly Mr. Eliot was not like these; so erect, indeed, did he hold himself in the strait and narrow path that his most admiring brethren, being, as became good Virginians, somewhat easy-going in their saintliness, were inclined to think that he leaned too far the other way. It was commendable to hate sin and reprove the sinner; but when it came to raining condemnation upon horse-racing, dancing, Cato at the playhouse, and like innocent diversions, Mr. Eliot was surely somewhat out of bounds. The most part accounted for his turn of mind by the fact that ere he came to Virginia he had been a sojourner in New England.

He was mighty in the pulpit, was Mr. Eliot; no droning reader of last year's sermons, but a thunderer forth of speech that was now acrid, now fiery, but that always came from an impassioned nature, vehement for the damnation of those whom God so strangely spared. When, as had perforce happened during the past week, he must sit with his brethren in the congregation and listen to lukewarm—nay, to dead and cold adjurations and expoundings, his very soul itched to mount the pulpit stairs, thrust down the Laodicean that chanced to occupy it, and himself awaken as with the sound of a trumpet this people who slept upon the verge of a precipice, between hell that gaped below and God who sat on high, serenely regardful of his creatures' plight. Though so short a time in Virginia, he was already become a man of note, the prophet not without honor, whom it was the fashion to admire, if not to follow. It was therefore natural enough that the Commissary, himself a man of plain speech from the pulpit, should appoint him to preach in Bruton church this Sunday morning, before his Excellency the Governor, the worshipful the Council, the clergy in convention, and as much of Williamsburgh, gentle and simple, as could crowd into the church. Mr. Eliot took the compliment as an answer to prayer, and chose for his text Daniel fifth and twenty-seventh.

Lodging as he did on Palace Street, the early hours of the past night, which he would have given to prayer and meditation, had been profaned by strains of music from the Governor's house, by laughter and swearing and much going to and fro in the street beneath his window. These disturbances filling him with righteous wrath, he came down to his breakfast next morning prepared to give his hostess, who kept him company at table, line and verse which should demonstrate that Jehovah shared his anger.

"Ay, sir!" she cried. "And if that were all, sir"—and straightway she embarked upon a colored narration of the occurrence at the Governor's ball. This was followed by a wonderfully circumstantial account of Mr. Marmaduke

Haward's sins of omission against old and new acquaintances who would have entertained him at their houses, and been entertained in turn at Fair View, and by as detailed a description of the toils that had been laid for him by that audacious piece who had forced herself upon the company last night.

Mr. Eliot listened aghast, and mentally amended his sermon. If he knew Virginia, even so flagrant a case as this might never come before a vestry. Should this woman go unreproved? When in due time he was in the church, and the congregation was gathering, he beckoned to him one of the sidesmen, asked a question, and when it was answered, looked fixedly at a dark girl sitting far away in a pew beneath the gallery.

It was a fine, sunny morning, with a tang of autumn in the air, and the concourse within the church was very great. The clergy showed like a wedge of black driven into the bright colors with which nave and transept overflowed. His Excellency the Governor sat in state, with the Council on either hand. One member of that body was not present. Well-nigh all Williamsburgh knew by now that Mr. Marmaduke Haward lay at Marot's ordinary, ill of a raging fever. Hooped petticoat and fragrant bodice found reason for whispering to laced coat and periwig; significant glances traveled from every quarter of the building toward the tall pew where, collected but somewhat palely smiling, sat Mistress Evelyn Byrd beside her father. All this was before the sermon. When the minister of the day mounted the pulpit, and, gaunt against the great black sounding-board, gave out his text in a solemn and ringing voice, such was the genuine power of the man that every face was turned toward him, and throughout the building there fell a sudden hush.

Audrey looked with the rest, but she could not have said that she listened,—not at first. She was there because she always went to church on Sunday. It had not occurred to her to ask that she might stay at home. She had come from her room that morning with the same still face, the same strained and startled look about the eyes, that she had carried to it the night before. Black Peggy, who found her bed unslept in, thought that she must have sat the night through beside the window. Mistress Stagg, meeting her at the stairfoot with the tidings (just gathered from the lips of a passer-by) of Mr. Haward's illness, thought that the girl took the news very quietly. She made no exclamation, said nothing good or bad; only drew her hand across her brow and eyes, as though she strove to thrust away a veil or mist that troubled her. This gesture she repeated now and again during the hour before church time. Mistress Stagg heard no more of the ball this morning than she had heard the night before. Something ailed the girl. She was not sullen, but she could not or would not talk. Perhaps, despite the fact of the Westover coach, she had not been kindly used at the Palace. The ex-actress pursed her lips, and confided to her Mirabell that times were not what they once were. Had she not, at Bath, been given a ticket to the Saturday ball by my Lord Squander himself? Ay, and she had footed it, too, in the country dance, with the best of them, with captains and French counts and gentlemen and ladies of title,—ay, and had gone down the middle with, the very pattern of Sir Harry Wildair! To be sure, no one had ever breathed a word against her character; but, for her part, she believed no great harm of Audrey, either. Look at the girl's eyes, now: they were like a child's or a saint's.

Mirabell nodded and looked wise, but said nothing.

When the church bells rang Audrey was ready, and she

walked to church with Mistress Stagg much as, the night before, she had walked between the lilacs to the green door when the Westover coach had passed from her sight. Now she sat in the church much as she had sat at the window the night through. She did not know that people were staring at her; nor had she caught the venomous glance of Mistress Deborah, already in the pew, and aware of more than had come to her friend's ears.

Audrey was not listening, was scarcely thinking. Her hands were crossed in her lap, and now and then she raised one and made the motion of pushing aside from her eyes something heavy that clung and blinded. What part of her spirit that was not wholly darkened and folded within itself was back in the mountains of her childhood, with those of her own blood whom she had loved and lost. What use to try to understand to-day,—to-day with its falling skies, its bewildered pondering over the words that were said to her last night? And the morrow,—she must leave that. Perhaps when it should dawn he would come to her, and call her "little maid," and laugh at her dreadful dream. But now, while it was to-day, she could not think of him without an agony of pain and bewilderment. He was ill, too, and suffering. Oh, she must leave the thought of him alone! Back then to the long yesterdays she traveled, and played quietly, dreamily, with Robin on the green grass beside the shining stream, or sat on the doorstep, her head on Molly's lap, and watched the evening star behind the Endless Mountains.

It was very quiet in the church save for that one great voice speaking. Little by little the voice impressed itself upon her consciousness. The eyes of her mind were upon long ranges of mountains distinct against the splendor of a sunset sky. Last seen in childhood, viewed now through the illusion of the years, the mountains were vastly higher than nature had planned them; the streamers of light shot to the zenith; the black forests were still; everywhere a fixed glory, a gigantic silence, a holding of the breath for things to happen.

By degrees the voice in her ears fitted in with the landscape, became, so solemn and ringing it was, like the voice of the archangel of that sunset land. Audrey listened at last; and suddenly the mountains were gone, and the light from the sky, and her people were dead and dust away in that hidden valley, and she was sitting in the church at Williamsburgh, alone, without a friend.

What was the preacher saying? What ball of the night before was he describing with bitter power, the while he gave warning of handwriting upon the wall such as had menaced Belshazzar's feast of old? Of what shameless girl was he telling,—what creature dressed in silks that should have gone in rags, brought to that ball by her paramour—

The gaunt figure in the pulpit trembled like a leaf with the passion of the preacher's convictions and the energy of his utterance. On had gone the stream of rhetoric, the denunciations, the satire, the tremendous assertions of God's mind and purposes. The lash that was wielded was far-reaching; all the vices of the age—irreligion, blasphemy, drunkenness, extravagance, vainglory, loose living—fell under its sting. The condemnation was general, and each man looked to see his neighbor wince. The occurrence at the ball last night,—he was on that for final theme, was he? There was a slight movement throughout the congregation. Some glanced to where would have sat Mr. Marmaduke Haward, had not the gentleman been at present in his bed, raving now of a great run of luck at the Cocoa Tree; now of an Indian who, with his knee upon his breast, was throttling him to death. Others looked over their shoulders to see if that gypsy yet sat beneath the gallery. Colonel Byrd took out his snuffbox and studied the picture on the lid, while his daughter sat like a carven lady, with a slight smile upon her lips.

On went the word picture that showed how vice could flaunt it in so fallen an age. The preacher spared not plain words, squarely turned himself toward the gallery, pointed out with voice and hand the object of his censure and of God's wrath. Had the law pilloried the girl before them all, it had been but little worse for her. She sat like a statue, staring with wide eyes at the window above the altar. This, then, was what the words in the coach last night had meant—this was what the princess thought— this was what his world thought—

There arose a commotion in the ranks of the clergy of Virginia. The Reverend Gideon Darden, quitting with an oath the company of his brethren, came down the aisle, and, pushing past his wife, took his stand in the pew beside the orphan who had lived beneath his roof, whom during many years he had cursed upon occasion and sometimes struck, and whom he had latterly made his tool, "Never mind him, Audrey, my girl," he said, and put an unsteady hand upon her shoulder. "You're a good child; they cannot harm ye."

He turned his great shambling body and heavy face toward the preacher, stemmed in the full tide of his eloquence by this unseemly interruption, "Ye beggarly Scot!" he exclaimed thickly. "Ye evil-thinking saint from Salem way, that know the very lining of the Lord's mind, and yet, walking through his earth, see but a poisonous weed in his every harmless flower! Shame on you to beat down the flower that never did you harm! The girl's as innocent a thing as lives! Ay, I've had my dram,—the more shame to you that are justly rebuked out of the mouth of a drunken man! I have done, Mr. Commissary," addressing himself to that dignitary, who had advanced to the altar rail with his arm raised in a command for silence. "I've no child of my own, thank God! but the maid has grown up in my house, and I'll not sit to hear her belied. I've heard of last night; 'twas the mad whim of a sick man. The girl's as guiltless of wrong as any lady here. I, Gideon Darden, vouch for it!"

He sat heavily down beside Audrey, who never stirred from her still regard of that high window. There was a moment of portentous silence; then, "Let us pray," said the minister from the pulpit.

Audrey knelt with the rest, but she did not pray. And when it was all over, and the benediction had been given, and she found herself without the church, she looked at the green trees against the clear autumnal skies and at the graves in the churchyard as though it were a new world into which she had stepped. She could not have said that she found it fair. Her place had been so near the door that well-nigh all the congregation was behind her, streaming out of the church, eager to reach the open air, where it might discuss the sermon, the futile and scandalous interruption by the notorious Mr. Darden, and what Mr. Marmaduke Haward might have said or done had he been present.

Only Mistress Stagg kept beside her; for Mistress Deborah hung back, unwilling to be seen in her company, and Darden, from that momentary awakening of his better nature, had sunk to himself again, and thought not how else he might aid this wounded member of his household. But Mary Stagg was a kindly soul, whose heart had led her comfortably through life with very little appeal to her head. The two or three young women—Oldfields and Porters of the Virginian stage—who were under indentures to her husband and herself found her as much their friend as mistress. Their triumphs in the petty playhouse of this town of a thousand souls were hers, and what woes they had came quickly to her ears. Now she would have slipped her hand into Audrey's and have given garrulous comfort, as the two passed alone through the churchyard gate and took their way up Palace Street toward the small white house. But Audrey gave not her hand, did not answer, made no moan, neither justified herself nor blamed another. She did not speak at all, but after the first glance about her moved like a sleepwalker.

When the house was reached she went up to the bedroom. Mistress Deborah, entering stormily ten minutes later, found herself face to face with a strange Audrey, who, standing in the middle of the floor, raised her hand for silence in a gesture so commanding that the virago stayed her tirade, and stood open-mouthed.

"I wish to speak," said the new Audrey. "I was waiting for you. There's a question I wish to ask, and I'll ask it of you who were never kind to me."

"Never kind to her!" cried the minister's wife to the four walls. "And she's been taught, and pampered, and treated more like a daughter than the beggar wench she is! And this is my return,—to sit by her in church to-day, and have all Virginia think her belonging to me"—

"I belong to no one," said Audrey. "Even God does not want me. Be quiet until I have done." She made again the gesture of pushing aside from face and eyes the mist that clung and blinded. "I know now what they say," she went on. "The preacher told me awhile ago. Last night a lady spoke to me: now I know what was her meaning. Because Mr. Haward, who saved my life, who brought me from the mountains, who left me, when he sailed away, where he thought I would be happy, was kind to me when he came again after so many years; because he has often been to the glebe house, and I to Fair View; because last night he would have me go with him to the Governor's ball, they think—they say out loud for all the people to hear—that I—that I am like Joan, who was whipped last month at the Court House. But it is not of the lies they tell that I wish to speak."

Her hand went again to her forehead, then dropped at her side. A look of fear and of piteous appeal came into her face. "The witch said that I dreamed, and that it was not well for dreamers to awaken." Suddenly the quiet of her voice and bearing was broken. With a cry, she hurried across the room, and, kneeling, caught at the other's gown. "Ah! that is no dream, is it? No dream that he is my friend, only my friend who has always been sorry for me, has always helped me! He is the noblest gentleman, the truest, the best—he loves the lady at Westover—they are to be married—he never knew what people were saying— he was not himself when he spoke to me so last night"— Her eyes appealed to the face above her. "I could never have dreamed all this," she said. "Tell me that I was awake!"

The minister's wife looked down upon her with a bitter smile. "So you've had your fool's paradise? Well, once I had mine, though 'twas not your kind. 'Tis a pretty country, Audrey, but it's not long before they turn you out." She laughed somewhat drearily, then in a moment turned shrew again. "He never knew what people were saying?" she cried. "You little fool, do you suppose he cared? 'Twas you that played your cards all wrong with your Governor's ball last night!—setting up for a lady, forsooth!—bringing all the town about your ears! You might have known that he would never have taken you there in his senses. At Fair View things went very well. He was entertained,—and I meant to see that no harm came of it,—and Darden got his support in the vestry. For he was bit,—there's no doubt of that,—though what he ever saw in you more than big eyes and a brown skin, the Lord knows, not I! Only your friend!—a fine gentleman just from London, with a whole Canterbury book of stories about his life there, to spend a'most a summer on the road between his plantation and a wretched glebe house because he was only your friend, and had saved you from the Indians when you were a child, and wished to be kind to you still! I'll tell you who did wish to be kind to you, and that was Jean Hugon, the trader, who wanted to marry you."

Audrey rose to her feet, and moved slowly backward to the wall. Mistress Deborah went shrilly on: "I dare swear you believe that Mr. Haward had you in mind all the years he was gone from Virginia? Well, he didn't. He puts you with Darden and me, and he says, 'There's the strip of Oronoko down by the swamp,—I've told my agent that you're to have from it so many pounds a year;' and he sails away to London and all the fine things there, and never thinks of you more until he comes back to Virginia and sees you last May Day at Jamestown. Next morning he comes riding to the glebe house. 'And so,' he says to Darden, 'and so my little maid that I brought for trophy out of the Appalachian Mountains is a woman grown? Faith, I'd quite forgot the child; but Saunderson tells me that you have not forgot to draw upon my Oronoko.' That's all the remembrance you were held in, Audrey."

She paused to take breath, and to look with shrewish

triumph at the girl who leaned against the wall. "I like not waking up," said Audrey to herself. "It were easier to die. Perhaps I am dying."

"And then out he walks to find and talk to you, and in sets your pretty summer of all play and no work!" went on the other, in a high voice. "Oh, there was kindness enough, once you had caught his fancy! I wonder if the lady at Westover praised his kindness? They say she is a proud young lady: I wonder if she liked your being at the ball last night? When she comes to Fair View, I'll take my oath that you'll walk no more in its garden! But perhaps she won't come now,—though her maid Chloe told Mistress Bray's Martha that she certainly loves him"—

"I wish I were dead," said Audrey. "I wish I were dead, like Molly." She stood up straight against the wall, and pushed her heavy hair from her forehead. "Be quiet now," she said. "You see that I am awake; there is no need for further calling. I shall not dream again." She looked at the older woman doubtfully. "Would you mind," she suggested,—"would you be so very kind as to leave me alone, to sit here awake for a while? I have to get used to it, you know. To-morrow, when we go back to the glebe house, I will work the harder. It must be easy to work when one is awake. Dreaming takes so much time."

Mistress Deborah could hardly have told why she did as she was asked. Perhaps the very strangeness of the girl made her uncomfortable in her presence; perhaps in her sour and withered heart there was yet some little soundness of pity and comprehension; or perhaps it was only that she had said her say, and was anxious to get to her friends below, and shake from her soul the dust of any possible complicity with circumstance in moulding the destinies of Darden's Audrey. Be that as it may, when she had flung her hood upon the bed and had looked at herself in the cracked glass above the dresser, she went out of the room, and closed the door somewhat softly behind her.

CHAPTER XXII

BY THE RIVERSIDE

"Yea, I am glad—I and my father and mother and Ephraim—that thee is returned to Fair View," answered Truelove. "And has thee truly no shoes of plain and sober stuffs? These be much too gaudy."

"There's a pair of black callimanco," said the storekeeper reluctantly; "but these of flowered silk would so become your feet, or this red-heeled pair with the buckles, or this of fine morocco. Did you think of me every day that I spent in Williamsburgh?"

"I prayed for thee every day," said Truelove simply,—"for thee and for the sick man who had called thee to his side. Let me see thy callimanco shoes. Thee knows that I may not wear these others."

The storekeeper brought the plainest footgear that his stock afforded. "They are of a very small size,—perhaps too small. Had you not better try them ere you buy? I could get a larger pair from Mr. Carter's store."

Truelove seated herself upon a convenient stool, and lifted her gray skirt an inch above a slender ankle.

"Perchance they may not be too small," she said, and in despite of her training and the whiteness of her soul two dimples made their appearance above the corners of her pretty mouth. MacLean knelt to remove the worn shoe, but found in the shoestrings an obstinate knot. The two had the store to themselves; for Ephraim waited for his sister at the landing, rocking in his boat on the bosom of the river, watching a flight of wild geese drawn like a snowy streamer across the dark blue sky. It was late autumn, and the forest was dressed in flame color.

"Thy fingers move so slowly that I fear thee is not well," said Truelove kindly. "They that have nursed men with fever do often fall ill themselves. Will thee not see a physician?"

MacLean, sanguine enough in hue, and no more gaunt of body than usual, worked languidly on. "I trust no lowland physician," he said. "In my own country, if I had need, I would send to the foot of Dun-da-gu for black Murdoch, whose fathers have been physicians to the MacLeans of Duart since the days of Galethus. The little man in this parish,—his father was a lawyer, his grandfather a merchant; he knows not what was his great-grandfather! There, the shoe is untied! If I came every day to your father's house, and if your mother gave me to drink of her elder-flower wine, and if I might sit on the sunny doorstep and watch you at your spinning, I should, I think, recover."

He slipped upon her foot the shoe of black cloth. Truelove regarded it gravely. "'Tis not too small, after all," she said. "And does thee not think it more comely than these other, with their silly pomp of colored heels and blossoms woven in the silk?" She indicated with her glance the vainglorious row upon the bench beside her; then looked down at the little foot in its sombre covering and sighed.

"I think that thy foot would be fair in the shoe of Donald Ross!" cried the storekeeper, and kissed the member which he praised.

Truelove drew back, her cheeks very pink, and the dimples quite uncertain whether to go or stay. "Thee is idle in thy behavior," she said severely. "I do think that thee is of the generation that will not learn. I pray thee to expeditiously put back my own shoe, and to give me in a parcel the callimanco pair."

MacLean set himself to obey, though with the expedition of a tortoise. Crisp autumn air and vivid sunshine pouring in at window and door filled and lit the store. The doorway framed a picture of blue sky, slow-moving water, and ragged landing; the window gave upon crimson sumac and the gold of a sycamore. Truelove, in her gray gown and close white cap, sat in the midst of the bouquet of colors afforded by the motley lining of the Fair View store, and gazed through the window at the riotous glory of this world. At last she looked at MacLean. "When, a year ago, thee was put to mind this store, and I, coming here to buy, made thy acquaintance," she said softly, "thee wore always so stern and sorrowful a look that my heart bled for thee. I knew that thee was unhappy. Is thee unhappy still?"

MacLean tied the shoestrings with elaborate care; then rose from his knees, and stood looking down from his great height upon the Quaker maiden. His face was softened, and when he spoke it was with a gentle voice. "No," he said, "I am not unhappy as at first I was. My king is an exile, and my chief is forfeited. I suppose that my father is dead. Ewin Mackinnon, my foe upon whom I swore revenge, lived untroubled by me, and died at another's hands. My country is closed against me; I shall never see it more. I am named a rebel, and chained to this soil, this dull and sluggish land, where from year's end to year's end the key keeps the house and the furze bush keeps the cow. The best years of my manhood—years in which I should have acquired honor—have gone from me here. There was a man of my name amongst those gentlemen, old officers of Dundee, who in France did not disdain to serve as private sentinels, that their maintenance might not burden a king as unfortunate as themselves. That MacLean fell in the taking of an island in the Rhine which to this day is called the Island of the Scots, so bravely did these gentlemen bear themselves. They made their lowly station honorable; marshals and princes applauded their deeds. The man of my name was unfortunate, but not degraded; his life was not amiss, and his death was glorious. But I, Angus MacLean, son and brother of chieftains, I serve as a slave; giving obedience where in nature it is not due, laboring in an alien land for that which profiteth not, looking to die peacefully in my bed! I should be no less than most unhappy."

He sat down upon the bench beside Truelove, and taking the hem of her apron began to plait it between his fingers. "But to-day," he said,—"but to-day the sky seems blue, the sunshine bright. Why is that, Truelove?"

Truelove, with her eyes cast down and a deeper wild rose in her cheeks, opined that it was because Friend Marmaduke Haward was well of his fever, and had that day returned to Fair View. "Friend Lewis Contesse did tell my father, when he was in Williamsburgh, that thee made a tenderer nurse than any woman, and that he did think that Marmaduke Haward owed his life to thee. I am glad that thee has made friends with him whom men foolishly call thy master."

"Credit to that the blue sky," said the storekeeper whimsically; "there is yet the sunshine to be accounted for. This room did not look so bright half an hour syne."

But Truelove shook her head, and would not reckon further; instead heard Ephraim calling, and gently drew her apron from the Highlander's clasp. "There will be a meeting of Friends at our house next fourth day," she said, in her most dovelike tones, as she rose and held out her hand for her new shoes. "Will thee come, Angus? Thee will be edified, for Friend Sarah Story, who hath the gift of prophecy, will be there, and we do think to hear of great things. Thee will come?"

"By St. Kattan, that will I!" exclaimed the storekeeper, with suspicious readiness. "The meeting lasts not long, does it? When the Friends are gone there will be reward? I mean I may sit on the doorstep and watch you—and watch *thee*—spin?"

Truelove dimpled once more, took her shoes, and would have gone her way sedately and alone, but MacLean must needs keep her company to the end of the landing and the waiting Ephraim. The latter, as he rowed away from the Fair View store, remarked upon his sister's looks: "What makes thy cheeks so pink, Truelove, and thy eyes so big and soft?"

Truelove did not know; thought that mayhap 'twas the sunshine and the blowing wind.

The sun still shone, but the wind had fallen, when, two hours later, MacLean pocketed the key of the store, betook himself again to the water's edge, and entering a small boat, first turned it sunwise for luck's sake, then rowed slowly downstream to the great-house landing. Here he found a handful of negroes—boatmen and house servants—basking in the sunlight. Juba was of the number, and at MacLean's call scrambled to his feet and came to the head of the steps. "No, sah, Marse Duke not on de place. He order Mirza an' ride off"—a pause—"an' ride off to de glebe house. Yes, sah, I done tol' him he ought to rest. Goin' to wait tel he come back?"

"No," answered MacLean, with a darkened face. "Tell him I will come to the great house to-night."

In effect, the storekeeper was now, upon Fair View plantation, master of his own time and person. Therefore, when he left the landing, he did not row back to the store, but, it being pleasant upon the water, kept on downstream, gliding beneath the drooping branches of red and russet and gold. When he came to the mouth of the little creek that ran past Haward's garden, he rested upon his oars, and with a frowning face looked up its silver reaches.

The sun was near its setting, and a still and tranquil light lay upon the river that was glassy smooth. Rowing close to the bank, the Highlander saw through the gold fretwork of the leaves above him far spaces of pale blue sky. All was quiet, windless, listlessly fair. A few birds were on the wing, and far toward the opposite shore an idle sail seemed scarce to hold its way. Presently the trees gave place to a grassy shore, rimmed by a fiery vine that strove to cool its leaves in the flood below. Behind it was a little rise of earth, a green hillock, fresh and vernal in the midst of the flame-colored autumn. In shape it was like those hills in his native land which the Highlander knew to be tenanted by the *daoine shi'* the men of peace. There, in glittering chambers beneath the earth, they dwelt, a potent, eerie, gossamer folk, and thence, men and women, they issued at times to deal balefully with the mortal race.

A woman was seated upon the hillock, quiet as a shadow, her head resting on her hand, her eyes upon the river. Dark-haired, dark-eyed, slight of figure, and utterly, mournfully still, sitting alone in the fading light, with the northern sky behind her, for the moment she wore to the Highlander an aspect not of earth, and he was startled. Then he saw that it was but Darden's Audrey. She watched the water where it gleamed far off, and did not see him in his boat below the scarlet vines. Nor when, after a moment's hesitation, he fastened the boat to a cedar stump, and stepped ashore, did she pay any heed. It was not until he spoke to her, standing where he could have touched her with his outstretched hand, that she moved or looked his way.

"How long since you left the glebe house?" he demanded abruptly.

"The sun was high," she answered, in a slow, even voice, with no sign of surprise at finding herself no longer alone. "I have been sitting here for a long time. I thought that Hugon might be coming this afternoon.... There is no use in hiding, but I thought if I stole down here he might not find me very soon."

Her voice died away, and she looked again at the water. The storekeeper sat down upon the bank, between the hillock and the fiery vine, and his keen eyes watched her closely. "The river," she said at last,—I like to watch it. There was a time when I loved the woods, but now I see that they are ugly. Now, when I can steal away, I come to the river always. I watch it and watch it, and think.... All that you give it is taken so surely, and hurried away, and buried out of sight forever. A little while ago I pulled a spray of farewell summer, and went down there where the bank shelves and gave it to the river. It was gone in a moment for all that the stream seems so stealthy and slow."

"The stream comes from afar," said the Highlander. "In the west, beneath the sun, it may be a torrent flashing through the mountains."

"The mountains!" cried Audrey. "Ah, they are uglier than the woods,—black and terrible! Once I loved them, too, but that was long ago." She put her chin upon her hand, and again studied the river. "Long ago," she said, beneath her breath.

There was a silence; then, "Mr. Haward is at Fair View again," announced the storekeeper.

The girl's face twitched.

"He has been nigh to death," went on her informant. "There were days when I looked for no morrow for him; one night when I held above his lips a mirror, and hardly thought to see the breath-stain."

Audrey laughed. "He can fool even Death, can he not?" The laugh was light and mocking, a tinkling, elvish sound which the Highlander frowned to hear. A book, worn and dog-eared, lay near her on the grass. He took it up and turned the leaves; then put it by, and glanced uneasily at the slender, brown-clad form seated upon the fairy mound.

"That is strange reading," he said.

Audrey looked at the book listlessly. "The schoolmaster gave it to me. It tells of things as they are, all stripped of make-believe, and shows how men love only themselves, and how ugly and mean is the world when we look at it aright. The schoolmaster says that to look at it aright you must not dream; you must stay awake,"—she drew her hand across her brow and eyes,—"you must stay awake."

"I had rather dream," said MacLean shortly. "I have no love for your schoolmaster."

"He is a wise man," she answered. "Now that I do not like the woods I listen to him when he comes to the glebe house. If I remember all he says, maybe I shall grow wise, also, and the pain will stop." Once more she dropped her chin upon her hand and fell to brooding, her eyes upon the river. When she spoke again it was to herself: "Sometimes of nights I hear it calling me. Last night, while I knelt by my window, it called so loud that I put my hands over my ears; but I could not keep out the sound,—the sound of the river that comes from the mountains, that goes to the sea. And then I saw that there was a light in Fair View house."

Her voice ceased, and the silence closed in around them. The sun was setting, and in the west were purple islands merging into a sea of gold. The river, too, was colored, and every tree was like a torch burning stilly in the quiet of the evening. For some time MacLean watched the girl, who now again seemed unconscious of his presence; but at last he got to his feet, and looked toward his boat. "I must be going," he said; then, as Audrey raised her head and the light struck upon her face, he continued more kindly than one would think so stern a seeming man could speak: "I am sorry for you, my maid. God knows that I should know how dreadful are the wounds of the spirit!

Should you need a friend"—

Audrey shook her head. "No more friends," she said, and laughed as she had laughed before. "They belong in dreams. When you are awake,—that is a different thing."

The storekeeper went his way, back to the Fair View store, rowing slowly, with a grim and troubled face, while Darden's Audrey sat still upon the green hillock and watched the darkening river. Behind her, at no great distance, was the glebe house; more than once she thought she heard Hugon coming through the bushes and calling her by name. The river darkened more and more, and in the west the sea of gold changed to plains of amethyst and opal. There was a crescent moon, and Audrey, looking at it with eyes that ached for the tears that would not gather, knew that once she would have found it fair.

Hugon was coming, for she heard the twigs upon the path from the glebe house snap beneath his tread. She did not turn or move; she would see him soon enough, hear him soon enough. Presently his black eyes would look into hers; it would be bird and snake over again, and the bird was tired of fluttering. The bird was so tired that when a hand was laid on her shoulder she did not writhe herself from under its touch; instead only shuddered slightly, and stared with wide eyes at the flowing river. But the hand was white, with a gleaming ring upon its forefinger, and it stole down to clasp her own. "Audrey," said a voice that was not Hugon's.

The girl flung back her head, saw Haward's face bending over her, and with a loud cry sprang to her feet. When he would have touched her again she recoiled, putting between them a space of green grass. "I have hunted you for an hour," he began. "At last I struck this path. Audrey"—

Audrey's hands went to her ears. Step by step she moved backward, until she stood against the trunk of a blood-red oak. When she saw that Haward followed her she uttered a terrified scream. At the sound and at the sight of her face he stopped short, and his outstretched hand fell to his side. "Why, Audrey, Audrey!" he exclaimed. "I would not hurt you, child. I am not Jean Hugon!"

The narrow path down which he had come was visible for some distance as it wound through field and copse, and upon it there now appeared another figure, as yet far off, but moving rapidly through the fading light toward the river. "Jean! Jean! Jean Hugon!" cried Audrey.

The blood rushed to Haward's face. "As bad as that!" he said, beneath his breath. Going over to the girl, he took her by the hands and strove to make her look at him; but her face was like marble, and her eyes would not meet his, and in a moment she had wrenched herself free of his clasp. "Jean Hugon! Help, Jean Hugon!" she called.

The half-breed in the distance heard her voice, and began to run toward them.

"Audrey, listen to me!" cried Haward. "How can I speak to you, how explain, how entreat, when you are like this? Child, child, I am no monster! Why do you shrink from me thus, look at me thus with frightened eyes? You know that I love you!"

She broke from him with lifted hands and a wailing cry. "Let me go! Let me go! I am running through the corn, in the darkness, and I hope to meet the Indians! I am awake,—oh, God! I am wide awake!"

With another cry, and with her hands shutting out the

sound of his voice, she turned and fled toward the approaching trader. Haward, after one deep oath and an impetuous, quickly checked movement to follow the flying figure, stood beneath the oak and watched that meeting: Hugon, in his wine-colored coat and Blenheim wig, fierce, inquisitive, bragging of what he might do; the girl suddenly listless, silent, set only upon an immediate return through the fields to the glebe house.

She carried her point, and the two went away without let or hindrance from the master of Fair View, who leaned against the stem of the oak and watched them go. He had been very ill, and the hour's search, together with this unwonted beating of his heart, had made him desperately weary,—too weary to do aught but go slowly and without overmuch of thought to the spot where he had left his horse, mount it, and ride as slowly homeward. To-morrow, he told himself, he would manage differently; at least, she should be made to hear him. In the mean time there was the night to be gotten through. MacLean, he remembered, was coming to the great house. What with wine and cards, thought might for a time be pushed out of doors.

CHAPTER XXIII

A DUEL

Juba, setting candles upon a table in Haward's bedroom, chanced to spill melted wax upon his master's hand, outstretched on the board. "Damn you!" cried Haward, moved by sudden and uncontrollable irritation. "Look what you are doing, sirrah!"

The negro gave a start of genuine surprise. Haward could punish,—Juba had more than once felt the weight of his master's cane,—but justice had always been meted out with an equable voice and a fine impassivity of countenance. "Don't stand there staring at me!" now ordered the master as irritably as before. "Go stir the fire, draw the curtains, shut out the night! Ha, Angus, is that you?"

MacLean crossed the room to the fire upon the hearth, and stood with his eyes upon the crackling logs. "You kindle too soon your winter fire," he said. "These forests, flaming red and yellow, should warm the land."

"Winter is at hand. The air strikes cold to-night," answered Haward, and, rising, began to pace the room, while MacLean watched him with compressed lips and gloomy eyes. Finally he came to a stand before a card table, set full in the ruddy light of the fire, and taking up the cards ran them slowly through his fingers. "When the lotus was all plucked and Lethe drained, then cards were born into the world," he said sententiously. "Come, my friend, let us forget awhile."

They sat down, and Haward dealt.

"I came to the house landing before sunset," began the storekeeper slowly. "I found you gone."

"Ay," said Haward, gathering up his cards. "'Tis yours to play."

"Juba told me that you had called for Mirza, and had ridden away to the glebe house."

"True," answered the other. "And what then?"

There was a note of warning in his voice, but MacLean did not choose to heed. "I rowed on down the river, past the mouth of the creek," he continued, with deliberation. "There was a mound of grass and a mass of colored vines"—

"And a blood-red oak," finished Haward coldly. "Shall we pay closer regard to what we are doing? I play the king."

"You were there!" exclaimed the Highlander. "You—not Jean Hugon—searched for and found the poor maid's hiding-place." The red came into his tanned cheek. "Now, by St. Andrew!" he began; then checked himself.

Haward tapped with his finger the bit of painted pasteboard before him. "I play the king," he repeated, in an even voice; then struck a bell, and when Juba appeared ordered the negro to bring wine and to stir the fire. The flames, leaping up, lent strange animation to the face of the lady above the mantelshelf, and a pristine brightness to the swords crossed beneath the painting. The slave moved about the room, drawing the curtains more closely, arranging all for the night. While he was present the players gave their attention to the game, but with the sound of the closing door MacLean laid down his cards.

"I must speak," he said abruptly. "The girl's face haunts me. You do wrong. It is not the act of a gentleman."

The silence that followed was broken by Haward, who spoke in the smooth, slightly drawling tones which with him spelled irritation and sudden, hardly controlled anger. "It is my home-coming," he said. "I am tired, and wish to-night to eat only of the lotus. Will you take up your cards again?"

A less impetuous man than MacLean, noting the signs of weakness, fatigue, and impatience, would have waited, and on the morrow have been listened to with equanimity. But the Highlander, fired by his cause, thought not of delay. "To forget!" he exclaimed. "That is the coward's part! I would have you remember: remember yourself, who are by nature a gentleman and generous; remember how alone and helpless is the girl; remember to cease from this pursuit!"

"We will leave the cards, and say good-night," said Haward, with a strong effort for self-control.

"Good-night with all my heart!" cried the other hotly,— "when you have promised to lay no further snare for that maid at your gates, whose name you have blasted, whose heart you have wrung, whose nature you have darkened and distorted"—

"Have you done?" demanded Haward. "Once more, 't were wise to say good-night at once."

"Not yet!" exclaimed the storekeeper, stretching out an eager hand. "That girl hath so haunting a face. Haward, see her not again! God wot, I think you have crushed the soul within her, and her name is bandied from mouth to mouth. 'T were kind to leave her to forget and be forgotten. Go to Westover: wed the lady there of whom you raved in your fever. You are her declared suitor; 'tis said that she loves you"—

Haward drew his breath sharply and turned in his chair. Then, spent with fatigue, irritable from recent illness, sore with the memory of the meeting by the river, determined upon his course and yet deeply perplexed, he narrowed his eyes and began to give poisoned arrow for poisoned arrow.

"Was it in the service of the Pretender that you became a squire of dames?" he asked. "'Gad, for a Jacobite you are particular!"

MacLean started as if struck, and drew himself up. "Have a care, sir! A MacLean sits not to hear his king or his chief defamed. In future, pray remember it."

"For my part," said the other, "I would have Mr. MacLean remember"—

The intonation carried his meaning. MacLean, flushing deeply, rose from the table. "That is unworthy of you," he said. "But since before to-night servants have rebuked masters, I spare not to tell you that you do most wrongly.

'Tis sad for the girl she died not in that wilderness where you found her."

"Ads my life!" cried Haward. "Leave my affairs alone!"

Both men were upon their feet. "I took you for a gentleman," said the Highlander, breathing hard. "I said to myself: 'Duart is overseas where I cannot serve him. I will take this other for my chief'"—

"That is for a Highland cateran and traitor," interrupted Haward, pleased to find another dart, but scarcely aware of how deadly an insult he was dealing.

In a flash the blow was struck. Juba, in the next room, hearing the noise of the overturned table, appeared at the door. "Set the table to rights and light the candles again," said his master calmly. "No, let the cards lie. Now begone to the quarters! 'Twas I that stumbled and overset the table."

Following the slave to the door he locked it upon him; then turned again to the room, and to MacLean standing waiting in the centre of it. "Under the circumstances, we may, I think, dispense with preliminaries. You will give me satisfaction here and now?"

"Do you take it at my hands?" asked the other proudly. "Just now you reminded me that I was your servant. But find me a sword"—

Haward went to a carved chest; drew from it two rapiers, measured the blades, and laid one upon the table. MacLean took it up, and slowly passed the gleaming steel between his fingers. Presently he began to speak, in a low, controlled, monotonous voice: "Why did you not leave me as I was? Six months ago I was alone, quiet, dead. A star had set for me; as the lights fail behind Ben More, it was lost and gone. You, long hated, long looked for, came, and the star arose again. You touched my scars, and suddenly I esteemed them honorable. You called me friend, and I turned from my enmity and clasped your hand. Now my soul goes back to its realm of solitude and hate; now you are my foe again." He broke off to bend the steel within his hands almost to the meeting of hilt and point. "A hated master," he ended, with bitter mirth, "yet one that I must thank for grace extended. Forty stripes is, I believe, the proper penalty."

Haward, who had seated himself at his escritoire and was writing, turned his head. "For my reference to your imprisonment in Virginia I apologize. I demand the reparation due from one gentleman to another for the indignity of a blow. Pardon me for another moment, when I shall be at your service."

He threw sand upon a sheet of gilt-edged paper, folded and superscribed it; then took from his breast a thicker document. "The Solebay, man-of-war, lying off James-town, sails at sunrise. The captain—Captain Meade—is my friend. Who knows the fortunes of war? If by chance I should fall to-night, take a boat at the landing, hasten upstream, and hail the Solebay. When you are aboard give Meade—who has reason to oblige me—this letter. He will carry you down the coast to Charleston, where, if you change your name and lurk for a while, you may pass for a buccaneer and be safe enough. For this other paper"— He hesitated, then spoke on with some constraint: "It is your release from servitude in Virginia,—in effect, your pardon. I have interest both here and at home—it hath been many years since Preston—the paper was not hard to obtain. I had meant to give it to you before we parted to-night. I regret that, should you prove the better swordsman, it may be of little service to you."

He laid the papers on the table, and began to divest himself of his coat, waistcoat, and long, curled periwig. MacLean took up the pardon and held it to a candle. It caught, but before the flame could reach the writing Haward had dashed down the other's hand and beaten out the blaze. "'Slife, Angus, what would you do!" he cried, and, taken unawares, there was angry concern in his voice. "Why, man, 't is liberty!"

"I may not accept it," said MacLean, with dry lips. "That letter, also, is useless to me. I would you were all villain."

"Your scruple is fantastic!" retorted the other, and as he spoke he put both papers upon the escritoire, weighting them with the sandbox. "You shall take them hence when our score is settled,—ay, and use them as best you may! Now, sir, are you ready?"

"You are weak from illness," said MacLean hoarsely, "Let the quarrel rest until you have recovered strength."

Haward laughed. "I was not strong yesterday," he said. "But Mr. Everard is pinked in the side, and Mr. Travis, who would fight with pistols, hath a ball through his shoulder."

The storekeeper started. "I have heard of those gentlemen! You fought them both upon the day when you left your sickroom?"

"Assuredly," answered the other, with a slight lift of his brows. "Will you be so good as to move the table to one side? So. On guard, sir!"

The man who had been ill unto death and the man who for many years had worn no sword acquitted themselves well. Had the room been a field behind Montagu House, had there been present seconds, a physician, gaping chairmen, the interest would have been breathless. As it was, the lady upon the wall smiled on, with her eyes forever upon the blossoms in her hand, and the river without, when it could be heard through the clashing of steel, made but a listless and dreamy sound. Each swordsman knew that he had provoked a friend to whom his debt was great, but each, according to his godless creed, must strive as though that friend were his dearest foe. The Englishman fought coolly, the Gael with fervor. The latter had an unguarded moment. Haward's blade leaped to meet it, and on the other's shirt appeared a bright red stain.

In the moment that he was touched the Highlander let fall his sword. Haward, not understanding, lowered his point, and with a gesture bade his antagonist recover the weapon. But the storekeeper folded his arms. "Where blood has been drawn there is satisfaction," he said. "I have given it to you, and now, by the bones of Gillean-na-Tuaidhe, I will not fight you longer!"

For a minute or more Haward stood with his eyes upon the ground and his hand yet closely clasping the rapier hilt; then, drawing a long breath, he took up the velvet scabbard and slowly sheathed his blade. "I am content," he said. "Your wound, I hope, is slight?"

MacLean thrust a handkerchief into his bosom to stanch the bleeding. "A pin prick," he said indifferently.

His late antagonist held out his hand. "It is well over. Come! We are not young hotheads, but men who have lived and suffered, and should know the vanity and the pity of such strife. Let us forget this hour, call each other friends again"—

"Tell me first," demanded MacLean, his arm rigid at his side,—"tell me first why you fought Mr. Everard and Mr. Travis."

Gray eyes and dark blue met. "I fought them," said Haward, "because, on a time, they offered insult to the woman whom I intend to make my wife."

So quiet was it in the room when he had spoken that the wash of the river, the tapping of walnut branches outside the window, the dropping of coals upon the hearth, became loud and insistent sounds. Then, "Darden's Audrey?" said MacLean in a whisper.

"Not Darden's Audrey, but mine," answered Haward,— "the only woman I have ever loved or shall love."

He walked to the window and looked out into the darkness. "To-night there is no light," he said to himself, beneath his breath. "By and by we shall stand here together, listening to the river, marking the wind in the trees." As upon paper heat of fire may cause to appear characters before invisible, so, when he turned, the flame of a great passion had brought all that was highest in this gentleman's nature into his countenance, softening and ennobling it. "Whatever my thoughts before," he said simply, "I have never, since I awoke from my fever and remembered that night at the Palace, meant other than this." Coming back to MacLean he laid a hand upon his shoulder. "Who made us knows we all do need forgiveness! Am I no more to you, Angus, than Ewin Mor Mackinnon?"

An hour later, those who were to be lifetime friends went together down the echoing stair and through the empty house to the outer door. When it was opened, they saw that upon the stone step without, in the square of light thrown by the candles behind them, lay an Indian arrow. MacLean picked it up. "'Twas placed athwart the door," he said doubtingly. "Is it in the nature of a challenge?"

Haward took the dart, and examined it curiously. "The trader grows troublesome," he remarked. "He must back to the woods and to the foes of his own class." As he spoke he broke the arrow in two, and flung the pieces from him.

It was a night of many stars and a keen wind. Moved each in his degree by its beauty, Haward and MacLean stood regarding it before they should go, the one back to his solitary chamber, the other to the store which was to be his charge no longer than the morrow. "I feel the air that blows from the hills," said the Highlander. "It comes over the heather; it hath swept the lochs, and I hear it in the sound of torrents." He lifted his face to the wind. "The breath of freedom! I shall have dreams to-night."

When he was gone, Haward, left alone, looked for a while upon the heights of stars. "I too shall dream to-night," he breathed to himself. "To-morrow all will be well." His gaze falling from the splendor of the skies to the swaying trees, gaunt, bare, and murmuring of their loss to the hurrying river, sadness and vague fear took sudden possession of his soul. He spoke her name over and over; he left the house and went into the garden. It was the garden of the dying year, and the change that in the morning he had smiled to see now appalled him. He would have had it June again. Now, when on the morrow he and Audrey should pass through the garden, it must be down dank and leaf-strewn paths, past yellow and broken stalks, with here and there wan ghosts of flowers.

He came to the dial, and, bending, pressed his lips against the carven words that, so often as they had stood there together, she had traced with her finger. "Love! thou mighty alchemist!" he breathed. "Life! that may now be gold, now iron, but never again dull lead! Death"—He paused; then, "There shall be no death," he said, and left the withered garden for the lonely, echoing house.

CHAPTER XXIV

AUDREY COMES TO WESTOVER

It was ten of the clock upon this same night when Hugon left the glebe house. Audrey, crouching in the dark beside her window, heard him bid the minister, as drunk as himself, good-night, and watched him go unsteadily down the path that led to the road. Once he paused, and made as if to return; then went on to his lair at the crossroads ordinary. Again Audrey waited,—this time by the door. Darden stumbled upstairs to bed. Mistress Deborah's voice was raised in shrill reproach, and the drunken minister answered her with oaths. The small house rang with their quarrel, but Audrey listened with indifference; not trembling and stopping her ears, as once she would have done. It was over at last, and the place sunk in silence; but still the girl waited and listened, standing close to the door. At last, as it was drawing toward midnight, she put her hand upon the latch, and, raising it very softly, slipped outside. Heavy breathing came from the room where slept her guardians; it went evenly on while she crept downstairs and unbarred the outer door. Sure and silent and light of touch, she passed like a spirit from the house that had given her shelter, nor once looked back upon it.

The boat, hidden in the reeds, was her destination; she loosed it, and taking the oars rowed down the creek. When she came to the garden wall, she bent her head and shut her eyes; but when she had left the creek for the great dim river, she looked at Fair View house as she rowed past it on her way to the mountains. No light to-night; the hour was late, and he was asleep, and that was well.

It was cold upon the river, and sere leaves, loosening their hold upon that which had given them life, drifted down upon her as she rowed beneath arching trees. When she left the dark bank for the unshadowed stream, the wind struck her brow and the glittering stars perplexed her. There were so many of them. When one shot, she knew that a soul had left the earth. Another fell, and another,— it must be a good night for dying. She ceased to row, and, leaning over, dipped her hand and arm into the black water. The movement brought the gunwale of the boat even with the flood.... Say that one leaned over a little farther ... there would fall another star. God gathered the stars in his hand, but he would surely be angry with one that came before it was called, and the star would sink past him into a night forever dreadful.... The water was cold and deep and black. Great fish throve in it, and below was a bed of ooze and mud....

The girl awoke from her dream of self-murder with a cry of terror. Not the river, good Lord, not the river! Not death, but life! With a second shuddering cry she lifted hand and arm from the water, and with frantic haste dried them upon the skirt of her dress. There had been none to hear her. Upon the midnight river, between the dim forests that ever spoke, but never listened, she was utterly alone. She took the oars again, and went on her way up the river, rowing swiftly, for the mountains were far away, and she might be pursued.

When she drew near to Jamestown she shot far out into the river, because men might be astir in the boats about the town landing. Anchored in midstream was a great ship,—a man-of-war, bristling with guns. Her boat touched its shadow, and the lookout called to her. She bent her head, put forth her strength, and left the black hull behind her. There was another ship to pass, a slaver that had come in the evening before, and would land its cargo at sunrise. The stench that arose from it was intolerable, and, as the girl passed, a corpse, heavily weighted, was thrown into the water. Audrey went swiftly by, and the river lay clean before her. The stars paled and the dawn came, but she could not see the shores for the thick white mist. A spectral boat, with a sail like a gray moth's wing, slipped past her. The shadow at the helm was whistling for the wind, and the sound came strange and shrill through the filmy, ashen morning. The mist began to lift. A few moments now, and the river would lie dazzlingly bare between the red and yellow forests. She turned her boat shorewards, and presently forced it beneath the bronze-leafed, drooping boughs of a sycamore. Here she left the boat, tying it to the tree, and hoping that it was well hidden. The great fear at her heart was that, when she was missed, Hugon would undertake to follow and to find her. He had the skill to do so. Perhaps, after many days, when she was in sight of the mountains, she might turn her head and, in that lonely land, see him coming toward her.

The sun was shining, and the woods were gay above her head and gay beneath her feet. When the wind blew, the colored leaves went before it like flights of birds. She was hungry, and as she walked she ate a piece of bread taken from the glebe-house larder. It was her plan to go rapidly through the settled country, keeping as far as possible to the great spaces of woodland which the axe had left untouched; sleeping in such dark and hidden hollows as she could find; begging food only when she must, and then from poor folk who would not stay her or be overcurious about her business. As she went on, the houses, she knew, would be farther and farther apart; the time would soon arrive when she might walk half a day and see never a clearing in the deep woods. Then the hills would rise about her, and far, far off she might see the mountains, fixed, cloudlike, serene, and still, beyond the miles of rustling forest. There would be no more great houses, built for ladies and gentlemen, but here and there, at far distances, rude cabins, dwelt in by kind and simple folk. At such a home, when the mountains had taken on a deeper blue, when the streams were narrow and the level land only a memory, she would pause, would ask if she might stay. What work was wanted she would do. Perhaps there would be children, or a young girl like Molly, or a kind woman like Mistress Stagg; and perhaps, after a long, long while, it would grow to seem to her like that other cabin.

These were her rose-colored visions. At other times a terror took her by the shoulders, holding her until her face whitened and her eyes grew wide and dark. The way was long and the leaves were falling fast, and she thought that it might be true that in this world into which she had awakened there was for her no home. The cold would come, and she might have no bread, and for all her wandering find none to take her in. In those forests of the west the wolves ran in packs, and the Indians burned and wasted. Some bitter night-time she would die.... Watching the sky from Fair View windows, perhaps he might idly mark a falling star.

All that day she walked, keeping as far as was possible to the woods, but forced now and again to traverse open fields and long stretches of sunny road. If she saw any one coming, she hid in the roadside bushes, or, if that could not be done, walked steadily onward, with her head bent and her heart beating fast. It must have been a day for minding one's own business, for none stayed or questioned her. Her dinner she begged from some children whom she found in a wood gathering nuts. Supper she had none. When night fell, she was glad to lay herself down upon a bed of leaves that she had raked together; but she slept little, for the wind moaned in the half-clad branches, and she could not cease from counting the stars that shot. In the morning, numbed and cold, she went slowly on until she came to a wayside house. Quaker folk lived there; and they asked her no question, but with kind words gave her of what they had, and let her rest and grow warm in the sunshine upon their doorstep. She thanked them with shy grace, but presently, when they were not looking, rose and went her way. Upon the second day she kept to the road. It was loss of time wandering in the woods, skirting thicket and marsh, forced ever and again to return to the beaten track. She thought, also, that she must be safe, so far was she now from Fair View. How could they guess that she was gone to the mountains?

About midday, two men on horseback looked at her in passing. One spoke to the other, and turning their horses they put after and overtook her. He who had spoken touched her with the butt of his whip. "Ecod!" he exclaimed. "It's the lass we saw run for a guinea last May Day at Jamestown! Why so far from home, light o' heels?"

A wild leap of her heart, a singing in her ears, and Audrey clutched at safety.

"I be Joan, the smith's daughter," she said stolidly. "I niver ran for a guinea. I niver saw a guinea. I be going an errand for feyther."

"Ecod, then!" said the other man. "You're on a wrong scent. 'Twas no dolt that ran that day!"

The man who had touched her laughed. "'Facks, you are right, Tom! But I'd ha' sworn 't was that brown girl. Go your ways on your errand for 'feyther'!" As he spoke, being of an amorous turn, he stooped from his saddle and kissed her. Audrey, since she was at that time not Audrey at all, but Joan, the smith's daughter, took the salute as stolidly as she had spoken. The two men rode away, and the second said to the first: "A Williamsburgh man told me that the girl who won the guinea could speak and look like a born lady. Didn't ye hear the story of how she went to the Governor's ball, all tricked out, dancing, and making people think she was some fine dame from Maryland maybe? And the next day she was scored in church before all the town. I don't know as they put a white sheet on her, but they say 't was no more than her deserts."

Audrey, left standing in the sunny road, retook her own countenance, rubbed her cheek where the man's lips had touched it, and trembled like a leaf. She was frightened, both at the encounter and because she could make herself so like Joan,—Joan who lived near the crossroads ordinary, and who had been whipped at the Court House.

Late that afternoon she came upon two or three rude dwellings clustered about a mill. A knot of men, the miller in the midst, stood and gazed at the mill-stream. They wore an angry look; and Audrey passed them hastily by. At the farthest house she paused to beg a piece of bread; but the woman who came to the door frowned and roughly bade her begone, and a child threw a stone at her. "One witch is enough to take the bread out of poor folks' mouths!" cried the woman. "Be off, or I'll set the dogs on ye!" The children ran after her as she hastened from the inhospitable neighborhood. "'T is a young witch," they cried, "going to help the old one swim to-night!" and a stone struck her, bruising her shoulder.

She began to run, and, fleet of foot as she was, soon distanced her tormentors. When she slackened pace it was sunset, and she was faint with hunger and desperately weary. From the road a bypath led to a small clearing in a wood, with a slender spiral of smoke showing between the trees. Audrey went that way, and came upon a crazy cabin whose door and window were fast closed. In the unkempt garden rose an apple-tree, with the red apples shriveling upon its boughs, and from the broken gate a line of cedars, black and ragged, ran down to a piece of water, here ghastly pale, there streaked like the sky above with angry crimson. The place was very still, and the air felt cold. When no answer came to her first knocking, Audrey beat upon the door; for she was suddenly afraid of the road behind her, and of the doleful woods and the coming night.

The window shutter creaked ever so slightly, and some one looked out; then the door opened, and a very old and wrinkled woman, with lines of cunning about her mouth, laid her hand upon the girl's arm. "Who be ye?" she whispered. "Did ye bring warning? I don't say, mind ye, that I can't make a stream go dry,—maybe I can and maybe I can't,—but I didn't put a word on the one yonder." She threw up her arms with a wailing cry. "But they won't believe what a poor old soul says! Are they in an evil temper, honey?"

"I don't know what you mean," said Audrey. "I have come a long way, and I am hungry and tired. Give me a piece of bread, and let me stay with you to-night."

The old woman moved aside, and the girl, entering a room that was mean and poor enough, sat down upon a stool beside the fire. "If ye came by the mill," demanded her hostess, with a suspicious eye, "why did ye not stop there for bite and sup?"

"The men were all talking together," answered Audrey wearily. "They looked so angry that I was afraid of them. I did stop at one house; but the woman bade me begone, and the children threw stones at me and called me a witch."

The crone stooped and stirred the fire; then from a cupboard brought forth bread and a little red wine, and set them before the girl. "They called you a witch, did they?" she mumbled as she went to and fro. "And the men were talking and planning together?"

Audrey ate the bread and drank the wine; then, because she was so tired, leaned her head against the table and fell half asleep. When she roused herself, it was to find her withered hostess standing over her with a sly and tooth-less smile. "I've been thinking," she whispered, "that since you're here to mind the house, I'll just step out to a neighbor's about some business I have in hand. You can stay by the fire, honey, and be warm and comfortable. Maybe I'll not come back to-night."

Going to the window, she dropped a heavy bar across the shutter. "Ye'll put the chain across the door when I'm out," she commanded. "There be evil-disposed folk may want to win in." Coming back to the girl, she laid a skinny hand upon her arm. Whether with palsy or with fright the hand shook like a leaf, but Audrey, half asleep again, noticed little beyond the fact that the fire warmed her, and that here at last was rest. "If there should come a knocking and a calling, honey," whispered the witch, "don't ye answer to it or unbar the door. Ye'll save time for me that way. But if they win in, tell them I went to the northward."

Audrey looked at her with glazed, uncomprehending eyes, while the gnome-like figure appeared to grow smaller, to melt out of the doorway. It was a minute or more before the wayfarer thus left alone in the hut could remember that she had been told to bar the door. Then her instinct of obedience sent her to the threshold. Dusk was falling, and the waters of the pool lay pale and still beyond the ebony cedars. Through the twilit landscape moved the crone who had housed her for the night; but she went not to the north, but southwards toward the river. Presently the dusk swallowed her up, and Audrey was left with the ragged garden and the broken fence and the tiny firelit hut. Reentering the room, she fastened the door, as she had been told to do, and then went back to the hearth. The fire blazed and the shadows danced; it was far better than last night, out in the cold, lying upon dead leaves, watching the falling stars. Here it was warm, warm as June in a walled garden; the fire was red like the roses ... the roses that had thorns to bring heart's blood.

Audrey fell fast asleep; and while she was asleep and the night was yet young, the miller whose mill stream had run dry, the keeper of a tippling house whose custom had dwindled, the ferryman whose child had peaked and pined and died, came with a score of men to reckon with the witch who had done the mischief. Finding door and window fast shut, they knocked, softly at first, then loudly and with threats. One watched the chimney, to see that the witch did not ride forth that way; and the father of the child wished to gather brush, pile it against the entrance, and set all afire. The miller, who was a man of strength, ended the matter by breaking in the door. They knew that the witch was there, because they had heard her moving about, and, when the door gave, a cry of affright. When, however, they had laid hands upon her, and dragged her out under the stars, into the light of the torches they carried, they found that the witch, who, as was well known, could slip her shape as a snake slips its skin, was no longer old and bowed, but straight and young.

"Let me go!" cried Audrey. "How dare you hold me! I never harmed one of you. I am a poor girl come from a long way off"—

"Ay, a long way!" exclaimed the ferryman. "More leagues, I'll warrant, than there are miles in Virginia! We'll see if ye can swim home, ye witch!"

"I'm no witch!" cried the girl again. "I never harmed you. Let me go!"

One of the torchbearers gave ground a little. "She do look mortal young. But where be the witch, then?"

Audrey strove to shake herself free. "The old woman left me alone in the house. She went to—to the northward."

"She lies!" cried the ferryman, addressing himself to the angry throng. The torches, flaming in the night wind, gave forth a streaming, uncertain, and bewildering light; to the excited imaginations of the rustic avengers, the form in the midst of them was not always that of a young girl, but now and again wavered toward the semblance of the hag who had wrought them evil. "Before the child died he talked forever of somebody young and fair that came and stood by him when he slept. We thought 't was his dead mother, but now—now I see who 't was!" Seizing the girl by the wrists, he burst with her through the crowd. "Let the water touch her, she'll turn witch again!"

The excited throng, blinded by its own imagination, took up the cry. The girl's voice was drowned; she set her lips, and strove dumbly with her captors; but they swept her through the weed-grown garden and broken gate, past the cedars that were so ragged and black, down to the cold and deep water. She thought of the night upon the river and of the falling stars, and with a sudden, piercing cry struggled fiercely to escape. The bank was steep; hands pushed her forward: she felt the ghastly embrace of the water, and saw, ere the flood closed over her upturned face, the cold and quiet stars.

So loud was the ringing in her ears that she heard no access of voices upon the bank, and knew not that a fresh commotion had arisen. She was sinking for the third time, and her mind had begun to wander in the Fair View garden, when an arm caught and held her up. She was borne to the shore; there were men on horseback; some one with a clear, authoritative voice was now berating, now good-humoredly arguing with, her late judges.

The man who had sprung to save her held her up to arms that reached down from the bank above; another moment and she felt the earth again beneath her feet, but could only think that, with half the dying past, these strangers had been cruel to bring her back. Her rescuer shook himself like a great dog. "I've saved the witch alive," he panted. "May God forgive and your Honor reward me!"

"Nay, worthy constable, you must look to Sathanas for

reward!" cried the gentleman who had been haranguing the miller and his company. These gentry, hardly convinced, but not prepared to debate the matter with a justice of the peace and a great man of those parts, began to slip away. The torchbearers, probably averse to holding a light to their own countenances, had flung the torches into the water, and now, heavily shadowed by the cedars, the place was in deep darkness. Presently there were left to berate only the miller and the ferryman, and at last these also went sullenly away without having troubled to mention the witch's late transformation from age to youth.

"Where is the rescued fair one?" continued the gentleman who, for his own pleasure, had led the conservers of law and order. "Produce the sibyl, honest Dogberry! Faith, if the lady be not an ingrate, you've henceforth a friend at court!"

"My name is Saunders,—Dick Saunders, your Honor," quoth the constable. "For the witch, she lies quiet on the ground beneath the cedar yonder."

"She won't speak!" cried another. "She just lies there trembling, with her face in her hands."

"But she said, 'O Christ!' when we took her from the water," put in a third.

"She was nigh drowned," ended the constable. "And I'm a-tremble myself, the water was that cold. Wauns! I wish I were in the chimney corner at the Court House ordinary!"

The master of Westover flung his riding cloak to one of the constable's men. "Wrap it around the shivering iniquity on the ground yonder; and you, Tom Hope, that brought warning of what your neighbors would do, mount and take the witch behind you. Master Constable, you will lodge Hecate in the gaol to-night, and in the morning bring her up to the great house. We would inquire why a lady so accomplished that she can dry a mill stream to plague a miller cannot drain a pool to save herself from drowning!"

At a crossing of the ways, shortly before Court House, gaol, and ordinary were reached, the adventurous Colonel gave a good-night to the constable and his company, and, with a negro servant at his heels, rode gayly on beneath the stars to his house at Westover. Hardy, alert, in love with living, he was well amused by the night's proceedings. The incident should figure in his next letter to Orrery or to his cousin Taylor.

It figured largely in the table-talk next morning, when the sprightly gentleman sat at breakfast with his daughter and his second wife, a fair and youthful kinswoman of Martha and Teresa Blount. The gentleman, launched upon the subject of witchcraft, handled it with equal wit and learning. The ladies thought that the water must have been very cold, and trusted that the old dame was properly grateful, and would, after such a lesson, leave her evil practices. As they were rising from table, word was brought to the master that constable and witch were outside.

The Colonel kissed his wife, promised his daughter to be merciful, and, humming a song, went through the hall to the open house door and the broad, three-sided steps of stone. The constable was awaiting him.

"Here be mysteries, your Honor! As I serve the King, 't weren't Goody Price for whom I ruined my new frieze, but a slip of a girl!" He waved his hand. "Will your Honor please to look?"

Audrey sat in the sunshine upon the stone steps with her head bowed upon her arms. The morning that was so bright was not bright for her; she thought that life had used her but unkindly. A great tree, growing close to the house, sent leaves of dull gold adrift, and they lay at her feet and upon the skirt of her dress. The constable spoke to her: "Now, mistress, here's a gentleman as stands for the King and the law. Look up!"

A white hand was laid upon the Colonel's arm. "I came to make sure that you were not harsh with the poor creature," said Evelyn's pitying voice. "There is so much misery. Where is she? Ah!"

To gain at last his prisoner's attention, the constable struck her lightly across the shoulders with his cane. "Get up!" he cried impatiently. "Get up and make your curtsy! Ecod, I wish I'd left you in Hunter's Pond!"

Audrey rose, and turned her face, not to the justice of the peace and arbiter of the fate of witches, but to Evelyn, standing above her,—Evelyn, slighter, paler, than she had been at Williamsburgh, but beautiful in her colored, fragrant silks and the air that was hers of sweet and mournful distinction. Now she cried out sharply, while "That girl again!" swore the Colonel, beneath his breath.

Audrey did as she had been told, and made her curtsy. Then, while father and daughter stared at her, the gentleman very red and biting his lip, the lady marble in her loveliness, she tried to speak, to ask them to let her go, but found no words. The face of Evelyn, at whom alone she looked, wavered into distance, gazing at her coldly and mournfully from miles away. She made a faint gesture of weariness and despair; then sank down at Evelyn's feet, and lay there in a swoon.

CHAPTER XXV

TWO WOMEN

Evelyn, hearing footsteps across the floor of the attic room above her own bedchamber, arose and set wide the door; then went back to her chair by the window that looked out upon green grass and party-colored trees and long reaches of the shining river. "Come here, if you please," she called to Audrey, as the latter slowly descended the stair from the room where, half asleep, half awake, she had lain since morning.

Audrey entered the pleasant chamber, furnished with what luxury the age afforded, and stood before the sometime princess of her dreams. "Will you not sit down?" asked Evelyn, in a low voice, and pointed to a chair.

"I had rather stand," answered Audrey. "Why did you call me? I was on my way"—

The other's clear eyes dwelt upon her. "Whither were you going?"

"Out of your house," said Audrey simply, "and out of your life."

Evelyn folded her hands in her silken lap, and looked out upon river and sky and ceaseless drift of colored leaves. "You can never go out of my life," she said. "Why the power to vex and ruin was given you I do not know, but you have used it. Why did you run away from Fair View?"

"That I might never see Mr. Haward again," answered Audrey. She held her head up, but she felt the stab. It had not occurred to her that hers was the power to vex and ruin; apparently that belonged elsewhere.

Evelyn turned from the window, and the two women, the princess and the herdgirl, regarded each other. "Oh, my God!" cried Evelyn. "I did not know that you loved him so!"

But Audrey shook her head, and spoke with calmness: "Once I loved and knew it not, and once I loved and knew it. It was all in a dream, and now I have waked up." She passed her hand across her brow and eyes, and pushed back her heavy hair. It was a gesture that was common to her. To Evelyn it brought a sudden stinging memory of the ballroom at the Palace; of how this girl had looked in her splendid dress, with the roses in her hair; of Haward's words at the coach door. She had not seen him since that night. "I am going a long way," continued Audrey. "It will be as though I died. I never meant to harm you."

The other gazed at her with wide, dry eyes, and with an unwonted color in her cheeks. "She is beautiful," thought Audrey; then wondered how long she must stay in this room and this house. Without the window the trees beckoned, the light was fair upon the river; in the south hung a cloud, silver-hued, and shaped like two mighty wings. Audrey, with her eyes upon the cloud, thought, "If the wings were mine, I would reach the mountains to-night."

"Do you remember last May Day?" asked Evelyn, in a voice scarcely above a whisper. "He and I, sitting side by side, watched your running, and I praised you to him. Then we went away, and while we gathered flowers on the road to Williamsburgh he asked me to be his wife. I said no, for he loved me not as I wished to be loved. Afterward, in Williamsburgh, he spoke again.... I said, 'When you come to Westover;' and he kissed my hand, and vowed that the next week should find him here." She turned once more to the window, and, with her chin in her hand, looked out upon the beauty of the autumn. "Day by day, and day by day," she said, in the same hushed voice, "I sat at this window and watched for him to come. The weeks went by, and he came not. I began to hear talk of you. Oh, I deny not that it was bitter!"

"Oh me! oh me!" cried Audrey. "I was so happy, and I thought no harm."

"He came at last," continued Evelyn. "For a month he stayed here, paying me court. I was too proud to speak of what I had heard. After a while I thought it must have been an idle rumor." Her voice changed, and with a sudden gesture of passion and despair she lifted her arms above her head, then clasped and wrung her hands. "Oh, for a month he forgot you! In all the years to come I shall have that comfort: for one little month, in the company of the woman whom, because she was of his own rank, because she had wealth, because others found her fair and honored her with heart as well as lip, he wished to make his wife,—for that short month he forgot you! The days were sweet to me, sweet, sweet! Oh, I dreamed my dreams!... And then we were called to Williamsburgh to greet the new Governor, and he went with us, and again I heard your name coupled with his.... There was between us no betrothal. I had delayed to say yes to his asking, for I wished to make sure,—to make sure that he loved me. No man can say he broke troth with me. For that my pride gives thanks!"

"What must I do?" said Audrey to herself. "Pain is hard to bear."

"That night at the ball," continued Evelyn, "when, coming down the stair, I saw you standing beside him ... and after that, the music, and the lights, and you dancing with him, in your dark beauty, with the flowers in your hair ... and after that, you and I in my coach and his face at the window!... Oh, I can tell you what he said! He said: 'Good-by, sweetheart.... The violets are for you; but the great white blossoms, and the boughs of rosy mist, and all the trees that wave in the wind are for Audrey.'"

"For me!" cried Audrey,—"for me an hour in Bruton church next morning!"

A silence followed her words. Evelyn, sitting in the great chair, rested her cheek upon her hand and gazed steadfastly at her guest of a day. The sunshine had stolen from the room, but dwelt upon and caressed the world without the window. Faint, tinkling notes of a harpsichord floated up from the parlor below, followed by young Madam Byrd's voice singing to the perturbed Colonel:—

"'O Love! they wrong thee much,
That say thy sweet is bitter,
When thy rich fruit is such
As nothing can be sweeter.
Fair house of joy and bliss'"—

The song came to an end, but after a pause the harpsichord sounded again, and the singer's voice rang out:—

"'Under the greenwood tree,
Who loves to lie with me'"—

Audrey gave an involuntary cry; then, with her lip between her teeth, strove for courage, failed, and with another strangled cry sank upon her knees before a chair and buried her face in its cushions.

When a little time had passed, Evelyn arose and went to her. "Fate has played with us both," she said, in a voice that strove for calmness. "If there was great bitterness in my heart toward you then, I hope it is not so now; if, on that night, I spoke harshly, unkindly, ungenerously, I—I am sorry. I thought what others thought. I—I cared not to touch you.... But now I am told that 't was not you that did unworthily. Mr. Haward has written to me; days ago I had this letter." It was in her hand, and she held it out to the kneeling girl. "Yes, yes, you must read; it concerns you." Her voice, low and broken, was yet imperious. Audrey raised her head, took and read the letter. There were but a few unsteady lines, written from Marot's ordinary at Williamsburgh. The writer was too weak as yet for many words; few words were best, perhaps. His was all the blame for the occurrence at the Palace, for all besides. That which, upon his recovery, he must strive to teach his acquaintance at large he prayed Evelyn to believe at once and forever. She whom, against her will and in the madness of his fever, he had taken to the Governor's house was most innocent,—guiltless of all save a child-like affection for the writer, a misplaced confidence, born of old days, and now shattered by his own hand. Before that night she had never guessed his passion, never known the use that had been made of her name. This upon the honor of a gentleman. For the rest, as soon as his strength was regained, he purposed traveling to Westover. There, if Mistress Evelyn Byrd would receive him for an hour, he might in some measure explain, excuse. For much, he knew, there was no excuse,—only pardon to be asked.

The letter ended abruptly, as though the writer's strength were exhausted. Audrey read it through, then with indifference gave it back to Evelyn. "It is true,—what he says?" whispered the latter, crumpling the paper in her hand.

Audrey gazed up at her with wide, tearless eyes. "Yes, it is true. There was no need for you to use those words to me in the coach, that night,—though even then I did not understand. There is no reason why you should fear to touch me."

Her head sank upon her arm. In the parlor below the singing came to an end, but the harpsichord, lightly fingered, gave forth a haunting melody. It was suited to the afternoon: to the golden light, the drifting leaves, the murmurs of wind and wave, without the window: to the shadows, the stillness, and the sorrow within the room. Evelyn, turning slowly toward the kneeling figure, of a sudden saw it through a mist of tears. Her clasped hands parted; she bent and touched the bowed head. Audrey looked up, and her dark eyes made appeal. Evelyn stooped lower yet; her tears fell upon Audrey's brow; a moment, and the two, cast by life in the selfsame tragedy, were in each other's arms.

"You know that I came from the mountains," whispered Audrey. "I am going back. You must tell no one; in a little while I shall be forgotten."

"To the mountains!" cried Evelyn. "No one lives there. You would die of cold and hunger. No, no! We are alike unhappy: you shall stay with me here at Westover."

She rose from her knees, and Audrey rose with her. They no longer clasped each other,—that impulse was past,—but their eyes met in sorrowful amity. Audrey shook her head. "That may not be," she said simply. "I must go away that we may not both be unhappy." She lifted her face to the cloud in the south, "I almost died last night. When you drown, there is at first fear and struggling, but at last it is like dreaming, and there is a lightness.... When that came I thought, 'It is the air of the mountains,—I am drawing near them.' ... Will you let me go now? I will slip from the house through the fields into the woods, and none will know"—

But Evelyn caught her by the wrist. "You are beside yourself! I would rouse the plantation; in an hour you would be found. Stay with me!"

A knock at the door, and the Colonel's secretary, a pale and grave young man, bowing on the threshold. He was just come from the attic room, where he had failed to find the young woman who had been lodged there that morning. The Colonel, supposing that by now she was recovered from her swoon and her fright of the night before, and having certain questions to put to her, desired her to descend to the parlor. Hearing voices in Mistress Evelyn's room—

"Very well, Mr. Drew," said the lady. "You need not wait. I will myself seek my father with—with our guest."

In the parlor Madam Byrd was yet at the harpsichord, but ceased to touch the keys when her step-daughter, followed by Darden's Audrey, entered the room. The master of Westover, seated beside his young wife, looked quickly up, arched his brows and turned somewhat red, as his daughter, with her gliding step, crossed the room to greet him. Audrey, obeying a motion of her companion's hand, waited beside a window, in the shadow of its heavy curtains. "Evelyn," quoth the Colonel, rising from his chair and taking his daughter's hand, "this is scarce befitting"—

Evelyn stayed his further speech by an appealing gesture. "Let me speak with you, sir. No, no, madam, do not go! There is naught the world might not hear."

Audrey waited in the shadow by the window, and her mind was busy, for she had her plans to lay. Sometimes Evelyn's low voice, sometimes the Colonel's deeper tones, pierced her understanding; when this was so she moved restlessly, wishing that it were night and she away. Presently she began to observe the room, which was richly furnished. There were garlands upon the ceiling; a table near her was set with many curious ornaments; upon a tall cabinet stood a bowl of yellow flowers; the lady at the harpsichord wore a dress to match the flowers, while Evelyn's dress was white; beyond them was a pier glass finer than the one at Fair View.

This glass reflected the doorway, and thus she was the first to see the man from whom she had fled. "Mr. Marmaduke Haward, massa!" announced the servant who had ushered him through the hall.

Haward, hat in hand, entered the room. The three beside the harpsichord arose; the one at the window slipped deeper into the shadow of the curtains, and so escaped the visitor's observation. The latter bowed to the master of

Westover, who ceremoniously returned the salute, and to the two ladies, who curtsied to him, but opened not their lips.

"This, sir," said Colonel Byrd, holding himself very erect, "is an unexpected honor."

"Rather, sir, an unwished-for intrusion," answered the other. "I beg you to believe that I will trouble you for no longer time than matters require."

The Colonel bit his lip. "There was a time when Mr. Haward was most welcome to my house. If 't is no longer thus"—

Haward made a gesture of assent. "I know that the time is past. I am sorry that 't is so. I had thought, sir, to find you alone. Am I to speak before these ladies?"

The Colonel hesitated, but Evelyn, leaving Madam Byrd beside the harpsichord, came to her father's side. That gentleman glanced at her keenly. There was no agitation to mar the pensive loveliness of her face; her eyes were steadfast, the lips faintly smiling. "If what you have to say concerns my daughter," said the Colonel, "she will listen to you here and now."

For a few moments dead silence; then Haward spoke, slowly, weighing his words: "I am on my way, Colonel Byrd, to the country beyond the falls. I have entered upon a search, and I know not when it will be ended or when I shall return. Westover lay in my path, and there was that which needed to be said to you, sir, and to your daughter. When it has been said I will take my leave." He paused; then, with a quickened breath, again took up his task: "Some months ago, sir, I sought and obtained your permission to make my suit to your daughter for her hand. The lady, worthy of a better mate, hath done well in saying no to my importunity. I accept her decision, withdraw my suit, wish her all happiness." He bowed again formally; then stood with lowered eyes, his hand griping the edge of the table.

"I am aware that my daughter has declined to entertain your proposals," said the Colonel coldly, "and I approve her determination. Is this all, sir?"

"It should, perhaps, be all," answered Haward. "And yet"—He turned to Evelyn, snow-white, calm, with that faint smile upon her face. "May I speak to you?" he said, in a scarcely audible voice.

She looked at him, with parting lips.

"Here and now," the Colonel answered for her. "Be brief, sir."

The master of Fair View found it hard to speak, "Evelyn"—he began, and paused, biting his lip. It was very quiet in the familiar parlor, quiet and dim, and drawing toward eventide. The lady at the harpsichord chanced to let fall her hand upon the keys. They gave forth a deep and melancholy sound that vibrated through the room. The chord was like an odor in its subtle power to bring crowding memories. To Haward, and perhaps to Evelyn, scenes long shifted, long faded, took on fresh colors, glowed anew, replaced the canvas of the present. For years the two had been friends; later months had seen him her avowed suitor. In this very room he had bent over her at the harpsichord when the song was finished; had sat beside her in the deep window seat while the stars brightened, before the candles were brought in.

Now, for a moment, he stood with his hand over his eyes; then, letting it fall, he spoke with firmness. "Evelyn," he said, "if I have wronged you, forgive me. Our friendship that has been I lay at your feet: forget it and forget me. You are noble, generous, high of mind: I pray you to let no remembrance of me trouble your life. May it be happy,—may all good attend you.... Evelyn, good-by!"

He kneeled and lifted to his lips the hem of her dress. As he rose, and bowing low would have taken formal leave of the two beside her, she put out her hand, staying him by the gesture and the look upon her colorless face. "You spoke of a search," she said. "What search?"

Haward raised his eyes to hers that were quiet, almost smiling, though darkly shadowed by past pain. "I will tell you, Evelyn. Why should not I tell you this, also?... Four days ago, upon my return to Fair View, I sought and found the woman that I love,—the woman that, by all that is best within me, I love worthily! She shrank from me; she listened not; she shut eye and ear, and fled. And I,— confident fool!—I thought, 'To-morrow I will make her heed,' and so let her go. When the morrow came she was gone indeed." He halted, made an involuntary gesture of distress, then went on, rapidly and with agitation: "There was a boat missing; she was seen to pass Jamestown, rowing steadily up the river. But for this I should have thought—I should have feared—God knows what I should not have feared! As it is I have searchers out, both on this side and on the southern shore. An Indian and myself have come up river in his canoe. We have not found her yet. If it be so that she has passed unseen through the settled country, I will seek her toward the mountains."

"And when you have found her, what then, sir?" cried the

Colonel, tapping his snuffbox.

"Then, sir," answered Haward with hauteur, "she will become my wife."

He turned again to Evelyn, but when he spoke it was less to her than to himself. "It grows late," he said. "Night is coming on, and at the fall of the leaf the nights are cold. One sleeping in the forest would suffer ... if she sleeps. I have not slept since she was missed. I must begone"—

"It grows late indeed," replied Evelyn, with lifted face and a voice low, clear, and sweet as a silver bell,—"so late that there is a rose flush in the sky beyond the river. Look! you may see it through yonder window."

She touched his hand and made him look to the far window. "Who is it that stands in the shadow, hiding her face in her hands?" he asked at last, beneath his breath.

"'Tis Audrey," answered Evelyn, in the same clear, sweet, and passionless tones. She took her hand from his and addressed herself to her father. "Dear sir," she said, "to my mind no quarrel exists between us and this gentleman. There is no reason"—she drew herself up—"no reason why we should not extend to Mr. Marmaduke Haward the hospitality of Westover." She smiled and leaned against her father's arm. "And now let us three,—you and Maria, whom I protest you keep too long at the harpsichord, and I, who love this hour of the evening,—let us go walk in the garden and see what flowers the frost has spared."

CHAPTER XXVI

SANCTUARY

"Child," demanded Haward, "why did you frighten me so?" He took her hands from her face, and drew her from the shadow of the curtain into the evening glow. Her hands lay passive in his; her eyes held the despair of a runner spent and fallen, with the goal just in sight. "Would have had me go again to the mountains for you, little maid?" Haward's voice trembled with the delight of his ended quest.

"Call me not by that name," Audrey said. "One that is dead used it."

"I will call you love," he answered,—"my love, my dear love, my true love!"

"Nor that either," she said, and caught her breath. "I know not why you should speak to me so."

"What must I call you then?" he asked, with the smile still upon his lips.

"A stranger and a dreamer," she answered. "Go your ways, and I will go mine."

There was silence in the room, broken by Haward. "For us two one path," he said; "why, Audrey, Audrey, Audrey!" Suddenly he caught her in his arms. "My love!" he whispered—"my love Audrey! my wife Audrey!" His kisses rained upon her face. She lay quiet until the storm had passed; then freed herself, looked at him, and shook her head.

"You killed him," she said, "that one whom I—worshiped. It was not well done of you.... There was a dream I had last summer. I told it to—to the one you killed. Now part of the dream has come true.... You never were! Oh, death had been easy pain, for it had left memory, hope! But you never were! you never were!"

"I am!" cried Haward ardently. "I am your lover! I am he who says to you, Forget the past, forget and forgive, and come with me out of your dreaming. Come, Audrey, come, come, from the dim woods into the sunshine,—into the sunshine of the garden! The night you went away I was there, Audrey, under the stars. The paths were deep in leaves, the flowers dead and blackening; but the trees will be green again, and the flowers bloom! When we are wed we will walk there, bringing the spring with us"—

"When we are wed!" she answered. "That will never be."

"It will be this week," he said, smiling. "Dear dryad, who have no friends to make a pother, no dowry to lug with you, no gay wedding raiment to provide; who have only to curtsy farewell to the trees and put your hand in mine"—

She drew away her hands that he had caught in his, and pressed them above her heart; then looked restlessly from window to door. "Will you let me pass, sir?" she asked at last. "I am tired. I have to think what I am to do, where I am to go."

"Where you are to go!" he exclaimed. "Why, back to the glebe house, and I will follow, and the minister shall marry us. Child, child! where else should you go? What else should you do?"

"God knows!" cried the girl, with sudden and extraordinary passion. "But not that! Oh, he is gone,—that other who would have understood!"

Haward let fall his outstretched hand, drew back a pace or two, and stood with knitted brows. The room was very quiet; only Audrey breathed hurriedly, and through the open window came the sudden, lonely cry of some river bird. The note was repeated ere Haward spoke again.

"I will try to understand," he said slowly. "Audrey, is it Evelyn that comes between us?"

Audrey passed her hand over her eyes and brow and pushed back her heavy hair. "Oh, I have wronged her!" she cried. "I have taken her portion. If once she was cruel to me, yet to-day she kissed me, her tears fell upon my face. That which I have robbed her of I want not.... Oh, my heart, my heart!"

"'T is I, not you, who have wronged this lady," said Haward, after a pause. "I have, I hope, her forgiveness. Is this the fault that keeps you from me?"

Audrey answered not, but leaned against the window and looked at the cloud in the south that was now an amethyst island. Haward went closer to her. "Is it," he said, "is it because in my mind I sinned against you, Audrey, because I brought upon you insult and calumny? Child, child! I am of the world. That I did all this is true, but now I would not purchase endless bliss with your least harm, and your name is more to me than my own. Forgive me, Audrey, forgive the past." He bowed his head as he stood before her.

Audrey gazed at him with wide, dry eyes whose lids burned. A hot color had risen to her cheek; at her heart was a heavier aching, a fuller knowledge of loss. "There is no past," she said. "It was a dream and a lie. There is only to-day ... *and you are a stranger*."

The purple cloud across the river began to darken; there came again the lonely cry of the bird; in the house quarter the slaves were singing as they went about their work. Suddenly Audrey laughed. It was sad laughter, as mocking and elfin and mirthless a sound as was ever heard in autumn twilight. "A stranger!" she repeated. "I know you by your name, and that is all. You are Mr. Marmaduke Haward of Fair View, while I—I am Darden's Audrey!"

She curtsied to him, so changed, so defiant, so darkly beautiful, that he caught his breath to behold her. "You are all the world to me!" he cried. "Audrey, Audrey! Look at me, listen to me!"

He would have approached her, would have seized her hand, but she waved him back. "Oh, the world! We must think of that! What would they say, the Governor and the Council, and the people who go to balls, and all the great folk you write to in England,—what would they say if you married me? Mr. Marmaduke Haward of Fair View, the richest man in Virginia! Mr. Marmaduke Haward, the man of taste, the scholar, the fine gentleman, proud of his name, jealous of his honor! And Darden's Audrey, who hath gone barefoot on errands to most houses in Fair View parish! Darden's Audrey, whom the preacher pointed out to the people in Bruton church! They would call you mad; they would give you cap and bells; they would say, 'Does he think that he can make her one of us?—her that we turned and looked long upon in Bruton church, when the preacher called her by a right name'"—

"Child, for God's sake!" cried Haward.

"There is the lady, too,—the lady who left us here together! We must not forget to think of her,—of her whose picture you showed me at Fair View, who was to be your wife, who took me by the hand that night at the Palace. There is reproach in her eyes. Ah, do you not think the look might grow, might come to haunt us? And yourself! Oh, sooner or later regret and weariness would come to dwell at Fair View! The lady who walks in the garden here is a fine lady and a fit mate for a fine gentleman, and I am a beggar maid and no man's mate, unless it be Hugon's. Hugon, who has sworn to have me in the house he has built! Hugon, who would surely kill you"—

Haward caught her by the wrists, bruising them in his grasp. "Audrey, Audrey! Let these fancies be! If we love each other"—

"If!" she echoed, and pulled her hands away. Her voice was strange, her eyes were bright and strained, her face was burning. "But if not, what then? And how should I love you who are a stranger to me? Oh, a generous stranger who, where he thinks he has done a wrong, would repair the damage." Her voice broke; she flung back her head and pressed her hands against her throat.

"You have done me no wrong," she said. "If you had, I would forgive you, would say good-by to you, would go my way.... as I am going now. Let me pass, sir!"

Haward barred her way. "A stranger!" he said, beneath his breath. "Is there then no tie between shadow and substance, dream and reality?"

"None!" answered Audrey, with defiance. "Why did you come to the mountains, eleven years ago? What business was it of yours whether I lived or died? Oh, God was not kind to send you there!"

"You loved me once!" he cried. "Audrey, Audrey, have I slain your love?"

"It was never yours!" she answered passionately, "It was that other's,—that other whom I imagined, who never lived outside my dream! Oh, let me pass, let me begone! You are cruel to keep me. I—I am so tired."

White to the lips, Haward moved backward a step or two, but yet stood between her and the door. Moments passed before he spoke; then, "Will you become my wife?" he asked, in a studiously quiet voice. "Marry me, Audrey, loving me not. Love may come in time, but give me now the right to be your protector, the power to clear your name."

She looked at him with a strange smile, a fine gesture of scorn. "Marry you, loving you not! That will I never do. Protector! That is a word I have grown to dislike. My name! It is a slight thing. What matter if folk look askance when it is only Darden's Audrey? And there are those whom an ill fame does not frighten. The schoolmaster will still give me books to read, and tell me what they mean. He will not care, nor the drunken minister, nor Hugon.... I am going back to them, to Mistress Deborah and the glebe house. She will beat me, and the minister will curse, but they will take me in.... I will work very hard, and never look to Fair View. I see now that I could never reach the mountains." She began to move toward the door. He kept with her, step for step, his eyes upon her face. "You will come no more to the glebe house," she said. "If you do, though the mountains be far the river is near."

He put his hand upon the latch of the door. "You will rest here to-night?" he asked gently, as of a child. "I will speak to Colonel Byrd; to-morrow he will send some one with you down the river. It will be managed for you, and as you wish. You will rest to-night? You go from me now to your room, Audrey?"

"Yes," she answered, and thought she spoke the truth.

"I love you,—love you greatly," he continued. "I will conquer,—conquer and atone! But now, poor tired one, I let you go. Sleep, Audrey, sleep and dream again." He held open the door for her, and stood aside with bent head.

She passed him; then turned, and after a moment of silence spoke to him with a strange and sorrowful state-liness. "You think, sir," she said, "that I have something to forgive?"

"Much," he answered,—"very much, Audrey."

"And you wish my forgiveness?"

"Ay, Audrey, your forgiveness and your love."

"The first is mine to give," she said. "If you wish it, take it. I forgive you, sir. Good-by."

"Good-night," he answered. "Audrey, good-night."

"Good-by," she repeated, and slowly mounting the broad staircase passed from his sight.

It was dark in the upper hall, but there was a great glimmer of sky, an opal space to mark a window that gave upon the sloping lawn and pallid river. The pale light seemed to beckon. Audrey went not on to her attic room, but to the window, and in doing so passed a small half-open door. As she went by she glanced through the aperture, and saw that there was a narrow stairway, built for the servants' use, winding down to a door in the western face of the house.

Once at the open window, she leaned forth and looked to the east and the west. The hush of the evening had fallen; the light was faint; above the last rose flush a great star palely shone. All was quiet, deserted; nothing stirring on the leaf-carpeted slope; no sound save the distant singing of the slaves. The river lay bare from shore to shore, save where the Westover landing stretched raggedly into the flood. To its piles small boats were tied, but there seemed to be no boatmen; wharf and river appeared as barren of movement and life as did the long expanse of dusky lawn.

"I will not sleep in this house to-night," said Audrey to herself. "If I can reach those boats unseen, I will go alone down the river. That will be well. I am not wanted here."

When she arrived at the foot of the narrow stair, she slipped through the door into a world all dusk and quiet, where was none to observe her, none to stay her.

Crouching by the wall she crept to the front of the house, stole around the stone steps where, that morning, she had sat in the sunshine, and came to the parlor windows. Close beneath one was a block of stone. After a moment's hesitation she stood upon this, and, pressing her face against the window pane, looked her last upon the room she had so lately left. A low fire upon the hearth, darkly illumined it: he sat by the table, with his arms outstretched and his head bowed upon them. Audrey dropped from the stone into the ever growing shadows, crossed the lawn, slipped below the bank, and took her way along the river edge to the long landing. When she was half way down its length, she saw that there was a canoe which she had not observed and that it held one man, who sat with his back to the shore. With a quick breath of dismay she stood still, then setting her lips went on; for the more she thought of having to see those two again, Evelyn and the master of Fair View, the stronger grew her determination to commence her backward journey alone and at once.

She had almost reached the end of the wharf when the man in the boat stood up and faced her. It was Hugon. The dusk was not so great but that the two, the hunter and his quarry, could see each other plainly. The latter turned with the sob of a stricken deer, but the impulse to flight lasted not. Where might she go? Run blindly, north or east or west, through the fields of Westover? That would shortly lead to cowering in some wood or swamp while the feet of the searchers came momently nearer. Return to the house, stand at bay once more? With all her strength of soul she put this course from her.

The quick strife in her mind ended in her moving slowly, as though drawn by an invisible hand, to the edge of the wharf, above Hugon and his canoe. She did not wonder to see him there. Every word that Haward had spoken in the Westover parlor was burned upon her brain, and he had said that he had come up river with an Indian. This was the Indian, and to hunt her down those two had joined forces.

"Ma'm'selle Audrey," whispered the trader, staring as at a spirit.

"Yes, Jean Hugon," she answered, and looked down the glimmering reaches of the James, then at the slender canoe and the deep and dark water that flowed between the piles. In the slight craft, with that strong man the river for ally, she were safe as in a tower of brass.

"I am going home, Jean," she said. "Will you row me down the river to-night, and tell me as we go your stories of the woods and your father's glories in France? If you speak of other things I will drown myself, for I am tired of hearing them. In the morning we will stop at some landing for food, and then go on again. Let us hasten"—

The trader moistened his lips. "And him," he demanded hoarsely,—"that Englishman, that Marmaduke Haward of Fair View, who came to me and said, 'Half-breed, seeing that an Indian and a bloodhound have gifts in common, we will take up the quest together. Find her, though it be to lose her to me that same hour! And look that in our travels you try no foul play, for this time I go armed,'— what of him?"

Audrey waved her hand toward the house she had left. "He is there. Let us make haste." As she spoke she descended the steps, and, evading his eager hand, stepped into the canoe. He looked at her doubtfully, half afraid, so strange was it to see her sitting there, so like a spirit from the land beyond the sun, a *revenant* out of one of old Pierre's wild tales, had she come upon him. With quickened breath he loosed the canoe from its mooring and took up the paddle. A moment, and they were quit of the Westover landing and embarked upon a strange journey, during which hour after hour Hugon made wild love, and hour after hour Audrey opened not her lips. As the canoe went swiftly down the flood, lights sprung up in the house it was leaving behind. A man, rising from his chair with a heavy sigh, walked to the parlor window and looked out upon lawn and sky and river, but, so dark had it grown, saw not the canoe; thought only how deserted, how desolate and lonely, was the scene.

* * * * *

In Williamsburgh as at Westover the autumn was dying, the winter was coming, but neither farewell nor greeting perturbed the cheerful town. To and fro through Palace and Nicholson and Duke of Gloucester streets were blown the gay leaves; of early mornings white frosts lay upon the earth like fairy snows, but midday and afternoon were warm and bright. Mistress Stagg's garden lay to the south, and in sheltered corners bloomed marigolds and asters, while a vine, red-leafed and purple-berried, made a splendid mantle for the playhouse wall.

Within the theatre a rehearsal of "Tamerlane" was in progress. Turk and Tartar spoke their minds, and Arpasia's death cry clave the air. The victorious Emperor passed final sentence upon Bajazet; then, chancing to glance toward the wide door, suddenly abdicated his throne, and in the character of Mr. Charles Stagg blew a kiss to his wife, who, applauding softly, stood in the opening that was framed by the red vine.

"Have you done, my dear?" she cried. "Then pray come with me a moment!"

The two crossed the garden, and entered the grape arbor where in September Mistress Stagg had entertained her old friend, my Lady Squander's sometime waiting-maid. Now the vines were bare of leaves, and the sunshine streaming through lay in a flood upon the earth. Mary Stagg's chair was set in that golden warmth, and upon the ground beside it had fallen some bright sewing. The silken stuff touched a coarser cloth, and that was the skirt of Darden's Audrey, who sat upon the ground asleep, with her arm across the chair, and her head upon her arm.

"How came she here?" demanded Mr. Stagg at last, when he had given a tragedy start, folded his arms, and bent his brows.

"She ran away," answered Mistress Stagg, in a low voice, drawing her spouse to a little distance from the sleeping figure. "She ran away from the glebe house and went up the river, wanting—the Lord knows why!—to reach the mountains. Something happened to bring her to her senses, and she turned back, and falling in with that trader, Jean Hugon, he brought her to Jamestown in his canoe. She walked from there to the glebe house,—that was yesterday. The minister was away, and Deborah, being in one of her passions, would not let her in. She's that hard, is Deborah, when she's angry, harder than the nether millstone! The girl lay in the woods last night. I vow I'll never speak again to Deborah, not though there were twenty Baths behind us!" Mistress Stagg's voice began to tremble. "I was sitting sewing in that chair, now listening to your voices in the theatre, and now harking back in my mind to old days when we weren't prosperous like we are now.... And at last I got to thinking of the babe, Charles, and how, if she had lived and grown up, I might ha' sat there sewing a pretty gown for my own child, and how happy I would have made her. I tried to see her standing beside me, laughing, pretty as a rose, waiting for me to take the last stitch. It got so real that I raised my head to tell my dead child how I was going to knot her ribbons, ... and there was this girl looking at me!"

"What, Millamant! a tear, my soul?" cried the theatric Mr. Stagg.

Millamant wiped away the tear. "I'll tell you what she said. She just said: 'You were kind to me when I was here before, but if you tell me to go away I'll go. You need not say it loudly.' And then she almost fell, and I put out my arm and caught her; and presently she was on her knees there beside me, with her head in my lap.... And then we talked together for a while. It was mostly me—she didn't say much—but, Charles, the girl's done no wrong, no more than our child that's dead and in Christ's bosom. She was so tired and worn. I got some milk and gave it to her, and directly she went to sleep like a baby, with her head on my knee."

The two went closer, and looked down upon the slender form and still, dark face. The sleeper's rest was deep. A tress of hair, fallen from its fastening, swept her cheek; Mistress Stagg, stooping, put it in place behind the small ear, then straightened herself and pressed her Mirabell's arm.

"Well, my love," quoth that gentleman, clearing his throat. "'Great minds, like Heaven, are pleased in doing good.' My Millamant, declare your thoughts!"

Mistress Stagg twisted her apron hem between thumb and

finger. "She's more than eighteen, Charles, and anyhow, if I understand it rightly, she was never really bound to Darden. The law has no hold on her, for neither vestry nor Orphan Court had anything to do with placing her with Darden and Deborah. She's free to stay."

"Free to stay?" queried Charles, and took a prodigious pinch of snuff. "To stay with us?"

"Why not?" asked his wife, and stole a persuasive hand into that of her helpmate. "Oh, Charles, my heart went out to her! I made her so beautiful once, and I could do it again and all the time. Don't you think her prettier than was Jane Day? And she's graceful, and that quick to learn! You're such a teacher, Charles, and I know she'd do her best.... Perhaps, after all, there would be no need to send away to Bristol for one to take Jane's place."

"H'm!" said the great man thoughtfully, and bit a curl of Tamerlane's vast periwig. "'Tis true I esteem her no dullard," he at last vouchsafed; "true also that she hath beauty. In fine, solely to give thee pleasure, my Millamant, I will give the girl a trial no later than this very afternoon."

Audrey stirred in her sleep, spoke Haward's name, and sank again to rest. Mr. Stagg took a second pinch of snuff. "There's the scandal, my love. His Excellency the Governor's ball, Mr. Eliot's sermon, Mr. Marmaduke Haward's illness and subsequent duels with Mr. Everard and Mr. Travis, are in no danger of being forgotten. If this girl ever comes to the speaking of an epilogue, there'll be in Williamsburgh a nine days' wonder indeed!"

"The wonder would not hurt," said Mistress Stagg simply.

"Far from it, my dear," agreed Mr. Stagg, and closing his snuffbox, went with a thoughtful brow back to the playhouse and the Tartar camp.

CHAPTER XXVII

THE MISSION OF TRUELOVE

Mistress Truelove Taberer, having read in a very clear and gentle voice the Sermon on the Mount to those placid Friends, Tobias and Martha Taberer, closed the book, and went about her household affairs with a quiet step, but a heart that somehow fluttered at every sound without the door. To still it she began to repeat to herself words she had read: "Blessed are the peacemakers, for they shall be called the children of God ... blessed are the peacemakers"—

Winter sunshine poured in at the windows and door. Truelove, kneeling to wipe a fleck of dust from her wheel, suddenly, with a catch of her breath and a lifting of her brown eyes, saw in the Scripture she had been repeating a meaning and application hitherto unexpected. "The peacemaker ... that is one who makes peace,—in the world, between countries, in families, yea, in the heart of one alone. Did he not say, last time he came, that with me he forgot this naughty world and all its strife; that if I were always with him"—

Truelove's countenance became exalted, her gaze fixed. "If it were a call"—she murmured, and for a moment bowed her head upon the wheel; then rose from her knees and went softly through the morning tasks. When they were over, she took down from a peg and put on a long gray cloak and a gray hood that most becomingly framed her wild-rose face; then came and stood before her father and mother. "I am going forth to walk by the creekside," she said, in her sweet voice. "It may be that I will meet Angus MacLean."

"If thee does," answered one tranquil Friend, "thee may tell him that upon next seventh day meeting will be held in this house."

"Truly," said the other tranquil Friend, "my heart is drawn toward that young man. His mind hath been filled with anger and resistance and the turmoil of the world. It were well if he found peace at last."

"Surely it were well," agreed Truelove sweetly, and went out into the crisp winter weather.

The holly, the pine, and the cedar made green places in the woods, and the multitude of leaves underfoot were pleasant to tread. Clouds were in the sky, but the spaces between were of serenest blue, and in the sunshine the creek flashed diamonds. Truelove stood upon the bank, and, with her hand shading her eyes, watched MacLean rowing toward her up the creek.

When he had fastened his boat and taken her hand, the two walked soberly on beside the sparkling water until they came to a rude seat built beneath an oak-tree, to which yet clung a number of brown leaves. Truelove sat down, drawing her cloak about her, for, though the sun shone, the air was keen. MacLean took off his coat, and kneeling put it beneath her feet. He laughed at her protest.

"Why, these winds are not bleak!" he said. "This land knows no true and honest cold. In my country, night after night have I lain in snow with only my plaid for cover, and heard the spirits call in the icy wind, the kelpie shriek beneath the frozen loch. I listened; then shut my eyes and dreamed warm of glory and—true love."

"Thy coat is new," said Truelove, with downcast eyes. "The earth will stain the good cloth."

MacLean laughed. "Then will I wear it stained, as 'tis said a courtier once wore his cloak."

"There is lace upon it," said Truelove timidly.

MacLean turned with a smile, and laid a fold of her cloak against his dark cheek. "Ah, the lace offends you,— offends thee,—Truelove. Why, 'tis but to mark me a gentleman again! Last night, at Williamsburgh, I supped with Haward and some gentlemen of Virginia. He would have me don this suit. I might not disoblige my friend."

"Thee loves it," said Truelove severely. "Thee loves the color, and the feel of the fine cloth, and the ruffles at thy wrists."

The Highlander laughed. "Why, suppose that I do! Look, Truelove, how brave and red are those holly berries, and how green and fantastically twisted the leaves! The sky is a bright blue, and the clouds are silver; and think what these woods will be when the winter is past! One might do worse, meseems, than to be of God's taste in such matters."

Truelove sighed, and drew her gray cloak more closely around her.

"Thee is in spirits to-day, Angus MacLean," she said, and sighed once more.

"I am free," he answered. "The man within me walks no longer with a hanging head."

"And what will thee do with thy freedom?"

The Highlander made no immediate reply, but, chin in hand, studied the drifts of leaves and the slow-moving water. "I am free," he said at last. "I wear to-day the dress of a gentleman. I could walk without shame into a hall that I know, and find there strangers, standers in dead men's shoon, brothers who want me not,—who would say behind their hands, 'He has been twelve years a slave, and the world has changed since he went away!' ... I will not trouble them."

His face was as sombre as when Truelove first beheld it. Suddenly, and against her will, tears came to her eyes. "I am glad—I and my father and mother and Ephraim—that thee goes not overseas, Angus MacLean," said the dove's voice. "We would have thee—I and my father and mother and Ephraim—we would have thee stay in Virginia."

"I am to stay," he answered. "I have felt no shame in taking a loan from my friend, for I shall repay it. He hath lands up river in a new-made county. I am to seat them for him, and there will be my home. I will build a house and name it Duart; and if there are hills they shall be Dun-da-gu and Grieg, and the sound of winter torrents shall be to me as the sound of the waters of Mull."

Truelove caught her breath. "Thee will be lonely in those forests."

"I am used to loneliness."

"There be Indians on the frontier. They burn houses and carry away prisoners. And there are wolves and dangerous beasts"—

"I am used to danger."

Truelove's voice trembled more and more. "And thee must dwell among negroes and rude men, with none to comfort thy soul, none to whom thee can speak in thy dark hours?"

"Before now I have spoken to the tobacco I have planted, the trees I have felled, the swords and muskets I have sold."

"But at last thee came and spoke to me!"

"Ay," he answered. "There have been times when you saved my soul alive. Now, in the forest, in my house of logs, when the day's work is done, and I sit upon my doorstep and begin to hear the voices of the past crying to me like the spirits in the valley of Glensyte, I will think of you instead."

"Oh!" cried Truelove. "Speak to me instead, and I will speak to thee ... sitting upon the doorstep of our house, when our day's work is done!"

Her hood falling back showed her face, clear pink, with dewy eyes. The carnation deepening from brow to throat, and the tears trembling upon her long lashes, she suddenly hid her countenance in her gray cloak. MacLean, on his knees beside her, drew away the folds. "Truelove, Truelove! do you know what you have said?"

Truelove put her hand upon her heart. "Oh, I fear," she whispered, "I fear that I have asked thee, Angus MacLean, to let me be—to let me be—thy wife."

The water shone, and the holly berries were gay, and a robin redbreast sang a cheerful song. Beneath the rustling oak-tree there was ardent speech on the part of MacLean, who found in his mistress a listener sweet and shy, and not garrulous of love. But her eyes dwelt upon him and her hand rested at ease within his clasp, and she liked to hear him speak of the home they were to make in the wilderness. It was to be thus, and thus, and thus! With impassioned eloquence the Gael adorned the shrine and advanced the merit of the divinity, and the divinity listened with a smile, a blush, a tear, and now and then a meek rebuke.

When an hour had passed, the sun went under a cloud and the air grew colder. The bird had flown away, but in the rising wind the dead leaves rustled loudly. MacLean and Truelove, leaving their future of honorable toil, peace of mind, and enduring affection, came back to the present.

"I must away," said the Highlander. "Haward waits for me at Williamsburgh. To-morrow, dearer to me than Deirdre to Naos! I will come again."

Hand in hand the two walked slowly toward that haunt of peace, Truelove's quiet home. "And Marmaduke Haward awaits thee at Williamsburgh?" said the Quakeress. "Last third day he met my father and me on the Fair View road, and checked his horse and spoke to us. He is changed."

"Changed indeed!" quoth the Highlander. "A fire burns him, a wind drives him; and yet to the world, last night"— He paused.

"Last night?" said Truelove.

"He had a large company at Marot's ordinary," went on the other. "There were the Governor and his fellow Councilors, with others of condition or fashion. He was the very fine gentleman, the perfect host, free, smiling, full of wit. But I had been with him before they came. I knew the fires beneath."

The two walked in silence for a few moments, when MacLean spoke again: "He drank to her. At the last, when this lady had been toasted, and that, he rose and drank to 'Audrey,' and threw his wineglass over his shoulder. He hath done what he could. The world knows that he loves her honorably, seeks her vainly in marriage. Something more I know. He gathered the company together last evening that, as his guests, the highest officers, the finest gentlemen of the colony, should go with him to the theatre to see her for the first time as a player. Being what they were, and his guests, and his passion known, he would insure for her, did she well or did she ill, order, interest, decent applause." MacLean broke off with a short, excited laugh. "It was not needed,—his mediation. But he could not know that; no, nor none of us. True, Stagg and his wife had bragged of the powers of this strangely found actress of theirs that they were training to do great things, but folk took it for a trick of their trade. Oh, there was curiosity enough, but 'twas on Haward's account.... Well, he drank to her, standing at the head of the table at Marot's ordinary, and the glass crashed over his shoulder, and we all went to the play."

"Yes, yes!" cried Truelove, breathing quickly, and quite forgetting how great a vanity was under discussion.

"'Twas 'Tamerlane,' the play that this traitorous generation calls for every 5th of November. It seems that the Governor—a Whig as rank as Argyle—had ordered it again for this week. 'Tis a cursed piece of slander that pictures the Prince of Orange a virtuous Emperor, his late Majesty of France a hateful tyrant. But for Haward, whose guest I was, I had not sat there with closed lips. I had sprung to my feet and given those flatterers, those traducers, the lie! The thing taunted and angered until she entered. Then I forgot."

"And she—and Audrey?"

"Arpasia was her name in the play. She entered late; her death came before the end; there was another woman who had more to do. It all mattered not, I have seen a great actress."

"Darden's Audrey!" said Truelove, in a whisper.

"That at the very first; not afterwards," answered MacLean. "She was dressed, they say, as upon the night at the Palace, that first night of Haward's fever. When she came upon the stage, there was a murmur like the wind in the leaves. She was most beautiful,—'beauteous in hatred,' as the Sultan in the play called her,—dark and wonderful, with angry eyes. For a little while she must stand in silence, and in these moments men and women stared at her, then turned and looked at Haward. But when she spoke we forgot that she was Darden's Audrey."

MacLean laughed again. "When the play was ended,—or rather, when her part in it was done,—the house did shake so with applause that Stagg had to remonstrate. There's naught talked of to-day in Williamsburgh but Arpasia; and when I came down Palace Street this morning, there was a great crowd about the playhouse door. Stagg might sell his tickets for to-night at a guinea apiece. 'Venice Preserved' is the play."

"And Marmaduke Haward,—what of him?" asked Truelove softly.

"He is English," said MacLean, after a pause. "He can make of his face a smiling mask, can keep his voice as even and as still as the pool that is a mile away from the fierce torrent its parent. It is a gift they have, the English. I remember at Preston"—He broke off with a sigh. "There will be an end some day, I suppose. He will win her at last to his way of thinking; and having gained her, he will be happy. And yet to my mind there is something unfortunate, strange and fatal, in the aspect of this girl. It hath always been so. She is such a one as the Lady in Green. On a Halloween night, standing in the twelfth rig, a man might hear her voice upon the wind. I would old Murdoch of Coll, who hath the second sight, were here: he could tell the ending of it all."

An hour later found the Highlander well upon his way to Williamsburgh, walking through wood and field with his long stride, his heart warm within him, his mind filled with the thought of Truelove and the home that he would make for her in the rude, upriver country. Since the two had sat beneath the oak, clouds had gathered, obscuring the sun. It was now gray and cold in the forest, and presently snow began to fall, slowly, in large flakes, between the still trees.

MacLean looked with whimsical anxiety at several white particles upon his suit of fine cloth, claret-colored and silver-laced, and quickened his pace. But the snow was but the lazy vanguard of a storm, and so few and harmless were the flakes that when, a, mile from Williamsburgh and at some little distance from the road, MacLean beheld a ring of figures seated upon the Gounod beneath a giant elm, he stopped to observe who and what they were that sat so still beneath the leafless tree in the winter weather.

The group, that at first glimpse had seemed some conclave of beings uncouth and lubberly and solely of the forest, resolved itself into the Indian teacher and his pupils, escaped for the afternoon from the bounds of William and Mary. The Indian lads—slender, bronze, and statuesque—sat in silence, stolidly listening to the words of the white man, who, standing in the midst of the ring, with his back to the elm-tree, told to his dusky charges a Bible tale. It was the story of Joseph and his brethren. The clear, gentle tones of the teacher reached MacLean's ears where he stood unobserved behind a roadside growth of bay and cedar.

A touch upon the shoulder made him turn, to find at his elbow that sometime pupil of Mr. Charles Griffin in whose company he had once trudged from Fair View store to Williamsburgh.

"I was lying in the woods over there," said Hugon sullenly. "I heard them coming, and I took my leave. 'Peste!' said I. 'The old, weak man who preaches quietness under men's injuries, and the young wolf pack, all brown, with Indian names!' They may have the woods; for me, I go back to the town where I belong."

He shrugged his shoulders, and stood scowling at the distant group. MacLean, in his turn, looked curiously at his quondam companion of a sunny day in May, the would-be assassin with whom he had struggled in wind and rain beneath the thunders of an August storm. The trader wore his great wig, his ancient steinkirk of tawdry lace, his high boots of Spanish leather, cracked and stained. Between the waves of coarse hair, out of coal-black, deep-set eyes looked the soul of the half-breed, fierce, vengeful, ignorant, and embittered.

"There is Meshawa," he said,—"Meshawa, who was a little boy when I went to school, but who used to laugh when I talked of France. Pardieu! one day I found him alone when it was cold, and there was a fire in the room. Next time I talked he did not laugh! They are all"—he swept his hand toward the circle beneath the elm—"they are all Saponies, Nottoways, Meherrins; their fathers are lovers of the peace pipe, and humble to the English. A Monacan is a great brave; he laughs at the Nottoways, and says that there are no men in the villages of the Meherrins."

"When do you go again to trade with your people?" asked MacLean.

Hugon glanced at him out of the corners of his black eyes. "They are not my people; my people are French. I am not going to the woods any more. I am so prosperous. Diable! shall not I as well as another stay at Williamsburgh, dress fine, dwell in an ordinary, play high, and drink of the best?"

"There is none will prevent you," said MacLean coolly. "Dwell in town, take your ease in your inn, wear gold lace, stake the skins of all the deer in Virginia, drink Burgundy and Champagne, but lay no more arrows athwart the threshold of a gentleman's door."

Hugon's lips twitched into a tigerish grimace. "So he found the arrow? Mortdieu! let him look to it that one day the arrow find not him!"

"If I were Haward," said MacLean, "I would have you taken up."

The trader again looked sideways at the speaker, shrugged his shoulders and waved his hand. "Oh, he—he despises me too much for that! Eh bien! to-day I love to see him live. When there is no wine in the cup, but only dregs that are bitter, I laugh to see it at his lips. She,—Ma'm'selle Audrey, that never before could I coax into my boat,—she reached me her hand, she came with me down the river, through the night-time, and left him behind at Westover. Ha! think you not that was bitter, that drink which she gave him, Mr. Marmaduke Haward of Fair View? Since then, if I go to that house, that garden at Williamsburgh, she hides, she will not see me; the man and his wife make excuse! Bad! But also he sees her never. He writes to her: she answers not. Good! Let him live, with the fire built around him and the splinters in his heart!"

He laughed again, and, dismissing the subject with airiness somewhat exaggerated, drew out his huge gilt snuffbox. The snow was now falling more thickly, drawing a white and fleecy veil between the two upon the road and the story-teller and his audience beneath the distant elm. "Are you for Williamsburgh?" demanded the Highlander, when he had somewhat abruptly declined to take snuff with Monsieur Jean Hugon.

That worthy nodded, pocketing his box and incidentally making a great jingling of coins.

"Then," quoth MacLean, "since I prefer to travel alone, twill wait here until you have passed the rolling-house in the distance yonder. Good-day to you!"

He seated himself upon the stump of a tree, and, giving all

his attention to the snow, began to whistle a thoughtful air. Hugon glanced at him with fierce black eyes and twitching lips, much desiring a quarrel; then thought better of it, and before the tune had come to an end was making with his long and noiseless stride his lonely way to Williamsburgh, and the ordinary in Nicholson Street.

Mary Johnston

CHAPTER XXVIII

THE PLAYER

About this time, Mr. Charles Stagg, of the Williamsburgh theatre in Virginia, sent by the Horn of Plenty, bound for London, a long letter to an ancient comrade and player of small parts at Drury Lane. A few days later, young Mr. Lee, writing by the Golden Lucy to an agreeable rake of his acquaintance, burst into a five-page panegyric upon the Arpasia, the Belvidera, the Monimia, who had so marvelously dawned upon the colonial horizon. The recipient of this communication, being a frequenter of Button's, and chancing one day to crack a bottle there with Mr. Colley Cibber, drew from his pocket and read to that gentleman the eulogy of Darden's Audrey, with the remark that the writer was an Oxford man and must know whereof he wrote.

Cibber borrowed the letter, and the next day, in the company of Wilks and a bottle of Burgundy, compared it with that of Mr. Charles Stagg,—the latter's correspondent having also brought the matter to the great man's notice.

"She might offset that pretty jade Fenton at the Fields, eh, Bob?" said Cibber. "They're of an age. If the town took to her"—

"If her Belvidera made one pretty fellow weep, why not another?" added Wilks. "Here—where is't he says that, when she went out, for many moments the pit was silent as the grave—and that then the applause was deep—not shrill—and very long? 'Gad, if 'tis a Barry come again, and we could lay hands on her, the house would be made!"

Gibber sighed. "You're dreaming, Bob," he said good-humoredly. "'Twas but a pack of Virginia planters, noisy over some *belle sauvage* with a ranting tongue."

"Men's passions are the same, I take it, in Virginia as in London," answered the other. "If the *belle sauvage* can move to that manner of applause in one spot of earth, she may do so in another. And here again he says, 'A dark beauty, with a strange, alluring air ... a voice of melting sweetness that yet can so express anguish and fear that the blood turns cold and the heart is wrung to hear it'—Zoons, sir! What would it cost to buy off this fellow Stagg, and to bring the phoenix overseas?"

"Something more than a lottery ticket," laughed the other, and beckoned to the drawer. "We'll wait, Bob, until we're sure 'tis a phoenix indeed! There's a gentleman in Virginia with whom I've some acquaintance, Colonel William Byrd, that was the colony's agent here. I'll write to him for a true account. There's time enough."

So thought honest Cibber, and wrote at leisure to his Virginia acquaintance. It made small difference whether he wrote or refrained from writing, for he had naught to do with the destinies of Darden's Audrey. 'Twas almost summer before there came an answer to his letter. He showed it to Wilks in the greenroom, between the acts of "The Provoked Husband." Mrs. Oldfield read it over their shoulders, and vowed that 'twas a moving story; nay, more, in her next scene there was a moisture in Lady Townly's eyes quite out of keeping with the vivacity of her lines.

Darden's Audrey had to do with Virginia, not London; with the winter, never more the summer. It is not known how acceptable her Monimia, her Belvidera, her Isabella, would have been to London playgoers. Perhaps they would have received them as did the Virginians, perhaps not. Cibber himself might or might not have drawn for us her portrait; might or might not have dwelt upon the speaking eye, the slow, exquisite smile with which she made more sad her saddest utterances, the wild charm of her mirth, her power to make each auditor fear as his own the impending harm, the tragic splendor in which, when the bolt had fallen, converged all the pathos, beauty, and tenderness of her earlier scenes. A Virginian of that winter, writing of her, had written thus; but then Williamsburgh was not London, nor its playhouse Drury Lane. Perhaps upon that ruder stage, before an audience less polite, with never a critic in the pit or footman in the gallery, with no Fops' Corner and no great number of fine ladies in the boxes, the jewel shone with a lustre that in a brighter light it had not worn. There was in Mr. Charles Stagg's company of players no mate for any gem; this one was set amongst pebbles, and perhaps by contrast alone did it glow so deeply.

However this may be, in Virginia, in the winter and the early spring of that year of grace Darden's Audrey was known, extravagantly praised, toasted, applauded to the echo. Night after night saw the theatre crowded, gallery, pit, and boxes. Even the stage had its row of chairs, seats held not too dear at half a guinea. Mr. Stagg had visions of a larger house, a fuller company, renown and prosperity undreamed of before that fortunate day when, in the grape arbor, he and his wife had stood and watched Darden's Audrey asleep, with her head pillowed upon her arm.

Darden's Audrey! The name clung to her, though the minister had no further lot or part in her fate. The poetasters called her Charmante, Anwet, Chloe,—what not! Young Mr. Lee in many a slight and pleasing set of verses addressed her as Sylvia, but to the community at large she was Darden's Audrey, and an enigma greater than the Sphinx. Why would she not marry Mr. Marmaduke Haward of Fair View? Was the girl looking for a prince to come overseas for her? Or did she prefer to a dazzling marriage the excitement of the theatre, the adulation, furious applause? That could hardly be, for these things seemed to frighten her. At times one could see her shrink and grow pale at some great clapping or loud "Again!" And only upon the stage did the town behold her. She rarely went abroad, and at the small white house in Palace Street she was denied to visitors. True, 'twas the way to keep upon curiosity the keenest edge, to pique interest and send the town to the playhouse as the one point of view from which the riddle might be studied. But wisdom such as this could scarce be expected of the girl. Given, then, that 'twas not her vanity which kept her Darden's Audrey, what was it? Was not Mr. Haward of Fair View rich, handsome, a very fine gentleman? Generous, too, for had he not sworn, as earnestly as though he expected to be believed, that the girl was pure innocence? His hand was ready to his sword, nor were men anxious to incur his cold enmity, so that the assertion passed without open challenge. He was mad for her,—that was plain enough. And she,—well she's woman and

Darden's Audrey, and so doubly an enigma. In the mean time, to-night she plays Monimia, and her madness makes you weep, so sad it is, so hopeless, and so piercing sweet.

In this new world that was so strange to her Darden's Audrey bore herself as best she might. While it was day she kept within the house, where the room that in September she had shared with Mistress Deborah was now for her alone. Hour after hour she sat there, book in hand, learning how those other women, those women of the past, had loved, had suffered, had fallen to dusty death. Other hours she spent with Mr. Charles Stagg in the long room downstairs, or, when Mistress Stagg had customers, in the theatre itself. As in the branded schoolmaster chance had given her a teacher skilled in imparting knowledge, so in this small and pompous man, who beneath a garb of fustian hugged to himself a genuine reverence and understanding of his art, she found an instructor more able, perhaps, than had been a greater actor. In the chill and empty playhouse, upon the narrow stage where, sitting in the September sunshine, she had asked of Haward her last favor, she now learned to speak for those sisters of her spirit, those dead women who through rapture, agony, and madness had sunk to their long rest, had given their hands to death and lain down in a common inn. To Audrey they were real; she was free of their company. The shadows were the people who lived and were happy; who night after night came to watch a soul caught in the toils, to thunder applause when death with rude and hasty hands broke the net, set free the prisoner.

The girl dreamed as she breathed. Wakened from a long, long fantasy, desolate and cold to the heart in an alien air, she sought for poppy and mandragora, and in some sort finding them dreamed again, though not for herself, not as before. It can hardly be said that she was unhappy. She walked in a pageant of strange miseries, and the pomp of woe was hers to portray. Those changelings from some fateful land, those passionate, pale women, the milestones of whose pilgrimage spelled love, ruin, despair, and death, they were her kindred, her sisters. Day and night they kept her company: and her own pain lessened, grew at last to a still and dreamy sorrow, never absent, never poignant.

Of necessity, importunate grief was drugged to sleep. In the daylight hours she must study, must rehearse with her fellow players; when night came she put on a beautiful dress, and to lights and music and loud applause there entered Monimia, or Belvidera, or Athenais. When the play was done and the curtain fallen, the crowd of those who would have stayed her ever gave way, daunted by her eyes, her closed lips, the atmosphere that yet wrapped her of passion, woe, and exaltation, the very tragedy of the soul that she had so richly painted. Like the ghost of that woman who had so direfully loved and died, she was wont to slip from the playhouse, through the dark garden, to the small white house and her quiet room. There she laid off her gorgeous dress, and drew the ornaments from her dark hair that was long as Molly's had been that day beneath the sugar-tree in the far-away valley.

She rarely thought of Molly now, or of the mountains. With her hair shadowing her face and streaming over bared neck and bosom she sat before her mirror. The candle burned low; the face in the glass seemed not her own. Dim, pale, dark-eyed, patient-lipped at last, out of a mist and from a great distance the other woman looked at her. Far countries, the burning noonday and utter love, night and woe and life, the broken toy, flung with haste away! The mist thickened; the face withdrew, farther, farther off; the candle burned low. Audrey put out the weak flame, and laid herself upon the bed. Sleep came soon, and it was still and dreamless. Sometimes Mary Stagg, light in hand, stole into the room and stood above the quiet form. The girl hardly seemed to breathe: she had a fashion of lying with crossed hands and head drawn slightly back, much as she might be laid at last in her final bed. Mistress Stagg put out a timid hand and felt the flesh if it were warm; then bent and lightly kissed hand or arm or the soft curve of the throat. Audrey stirred not, and the other went noiselessly away; or Audrey opened dark eyes, faintly smiled and raised herself to meet the half-awed caress, then sank to rest again.

Into Mistress Stagg's life had struck a shaft of colored light, had come a note of strange music, had flown a bird of paradise. It was and it was not her dead child come again. She knew that her Lucy had never been thus, and the love that she gave Audrey was hardly mother love. It was more nearly an homage, which, had she tried, she could not have explained. When they were alone together, Audrey called the older woman "mother," often knelt and laid her head upon the other's lap or shoulder. In all her ways she was sweet and duteous, grateful and eager to serve. But her spirit dwelt in a rarer air, and there were heights and depths where the waif and her protectress might not meet. To this the latter gave dumb recognition, and though she could not understand, yet loved her protegee. At night, in the playhouse, this love was heightened into exultant worship. At all times there was delight in the girl's beauty, pride in the comment and wonder of the town, self-congratulation and the pleasing knowledge that wisdom is vindicated of its children. Was not all this of her bringing about? Did it not first occur to her that the child might take Jane Day's place? Even Charles, who strutted and plumed himself and offered his snuffbox to every passer-by, must acknowledge that!

Mistress Stagg stopped her sewing to laugh triumphantly, then fell to work more diligently than ever; for it was her pleasure to dress Darden's Audrey richly, in soft colors, heavy silken stuffs upon which was lavished a wealth of delicate needlework. It was chiefly while she sat and sewed upon these pretty things, with Audrey, book on knee, close beside her, that her own child seemed to breathe again.

Audrey thanked her and kissed her, and wore what she was given to wear, nor thought how her beauty was enhanced. If others saw it, if the wonder grew by what it fed on, if she was talked of, written of, pledged, and lauded by a frank and susceptible people, she knew of all this little enough, and for what she knew cared not at all. Her days went dreamily by, nor very sad nor happy; full of work, yet vague and unmarked as desert sands. What was real was a past that was not hers, and those dead women to whom night by night she gave life and splendor.

There were visitors to whom she was not denied. Darden came at times, sat in Mistress Stagg's sunny parlor, and talked to his sometime ward much as he had talked in the glebe-house living room,—discursively, of men and parochial affairs and his own unmerited woes. Audrey sat and heard him, with her eyes upon the garden without the window. When he lifted from the chair his great shambling figure, and took his stained old hat and heavy cane, Audrey rose also, curtsied, and sent her duty to Mistress Deborah, but she asked no questions as to that past home of hers. It seemed not to interest her that the creek was frozen so hard that one could walk upon it to Fair View, or that the minister had bought a field from his wealthy neighbor, and meant to plant it with Oronoko. Only when he told her that the little wood—the wood that she had called her own—was being cleared, and that all day could be heard the falling of the trees, did she lift startled eyes and draw a breath like a moan. The minister looked at her from under shaggy brows, shook his head, and went his way to his favorite ordinary, rum, and a hand at cards.

Mistress Deborah she beheld no more; but once the Widow Constance brought Barbara to town, and the two, being very simple women, went to the play to see the old Audrey, and saw instead a queen, tinseled, mock-jeweled, clad in silk, who loved and triumphed, despaired and died. The rude theatre shook to the applause. When it was all over, the widow and Barbara went dazed to their lodging, and lay awake through the night talking of these marvels. In the morning they found the small white house, and Audrey came to them in the garden. When she had kissed them, the three sat down in the arbor; for it was a fine, sunny morning, and not cold. But the talk was not easy; Barbara's eyes were so round, and the widow kept mincing her words. Only when they were joined by Mistress Stagg, to whom the widow became voluble, the two girls spoke aside.

"I have a guinea, Barbara," said Audrey. "Mr. Stagg gave it to me, and I need it not,—I need naught in the world. Barbara, here!—'tis for a warm dress and a Sunday hood."

"Oh, Audrey," breathed Barbara, "they say you might live at Fair View,—that you might marry Mr. Haward and be a fine lady"—

Audrey laid her hand upon the other's lips. "Hush! See, Barbara, you must have the dress made thus, like mine."

"But if 'tis so, Audrey!" persisted poor Barbara. "Mother

and I talked of it last night. She said you would want a waiting-woman, and I thought—Oh, Audrey!"

Audrey bit her quivering lip and dashed away the tears. "I'll want no waiting-woman, Barbara. I'm naught but Audrey that you used to be kind to. Let's talk of other things. Have you missed me from the woods all these days?"

"It has been long since you were there," said Barbara dully. "Now I go with Joan at times, though mother frowns and says she is not fit. Eh, Audrey, if I could have a dress of red silk, with gold and bright stones, like you wore last night! Old days I had more than you, but all's changed now. Joan says"—

The Widow Constance rising to take leave, it did not appear what Joan had said. The visitors from the country went away, nor came again while Audrey dwelt in Williamsburgh. The schoolmaster came, and while he waited for his sometime pupil to slowly descend the stairs talked learnedly to Mr. Stagg of native genius, of the mind drawn steadily through all accidents and adversities to the end of its own discovery, and of how time and tide and all the winds of heaven conspire to bring the fate assigned, to make the puppet move in the stated measure. Mr. Stagg nodded, took out his snuffbox, and asked what now was the schoolmaster's opinion of the girl's Monimia last night,—the last act, for instance. Good Lord, how still the house was!—and then one long sigh!

The schoolmaster fingered the scars in his bands, as was his manner at times, but kept his eyes upon the ground. When he spoke, there was in his voice unwonted life. "Why, sir, I could have said with Lear, *'Hysterica passio! down, thou climbing sorrow!'*—and I am not a man, sir, that's easily moved. The girl is greatly gifted. I knew that before either you or the town, sir. Audrey, good-morrow!"

Such as these from out her old life Darden's Audrey saw and talked with. Others sought her, watched for her, laid traps that might achieve at least her presence, but largely in vain. She kept within the house; when the knocker sounded she went to her own room. No flowery message, compliment, or appeal, not even Mary Stagg's kindly importunity, could bring her from that coign of vantage. There were times when Mistress Stagg's showroom was crowded with customers; on sunny days young men left the bowling green to stroll in the shell-bordered garden paths; gentlemen and ladies of quality passing up and down Palace Street walked more slowly when they came to the small white house, and looked to see if the face of Darden's Audrey showed at any window.

Thus the winter wore away. The springtime was at hand, when one day the Governor, wrought upon by Mistress Evelyn Byrd, sent to Mr. Stagg, bidding him with his wife and the new player to the Palace. The three, dressed in their best, were ushered into the drawing-room, where they found his Excellency at chess with the Attorney-General; a third gentleman, seated somewhat in the shadow, watching the game. A servant placed, chairs for the people from the theatre. His Excellency checkmated his antagonist, and, leaning back in his great chair, looked at Darden's Audrey, but addressed his conversation to Mr. Charles Stagg. The great man was condescendingly affable, the lesser one obsequious; while they talked the gentleman in the shadow arose and drew his chair to Audrey's side. 'Twas Colonel Byrd, and he spoke to the girl kindly and courteously; asking after her welfare, giving her her meed of praise, dwelling half humorously upon the astonishment and delight into which she had surprised the play-loving town. Audrey listened with downcast eyes to the suave tones, the well-turned compliments, but when she must speak spoke quietly and well.

At last the Governor turned toward her, and began to ask well-meant questions and to give pompous encouragement to the new player. No reference was made to that other time when she had visited the Palace. A servant poured for each of the three a glass of wine. His Excellency graciously desired that they shortly give 'Tamerlane' again, that being a play which, as a true Whig and a hater of all tyrants, he much delighted in, and as graciously announced his intention of bestowing upon the company two slightly tarnished birthday suits. The great man then arose, and the audience was over.

Outside the house, in the sunny walk leading to the gates, the three from the theatre met, full face, a lady and two gentlemen who had been sauntering up and down in the pleasant weather. The lady was Evelyn Byrd; the gentlemen were Mr. Lee and Mr. Grymes.

Audrey, moving slightly in advance of her companions, halted at the sight of Evelyn, and the rich color surged to her face; but the other, pale and lovely, kept her composure, and, with a smile and a few graceful words of greeting, curtsied deeply to the player. Audrey, with a little catch of her breath, returned the curtsy. Both women were richly dressed, both were beautiful; it seemed a ceremonious meeting of two ladies of quality. The gentlemen also bowed profoundly, pressing their hats against their hearts. Mistress Stagg, to whom her protegee's aversion to company was no light cross, twitched her Mirabell by the sleeve and, hanging upon his arm, prevented his further advance. The action said: "Let the child alone; maybe when the ice is once broken she'll see people, and not be so shy and strange!"

"Mr. Lee," said Evelyn sweetly, "I have dropped my glove,—perhaps in the summer-house on the terrace. If you will be so good? Mr. Grymes, will you desire Mr. Stagg yonder to shortly visit me at my lodging? I wish to bespeak a play, and would confer with him on the matter."

The gentlemen bowed and hasted upon their several errands, leaving Audrey and Evelyn standing face to face in the sunny path. "You are well, I hope," said the latter, in her low, clear voice, "and happy?"

"I am well, Mistress Evelyn," answered Audrey. "I think that I am not unhappy."

The other gazed at her in silence; then, "We have all been blind," she said. "'Tis not a year since May Day and the Jaquelins' merrymaking. It seems much longer. You won the race,—do you remember?—and took the prize from my hand. And neither of us thought of all that should follow—did we?—or guessed at other days. I saw you last night at the theatre, and you made my heart like to burst for pity and sorrow. You were only playing at woe? You are not unhappy, not like that?"

Audrey shook her head. "No, not like that."

There was a pause, broken by Evelyn. "Mr. Haward is in town," she said, in a low but unfaltering voice, "He was at the playhouse last night. I watched him sitting in a box, in the shadow.... You also saw him?"

"Yes," said Audrey. "He had not been there for a long,

long time. At first he came night after night.... I wrote to him at last and told him how he troubled me,—made me forget my lines,—and then he came no more."

There was in her tone a strange wistfulness. Evelyn drew her breath sharply, glanced swiftly at the dark face and liquid eyes. Mr. Grymes yet held the manager and his wife in conversation, but Mr. Lee, a small jessamine-scented glove in hand, was hurrying toward them from the summer-house.

"You think that you do not love Mr. Haward?" said Evelyn, in a low voice.

"I loved one that never lived," said Audrey simply. "It was all in a dream from which I have waked. I told him that at Westover, and afterwards here in Williamsburgh. I grew so tired at last—it hurt me so to tell him ... and then I wrote the letter. He has been at Fair View this long time, has he not?"

"Yes," said Evelyn quietly. "He has been alone at Fair View." The rose in her cheeks had faded; she put her lace handkerchief to her lips, and shut her hand so closely that the nails bit into the palm. In a moment, however, she was smiling, a faint, inscrutable smile, and presently she came a little nearer and took Audrey's hand in her own.

The soft, hot, lingering touch thrilled the girl. She began to speak hurriedly, not knowing why she spoke nor what she wished to say: "Mistress Evelyn"—

"Yes, Audrey," said Evelyn, and laid a fluttering touch upon the other's lips, then in a moment spoke herself: "You are to remember always, though you love him not, Audrey, that he never was true lover of mine; that now and forever, and though you died to-night, he is to me but an old acquaintance,—Mr. Marmaduke Haward of Fair View. Remember also that it was not your fault, nor his perhaps, nor mine, and that with all my heart I wish his happiness.... Ah, Mr. Lee, you found it? My thanks, sir."

Mr. Lee, having restored the glove with all the pretty froth of words which the occasion merited, and seen Mistress Evelyn turn aside to speak with Mr. Stagg, found himself mightily inclined to improve the golden opportunity and at once lay siege to this paragon from the playhouse. Two low bows, a three-piled, gold-embroidered compliment, a quotation from his "To Sylvia upon her Leaving the Theatre," and the young gentleman thought his lines well laid. But Sylvia grew restless, dealt in monosyllables, and finally retreated to Mistress Stagg's side. "Shall we not go home?" she whispered. "I—I am tired, and I have my part to study, the long speech at the end that I stumbled in last night. Ah, let us go!"

Mistress Stagg sighed over the girl's contumacy. It was not thus in Bath when she was young, and men of fashion flocked to compliment a handsome player. Now there was naught to do but to let the child have her way. She and Audrey made their curtsies, and Mr. Charles Stagg his bow, which was modeled after that of Beau Nash. Then the three went down the sunny path to the Palace gates, and Evelyn with the two gentlemen moved toward the house and the company within.

CHAPTER XXIX

AMOR VINCIT

By now it was early spring in Virginia, and a time of balm and pleasantness. The season had not entered into its complete heritage of gay hues, sweet odors, song, and wealth of bliss. Its birthday robe was yet a-weaving, its coronal of blossoms yet folded buds, its choristers not ready with their fullest paeans. But everywhere was earnest of future riches. In the forest the bloodroot was in flower, and the bluebird and the redbird flashed from the maple that was touched with fire to the beech just lifted from a pale green fountain. In Mistress Stagg's garden daffodils bloomed, and dim blue hyacinths made sweet places in the grass. The sun lay warm upon upturned earth, blackbirds rose in squadrons and darkened the yet leafless trees, and every wind brought rumors of the heyday toward which the earth was spinning. The days were long and sweet; at night a moon came up, and between it and the earth played soft and vernal airs. Then a pale light flooded the garden, the shells bordering its paths gleamed like threaded pearls, and the house showed whiter than a marble sepulchre. Mild incense, cool winds, were there, but quiet came fitfully between the bursts of noise from the lit theatre.

Mary Johnston

On such a night as this Audrey, clothed in red silk, with a band of false jewels about her shadowy hair, slipped through the stage door into the garden, and moved across it to the small white house and rest. Her part in the play was done; for all their storming she would not stay. Silence and herself alone, and the mirror in her room; then, sitting before the glass, to see in it darkly the woman whom she had left dead upon the boards yonder,—no, not yonder, but in a far country, and a fair and great city. Love! love! and death for love! and her own face in the mirror gazing at her with eyes of that long-dead Greek. It was the exaltation and the dream, mournful, yet not without its luxury, that ended her every day. When the candle burned low, when the face looked but dimly from the glass, then would she rise and quench the flame, and lay herself down to sleep, with the moonlight upon her crossed hands and quiet brow.

*　*　*　*　*

She passed through the grape arbor, and opened the door at which Haward had knocked that September night of the Governor's ball. She was in Mistress Stagg's long room; at that hour it should have been lit only by a dying fire and a solitary candle. Now the fire was low enough, but the room seemed aflare with myrtle tapers. Audrey, coming from the dimness without, shaded her eyes with her hand. The heavy door shut to behind her; unseeing still she moved toward the fire, but in a moment let fall her hand and began to wonder at the unwonted lights. Mistress Stagg was yet in the playhouse; who then had lit these candles? She turned, and saw Haward standing with folded arms between her and the door.

The silence was long. He was Marmaduke Haward with all his powers gathered, calm, determined, so desperate to have done with this thing, to at once and forever gain his own and master fate, that his stillness was that of deepest waters, his cool equanimity that of the gamester who knows how will fall the loaded dice. Dressed with his accustomed care, very pale, composed and quiet, he faced her whose spirit yet lingered in a far city, who in the dreamy exaltation of this midnight hour was ever half Audrey of the garden, half that other woman in a dress of red silk, with jewels in her hair, who, love's martyr, had exulted, given all, and died.

"How did you come here?" she breathed at last. "You said that you would come never again."

"After to-night, never again," he answered. "But now, Audrey, this once again, this once again!"

Gazing past him she made a movement toward the door. He shook his head. "This is my hour, Audrey. You may not leave the room, nor will Mistress Stagg enter it. I will not touch you, I will come no nearer to you. Stand there in silence, if you choose, or cover the sight of me from your eyes, while for my own ease, my own unhappiness, I say farewell."

"Farewell!" she echoed. "Long ago, at Westover, that was said between you and me.... Why do you come like a ghost to keep me and peace apart?"

He did not answer, and she locked her hands across her brow that burned beneath the heavy circlet of mock gems. "Is it kind?" she demanded, with a sob in her voice. "Is it kind to trouble me so, to keep me here"—

"Was I ever kind?" he asked. "Since the night when I followed you, a child, and caught you from the ground when you fell between the corn rows, what kindness, Audrey?"

"None!" she answered, with sudden passion. "Nor kindness then! Why went you not some other way?"

"Shall I tell you why I was there that night,—why I left my companions and came riding back to the cabin in the valley?"

She uncovered her eyes, "I thought—I thought then—that you were sent"—

He looked at her with strange compassion. "My own will sent me.... When, that sunny afternoon, we spurred from the valley toward the higher mountains, we left behind us a forest flower, a young girl of simple sweetness, with long dark hair,—like yours, Audrey.... It was to pluck that flower that I deserted the expedition, that I went back to the valley between the hills."

Her eyes dilated, and her hands very slowly rose to press her temples, to make a shadow from which she might face the cup of trembling he was pouring for her.

"*Molly!*" she said, beneath her breath.

He nodded. "Well, Death had gathered the flower.... Accident threw across my path a tinier blossom, a helpless child. Save you then, care for you then, I must, or I had been not man, but monster. Did I care for you tenderly, Audrey? Did I make you love me with all your childish heart? Did I become to you father and mother and sister and fairy prince? Then what were you to me in those old days? A child fanciful and charming, too fine in all her moods not to breed wonder, to give the feeling that

Nature had placed in that mountain cabin a changeling of her own. A child that one must regard with fondness and some pity,—what is called a dear child. Moreover, a child whose life I had saved, and to whom it pleased me to play Providence. I was young, not hard of heart, sedulous to fold back to the uttermost the roseleaves of every delicate and poetic emotion, magnificently generous also, and set to play my life *au grand seigneur*. To myself assume a responsibility which with all ease might have been transferred to an Orphan Court, to put my stamp upon your life to come, to watch you kneel and drink of my fountain of generosity, to open my hand and with an indulgent smile shower down upon you the coin of pleasure and advantage,—why, what a tribute was this to my own sovereignty, what subtle flattery of self-love, what delicate taste of power! Well, I kissed you good-by, and unclasped your hands from my neck, chided you, laughed at you, fondled you, promised all manner of pretty things and engaged you never to forget me—and sailed away upon the Golden Rose to meet my crowded years with their wine and roses, upas shadows and apples of Sodom. How long before I forgot you, Audrey? A year and a day, perhaps. I protest that I cannot remember exactly."

He slightly changed his position, but came no nearer to her. It was growing quiet in the street beyond the curtained windows. One window was bare, but it gave only upon an unused nook of the garden where were merely the moonlight and some tall leafless bushes.

"I came back to Virginia," he said, "and I looked for and found you in the heart of a flowering wood.... All that you imagined me to be, Audrey, that was I not. Knight-errant, paladin, king among men,—what irony, child, in that strange dream and infatuation of thine! I was—I am—of my time and of myself, and he whom that day you thought me had not then nor afterwards form or being. I wish you to be perfect in this lesson, Audrey. Are you so?"

"Yes," she sighed. Her hands had fallen; she was looking at him with slowly parting lips, and a strange expression in her eyes.

He went on quietly as before, every feature controlled to impassivity and his arms lightly folded: "That is well. Between the day when I found you again and a night in the Palace yonder lies a summer,—a summer! To me all the summers that ever I had or will have,—ten thousand summers! Now tell me how I did in this wonderful summer."

"Ignobly," she answered.

He bowed his head gravely. "Ay, Audrey, it is a good word." With a quick sigh he left his place, and walking to the uncurtained window stood there looking out upon the strip of moonlight and the screen of bushes; but when he turned again to the room his face and bearing were as impressive as before in their fine, still gravity, their repose of determination. "And that evening by the river when you fled from me to Hugon"—

"I had awaked," she said, in a low voice. "You were to me a stranger, and I feared you."

"And at Westover?"

"A stranger."

"Here in Williamsburgh, when by dint of much striving I

saw you, when I wrote to you, when at last you sent me that letter, that piteous and cruel letter, Audrey?"

For one moment her dark eyes met his, then fell to her clasped hands. "A stranger," she said.

"The letter was many weeks ago. I have been alone with my thoughts at Fair View. And to-night, Audrey?"

"A stranger," she would have answered, but her voice broke. There were shadows under her eyes; her lifted face had in it a strained, intent expectancy as though she saw or heard one coming.

"A stranger," he acquiesced. "A foreigner in your world of dreams and shadows. No prince, Audrey, or great white knight and hero. Only a gentleman of these latter days, compact like his fellows of strength and weakness; now very wise and now the mere finger-post of folly; set to travel his own path; able to hear above him in the rarer air the trumpet call, but choosing to loiter on the lower slopes. In addition a man who loves at last, loves greatly, with a passion that shall ennoble. A stranger and your lover, Audrey, come to say farewell."

Her voice came like an echo, plaintive and clear and from far away: "Farewell."

"How steadily do I stand here to say farewell!" he said. "Yet I am eaten of my passion. A fire burns me, a voice within me ever cries aloud. I am whirled in a resistless wind.... Ah, my love, the garden at Fair View! The folded rose that will never bloom, the dial where linger the heavy hours, the heavy, heavy, heavy hours!"

"The garden," she whispered. "I smell the box.... The path

was all in sunshine. So quiet, so hushed.... I went a little farther, and I heard your voice where you sat and read— and read of Eloisa.... *Oh, Evelyn, Evelyn!*"

"The last time—the last farewell!" he said. "When the Golden Rose is far at sea, when the winds blow, when the stars drift below the verge, when the sea speaks, then may I forget you, may the vision of you pass! Now at Fair View it passes not; it dwells. Night and day I behold you, the woman that I love, the woman that I love in vain!"

"The Golden Rose!" she answered. "The sea.... Alas!"

Her voice had risen into a cry. The walls of the room were gone, the air pressed upon her heavily, the lights wavered, the waters were passing over her as they had passed that night of the witch's hut. How far away the bank upon which he stood! He spoke to her, and his voice came faintly as from that distant shore or from the deck of a swiftly passing ship. "And so it is good-by, sweetheart; for why should I stay in Virginia? Ah, if you loved me, Audrey! But since it is not so—Good-by, good-by. This time I'll not forget you, but I will not come again. Good-by!"

Her lips moved, but there came no words. A light had dawned upon her face, her hand was lifted as though to stay a sound of music. Suddenly she turned toward him, swayed, and would have fallen but that his arm caught and upheld her. Her head was thrown back; the soft masses of her wonderful hair brushed his cheek and shoulder; her eyes looked past him, and a smile, pure and exquisite past expression, just redeemed her face from sadness. "Good-morrow, Love!" she said clearly and sweetly.

At the sound of her own words came to her the full realization and understanding of herself. With a cry she freed herself from his supporting arm, stepped backward and looked at him. The color surged over her face and throat, her eyelids drooped; while her name was yet upon his lips she answered with a broken cry of ecstasy and abandonment. A moment and she was in his arms and their lips had met.

How quiet it was in the long room, where the myrtle candles gave out their faint perfume and the low fire leaped upon the hearth! Thus for a time; then, growing faint with her happiness, she put up protesting hands. He made her sit in the great chair, and knelt before her, all youth and fire, handsome, ardent, transfigured by his passion into such a lover as a queen might desire.

"Hail, Sultana!" he said, smiling, his eyes upon her diadem. "Now you are Arpasia again, and I am Moneses, and ready, ah, most ready, to die for you."

She also smiled. "Remember that I am to quickly follow you."

"When shall we marry?" he demanded. "The garden cries out for you, my love, and I wish to hear your footstep in my house. It hath been a dreary house, filled with shadows, haunted by keen longings and vain regrets. Now the windows shall be flung wide and the sunshine shall pour in. Oh, your voice singing through the rooms, your foot upon the stairs!" He took her hands and put them to his lips. "I love as men loved of old," he said. "I am far from myself and my times. When will you become my wife?"

She answered him simply, like the child that at times she

seemed: "When you will. But I must be Arpasia again to-morrow night. The Governor hath ordered the play repeated, and Margery Linn could not learn my part in time."

He laughed, fingering the red silk of her hanging sleeve, feasting his eyes upon her dark beauty, so heightened and deepened in the year that had passed. "Then play to them—and to me who shall watch you well—to-morrow night. But after that to them never again! only to me, Audrey, to me when we walk in the garden at home, when we sit in the book-room and the candles are lighted. That day in May when first you came into my garden, when first I showed you my house, when first I rowed you home with the sunshine on the water and the roses in your hair! Love, love! do you remember?"

"Remember?" she answered, in a thrilling voice. "When I am dead I shall yet remember! And I will come when you want me. After to-morrow night I will come.... Oh, cannot you hear the river? And the walls of the box will be freshly green, and the fruit-trees all in bloom! The white leaves drift down upon the bench beneath the cherry-tree.... I will sit in the grass at your feet. Oh, I love you, have loved you long!"

They had risen and now with her head upon his breast and his arm about her, they stood in the heart of the soft radiance of many candles. His face was bowed upon the dark wonder of her hair; when at last he lifted his eyes, they chanced to fall upon the one uncurtained window. Audrey, feeling his slight, quickly controlled start, turned within his arm and also saw the face of Jean Hugon, pressed against the glass, staring in upon them.

Before Haward could reach the window the face was

gone. A strip of moonlight, some leafless bashes, beyond, the blank wall of the theatre,—that was all. Raising the sash, Haward leaned forth until he could see the garden at large. Moonlight still and cold, winding paths, and shadows of tree and shrub and vine, but no sign of living creature. He closed the window and drew the curtain across, then turned again to Audrey. "A phantom of the night," he said, and laughed.

She was standing in the centre of the room, with her red dress gleaming in the candlelight. Her brow beneath its mock crown had no lines of care, and her wonderful eyes smiled upon him. "I have no fear of it," she answered. "That is strange, is it not, when I have feared it for so long? I have no other fear to-night than that I shall outlive your love for me."

"I will love you until the stars fall," he said.

"They are falling to-night. When you are without the door look up, and you may see one pass swiftly down the sky. Once I watched them from the dark river"—

"I will love you until the sun grows old," he said. "Through life and death, through heaven or hell, past the beating of my heart, while lasts my soul!... Audrey, Audrey!"

"If it is so," she answered, "then all is well. Now kiss me good-night, for I hear Mistress Stagg's voice. You will come again to-morrow? And to-morrow night,—oh, to-morrow night I shall see only you, think of only you while I play! Good-night, good-night."

They kissed and parted, and Haward, a happy man, went with raised face through the stillness and the moonlight to his lodging at Marot's ordinary. No phantoms of the night disturbed him. He had found the philosopher's stone, had drunk of the divine elixir. Life was at last a thing much to be desired, and the Giver of life was good, and the *summum bonum* was deathless love.

CHAPTER XXX

THE LAST ACT

Before eight of the clock, Mr. Stagg, peering from behind the curtain, noted with satisfaction that the house was filling rapidly; upon the stroke of the hour it was crowded to the door, without which might be heard angry voices contending that there must be yet places for the buying. The musicians began to play and more candles were lighted. There were laughter, talk, greetings from one part of the house to another, as much movement to and fro as could be accomplished in so crowded a space. The manners of the London playhouses were aped not unsuccessfully. To compare small things with great, it might have been Drury Lane upon a gala night. If the building was rude, yet it had no rival in the colonies, and if the audience was not so gay of hue, impertinent of tongue, or paramount in fashion as its London counterpart, yet it was composed of the rulers and makers of a land destined to greatness.

In the centre box sat his Excellency, William Gooch, Lieutenant-Governor of Virginia, resplendent in velvet and gold lace, and beside him Colonel Alexander Spotswood, arrived in town from Germanna that day, with his heart much set upon the passage, by the Assembly, of an act which would advantage his iron works. Colonel Byrd of Westover, Colonel Esmond of Castlewood, Colonel Carter, Colonel Page, and Colonel Ludwell were likewise of the Governor's party, while seated or standing in the pit, or mingling with the ladies who made gay the boxes, were other gentlemen of consequence,—Councilors, Burgesses, owners of vast tracts of land, of ships and many slaves. Of their number some were traveled men, and some had fought in England's wars, and some had studied in her universities. Many were of gentle blood, sprung from worthy and venerable houses in that green island which with fondness they still called home, and many had made for themselves name and fortune, hewing their way to honor through a primeval forest of adversities. Lesser personages were not lacking, but crowded the gallery and invaded the pit. Old fighters of Indians were present, and masters of ships trading from the Spanish islands or from the ports of home. Rude lumbermen from Norfolk or the borders of the Dismal Swamp stared about them, while here and there showed the sad-colored coat of a minister, or the broad face of some Walloon from Spotswood's settlement on the Rapidan, or the keener countenances of Frenchmen from Monacan-Town. The armorer from the Magazine elbowed a great proprietor from the Eastern shore, while a famous guide and hunter, long and lean and brown, described to a magnate of Yorktown a buffalo capture in the far west, twenty leagues beyond the falls. Masters and scholars from William and Mary were there, with rangers, traders, sailors ashore, small planters, merchants, loquacious keepers of ordinaries, and with men, now free and with a stake in the land, who had come there as indentured servants, or as convicts, runaways, and fugitives from justice. In the upper gallery, where no payment was exacted, many servants with a sprinkling of favorite mulatto or mustee slaves; in the boxes the lustre and sweep of damask and brocade, light laughter, silvery voices, the flutter of fans; everywhere the vividness and animation of a strangely compounded society, where the shadows were deep and the lights were high.

Nor did the conversation of so motley an assemblage lack a certain pictorial quality, a somewhat fantastic opulence of reference and allusion. Of what might its members speak while they waited for the drawing aside of the piece of baize which hung between them and an Oriental camp? There was the staple of their wealth, a broad-leafed plant, the smoke of whose far-spread burning might have wrapped its native fields in a perpetual haze as of Indian summer; and there was the warfare, bequeathed from generation to generation, against the standing armies of the forest, that subtle foe that slept not, retreated not, whose vanguard, ever falling, ever showed unbroken ranks beyond. Trapper and trader and ranger might tell of trails through the wilderness vast and hostile, of canoes upon unknown waters, of beasts of prey, creatures screaming in the night-time through the ebony woods. Of Indian villages, also, and of red men who, in the fastnesses that were left them, took and tortured and slew after strange fashions. The white man, strong as the wind, drove the red man before his face like an autumn leaf, but he beckoned to the black man, and the black man came at his call. He came in numbers from a far country, and the manner of his coming was in chains. What he had to sell was valuable, but the purchase price came not into his hands. Of him also mention was made to-night. The master of the tall ship that had brought him into the James or the York, the dealer to whom he was consigned, the officer of the Crown who had cried him for sale, the planter who had bought him, the divine who preached that he was of a race accursed,—all were there, and all had interest in this merchandise. Others in the throng talked of ships both great and small, and the quaintness of their names, the golden flowers and golden women, the swift birds and beasts, the namesakes of Fortune or of Providence, came pleasantly upon the ear. The still-vexed Bermoothes, Barbadoes, and all the Indies were spoken of; ports to the north and ports to the south, pirate craft and sunken treasure, a flight, a fight, a chase at sea. The men from Norfolk talked of the great Dismal and its trees of juniper and cypress, the traders of trading, the masters from William and Mary of the humanities. The greater men, authoritative and easy, owners of flesh and blood and much land, holders of many offices and leaders of the people, paid their respects to horse-racing and cock-fighting, cards and dice; to building, planting, the genteelest mode of living, and to public affairs both in Virginia and at home in England. Old friends, with oaths of hearty affection, and from opposite quarters of the house, addressed each other as Tom, or Ned, or Dick, while old enemies, finding themselves side by side, exchanged extremely civil speeches, and so put a keener edge upon their mutual disgust. In the boxes where glowed the women there was comfit talk, vastly pretty speeches, asseverations, denials, windy sighs, the politest oaths, whispering, talk of the play, and, last but not least, of Mr. Haward of Fair View, and Darden's Audrey.

Haward, entering the pit, made his way quietly to where a servant was holding for him a place. The fellow pulled his forelock in response to his master's nod, then shouldered his way through the press to the ladder-like stairs that led to the upper gallery. Haward, standing at his ease, looked about him, recognizing this or that acquaintance with his slow, fine smile and an inclination of his head. He was much observed, and presently a lady leaned from her box, smiled, waved her fan, and slightly beckoned to him. It was young Madam Byrd, and Evelyn sat beside her.

Five minutes later, as Haward entered the box of the ladies of Westover, music sounded, the curtain was drawn back, and the play began. Upon the ruder sort in the audience silence fell at once: they that followed the sea, and they that followed the woods, and all the simple folk ceased their noise and gesticulation, and gazed spellbound at the pomp before them of rude scenery and indifferent actors. But the great ones of the earth talked on, attending to their own business in the face of Tamerlane and his victorious force. It was the fashion to do so, and in the play to-night the first act counted nothing, for Darden's Audrey had naught to do with it. In the second act, when she entered as Arpasia, the entire house would fall quiet, staring and holding its breath.

Haward bent over Madam Byrd's hand; then, as that lady turned from him to greet Mr. Lee, addressed himself with grave courtesy to Evelyn, clothed in pale blue, and more lovely even than her wont. For months they had not met. She had written him one letter,—had written the night of the day upon which she had encountered Audrey in the Palace walk,—and he had answered it with a broken line of passionate thanks for unmerited kindness. Now as he bent over her she caught his wrist lightly with her hand, and her touch burned him through the lace of his ruffles. With her other hand she spread her fan; Mr. Lee's shoulder knot also screened them while Mr. Grymes had engaged its owner's attention, and pretty Madam Byrd was in animated conversation with the occupants of a neighboring box. "Is it well?" asked Evelyn, very low.

Haward's answer was as low, and bravely spoken with his eyes meeting her clear gaze, and her touch upon his wrist. "For me, Evelyn, it is very well," he said. "For her—may I live to make it well for her, forever and a day well for her! She is to be my wife."

"I am glad," said Evelyn,—"very glad."

"You are a noble lady," he answered. "Once, long ago, I styled myself your friend, your equal. Now I know better my place and yours, and as from a princess I take your alms. For your letter—that letter, Evelyn, which told me what you thought, which showed me what to do—I humbly thank you."

She let fall her hand from her silken lap, and watched with unseeing eyes the mimicry of life upon the stage before them, where Selima knelt to Tamerlane, and Moneses mourned for Arpasia. Presently she said again, "I am glad;" and then, when they had kept silence for a while, "You will live at Fair View?"

"Ay," he replied. "I will make it well for her here in Virginia."

"You must let me help you," she said. "So old a friend as I may claim that as a right. To-morrow I may visit her, may I not? Now we must look at the players. When she enters there is no need to cry for silence. It comes of itself, and stays; we watch her with straining eyes. Who is that man in a cloak, staring at us from the pit? See, with the great peruke and the scar!"

Haward, bending, looked over the rail, then drew back with a smile. "A half-breed trader," he said, "by name Jean Hugon. Something of a character."

"He looked strangely at us," said Evelyn, "with how haggard a face! My scarf, Mr. Lee? Thank you. Madam, have you the right of the matter from Kitty Page?"

The conversation became general, and soon, the act

approaching its end, and other gentlemen pressing into the box which held so beautiful a woman, so great a catch, and so assured a belle as Mistress Evelyn Byrd, Haward arose and took his leave. To others of the brilliant company assembled in the playhouse he paid his respects, speaking deferentially to the Governor, gayly to his fellow Councilors and planters, and bowing low to many ladies. All this was in the interval between the acts. At the second parting of the curtain he resumed his former station in the pit. With intention he had chosen a section of it where were few of his own class. From the midst of the ruder sort he could watch her more freely, could exult at his ease in her beauty both of face and mind.

The curtains parted, and the fiddlers strove for warlike music. Tamerlane, surrounded by the Tartar host, received his prisoners, and the defiant rant of Bajazet shook the rafters. All the sound and fury of the stage could not drown the noise of the audience. Idle talk and laughter, loud comment upon the players, went on,—went on until there entered Darden's Audrey, dressed in red silk, with a jeweled circlet like a line of flame about her dark flowing hair. The noise sank, voices of men and women died away; for a moment the rustle of silk, the flutter of fans, continued, then this also ceased.

She stood before the Sultan, wide-eyed, with a smile of scorn upon her lips; then spoke in a voice, low, grave, monotonous, charged like a passing bell with warning and with solemn woe. The house seemed to grow more still; the playgoers, box and pit and gallery, leaned slightly forward: whether she spoke or moved or stood in silence, Darden's Audrey, that had been a thing of naught, now held every eye, was regnant for an hour in this epitome of the world. The scene went on, and now it was to Moneses that she spoke. All the bliss and anguish of unhappy love sounded in her voice, dwelt in her eye and most exquisite smile, hung upon her every gesture. The curtains closed; from the throng that had watched her came a sound like a sigh, after which, slowly, tongues were loosened. An interval of impatient waiting, then the music again and the parting curtains, and Darden's Audrey,—the girl who could so paint very love, very sorrow, very death; the girl who had come strangely and by a devious path from the height and loneliness of the mountains to the level of this stage and the watching throng.

At the close of the fourth act of the play, Haward left his station in the pit, and quietly made his way to the regions behind the curtain, where in the very circumscribed space that served as greenroom to the Williamsburgh theatre he found Tamerlane, Bajazet, and their satellites, together with a number of gentlemen invaders from the front of the house. Mistress Stagg was there, and Selima, perched upon a table, was laughing with the aforesaid gentlemen, but no Arpasia. Haward drew the elder woman aside. "I wish to see her," he said, in a low voice, kindly but imperious. "A moment only, good woman."

With her finger at her lips Mistress Stagg glanced about her. "She hides from them always, she's that strange a child: though indeed, sir, as sweet a young lady as a prince might wed! This way, sir,—it's dark; make no noise."

She led him through a dim passageway, and softly opened a door. "There, sir, for just five minutes! I'll call her in time."

The door gave upon the garden, and Audrey sat upon the step in the moonshine and the stillness. Her hand propped her chin, and her eyes were raised to the few silver stars.

That mock crown which she wore sparkled palely, and the light lay in the folds of her silken dress. At the opening of the door she did not turn, thinking that Mistress Stagg stood behind her. "How bright the moon shines!" she said. "A mockingbird should be singing, singing! Is it time for Arpasia?"

As she rose from the step Haward caught her in his arms. "It is I, my love! Ah, heart's desire! I worship you who gleam in the moonlight, with your crown like an aureole"—

Audrey rested against him, clasping her hands upon his shoulder. "There were nights like this," she said dreamily. "If I were a little child again, you could lift me in your arms and carry me home, I am tired ... I would that I needed not to go back to the glare and noise. The moon shines so bright! I have been thinking"—

He bent his head and kissed her twice. "Poor Arpasia! Poor tired child! Soon we shall go home, Audrey,—we two, my love, we two!"

"I have been thinking, sitting here in the moonlight," she went on, her hands clasped upon his shoulder, and her cheek resting on them. "I was so ignorant. I never dreamed that I could wrong her ... and when I awoke it was too late. And now I love you,—not the dream, but you. I know not what is right or wrong; I know only that I love. I think she understands—forgives. I love you so!" Her hands parted, and she stood from him with her face raised to the balm of the night. "I love you so," she repeated, and the low cadence of her laugh broke the silver stillness of the garden. "The moon up there, she knows it. And the stars,—not one has fallen to-night! Smell the flowers. Wait, I will pluck you hyacinths."

They grew by the doorstep, and she broke the slender stalks and gave them into his hand. But when he had kissed them he would give them back, would fasten them himself in the folds of silk, that rose and fell with her quickened breathing. He fastened them with a brooch which he took from the Mechlin at his throat. It was the golden horseshoe, the token that he had journeyed to the Endless Mountains.

"Now I must go," said Audrey. "They are calling for Arpasia. Follow me not at once. Good-night, good-night! Ah, I love you so! Remember always that I love you so!"

She was gone. In a few minutes he also reentered the playhouse, and went to his former place where, with none of his kind about him, he might watch her undisturbed. As he made his way with some difficulty through the throng, he was aware that he brushed against a man in a great peruke, who, despite the heat of the house, was wrapped in an old roquelaure tawdrily laced; also that the man was keeping stealthy pace with him, and that when he at last reached his station the cloaked figure fell into place immediately behind him.

Haward shrugged his shoulders, but would not turn his head, and thereby grant recognition to Jean Hugon, the trader. Did he so, the half-breed might break into speech, provoke a quarrel, make God knew what assertion, what disturbance. To-morrow steps should be taken—Ah, the curtain!

The silence deepened, and men and women leaned forward holding their breath. Darden's Audrey, robed and crowned as Arpasia, sat alone in the Sultan's tent, staring before her with wide dark eyes, then slowly rising began to speak. A sound, a sigh as of wonder, ran from the one to the other of the throng that watched her. Why did she look thus, with contracted brows, toward one quarter of the house? What inarticulate words was she uttering? What gesture, quickly controlled, did she make of ghastly fear and warning? And now the familiar words came halting from her lips:—

> "'Sure 'tis a horror, more than darkness brings,
> That sits upon the night!'"

With the closing words of her speech the audience burst into a great storm of applause. 'Gad! how she acts! But what now? Why, what is this?

It was quite in nature and the mode for an actress to pause in the middle of a scene to curtsy thanks for generous applause, to smile and throw a mocking kiss to pit and boxes, but Darden's Audrey had hitherto not followed the fashion. Also it was not uncustomary for some spoiled favorite of a player to trip down, between her scenes, the step or two from the stage to the pit, and mingle with the gallants there, laugh, jest, accept languishing glances, audacious comparisons, and such weighty trifles as gilt snuffboxes and rings of price. But this player had not heretofore honored the custom; moreover, at present she was needed upon the stage. Bajazet must thunder and she defy; without her the play could not move, and indeed the actors were now staring with the audience. What was it? Why had she crossed the stage, and, slowly, smilingly, beautiful and stately in her gleaming robes, descended those few steps which led to the pit? What had she to do there, throwing smiling glances to right and left, lightly waving the folk, gentle and simple, from her path, pressing steadily onward to some unguessed-at goal. As though held by a spell they watched her, one and all,—Haward, Evelyn, the Governor, the man in the cloak, every soul in that motley assemblage. The wonder had not time to dull, for the moments were few between her final leave-taking of those boards which she had trodden supreme and the crashing and terrible chord which was to close the entertainment of this night.

Her face was raised to the boxes, and it seemed as though her dark eyes sought one there. Then, suddenly, she swerved. There were men between her and Haward. She raised her hand, and they fell back, making for her a path. Haward, bewildered, started forward, but her cry was not to him. It was to the figure just behind him,—the cloaked figure whose hand grasped the hunting-knife which from the stage, as she had looked to where stood her lover, she had seen or divined. "Jean! Jean Hugon!" she cried.

Involuntarily the trader pushed toward her, past the man whom he meant to stab to the heart. The action, dragging his cloak aside, showed the half-raised arm and the gleaming steel. For many minutes the knife had been ready. The play was nearly over, and she must see this man who had stolen her heart, this Haward of Fair View, die. Else Jean Hugon's vengeance were not complete. For his own safety the maddened half-breed had ceased to care. No warning cried from the stage could have done aught but precipitate the deed, but now for the moment, amazed and doubtful, he turned his back upon his prey.

In that moment the Audrey of the woods, a creature lithe and agile and strong of wrist as of will, had thrown herself upon him, clutching the hand that held the knife. He strove to dash her from him, but in vain; the house was in an uproar; and now Haward's hands were at his throat, Haward's voice was crying to that fair devil, that Audrey for whom he had built his house, who was balking him of revenge, whose body was between him and his enemy!

Suddenly he was all savage; as upon a night in Fair View house he had cast off the trammels of his white blood, so now. An access of furious strength came to him; he shook himself free; the knife gleamed in the air, descended.... He drew it from the bosom into which he had plunged it, and as Haward caught her in his arms, who would else have sunk to the floor, the half-breed burst through the horror-stricken throng, brandishing the red blade and loudly speaking in the tongue of the Monacans. Like a whirlwind he was gone from the house, and for a time none thought to follow him.

They bore her into the small white house, and up the stair to her own room, and laid her upon the bed. Dr. Contesse came and went away, and came again. There was a crowd in Palace Street before the theatre. A man mounting the doorstep so that he might be heard of all, said clearly, "She may live until dawn,—no longer." Later, one came out of the house and asked that there might be quiet. The crowd melted away, but throughout the mild night, filled with the soft airs and thousand odors of the spring, people stayed about the place, standing silent in the street or sitting on the garden benches.

In the room upstairs lay Darden's Audrey, with crossed hands and head put slightly back. She lay still, upon the edge of death, nor seemed to care that it was so. Her eyes were closed, and at intervals one sitting at the bed head laid touch upon her pulse, or held before her lips a slight ringlet of her hair. Mary Stagg sat by the window and wept, but Haward, kneeling, hid his face in the covering of the bed. The form upon it was not more still than he; Mistress Stagg, also, stifled her sobs, for it seemed not a place for loud grief.

In the room below, amidst the tinsel frippery of small

wares, waited others whose lives had touched the life that was ebbing away. Now and then one spoke in a hushed voice, a window was raised, a servant bringing in fresh candles trod too heavily; then the quiet closed in again. Late in the night came through the open windows a distant clamor, and presently a man ran down Palace Street, and as he ran called aloud some tidings. MacLean, standing near the door, went softly out. When he returned, Colonel Byrd, sitting at the table, lifted inquiring brows. "They took him in the reeds near the Capitol landing," said the Highlander grimly. "He's in the gaol now, but whether the people will leave him there"—

The night wore on, grew old, passed into the cold melancholy of its latest hour. Darden's Audrey sighed and stirred, and a little strength coming to her parting spirit, she opened her eyes and loosed her hands. The physician held to her lips the cordial, and she drank a very little. Haward lifted his head, and as Contesse passed him to set down the cup, caught him by the sleeve. The other looked pityingly at the man into whose face had come a flush of hope. "'T is but the last flickering of the flame," he said. "Soon even the spark will vanish."

Audrey began to speak. At first her words were wild and wandering, but, the mist lifting somewhat, she presently knew Mistress Stagg, and liked to have her take the doctor's place beside her. At Haward she looked doubtfully, with wide eyes, as scarce understanding. When he called her name she faintly shook her head, then turned it slightly from him and veiled her eyes. It came to him with a terrible pang that the memory of their latest meetings was wiped from her brain, and that she was afraid of his broken words and the tears upon her hand.

When she spoke again it was to ask for the minister. He

was below, and Mistress Stagg went weeping down the stairs to summon him. He came, but would not touch the girl; only stood, with his hat in his hand, and looked down upon her with bleared eyes and a heavy countenance.

"I am to die, am I not?" she asked, with her gaze upon him.

"That is as God wills, Audrey," he answered.

"I am not afraid to die."

"You have no need," he said, and going out of the room and down the stairs, made Stagg pour for him a glass of aqua vitae.

Audrey closed her eyes, and when she opened them again there seemed to be many persons in the room. One was bending over her whom at first she thought was Molly, but soon she saw more clearly, and smiled at the pale and sorrowful face. The lady bent lower yet, and kissed her on the forehead. "Audrey," she said, and Audrey looking up at her answered, "Evelyn."

When the dawn came glimmering in the windows, when the mist was cold and the birds were faintly heard, they raised her upon her pillows, and wiped the death dew from her forehead. "Audrey, Audrey, Audrey!" cried Haward, and caught at her hands.

She looked at him with a faint and doubtful smile, remembering nothing of that hour in the room below, of those minutes in the moonlit garden. "Gather the rosebuds while ye may," she said; and then, "The house is large. Good giant, eat me not!"

The man upon his knees beside her uttered a cry, and began to speak to her, thickly, rapidly, words of agony, entreaty, and love. To-morrow and for all life habit would resume its sway, and lost love, remorse, and vain regrets put on a mask that was cold and fine and able to deceive. To-night there spoke the awakened heart. With her hands cold in his, with his agonized gaze upon the face from which the light was slowly passing, he poured forth his passion and his anguish, and she listened not. They moistened her lips, and one opened wide the window that gave upon the east. "It was all a dream," she said; and again, "All a dream." A little later, while the sky flushed slowly and the light of the candles grew pale, she began suddenly, and in a stronger voice, to speak as Arpasia:—

"'If it be happiness, alas! to die,
To lie forgotten in the silent grave'"—

"Forgotten!" cried Haward. "Audrey, Audrey, Audrey! Go not from me! Oh, love, love, stay awhile!"

"The mountains," said Audrey clearly. "The sun upon them and the lifting mist."

"The mountains!" he cried. "Ay, we will go to them, Audrey, we will go together! Why, you are stronger, sweetheart! There is strength in your voice and your hands, and a light in your eyes. Oh, if you will live, Audrey, I will make you happy! You shall take me to the mountains—we will go together, you and I! Audrey, Audrey"—

But Audrey was gone already.

Choose from Thousands of 1stWorldLibrary Classics By

A. M. Barnard
Ada Leverson
Adolphus William Ward
Aesop
Agatha Christie
Alexander Aaronsohn
Alexander Kielland
Alexandre Dumas
Alfred Gatty
Alfred Ollivant
Alice Duer Miller
Alice Turner Curtis
Alice Dunbar
Allen Chapman
Alleyne Ireland
Ambrose Bierce
Amelia E. Barr
Amory H. Bradford
Andrew Lang
Andrew McFarland Davis
Andy Adams
Angela Brazil
Anna Alice Chapin
Anna Sewell
Annie Besant
Annie Hamilton Donnell
Annie Payson Call
Annie Roe Carr
Annonaymous
Anton Chekhov
Archibald Lee Fletcher
Arnold Bennett
Arthur C. Benson
Arthur Conan Doyle
Arthur M. Winfield
Arthur Ransome
Arthur Schnitzler
Arthur Train
Atticus
B.H. Baden-Powell
B. M. Bower
B. C. Chatterjee
Baroness Emmuska Orczy
Baroness Orczy
Basil King
Bayard Taylor
Ben Macomber
Bertha Muzzy Bower
Bjornstjerne Bjornson

Booth Tarkington
Boyd Cable
Bram Stoker
C. Collodi
C. E. Orr
C. M. Ingleby
Carolyn Wells
Catherine Parr Traill
Charles A. Eastman
Charles Amory Beach
Charles Dickens
Charles Dudley Warner
Charles Farrar Browne
Charles Ives
Charles Kingsley
Charles Klein
Charles Hanson Towne
Charles Lathrop Pack
Charles Romyn Dake
Charles Whibley
Charles Willing Beale
Charlotte M. Braeme
Charlotte M. Yonge
Charlotte Perkins Stetson
Clair W. Hayes
Clarence Day Jr.
Clarence E. Mulford
Clemence Housman
Confucius
Coningsby Dawson
Cornelis DeWitt Wilcox
Cyril Burleigh
D. H. Lawrence
Daniel Defoe
David Garnett
Dinah Craik
Don Carlos Janes
Donald Keyhoe
Dorothy Kilner
Dougan Clark
Douglas Fairbanks
E. Nesbit
E. P. Roe
E. Phillips Oppenheim
E. S. Brooks
Earl Barnes
Edgar Rice Burroughs
Edith Van Dyne
Edith Wharton

Edward Everett Hale
Edward J. O'Biren
Edward S. Ellis
Edwin L. Arnold
Eleanor Atkins
Eleanor Hallowell Abbott
Eliot Gregory
Elizabeth Gaskell
Elizabeth McCracken
Elizabeth Von Arnim
Ellem Key
Emerson Hough
Emilie F. Carlen
Emily Bronte
Emily Dickinson
Enid Bagnold
Enilor Macartney Lane
Erasmus W. Jones
Ernie Howard Pie
Ethel May Dell
Ethel Turner
Ethel Watts Mumford
Eugene Sue
Eugenie Foa
Eugene Wood
Eustace Hale Ball
Evelyn Everett-green
Everard Cotes
F. H. Cheley
F. J. Cross
F. Marion Crawford
Fannie E. Newberry
Federick Austin Ogg
Ferdinand Ossendowski
Fergus Hume
Florence A. Kilpatrick
Fremont B. Deering
Francis Bacon
Francis Darwin
Frances Hodgson Burnett
Frances Parkinson Keyes
Frank Gee Patchin
Frank Harris
Frank Jewett Mather
Frank L. Packard
Frank V. Webster
Frederic Stewart Isham
Frederick Trevor Hill
Frederick Winslow Taylor

Friedrich Kerst
Friedrich Nietzsche
Fyodor Dostoyevsky
G.A. Henty
G.K. Chesterton
Gabrielle E. Jackson
Garrett P. Serviss
Gaston Leroux
George A. Warren
George Ade
Geroge Bernard Shaw
George Cary Eggleston
George Durston
George Ebers
George Eliot
George Gissing
George MacDonald
George Meredith
George Orwell
George Sylvester Viereck
George Tucker
George W. Cable
George Wharton James
Gertrude Atherton
Gordon Casserly
Grace E. King
Grace Gallatin
Grace Greenwood
Grant Allen
Guillermo A. Sherwell
Gulielma Zollinger
Gustav Flaubert
H. A. Cody
H. B. Irving
H.C. Bailey
H. G. Wells
H. H. Munro
H. Irving Hancock
H. R. Naylor
H. Rider Haggard
H. W. C. Davis
Haldeman Julius
Hall Caine
Hamilton Wright Mabie
Hans Christian Andersen
Harold Avery
Harold McGrath
Harriet Beecher Stowe
Harry Castlemon
Harry Coghill
Harry Houidini

Hayden Carruth
Helent Hunt Jackson
Helen Nicolay
Hendrik Conscience
Hendy David Thoreau
Henri Barbusse
Henrik Ibsen
Henry Adams
Henry Ford
Henry Frost
Henry James
Henry Jones Ford
Henry Seton Merriman
Henry W Longfellow
Herbert A. Giles
Herbert Carter
Herbert N. Casson
Herman Hesse
Hildegard G. Frey
Homer
Honore De Balzac
Horace B. Day
Horace Walpole
Horatio Alger Jr.
Howard Pyle
Howard R. Garis
Hugh Lofting
Hugh Walpole
Humphry Ward
Ian Maclaren
Inez Haynes Gillmore
Irving Bacheller
Isabel Cecilia Williams
Isabel Hornibrook
Israel Abrahams
Ivan Turgenev
J.G.Austin
J. Henri Fabre
J. M. Barrie
J. M. Walsh
J. Macdonald Oxley
J. R. Miller
J. S. Fletcher
J. S. Knowles
J. Storer Clouston
J. W. Duffield
Jack London
Jacob Abbott
James Allen
James Andrews
James Baldwin

James Branch Cabell
James DeMille
James Joyce
James Lane Allen
James Lane Allen
James Oliver Curwood
James Oppenheim
James Otis
James R. Driscoll
Jane Abbott
Jane Austen
Jane L. Stewart
Janet Aldridge
Jens Peter Jacobsen
Jerome K. Jerome
Jessie Graham Flower
John Buchan
John Burroughs
John Cournos
John F. Kennedy
John Gay
John Glasworthy
John Habberton
John Joy Bell
John Kendrick Bangs
John Milton
John Philip Sousa
John Taintor Foote
Jonas Lauritz Idemil Lie
Jonathan Swift
Joseph A. Altsheler
Joseph Carey
Joseph Conrad
Joseph E. Badger Jr
Joseph Hergesheimer
Joseph Jacobs
Jules Vernes
Julian Hawthrone
Julie A Lippmann
Justin Huntly McCarthy
Kakuzo Okakura
Karle Wilson Baker
Kate Chopin
Kenneth Grahame
Kenneth McGaffey
Kate Langley Bosher
Kate Langley Bosher
Katherine Cecil Thurston
Katherine Stokes
L. A. Abbot
L. T. Meade

L. Frank Baum
Latta Griswold
Laura Dent Crane
Laura Lee Hope
Laurence Housman
Lawrence Beasley
Leo Tolstoy
Leonid Andreyev
Lewis Carroll
Lewis Sperry Chafer
Lilian Bell
Lloyd Osbourne
Louis Hughes
Louis Joseph Vance
Louis Tracy
Louisa May Alcott
Lucy Fitch Perkins
Lucy Maud Montgomery
Luther Benson
Lydia Miller Middleton
Lyndon Orr
M. Corvus
M. H. Adams
Margaret E. Sangster
Margret Howth
Margaret Vandercook
Margaret W. Hungerford
Margret Penrose
Maria Edgeworth
Maria Thompson Daviess
Mariano Azuela
Marion Polk Angellotti
Mark Overton
Mark Twain
Mary Austin
Mary Catherine Crowley
Mary Cole
Mary Hastings Bradley
Mary Roberts Rinehart
Mary Rowlandson
M. Wollstonecraft Shelley
Maud Lindsay
Max Beerbohm
Myra Kelly
Nathaniel Hawthrone
Nicolo Machiavelli
O. F. Walton
Oscar Wilde

Owen Johnson
P.G. Wodehouse
Paul and Mabel Thorne
Paul G. Tomlinson
Paul Severing
Percy Brebner
Percy Keese Fitzhugh
Peter B. Kyne
Plato
Quincy Allen
R. Derby Holmes
R. L. Stevenson
R. S. Ball
Rabindranath Tagore
Rahul Alvares
Ralph Bonehill
Ralph Henry Barbour
Ralph Victor
Ralph Waldo Emmerson
Rene Descartes
Ray Cummings
Rex Beach
Rex E. Beach
Richard Harding Davis
Richard Jefferies
Richard Le Gallienne
Robert Barr
Robert Frost
Robert Gordon Anderson
Robert L. Drake
Robert Lansing
Robert Lynd
Robert Michael Ballantyne
Robert W. Chambers
Rosa Nouchette Carey
Rudyard Kipling
Saint Augustine
Samuel B. Allison
Samuel Hopkins Adams
Sarah Bernhardt
Sarah C. Hallowell
Selma Lagerlof
Sherwood Anderson
Sigmund Freud
Standish O'Grady
Stanley Weyman
Stella Benson
Stella M. Francis

Stephen Crane
Stewart Edward White
Stijn Streuvels
Swami Abhedananda
Swami Parmananda
T. S. Ackland
T. S. Arthur
The Princess Der Ling
Thomas A. Janvier
Thomas A Kempis
Thomas Anderton
Thomas Bailey Aldrich
Thomas Bulfinch
Thomas De Quincey
Thomas Dixon
Thomas H. Huxley
Thomas Hardy
Thomas More
Thornton W. Burgess
U. S. Grant
Upton Sinclair
Valentine Williams
Various Authors
Vaughan Kester
Victor Appleton
Victor G. Durham
Victoria Cross
Virginia Woolf
Wadsworth Camp
Walter Camp
Walter Scott
Washington Irving
Wilbur Lawton
Wilkie Collins
Willa Cather
Willard F. Baker
William Dean Howells
William le Queux
W. Makepeace Thackeray
William W. Walter
William Shakespeare
Winston Churchill
Yei Theodora Ozaki
Yogi Ramacharaka
Young E. Allison
Zane Grey